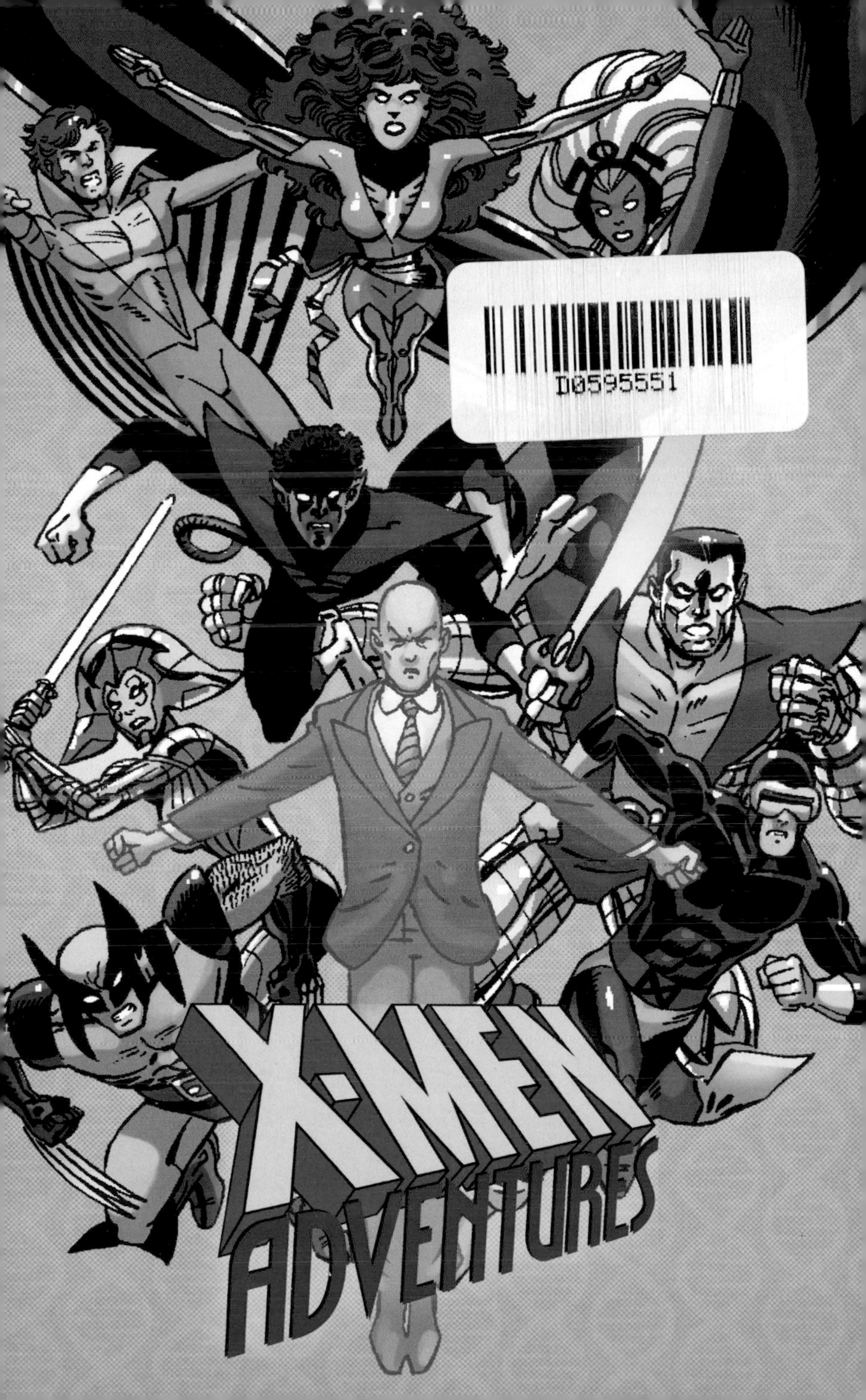
X-MEN
ADVENTURES

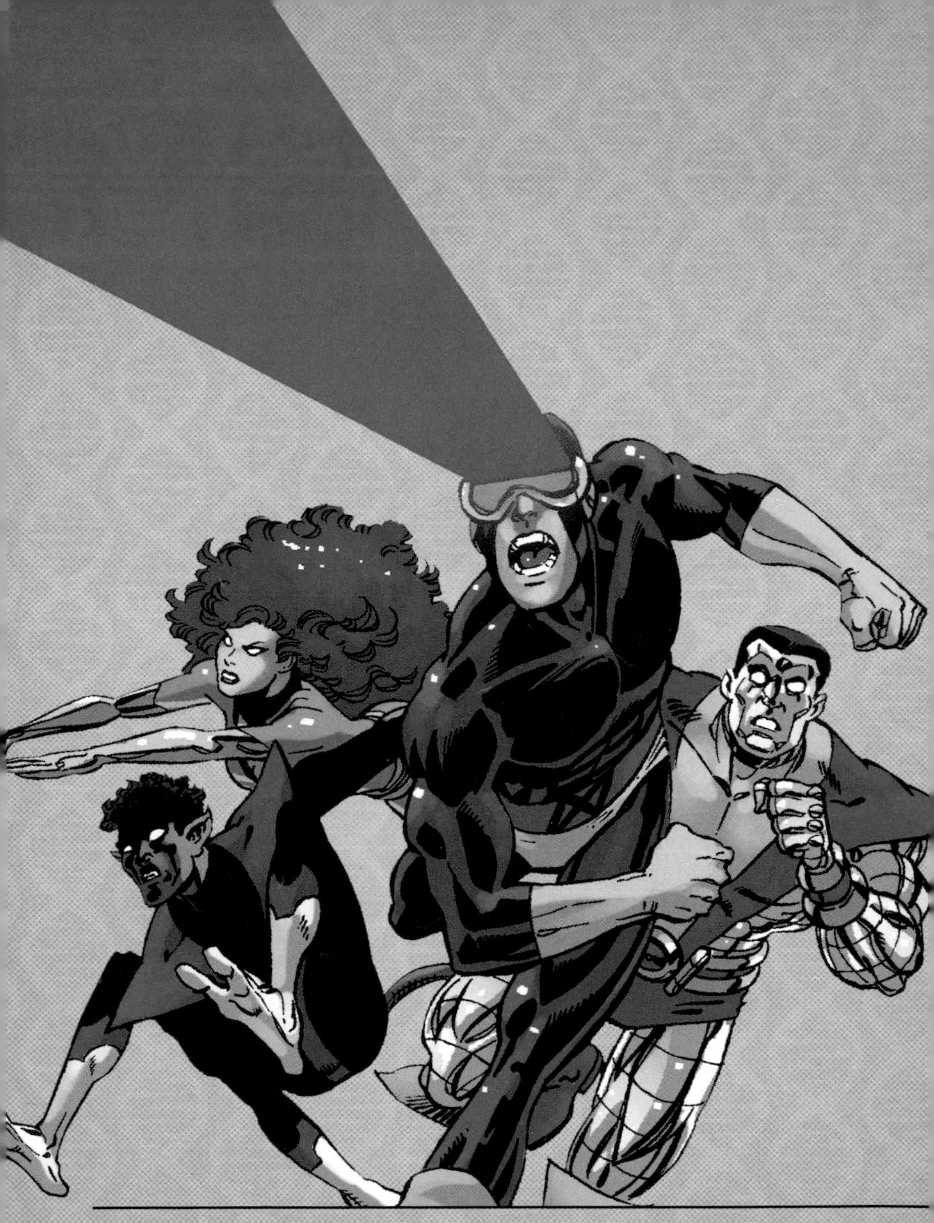

X-MEN ADVENTURES. Contains material originally published in magazine form as X-MEN #1 and #19, and UNCANNY X-MEN: FIRST CLASS #5-7. First printing 2018. ISBN 978-1-302-91211-6. Published by MARVEL WORLDWIDE, INC., a subsidiary of MARVEL ENTERTAINMENT, LLC. OFFICE OF PUBLICATION: 135 West 50th Street, New York, NY 10020. Copyright © 2018 MARVEL No similarity between any of the names, characters, persons, and/or institutions in this magazine with those of any living or dead person or institution is intended, and any such similarity which may exist is purely coincidental. **Printed in the U.S.A.** DAN BUCKLEY, President, Marvel Entertainment; JOHN NEE, Publisher; JOE QUESADA, Chief Creative Officer; TOM BREVOORT, SVP of Publishing; DAVID BOGART, SVP of Business Affairs & Operations, Publishing & Partnership; DAVID GABRIEL, SVP of Sales & Marketing, Publishing; JEFF YOUNGQUIST, VP of Production & Special Projects; DAN CARR, Executive Director of Publishing Technology; ALEX MORALES, Director of Publishing Operations; DAN EDINGTON, Managing Editor; SUSAN CRESPI, Production Manager; STAN LEE, Chairman Emeritus. For information regarding advertising in Marvel Comics or on Marvel.com, please contact Vit DeBellis, Custom Solutions & Integrated Advertising Manager, at vdebellis@marvel.com. For Marvel subscription inquiries, please call 888-511-5480. **Manufactured between 6/22/2018 and 7/24/2018 by SHERIDAN, CHELSEA, MI, USA.**

10 9 8 7 6 5 4 3 2 1

X-MEN #1

Writer: **Stan Lee**
Penciler: **Jack Kirby**
Inker: **Paul Reinman**
Letterer: **Sam Rosen**

X-MEN #19

Writer: **Stan Lee**
Penciler: **Werner Roth**
Inker: **Dick Ayers**
Letterer: **Art Simek**

UNCANNY X-MEN: FIRST CLASS #5-7

Writer: **Scott Gray**

Artists: **Nelson DeCastro** & **Scott Koblish**

Colorist: **Val Staples**

Letterers: **Blambot's Nate Piekos**

Cover Art: **Roger Cruz** & **Chris Sotomayor** (#5);
 Paul Pelletier, Terry Pallot & **Val Staples** (#6);
 and **Reilly Brown, Jason Paz** & **Val Staples** (#7)

Editor: **Jordan D. White**

Supervising Editor: **Nathan Cosby**

X-Men created by
Stan Lee & **Jack Kirby**

Collection Editor **Jennifer Grünwald**
Assistant Editor **Caitlin O'Connell**
Associate Managing Editor **Kateri Woody**
Editor, Special Projects **Mark D. Beazley**
VP Production & Special Projects **Jeff Youngquist**
SVP Print, Sales & Marketing **David Gabriel**

Book Designer **Adam Del Re**

Editor in Chief **C.B. Cebulski**
Chief Creative Officer **Joe Quesada**
President **Dan Buckley**
Executive Producer **Alan Fine**

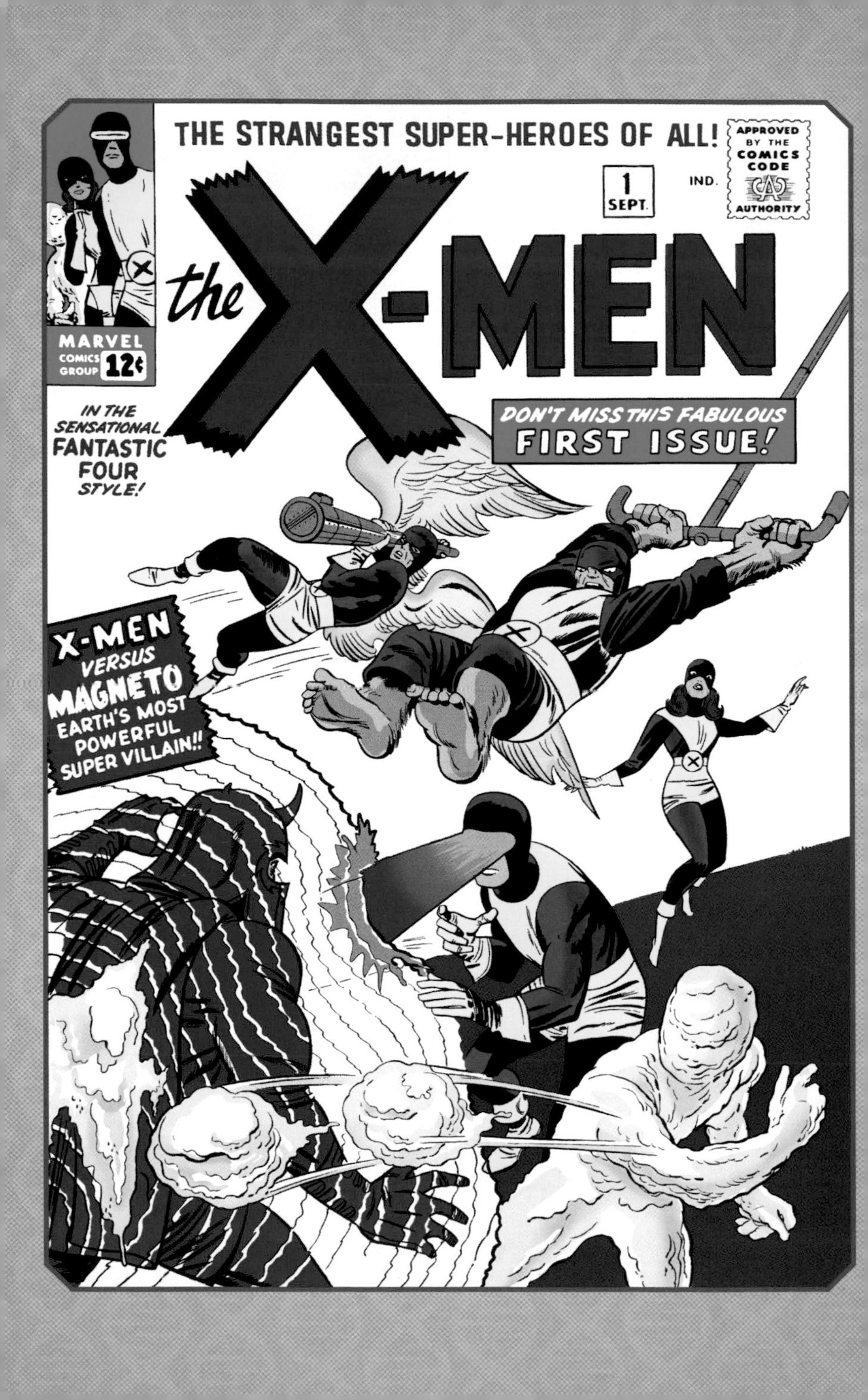
THE STRANGEST SUPER-HEROES OF ALL!
APPROVED BY THE COMICS CODE AUTHORITY
1 SEPT.
IND.
MARVEL COMICS GROUP 12¢
the X-MEN
IN THE SENSATIONAL FANTASTIC FOUR STYLE!
DON'T MISS THIS FABULOUS FIRST ISSUE!
X-MEN VERSUS MAGNETO EARTH'S MOST POWERFUL SUPER VILLAIN!!

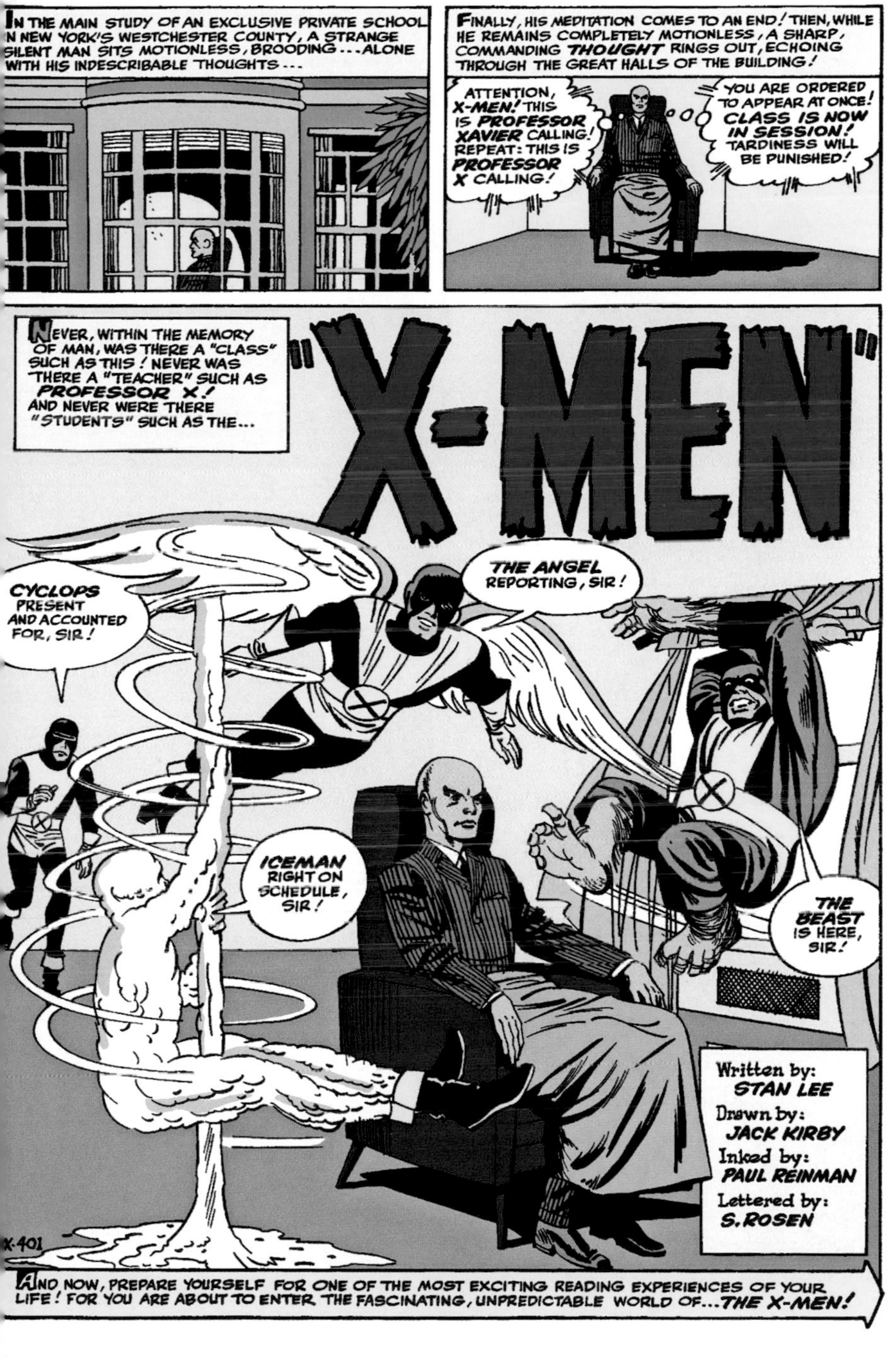
IN THE MAIN STUDY OF AN EXCLUSIVE PRIVATE SCHOOL IN NEW YORK'S WESTCHESTER COUNTY, A STRANGE SILENT MAN SITS MOTIONLESS, BROODING... ALONE WITH HIS INDESCRIBABLE THOUGHTS...
FINALLY, HIS MEDITATION COMES TO AN END! THEN, WHILE HE REMAINS COMPLETELY MOTIONLESS, A SHARP, COMMANDING THOUGHT RINGS OUT, ECHOING THROUGH THE GREAT HALLS OF THE BUILDING!
ATTENTION, X-MEN! THIS IS PROFESSOR XAVIER CALLING! REPEAT: THIS IS PROFESSOR X CALLING!
YOU ARE ORDERED TO APPEAR AT ONCE! CLASS IS NOW IN SESSION! TARDINESS WILL BE PUNISHED!
NEVER, WITHIN THE MEMORY OF MAN, WAS THERE A "CLASS" SUCH AS THIS! NEVER WAS THERE A "TEACHER" SUCH AS PROFESSOR X! AND NEVER WERE THERE "STUDENTS" SUCH AS THE...
"X-MEN"
CYCLOPS PRESENT AND ACCOUNTED FOR, SIR!
THE ANGEL REPORTING, SIR!
ICEMAN RIGHT ON SCHEDULE, SIR!
THE BEAST IS HERE, SIR!
Written by: STAN LEE
Drawn by: JACK KIRBY
Inked by: PAUL REINMAN
Lettered by: S. ROSEN
X-401
AND NOW, PREPARE YOURSELF FOR ONE OF THE MOST EXCITING READING EXPERIENCES OF YOUR LIFE! FOR YOU ARE ABOUT TO ENTER THE FASCINATING, UNPREDICTABLE WORLD OF... THE X-MEN!

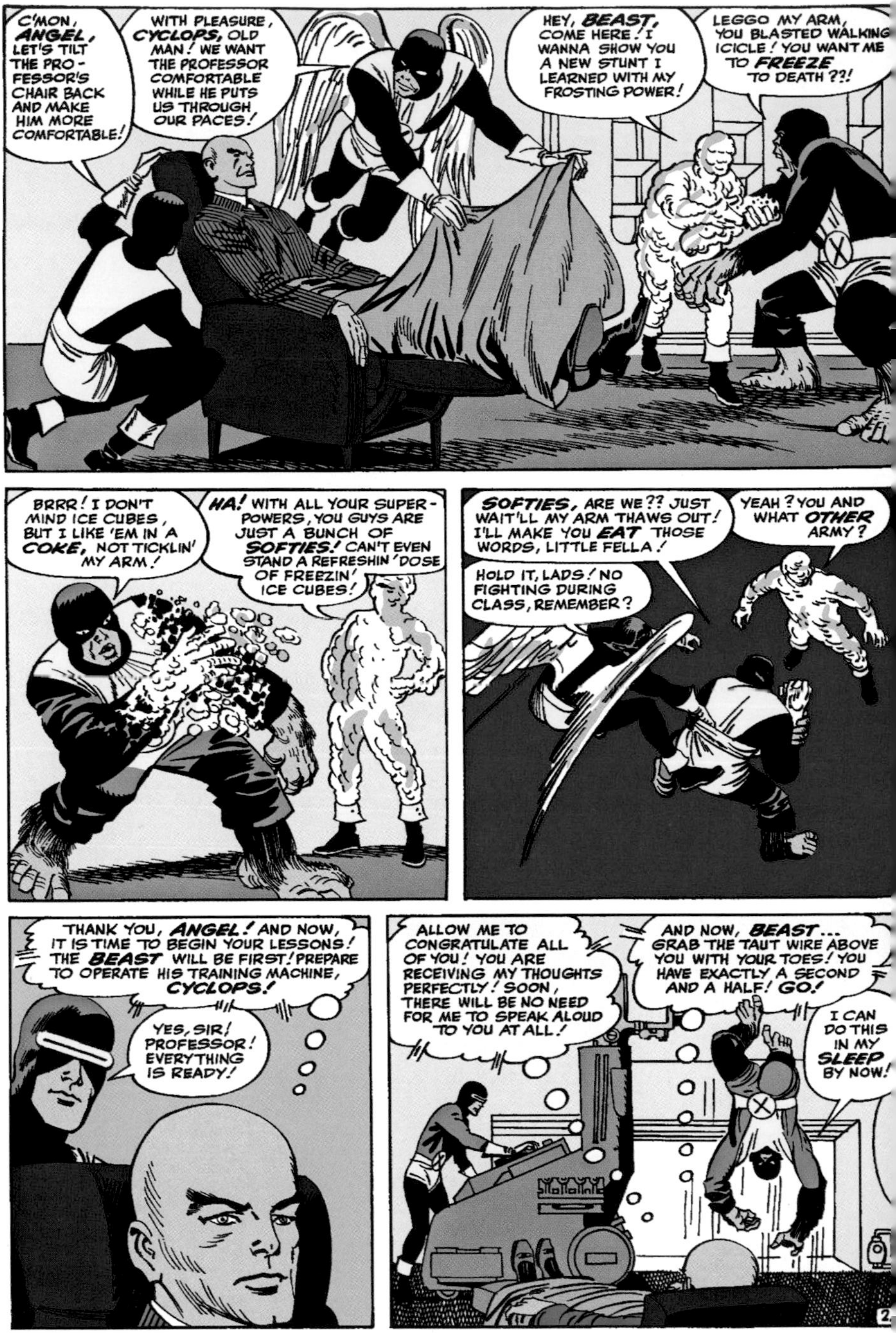
C'MON, ANGEL, LET'S TILT THE PRO-FESSOR'S CHAIR BACK AND MAKE HIM MORE COMFORTABLE!
WITH PLEASURE, CYCLOPS, OLD MAN! WE WANT THE PROFESSOR COMFORTABLE WHILE HE PUTS US THROUGH OUR PACES!
HEY, BEAST, COME HERE! I WANNA SHOW YOU A NEW STUNT I LEARNED WITH MY FROSTING POWER!
LEGGO MY ARM, YOU BLASTED WALKING ICICLE! YOU WANT ME TO FREEZE TO DEATH??!
BRRR! I DON'T MIND ICE CUBES, BUT I LIKE 'EM IN A COKE, NOT TICKLIN' MY ARM!
HA! WITH ALL YOUR SUPER-POWERS, YOU GUYS ARE JUST A BUNCH OF SOFTIES! CAN'T EVEN STAND A REFRESHIN' DOSE OF FREEZIN' ICE CUBES!
SOFTIES, ARE WE?? JUST WAIT'LL MY ARM THAWS OUT! I'LL MAKE YOU EAT THOSE WORDS, LITTLE FELLA!
YEAH? YOU AND WHAT OTHER ARMY?
HOLD IT, LADS! NO FIGHTING DURING CLASS, REMEMBER?
THANK YOU, ANGEL! AND NOW, IT IS TIME TO BEGIN YOUR LESSONS! THE BEAST WILL BE FIRST! PREPARE TO OPERATE HIS TRAINING MACHINE, CYCLOPS!
YES, SIR! PROFESSOR! EVERYTHING IS READY!
ALLOW ME TO CONGRATULATE ALL OF YOU! YOU ARE RECEIVING MY THOUGHTS PERFECTLY! SOON, THERE WILL BE NO NEED FOR ME TO SPEAK ALOUD TO YOU AT ALL!
AND NOW, BEAST... GRAB THE TAUT WIRE ABOVE YOU WITH YOUR TOES! YOU HAVE EXACTLY A SECOND AND A HALF! GO!
I CAN DO THIS IN MY SLEEP BY NOW!

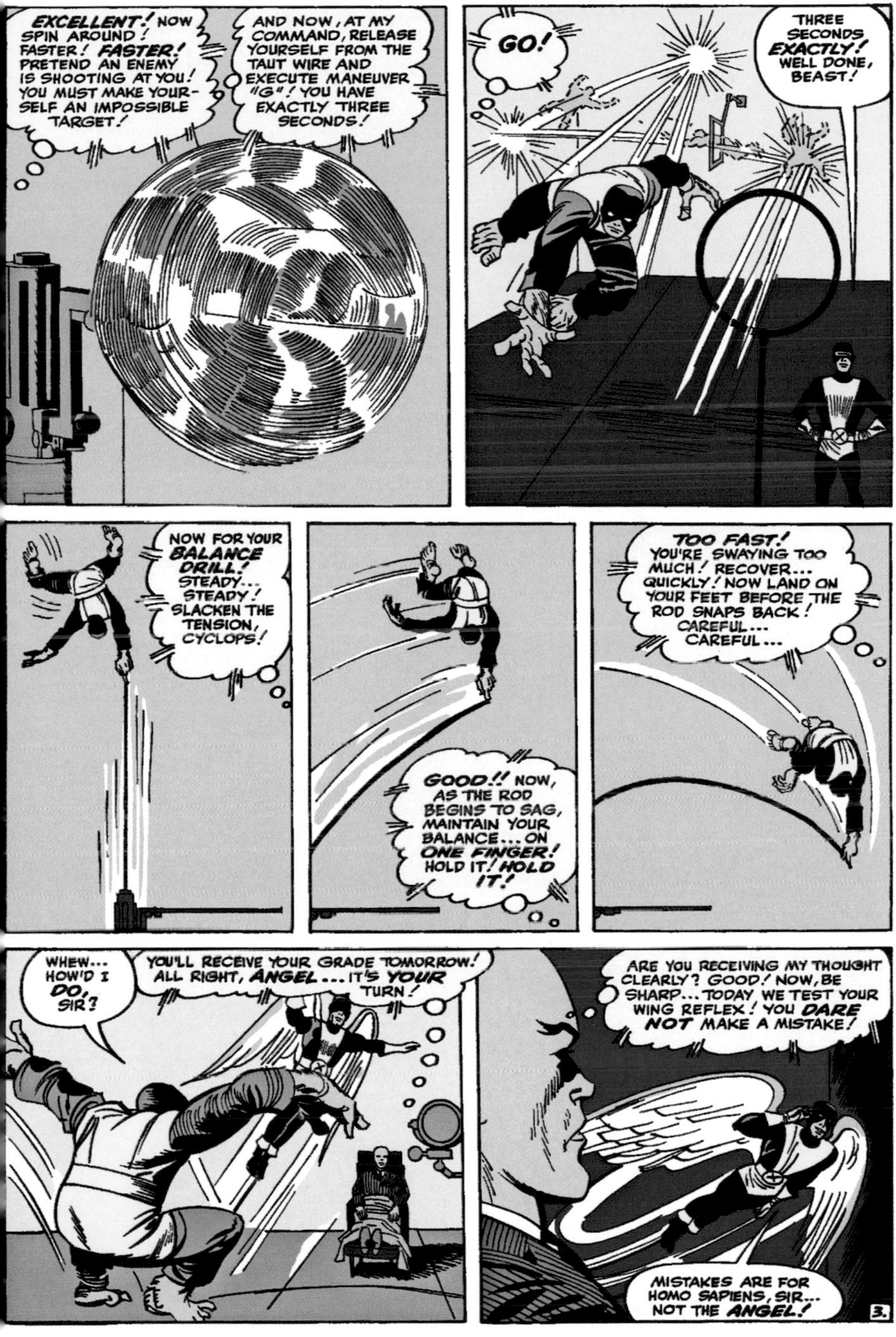
EXCELLENT! NOW SPIN AROUND! FASTER! FASTER! PRETEND AN ENEMY IS SHOOTING AT YOU! YOU MUST MAKE YOURSELF AN IMPOSSIBLE TARGET!
AND NOW, AT MY COMMAND, RELEASE YOURSELF FROM THE TAUT WIRE AND EXECUTE MANEUVER "G"! YOU HAVE EXACTLY THREE SECONDS!
GO!
THREE SECONDS EXACTLY! WELL DONE, BEAST!
NOW FOR YOUR BALANCE DRILL! STEADY... STEADY! SLACKEN THE TENSION, CYCLOPS!
GOOD!! NOW, AS THE ROD BEGINS TO SAG, MAINTAIN YOUR BALANCE... ON ONE FINGER! HOLD IT! HOLD IT!
TOO FAST! YOU'RE SWAYING TOO MUCH! RECOVER... QUICKLY! NOW LAND ON YOUR FEET BEFORE THE ROD SNAPS BACK! CAREFUL... CAREFUL...
WHEW... HOW'D I DO, SIR?
YOU'LL RECEIVE YOUR GRADE TOMORROW! ALL RIGHT, ANGEL... IT'S YOUR TURN!
ARE YOU RECEIVING MY THOUGHT CLEARLY? GOOD! NOW, BE SHARP... TODAY WE TEST YOUR WING REFLEX! YOU DARE NOT MAKE A MISTAKE!
MISTAKES ARE FOR HOMO SAPIENS, SIR... NOT THE ANGEL!
3.

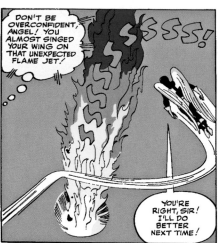

DON'T BE OVERCONFIDENT, ANGEL! YOU ALMOST SINGED YOUR WING ON THAT UNEXPECTED FLAME JET!

SSSSSS!

YOU'RE RIGHT, SIR! I'LL DO BETTER NEXT TIME!

GOOD! YOU AVOIDED THE SECOND OBSTACLE WITH SECONDS TO SPARE!

KLACK!

AHHH! NOW I'M GETTING WARMED UP!

FIRST TIME I EVER FLEW THE SPANNER WITHOUT A SLIP!

WHA... WHAT'S THIS??

I WARNED YOU AGAINST OVER-CONFIDENCE! THIS SUDDEN SOUND CONCUSSION IS TO TEST YOUR SURVIVAL ABILITY! YOU MUST NOT FALL TO THE GROUND!

HOLD ON, ANGEL! FLAP YOUR WINGS! KEEP FLAPPING... DON'T STOP! YOU CAN DO IT, BOY! YOU MUSTN'T FALL!

THAT WAS A CLOSE ONE, SIR! BUT I THINK I'M ALL RIGHT NOW!

YES! YOU'RE BEGINNING TO MASTER THE HOVERING MANEUVER... IT MAY SOME DAY SAVE YOUR LIFE! THAT WILL BE ALL NOW!

4.

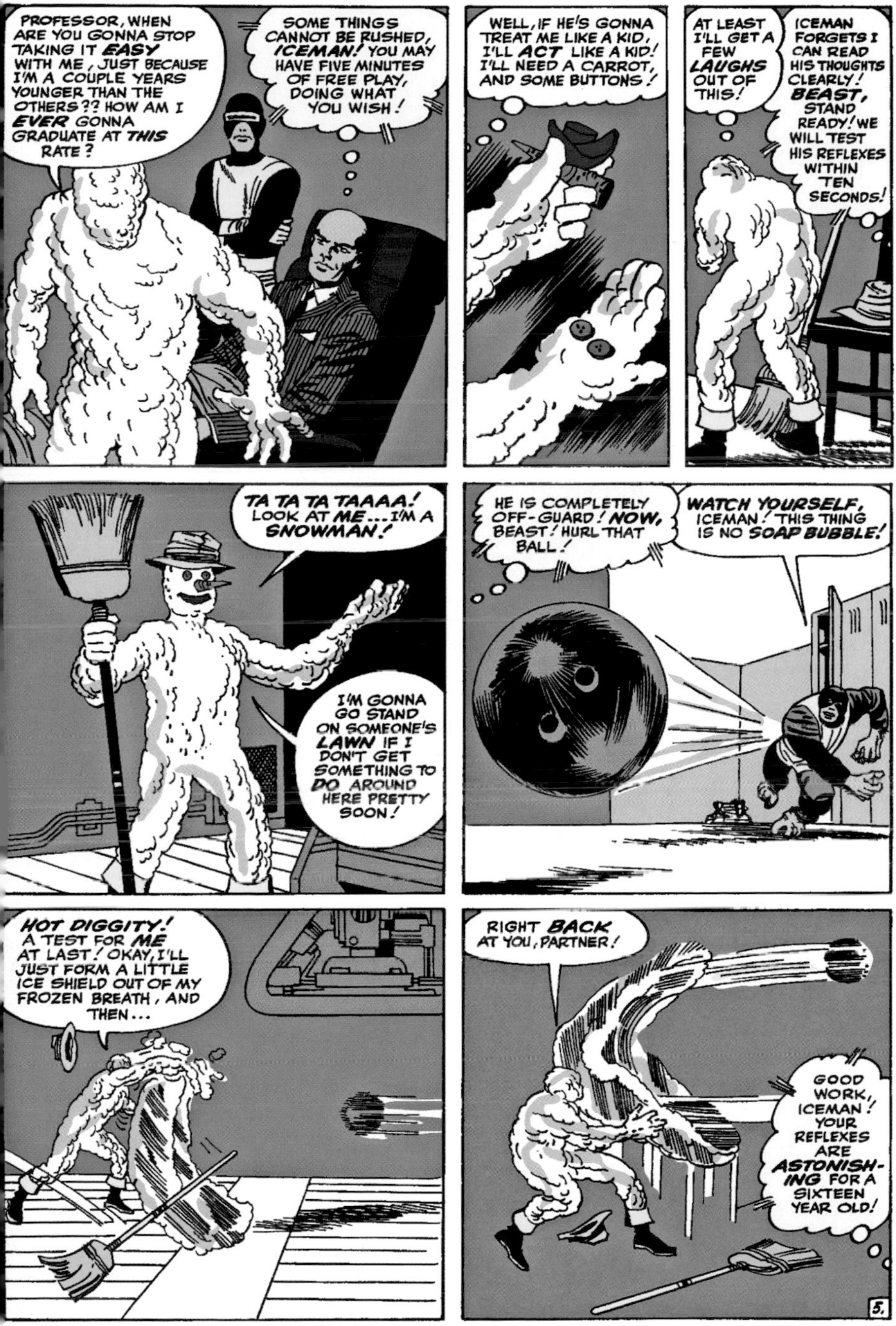
PROFESSOR, WHEN ARE YOU GONNA STOP TAKING IT EASY WITH ME, JUST BECAUSE I'M A COUPLE YEARS YOUNGER THAN THE OTHERS?? HOW AM I EVER GONNA GRADUATE AT THIS RATE?
SOME THINGS CANNOT BE RUSHED, ICEMAN! YOU MAY HAVE FIVE MINUTES OF FREE PLAY, DOING WHAT YOU WISH!
WELL, IF HE'S GONNA TREAT ME LIKE A KID, I'LL ACT LIKE A KID! I'LL NEED A CARROT, AND SOME BUTTONS!
AT LEAST I'LL GET A FEW LAUGHS OUT OF THIS!
ICEMAN FORGETS I CAN READ HIS THOUGHTS CLEARLY! BEAST, STAND READY! WE WILL TEST HIS REFLEXES WITHIN TEN SECONDS!
TA TA TA TAAAA! LOOK AT ME... I'M A SNOWMAN!
I'M GONNA GO STAND ON SOMEONE'S LAWN IF I DON'T GET SOMETHING TO DO AROUND HERE PRETTY SOON!
HE IS COMPLETELY OFF-GUARD! NOW, BEAST! HURL THAT BALL!
WATCH YOURSELF, ICEMAN! THIS THING IS NO SOAP BUBBLE!
HOT DIGGITY! A TEST FOR ME AT LAST! OKAY, I'LL JUST FORM A LITTLE ICE SHIELD OUT OF MY FROZEN BREATH, AND THEN...
RIGHT BACK AT YOU, PARTNER!
GOOD WORK, ICEMAN! YOUR REFLEXES ARE ASTONISHING FOR A SIXTEEN YEAR OLD!
5.

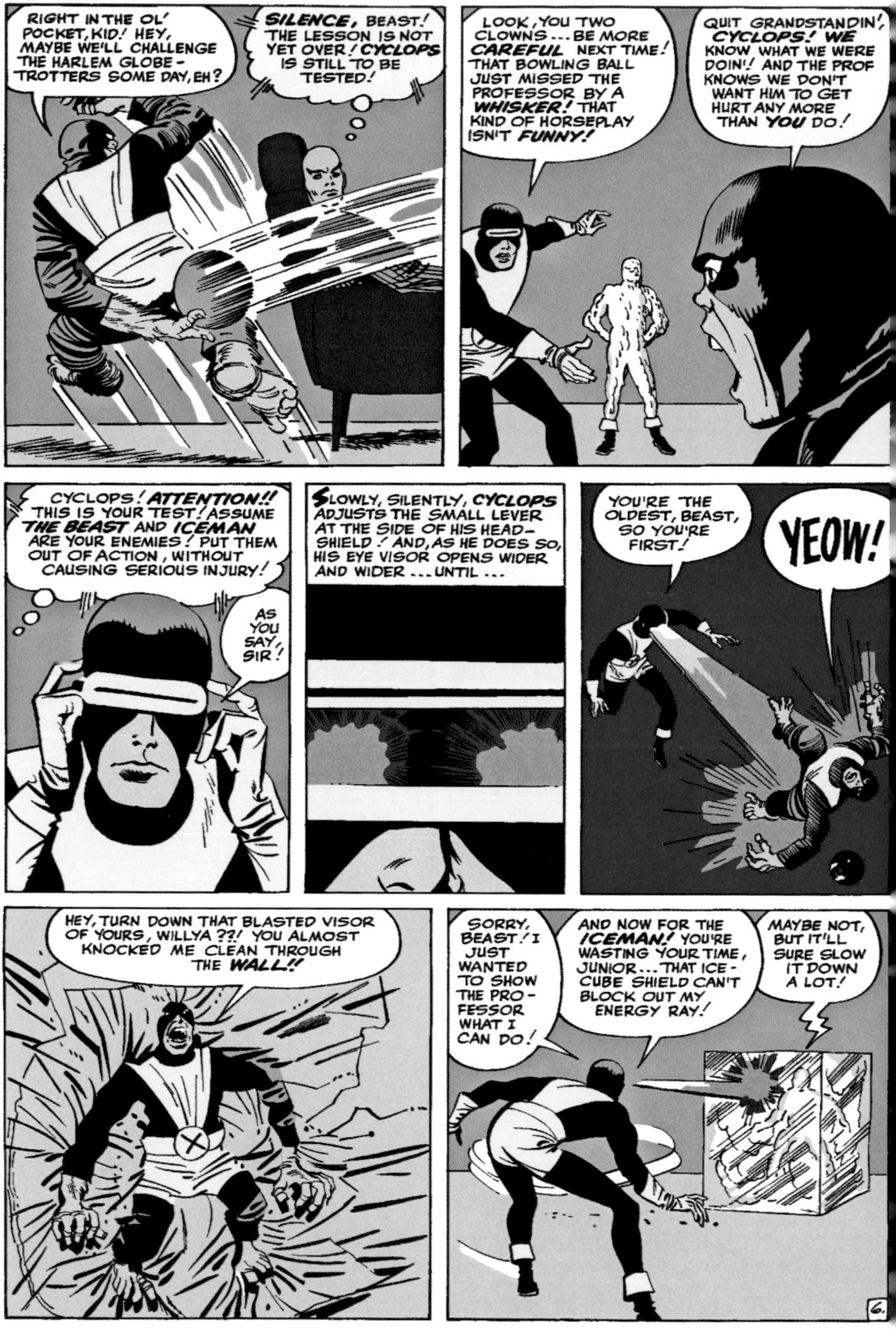
RIGHT IN THE OL' POCKET, KID! HEY, MAYBE WE'LL CHALLENGE THE HARLEM GLOBE-TROTTERS SOME DAY, EH?
SILENCE, BEAST! THE LESSON IS NOT YET OVER! CYCLOPS IS STILL TO BE TESTED!
LOOK, YOU TWO CLOWNS... BE MORE CAREFUL NEXT TIME! THAT BOWLING BALL JUST MISSED THE PROFESSOR BY A WHISKER! THAT KIND OF HORSEPLAY ISN'T FUNNY!
QUIT GRANDSTANDIN', CYCLOPS! WE KNOW WHAT WE WERE DOIN'! AND THE PROF KNOWS WE DON'T WANT HIM TO GET HURT ANY MORE THAN YOU DO!
CYCLOPS! ATTENTION!! THIS IS YOUR TEST! ASSUME THE BEAST AND ICEMAN ARE YOUR ENEMIES! PUT THEM OUT OF ACTION, WITHOUT CAUSING SERIOUS INJURY!
AS YOU SAY, SIR!
SLOWLY, SILENTLY, CYCLOPS ADJUSTS THE SMALL LEVER AT THE SIDE OF HIS HEAD-SHIELD! AND, AS HE DOES SO, HIS EYE VISOR OPENS WIDER AND WIDER... UNTIL...
YOU'RE THE OLDEST, BEAST, SO YOU'RE FIRST!
YEOW!
HEY, TURN DOWN THAT BLASTED VISOR OF YOURS, WILLYA ??! YOU ALMOST KNOCKED ME CLEAN THROUGH THE WALL!!
SORRY, BEAST! I JUST WANTED TO SHOW THE PROFESSOR WHAT I CAN DO!
AND NOW FOR THE ICEMAN! YOU'RE WASTING YOUR TIME, JUNIOR... THAT ICE-CUBE SHIELD CAN'T BLOCK OUT MY ENERGY RAY!
MAYBE NOT, BUT IT'LL SURE SLOW IT DOWN A LOT!
6.

HEY!! THAT'S NOT **FAIR!** YOU'RE OPENIN' THAT COTTON-PICKIN' **VISOR** OF YOURS **WIDER!**

ICEMAN, FOR THE KIND OF CAREER **WE'RE** TRAINING FOR, THERE'S NO SUCH WORD AS "**FAIR**"!

NOW **PROTECT YOURSELF!** MY ENERGY BEAM IS SMASHING THROUGH!

THIS IS **ONE** DAY I SHOULDA STOOD IN BED!

OKAY... TURN THAT BLAMED BEAM **OFF,** WILLYA?

WHUP!

ANGEL! BEAST! JOIN **ICEMAN!** TRY TO SUBDUE **CYCLOPS!**

THANKS, PROF! I COULD **USE** A LITTLE HELP!

IT IS NOT FOR YOUR SAKE ALONE, LAD! A FEW MINUTES OF ROUGHHOUSE IS GOOD FOR **ALL** OF YOU...TO HELP YOU LET OFF STEAM!

THEN, SUDDENLY, MINUTES LATER, A SHARP COMMANDING THOUGHT PIERCES THE BRAIN OF EACH OF THE FOUR RAMPAGING YOUTHS...

ENOUGH! THE LESSON IS OVER! WE MUST TURN OUR ENERGIES TO **DIFFERENT** MATTERS! RETURN TO YOUR PLACES.... **AT ONCE!!**

STUNNED BY THE FORCE AND EXPLOSIVE POWER OF **PROFESSOR XAVIER'S** MENTAL COMMAND, THE **X-MEN** RECOIL AND DRAW BACK, THEIR FRIENDLY FREE-FOR-ALL COMPLETELY FORGOTTEN!

WHEW! HE ALMOST BOWLED ME OVER WITH **THAT** ONE!

LET'S SIMMER DOWN AND SEE WHAT HAPPENS NEXT!

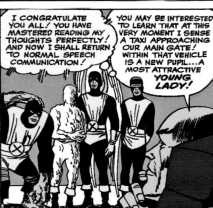

I CONGRATULATE YOU ALL! YOU HAVE MASTERED READING MY THOUGHTS PERFECTLY! AND NOW I SHALL RETURN TO NORMAL SPEECH COMMUNICATION!

YOU MAY BE INTERESTED TO LEARN THAT AT THIS VERY MOMENT I SENSE A TAXI APPROACHING OUR MAIN GATE! WITHIN THAT VEHICLE IS A NEW PUPIL...A MOST ATTRACTIVE **YOUNG LADY!**

7

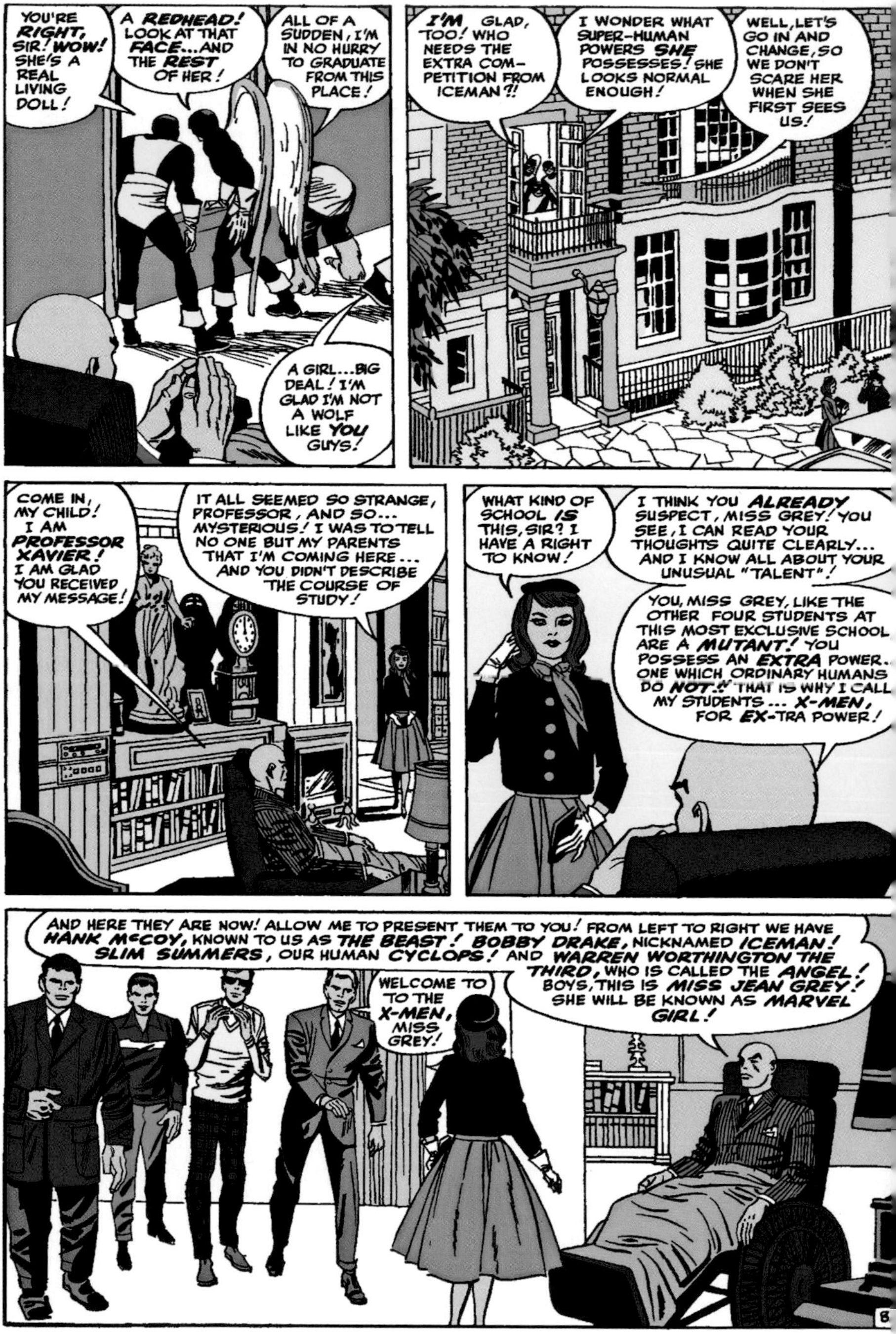

YOU'RE RIGHT, SIR! WOW! SHE'S A REAL LIVING DOLL!
A REDHEAD! LOOK AT THAT FACE...AND THE REST OF HER!
ALL OF A SUDDEN, I'M IN NO HURRY TO GRADUATE FROM THIS PLACE!
A GIRL...BIG DEAL! I'M GLAD I'M NOT A WOLF LIKE YOU GUYS!
I'M GLAD, TOO! WHO NEEDS THE EXTRA COM-PETITION FROM ICEMAN?!
I WONDER WHAT SUPER-HUMAN POWERS SHE POSSESSES! SHE LOOKS NORMAL ENOUGH!
WELL, LET'S GO IN AND CHANGE, SO WE DON'T SCARE HER WHEN SHE FIRST SEES US!
COME IN, MY CHILD! I AM PROFESSOR XAVIER! I AM GLAD YOU RECEIVED MY MESSAGE!
IT ALL SEEMED SO STRANGE, PROFESSOR, AND SO... MYSTERIOUS! I WAS TO TELL NO ONE BUT MY PARENTS THAT I'M COMING HERE... AND YOU DIDN'T DESCRIBE THE COURSE OF STUDY!
WHAT KIND OF SCHOOL IS THIS, SIR? I HAVE A RIGHT TO KNOW!
I THINK YOU ALREADY SUSPECT, MISS GREY! YOU SEE, I CAN READ YOUR THOUGHTS QUITE CLEARLY... AND I KNOW ALL ABOUT YOUR UNUSUAL "TALENT"!
YOU, MISS GREY, LIKE THE OTHER FOUR STUDENTS AT THIS MOST EXCLUSIVE SCHOOL ARE A MUTANT! YOU POSSESS AN EXTRA POWER.. ONE WHICH ORDINARY HUMANS DO NOT!! THAT IS WHY I CALL MY STUDENTS... X-MEN, FOR EX-TRA POWER!
AND HERE THEY ARE NOW! ALLOW ME TO PRESENT THEM TO YOU! FROM LEFT TO RIGHT WE HAVE HANK McCOY, KNOWN TO US AS THE BEAST! BOBBY DRAKE, NICKNAMED ICEMAN! SLIM SUMMERS, OUR HUMAN CYCLOPS! AND WARREN WORTHINGTON THE THIRD, WHO IS CALLED THE ANGEL! BOYS, THIS IS MISS JEAN GREY! SHE WILL BE KNOWN AS MARVEL GIRL!
WELCOME TO TO THE X-MEN, MISS GREY!
8

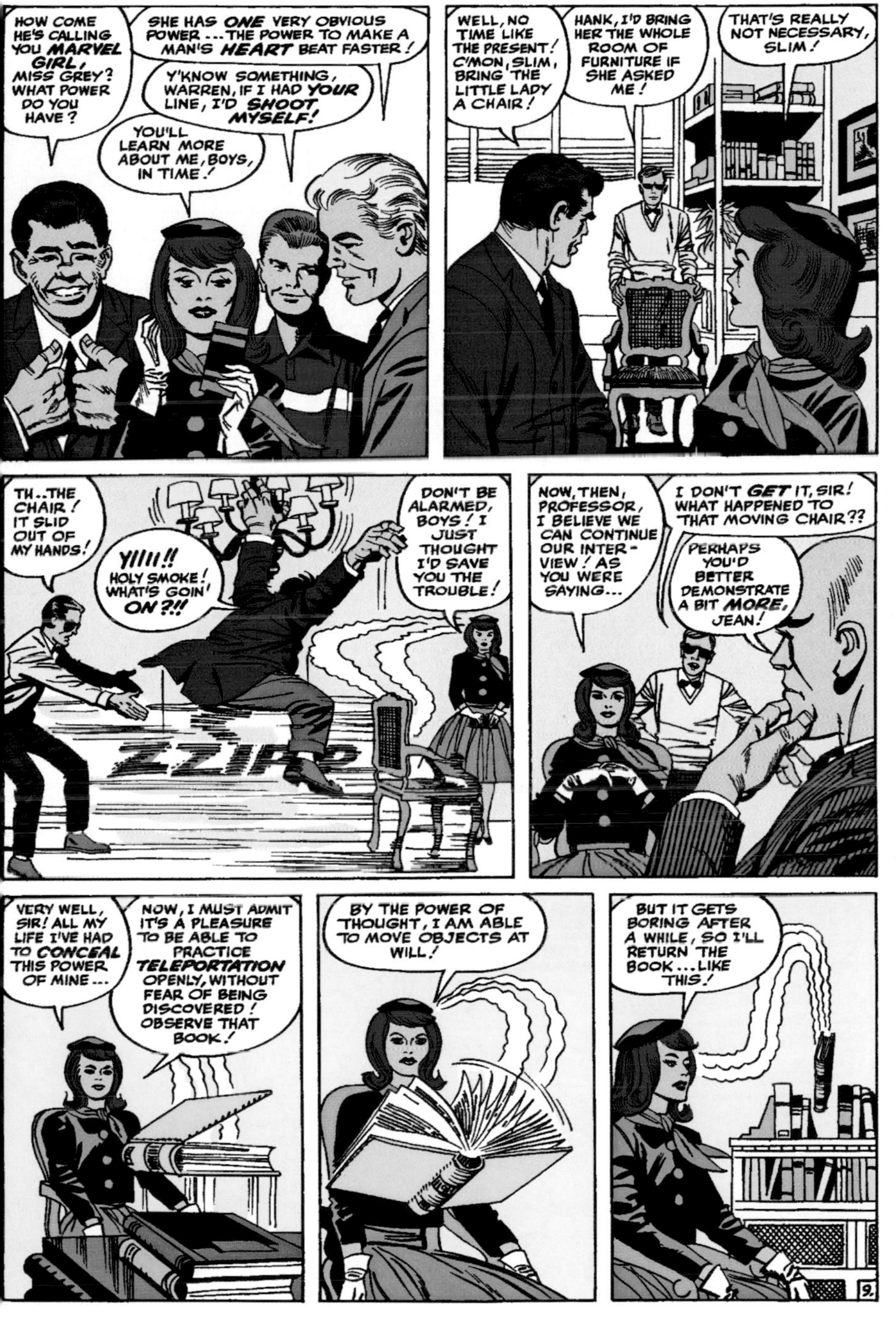
HOW COME HE'S CALLING YOU MARVEL GIRL, MISS GREY? WHAT POWER DO YOU HAVE?
SHE HAS ONE VERY OBVIOUS POWER ... THE POWER TO MAKE A MAN'S HEART BEAT FASTER!
Y'KNOW SOMETHING, WARREN, IF I HAD YOUR LINE, I'D SHOOT MYSELF!
YOU'LL LEARN MORE ABOUT ME, BOYS, IN TIME!
WELL, NO TIME LIKE THE PRESENT! C'MON, SLIM, BRING THE LITTLE LADY A CHAIR!
HANK, I'D BRING HER THE WHOLE ROOM OF FURNITURE IF SHE ASKED ME!
THAT'S REALLY NOT NECESSARY, SLIM!
TH..THE CHAIR! IT SLID OUT OF MY HANDS!
YIIII!! HOLY SMOKE! WHAT'S GOIN' ON?!!
ZZIPP
DON'T BE ALARMED, BOYS! I JUST THOUGHT I'D SAVE YOU THE TROUBLE!
NOW, THEN, PROFESSOR, I BELIEVE WE CAN CONTINUE OUR INTER-VIEW! AS YOU WERE SAYING...
I DON'T GET IT, SIR! WHAT HAPPENED TO THAT MOVING CHAIR??
PERHAPS YOU'D BETTER DEMONSTRATE A BIT MORE, JEAN!
VERY WELL, SIR! ALL MY LIFE I'VE HAD TO CONCEAL THIS POWER OF MINE...
NOW, I MUST ADMIT IT'S A PLEASURE TO BE ABLE TO PRACTICE TELEPORTATION OPENLY, WITHOUT FEAR OF BEING DISCOVERED! OBSERVE THAT BOOK!
BY THE POWER OF THOUGHT, I AM ABLE TO MOVE OBJECTS AT WILL!
BUT IT GETS BORING AFTER A WHILE, SO I'LL RETURN THE BOOK ... LIKE THIS!
9.

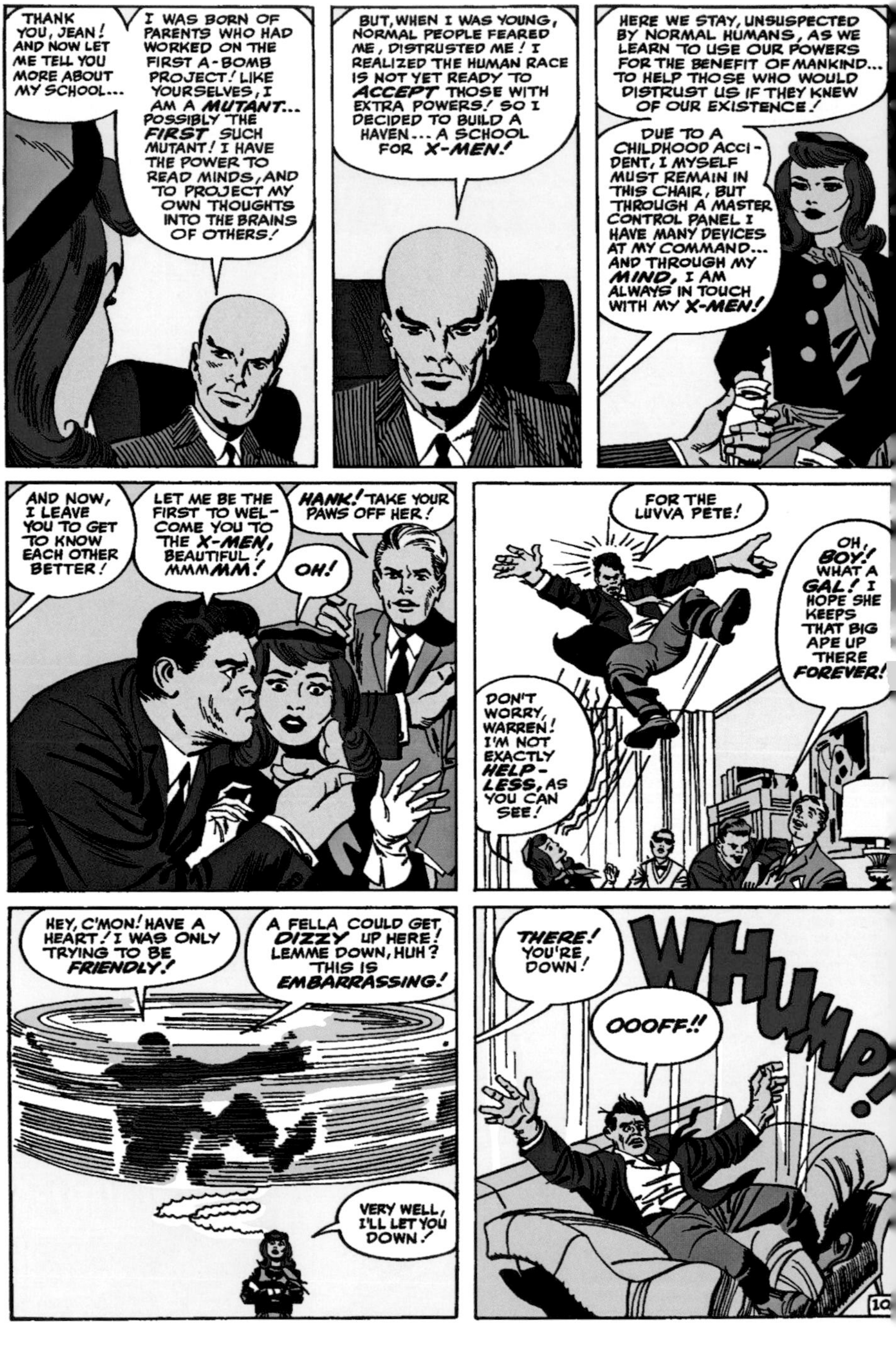
THANK YOU, JEAN! AND NOW LET ME TELL YOU MORE ABOUT MY SCHOOL...
I WAS BORN OF PARENTS WHO HAD WORKED ON THE FIRST A-BOMB PROJECT! LIKE YOURSELVES, I AM A MUTANT... POSSIBLY THE FIRST SUCH MUTANT! I HAVE THE POWER TO READ MINDS, AND TO PROJECT MY OWN THOUGHTS INTO THE BRAINS OF OTHERS!
BUT, WHEN I WAS YOUNG, NORMAL PEOPLE FEARED ME, DISTRUSTED ME! I REALIZED THE HUMAN RACE IS NOT YET READY TO ACCEPT THOSE WITH EXTRA POWERS! SO I DECIDED TO BUILD A HAVEN... A SCHOOL FOR X-MEN!
HERE WE STAY, UNSUSPECTED BY NORMAL HUMANS, AS WE LEARN TO USE OUR POWERS FOR THE BENEFIT OF MANKIND... TO HELP THOSE WHO WOULD DISTRUST US IF THEY KNEW OF OUR EXISTENCE!
DUE TO A CHILDHOOD ACCI-DENT, I MYSELF MUST REMAIN IN THIS CHAIR, BUT THROUGH A MASTER CONTROL PANEL I HAVE MANY DEVICES AT MY COMMAND... AND THROUGH MY MIND, I AM ALWAYS IN TOUCH WITH MY X-MEN!
AND NOW, I LEAVE YOU TO GET TO KNOW EACH OTHER BETTER!
LET ME BE THE FIRST TO WEL-COME YOU TO THE X-MEN, BEAUTIFUL! MMMMM!
HANK! TAKE YOUR PAWS OFF HER!
OH!
FOR THE LUVVA PETE!
OH, BOY! WHAT A GAL! I HOPE SHE KEEPS THAT BIG APE UP THERE FOREVER!
DON'T WORRY, WARREN! I'M NOT EXACTLY HELP-LESS, AS YOU CAN SEE!
HEY, C'MON! HAVE A HEART! I WAS ONLY TRYING TO BE FRIENDLY!
A FELLA COULD GET DIZZY UP HERE! LEMME DOWN, HUH? THIS IS EMBARRASSING!
VERY WELL, I'LL LET YOU DOWN!
THERE! YOU'RE DOWN!
WHUMP!
OOOFF!!
10

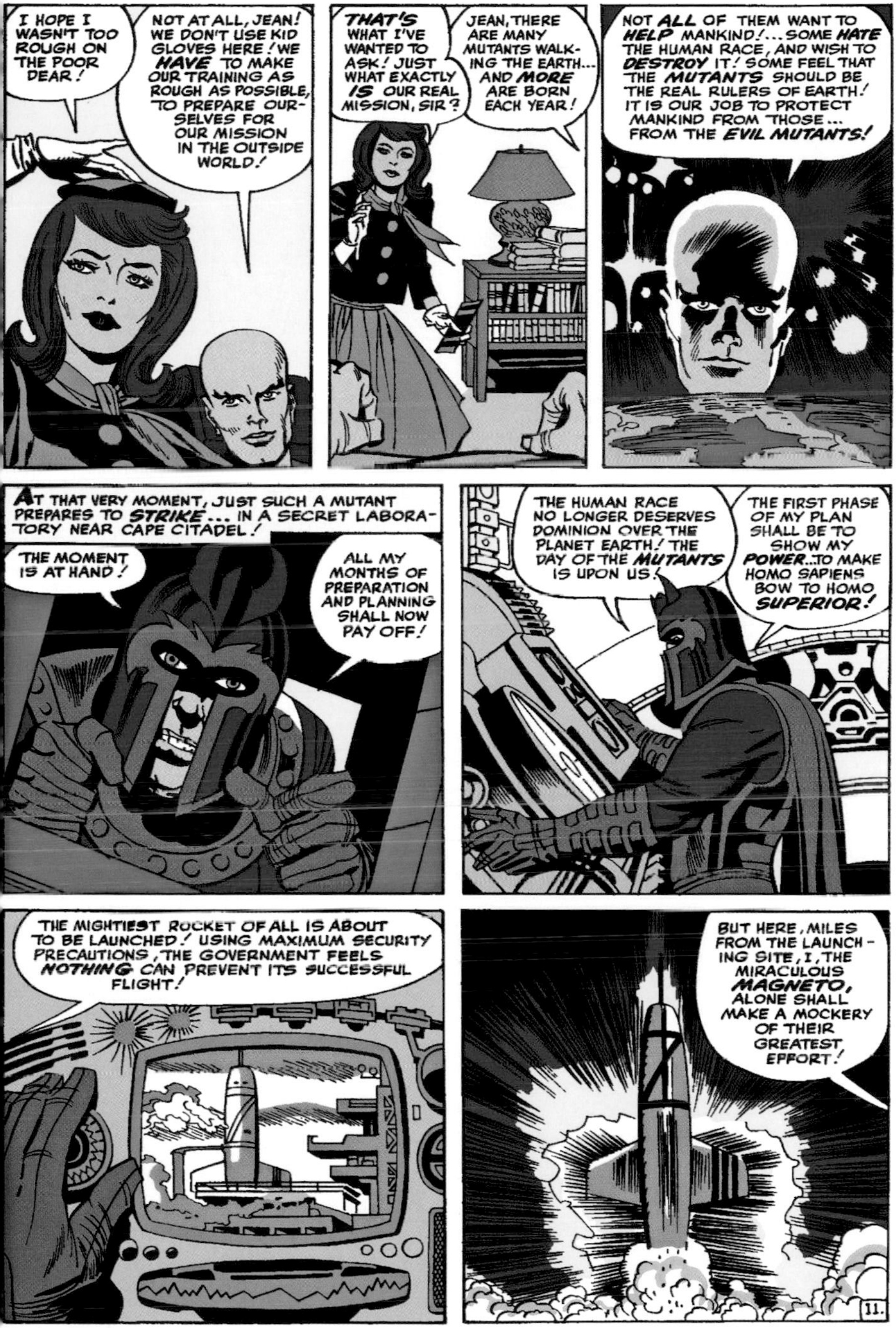
I HOPE I WASN'T TOO ROUGH ON THE POOR DEAR!
NOT AT ALL, JEAN! WE DON'T USE KID GLOVES HERE! WE HAVE TO MAKE OUR TRAINING AS ROUGH AS POSSIBLE, TO PREPARE OURSELVES FOR OUR MISSION IN THE OUTSIDE WORLD!
THAT'S WHAT I'VE WANTED TO ASK! JUST WHAT EXACTLY IS OUR REAL MISSION, SIR?
JEAN, THERE ARE MANY MUTANTS WALKING THE EARTH... AND MORE ARE BORN EACH YEAR!
NOT ALL OF THEM WANT TO HELP MANKIND!... SOME HATE THE HUMAN RACE, AND WISH TO DESTROY IT! SOME FEEL THAT THE MUTANTS SHOULD BE THE REAL RULERS OF EARTH! IT IS OUR JOB TO PROTECT MANKIND FROM THOSE... FROM THE EVIL MUTANTS!
AT THAT VERY MOMENT, JUST SUCH A MUTANT PREPARES TO STRIKE... IN A SECRET LABORATORY NEAR CAPE CITADEL!
THE MOMENT IS AT HAND!
ALL MY MONTHS OF PREPARATION AND PLANNING SHALL NOW PAY OFF!
THE HUMAN RACE NO LONGER DESERVES DOMINION OVER THE PLANET EARTH! THE DAY OF THE MUTANTS IS UPON US!
THE FIRST PHASE OF MY PLAN SHALL BE TO SHOW MY POWER... TO MAKE HOMO SAPIENS BOW TO HOMO SUPERIOR!
THE MIGHTIEST ROCKET OF ALL IS ABOUT TO BE LAUNCHED! USING MAXIMUM SECURITY PRECAUTIONS, THE GOVERNMENT FEELS NOTHING CAN PREVENT ITS SUCCESSFUL FLIGHT!
BUT HERE, MILES FROM THE LAUNCHING SITE, I, THE MIRACULOUS MAGNETO, ALONE SHALL MAKE A MOCKERY OF THEIR GREATEST EFFORT!
11.

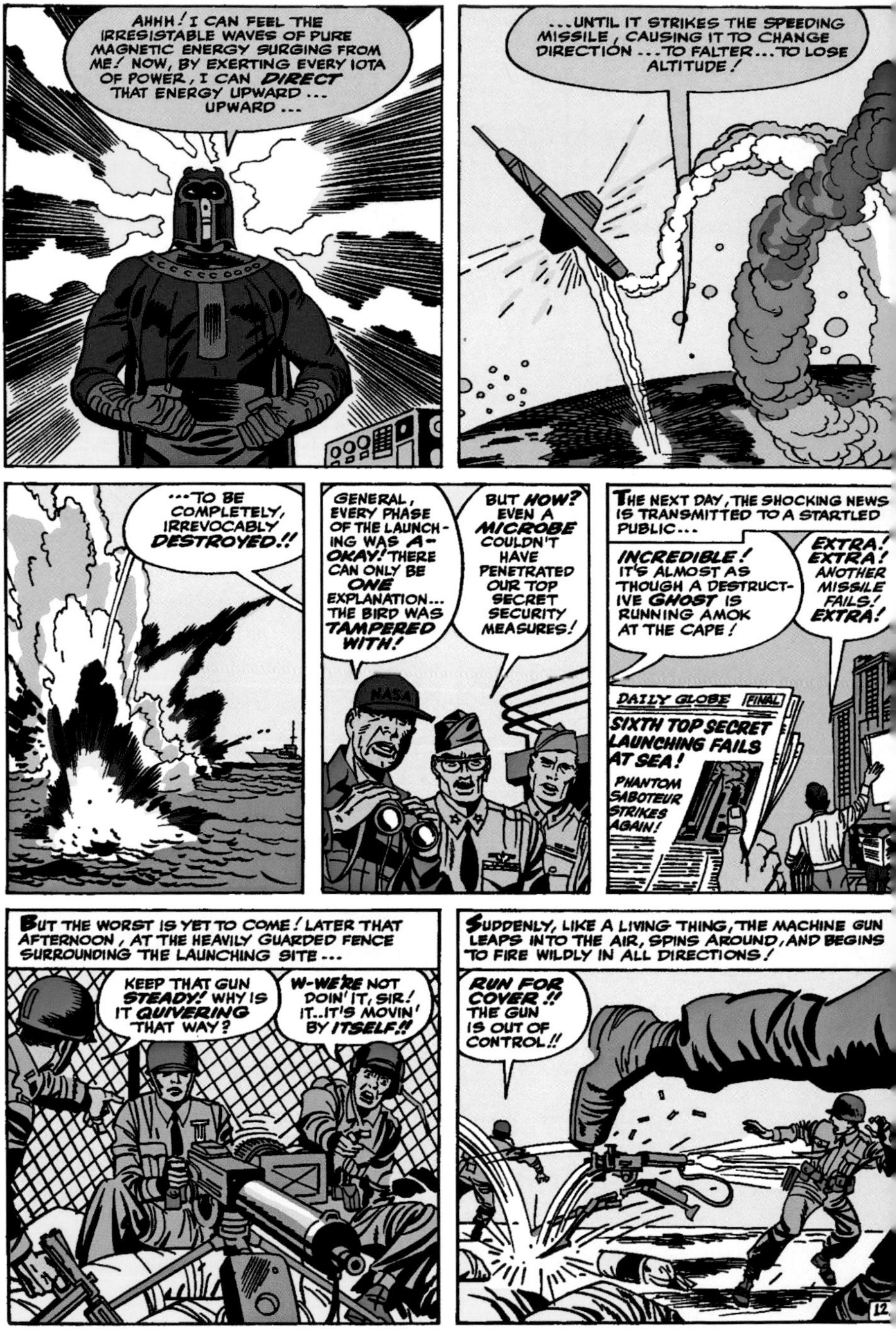
AHHH! I CAN FEEL THE IRRESISTABLE WAVES OF PURE MAGNETIC ENERGY SURGING FROM ME! NOW, BY EXERTING EVERY IOTA OF POWER, I CAN DIRECT THAT ENERGY UPWARD... UPWARD...
...UNTIL IT STRIKES THE SPEEDING MISSILE, CAUSING IT TO CHANGE DIRECTION...TO FALTER...TO LOSE ALTITUDE!
...TO BE COMPLETELY, IRREVOCABLY DESTROYED.!!
GENERAL, EVERY PHASE OF THE LAUNCHING WAS A-OKAY! THERE CAN ONLY BE ONE EXPLANATION... THE BIRD WAS TAMPERED WITH!
BUT HOW? EVEN A MICROBE COULDN'T HAVE PENETRATED OUR TOP SECRET SECURITY MEASURES!
NASA
THE NEXT DAY, THE SHOCKING NEWS IS TRANSMITTED TO A STARTLED PUBLIC...
INCREDIBLE! IT'S ALMOST AS THOUGH A DESTRUCTIVE GHOST IS RUNNING AMOK AT THE CAPE!
EXTRA! EXTRA! ANOTHER MISSILE FAILS! EXTRA!
DAILY GLOBE FINAL
SIXTH TOP SECRET LAUNCHING FAILS AT SEA!
PHANTOM SABOTEUR STRIKES AGAIN!
BUT THE WORST IS YET TO COME! LATER THAT AFTERNOON, AT THE HEAVILY GUARDED FENCE SURROUNDING THE LAUNCHING SITE...
KEEP THAT GUN STEADY! WHY IS IT QUIVERING THAT WAY?
W-WE'RE NOT DOIN' IT, SIR! IT...IT'S MOVIN' BY ITSELF!!
SUDDENLY, LIKE A LIVING THING, THE MACHINE GUN LEAPS INTO THE AIR, SPINS AROUND, AND BEGINS TO FIRE WILDLY IN ALL DIRECTIONS!
RUN FOR COVER!! THE GUN IS OUT OF CONTROL!!
12

BUT, THE MACHINE GUN IS NOT THE *ONLY* THING THAT SUDDENLY, MADDENINGLY SEEM TO GO AMOK!

RUN! THE TANK IS MOVING BY *ITSELF!* GANGWAY!

IT..IT'S IMPOSSIBLE! AND YET...IT'S ACTING LIKE IT HAS A MIND OF ITS OWN! LIKE IT'S *TRYING* TO MENACE US!

SWISH!

CLANK!

CLANK!

WITHIN SECONDS, THE ENTIRE INSTALLATION IS ALARMED, AS EMERGENCY MEASURES ARE SWIFTLY BROUGHT INTO PLAY! AND THEN...

SOUND THE ALARM! CONDITION RED! ALERT THE PENTAGON!

GENERAL! LOOK! ABOVE US... IN THE SKY!

APPEARING AS THOUGH BY MAGIC, OVER THE HEADS OF THE ASTONISHED TROOPS, HUGE LETTERS TAKE SHAPE...COMPOSED OF THE DUST PARTICLES FROM THE AIR ITSELF, SKILLFULLY MAGNETIZED INTO A MESSAGE BY THE UNSEEN MUTANT!

SURRENDER THE BASE OR I'LL TAKE IT BY FORCE!

Magneto

MAGNETO? WHO... *WHAT* IS MAGNETO??

GENERAL, WHAT DOES IT *MEAN?* IS SOMEONE PLAYING A GRIM *PRANK?*

YOU SAW THAT MACHINE GUN... THAT TANK... RAMPAGING OUT OF CONTROL! THIS IS *NO JOKE,* COLONEL!

THEY ARE STARTLED! *GOOD!* THE ELEMENT OF SURPRISE IS IN MY FAVOR!

BUT THEY'RE MAKING NO MOVE TO SURRENDER! PERHAPS THEY NEED *ANOTHER* DEMONSTRATION OF MY POWER!

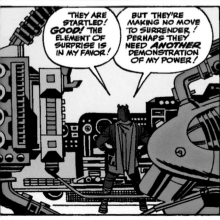

I'LL DIRECT MY MAGNETIC IMPULSES INTO THIS ENERGIZER, TO INCREASE THEIR POWER, AND THEN I'LL LEAVE THE HELPLESS HOMO SAPIENS WITH NO ROOM FOR DOUBT!

13.

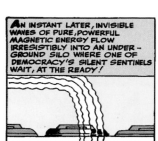

AN INSTANT LATER, INVISIBLE WAVES OF PURE, POWERFUL MAGNETIC ENERGY FLOW IRRESISTIBLY INTO AN UNDER-GROUND SILO WHERE ONE OF DEMOCRACY'S SILENT SENTINELS WAIT, AT THE READY!

AND THEN, MANIPULATED BY A SINISTER INTELLIGENCE, MANY HUNDREDS OF YARDS AWAY, THE MAGNETIC FORCE LIFTS THE SILO HEAD, ACTIVATING THE MIGHTY MISSILE!!

DEMONSTRATING A POWER WHICH THE HUMAN BRAIN IS ALMOST UNABLE TO COMPREHEND, MAGNETO CAUSES THE GRIM ROCKET TO FALL INTO THE SEA MANY MILES FROM SHORE, NEXT TO AN UNMANNED TARGET SHIP!

BUT STILL, THE THOUGHT OF SURRENDER NEVER CROSSES THE MINDS OF THE FIGHTING-MAD BASE PERSONNEL!

SERGEANT! ORDER THE GUARD DOUBLED AT EVERY MISSILE CONTROL CENTER! ANY ROCKET DEEMED A MENACE IS TO BE DESTROYED INSTANTLY!

SOME POWER BEYOND OUR UNDERSTANDING IS AFFECTING OUR WEAPONS! WE MUST FIND THIS MAGNETO!

GENERAL, LOOK! THAT COMMOTION AT THE MAIN GATE! IT SEEMS THAT HE HAS FOUND US FIRST!

HOLD IT, MAC! IF YOU'RE LOOKIN' FOR A MASQUERADE PARTY, YOU'VE COME TO THE WRONG PLACE! BEAT IT!

WELL SAID, GUARD! WHAT A PITY YOU HAVE NO POWER TO BACK UP SUCH IMPRESSIVE WORDS! YOUR PUNY WEAPONS CANNOT STOP ME!

THEY CAN'T, EH? ONE LITTLE BURST OVER YOUR HEAD WILL SURELY CHANGE YOUR MIND!

HEY! WHA—WHAT GIVES? THE GUN WON'T FIRE! THE TRIGGER SEEMS LOCKED IN PLACE!

I CAN'T EVEN LIFT MY GUN! FEELS LIKE IT WEIGHS A TON!

14.

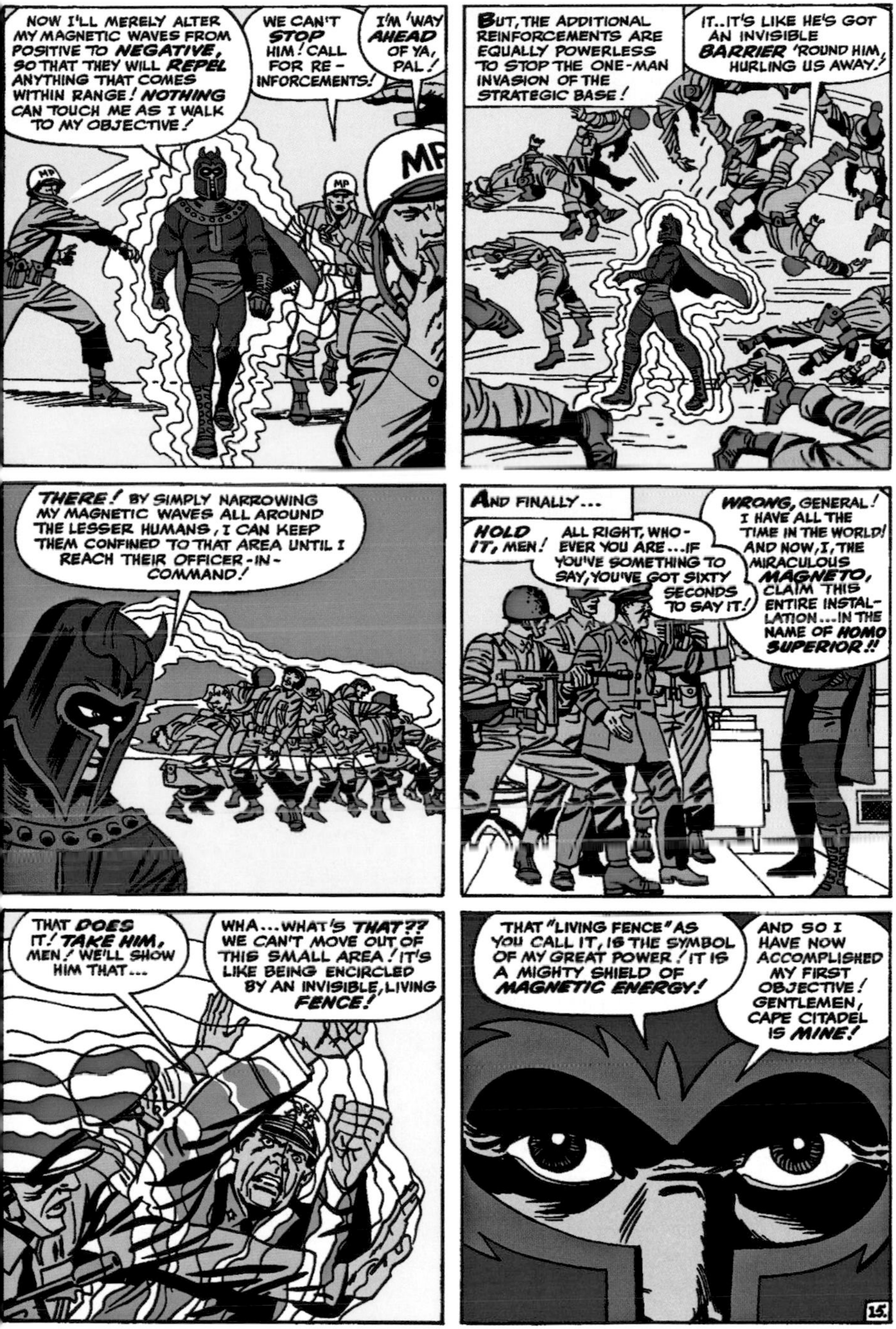
NOW I'LL MERELY ALTER MY MAGNETIC WAVES FROM POSITIVE TO NEGATIVE, SO THAT THEY WILL REPEL ANYTHING THAT COMES WITHIN RANGE! NOTHING CAN TOUCH ME AS I WALK TO MY OBJECTIVE!
WE CAN'T STOP HIM! CALL FOR RE-INFORCEMENTS!
I'M 'WAY AHEAD OF YA, PAL!
MP
MP
MP
BUT, THE ADDITIONAL REINFORCEMENTS ARE EQUALLY POWERLESS TO STOP THE ONE-MAN INVASION OF THE STRATEGIC BASE!
IT..IT'S LIKE HE'S GOT AN INVISIBLE BARRIER 'ROUND HIM, HURLING US AWAY!
THERE! BY SIMPLY NARROWING MY MAGNETIC WAVES ALL AROUND THE LESSER HUMANS, I CAN KEEP THEM CONFINED TO THAT AREA UNTIL I REACH THEIR OFFICER-IN-COMMAND!
MP
AND FINALLY...
HOLD IT, MEN!
ALL RIGHT, WHO-EVER YOU ARE...IF YOU'VE SOMETHING TO SAY, YOU'VE GOT SIXTY SECONDS TO SAY IT!
WRONG, GENERAL! I HAVE ALL THE TIME IN THE WORLD! AND NOW, I, THE MIRACULOUS MAGNETO, CLAIM THIS ENTIRE INSTAL-LATION...IN THE NAME OF HOMO SUPERIOR!!
THAT DOES IT! TAKE HIM, MEN! WE'LL SHOW HIM THAT...
WHA...WHAT'S THAT?? WE CAN'T MOVE OUT OF THIS SMALL AREA! IT'S LIKE BEING ENCIRCLED BY AN INVISIBLE, LIVING FENCE!
THAT "LIVING FENCE" AS YOU CALL IT, IS THE SYMBOL OF MY GREAT POWER! IT IS A MIGHTY SHIELD OF MAGNETIC ENERGY!
AND SO I HAVE NOW ACCOMPLISHED MY FIRST OBJECTIVE! GENTLEMEN, CAPE CITADEL IS MINE!
15.

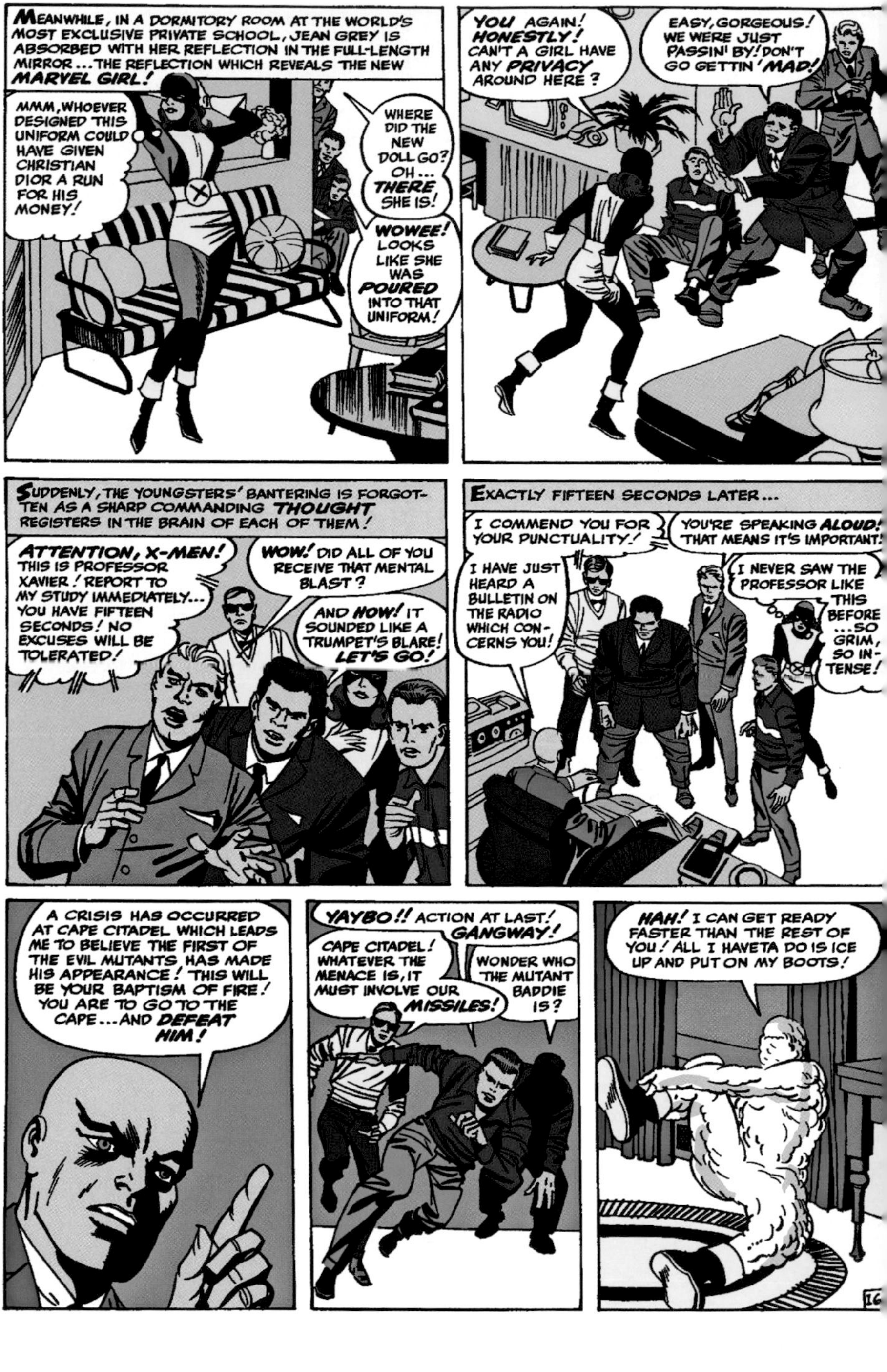
MEANWHILE, IN A DORMITORY ROOM AT THE WORLD'S MOST EXCLUSIVE PRIVATE SCHOOL, JEAN GREY IS ABSORBED WITH HER REFLECTION IN THE FULL-LENGTH MIRROR ... THE REFLECTION WHICH REVEALS THE NEW MARVEL GIRL!
MMM, WHOEVER DESIGNED THIS UNIFORM COULD HAVE GIVEN CHRISTIAN DIOR A RUN FOR HIS MONEY!
WHERE DID THE NEW DOLL GO? OH ... THERE SHE IS!
WOWEE! LOOKS LIKE SHE WAS POURED INTO THAT UNIFORM!
YOU AGAIN! HONESTLY! CAN'T A GIRL HAVE ANY PRIVACY AROUND HERE?
EASY, GORGEOUS! WE WERE JUST PASSIN' BY! DON'T GO GETTIN' MAD!
SUDDENLY, THE YOUNGSTERS' BANTERING IS FORGOTTEN AS A SHARP COMMANDING THOUGHT REGISTERS IN THE BRAIN OF EACH OF THEM!
ATTENTION, X-MEN! THIS IS PROFESSOR XAVIER! REPORT TO MY STUDY IMMEDIATELY... YOU HAVE FIFTEEN SECONDS! NO EXCUSES WILL BE TOLERATED!
WOW! DID ALL OF YOU RECEIVE THAT MENTAL BLAST?
AND HOW! IT SOUNDED LIKE A TRUMPET'S BLARE! LET'S GO!
EXACTLY FIFTEEN SECONDS LATER...
I COMMEND YOU FOR YOUR PUNCTUALITY!
YOU'RE SPEAKING ALOUD! THAT MEANS IT'S IMPORTANT!
I HAVE JUST HEARD A BULLETIN ON THE RADIO WHICH CONCERNS YOU!
I NEVER SAW THE PROFESSOR LIKE THIS BEFORE ...SO GRIM, SO INTENSE!
A CRISIS HAS OCCURRED AT CAPE CITADEL WHICH LEADS ME TO BELIEVE THE FIRST OF THE EVIL MUTANTS HAS MADE HIS APPEARANCE! THIS WILL BE YOUR BAPTISM OF FIRE! YOU ARE TO GO TO THE CAPE ... AND DEFEAT HIM!
YAYBO!! ACTION AT LAST! GANGWAY!
CAPE CITADEL! WHATEVER THE MENACE IS, IT MUST INVOLVE OUR MISSILES!
WONDER WHO THE MUTANT BADDIE IS?
HAH! I CAN GET READY FASTER THAN THE REST OF YOU! ALL I HAVETA DO IS ICE UP AND PUT ON MY BOOTS!
16

AS FOR **ME**, IT'LL BE A PLEASURE TO GET OUT OF THIS HARNESS I HAVE TO WEAR!

HAVING A PAIR OF WINGS CAN BE MORE TROUBLE THAN YOU'D GUESS!

THESE RESTRAINING BELTS OF MINE KEEP MY WINGS FROM BULGING UNDER MY SUIT, BUT AFTER A WHILE THEY FEEL LIKE I'M WEARING A **STRAIT-JACKET!**

AHHH! THAT'S MORE LIKE IT! NOW I FEEL LIKE MYSELF AGAIN! NOW THE **ANGEL** IS READY TO SPREAD HIS WINGS ..AND **FLY!**

BUT THE TIME HAS NOT YET COME FOR THE ANGEL TO FLY! INSTEAD, THE BAND OF SUPER-HUMAN TEEN-AGERS ARE **DRIVEN** TO THE AIRPORT IN PROFESSOR XAVIER'S SPECIALLY-BUILT ROLLS ROYCE, WITH ITS DARK-TINTED WINDOWS!

BOY! IT MUSTA TAKEN A HEAP OF GREEN STAMPS TO BY A CHARIOT LIKE THIS!

NO JOKING, PLEASE! CONCENTRATE ON YOUR MISSION! REVIEW YOUR POWERS! YOUR FOE IS CERTAIN TO BE HIGHLY DANGEROUS!

MINUTES LATER, IN THE PROFESSOR'S REMOTE-CONTROL PRIVATE JET, THE **X-MEN** AND **MARVEL GIRL** ARE WINGING TOWARDS **CAPE CITADEL** AT NEARLY THE SPEED OF SOUND!

YOU MEAN THE PROFESSOR IS GUIDING THIS PLANE FROM THE GROUND... BY **THOUGHT IMPULSES?!** IT'S **UN-BELIEVABLE!**

LOOK, DOLL... WHEN YOU JOIN THE X-MEN, YOU REALIZE **NOTHING'S** UN-BELIEVABLE!

A SHORT TIME LATER, AT THE CAPE!...

CEASE FIRING! IT'S USELESS! WE HAVEN'T ANYTHING IN OUR ARSENAL THAT'LL PENETRATE **MAGNETO'S** MAGNETIC FORCE FIELD!

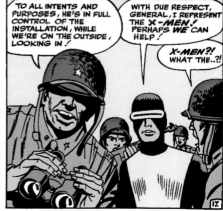

TO ALL INTENTS AND PURPOSES, HE'S IN FULL CONTROL OF THE INSTALLATION, WHILE WE'RE ON THE OUTSIDE, LOOKING IN!

WITH DUE RESPECT, GENERAL, I REPRESENT THE **X-MEN!** PERHAPS **WE** CAN HELP!

X-MEN?! WHAT THE..?!

17

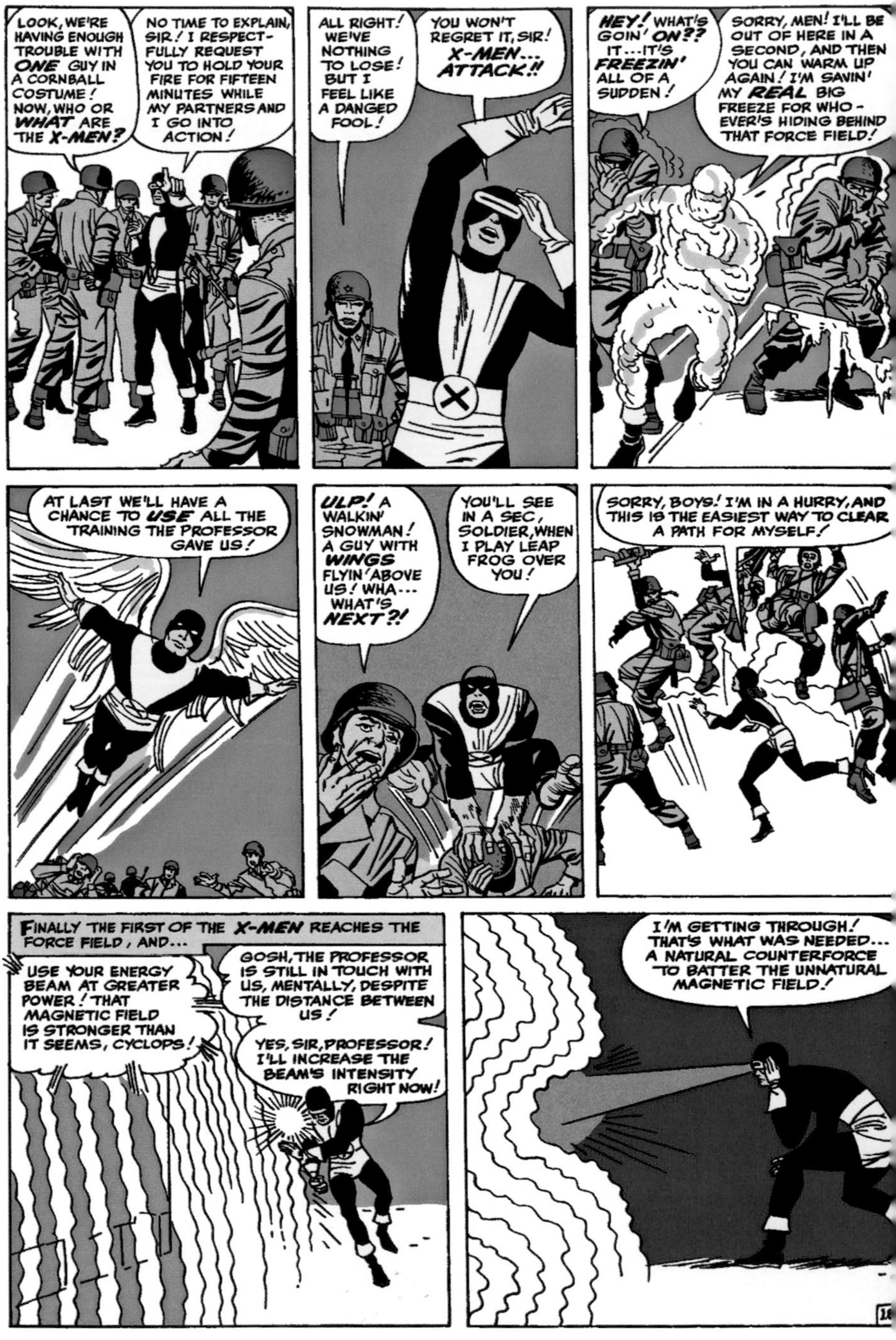

LOOK, WE'RE HAVING ENOUGH TROUBLE WITH ONE GUY IN A CORNBALL COSTUME! NOW, WHO OR WHAT ARE THE X-MEN?
NO TIME TO EXPLAIN, SIR! I RESPECTFULLY REQUEST YOU TO HOLD YOUR FIRE FOR FIFTEEN MINUTES WHILE MY PARTNERS AND I GO INTO ACTION!
ALL RIGHT! WE'VE NOTHING TO LOSE! BUT I FEEL LIKE A DANGED FOOL!
YOU WON'T REGRET IT, SIR! X-MEN... ATTACK!!
HEY! WHAT'S GOIN' ON?? IT...IT'S FREEZIN' ALL OF A SUDDEN!
SORRY, MEN! I'LL BE OUT OF HERE IN A SECOND, AND THEN YOU CAN WARM UP AGAIN! I'M SAVIN' MY REAL BIG FREEZE FOR WHOEVER'S HIDING BEHIND THAT FORCE FIELD!
AT LAST WE'LL HAVE A CHANCE TO USE ALL THE TRAINING THE PROFESSOR GAVE US!
ULP! A WALKIN' SNOWMAN! A GUY WITH WINGS FLYIN' ABOVE US! WHA... WHAT'S NEXT?!
YOU'LL SEE IN A SEC, SOLDIER, WHEN I PLAY LEAP FROG OVER YOU!
SORRY, BOYS! I'M IN A HURRY, AND THIS IS THE EASIEST WAY TO CLEAR A PATH FOR MYSELF!
FINALLY THE FIRST OF THE X-MEN REACHES THE FORCE FIELD, AND...
USE YOUR ENERGY BEAM AT GREATER POWER! THAT MAGNETIC FIELD IS STRONGER THAN IT SEEMS, CYCLOPS!
GOSH, THE PROFESSOR IS STILL IN TOUCH WITH US, MENTALLY, DESPITE THE DISTANCE BETWEEN US!
YES, SIR, PROFESSOR! I'LL INCREASE THE BEAM'S INTENSITY RIGHT NOW!
I'M GETTING THROUGH! THAT'S WHAT WAS NEEDED... A NATURAL COUNTERFORCE TO BATTER THE UNNATURAL MAGNETIC FIELD!

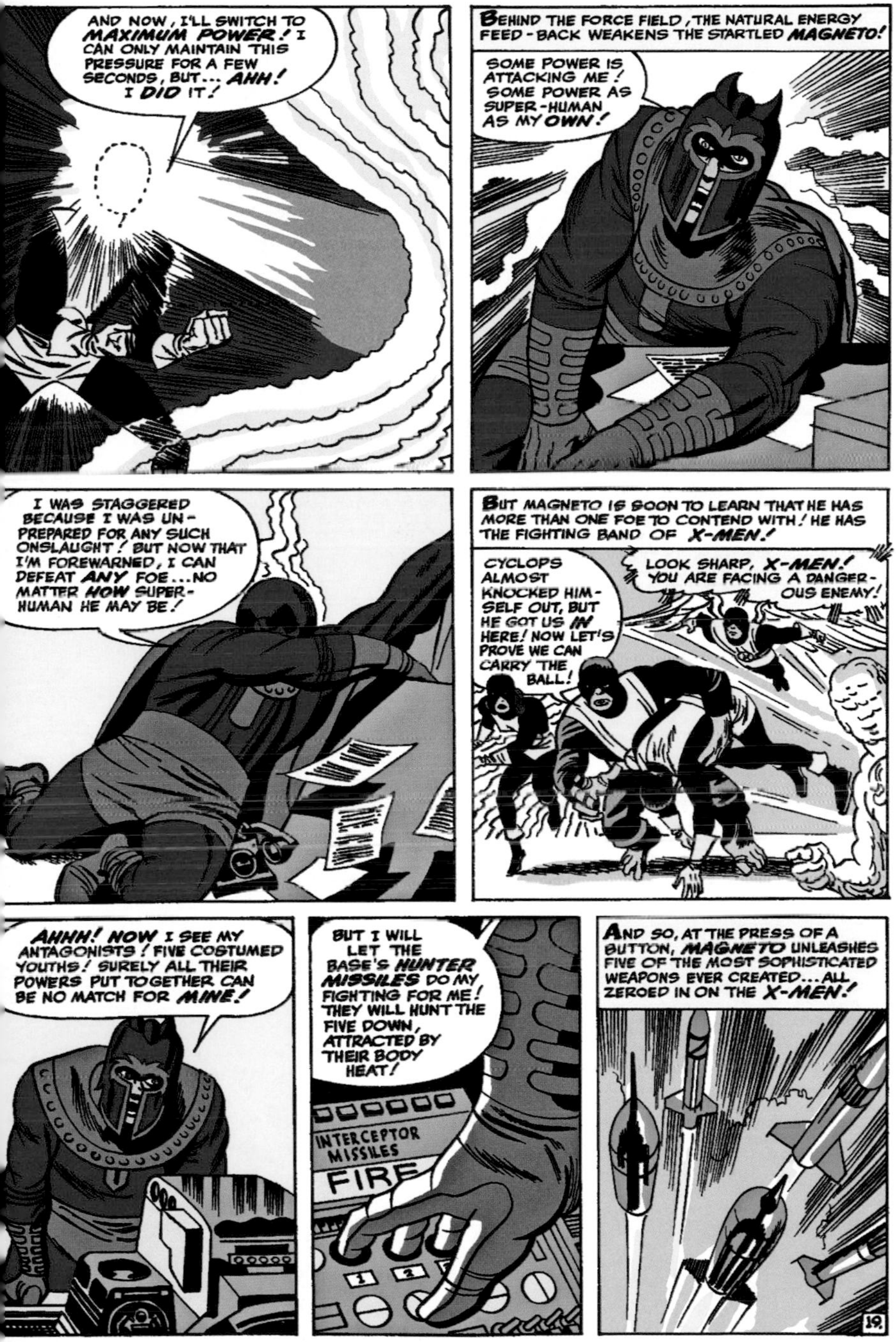
AND NOW, I'LL SWITCH TO MAXIMUM POWER! I CAN ONLY MAINTAIN THIS PRESSURE FOR A FEW SECONDS, BUT... AHH! I DID IT!
BEHIND THE FORCE FIELD, THE NATURAL ENERGY FEED-BACK WEAKENS THE STARTLED MAGNETO!
SOME POWER IS ATTACKING ME! SOME POWER AS SUPER-HUMAN AS MY OWN!
I WAS STAGGERED BECAUSE I WAS UN-PREPARED FOR ANY SUCH ONSLAUGHT! BUT NOW THAT I'M FOREWARNED, I CAN DEFEAT ANY FOE...NO MATTER HOW SUPER-HUMAN HE MAY BE!
BUT MAGNETO IS SOON TO LEARN THAT HE HAS MORE THAN ONE FOE TO CONTEND WITH! HE HAS THE FIGHTING BAND OF X-MEN!
CYCLOPS ALMOST KNOCKED HIM-SELF OUT, BUT HE GOT US IN HERE! NOW LET'S PROVE WE CAN CARRY THE BALL!
LOOK SHARP, X-MEN! YOU ARE FACING A DANGER-OUS ENEMY!
AHHH! NOW I SEE MY ANTAGONISTS! FIVE COSTUMED YOUTHS! SURELY ALL THEIR POWERS PUT TOGETHER CAN BE NO MATCH FOR MINE!
BUT I WILL LET THE BASE'S HUNTER MISSILES DO MY FIGHTING FOR ME! THEY WILL HUNT THE FIVE DOWN, ATTRACTED BY THEIR BODY HEAT!
INTERCEPTOR MISSILES
FIRE
1
2
AND SO, AT THE PRESS OF A BUTTON, MAGNETO UNLEASHES FIVE OF THE MOST SOPHISTICATED WEAPONS EVER CREATED... ALL ZEROED IN ON THE X-MEN!
19

THE FIRST TARGET FOR THE MERCILESS MISSILES IS THE *ANGEL*, FLYING CLOSEST TO THEM!

GOT TO *DODGE* THEM, SOME-HOW!

IT'S NO USE! THEY'RE TOO *FAST!* GAINING ON ME....!

HANG ON, ANGEL! I CAN HELP YOU...WHILE THEY'RE STILL WITHIN RANGE!

THESE *ICE GRENADES* MUSTN'T MISS! THEY'RE THE ANGEL'S ONLY CHANCE!

JUST AS THE HUNTER MISSILES ARE ATTRACTED BY HEAT, SO ARE THE ICEMAN'S ICE GRENADES ATTRACTED BY THE MISSILES' SPEED, AND SO...

BULL'S EYE!

IT *WORKED!* THE ICE COVERED THEIR NOSES, PREVENTING 'EM FROM EXPLODING! NOW, WITH THEIR GUIDANCE SYSTEMS KNOCKED OUT, THEY'VE GOT TO DROP TO THE GROUND!

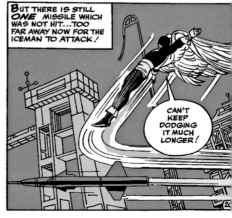

BUT THERE IS STILL *ONE* MISSILE WHICH WAS NOT HIT...TOO FAR AWAY NOW FOR THE ICEMAN TO ATTACK!

CAN'T KEEP DODGING IT MUCH LONGER!

24

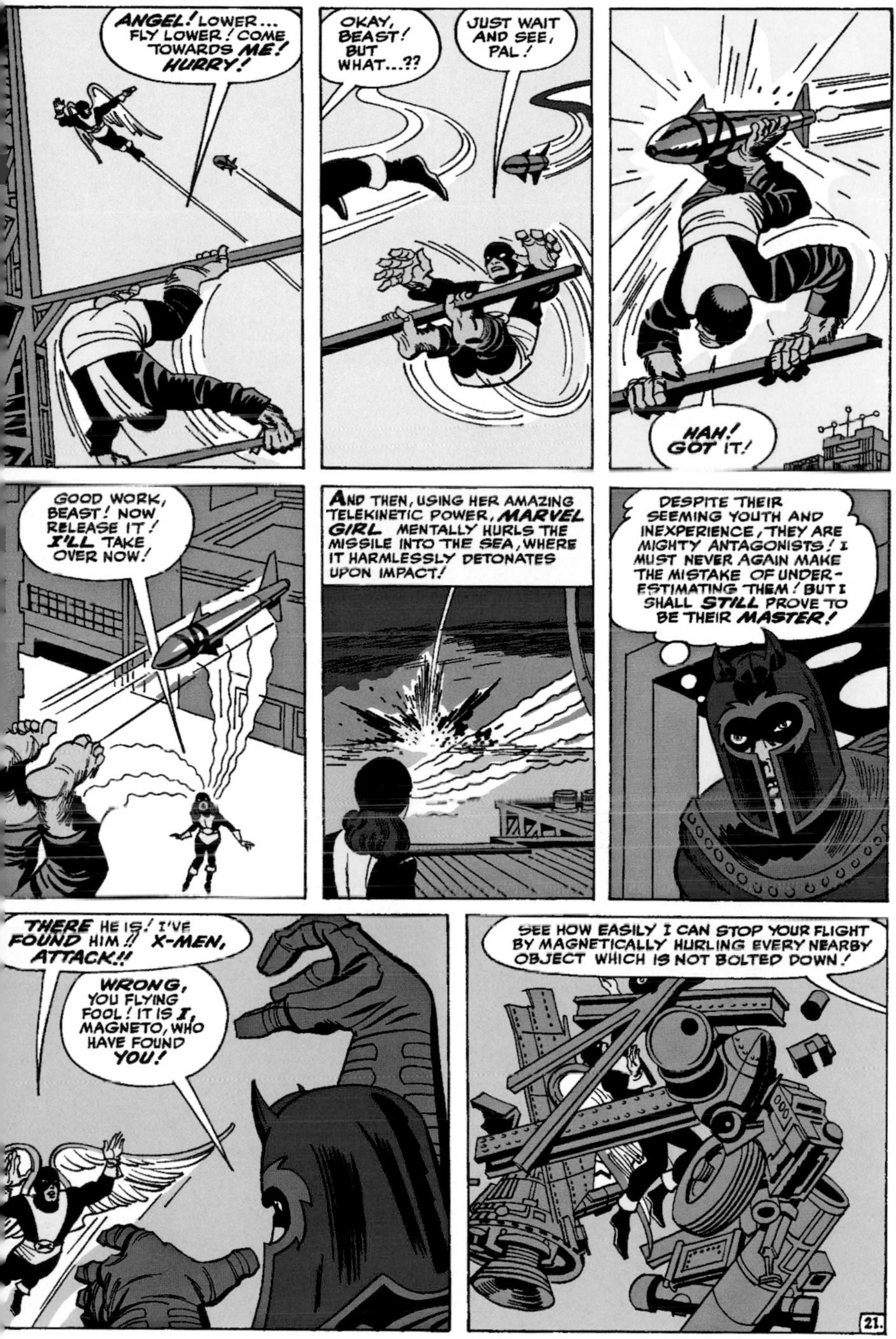
ANGEL! LOWER... FLY LOWER! COME TOWARDS ME! HURRY!
OKAY, BEAST! BUT WHAT...??
JUST WAIT AND SEE, PAL!
HAH! GOT IT!
GOOD WORK, BEAST! NOW RELEASE IT! I'LL TAKE OVER NOW!
AND THEN, USING HER AMAZING TELEKINETIC POWER, MARVEL GIRL MENTALLY HURLS THE MISSILE INTO THE SEA, WHERE IT HARMLESSLY DETONATES UPON IMPACT!
DESPITE THEIR SEEMING YOUTH AND INEXPERIENCE, THEY ARE MIGHTY ANTAGONISTS! I MUST NEVER AGAIN MAKE THE MISTAKE OF UNDER-ESTIMATING THEM! BUT I SHALL STILL PROVE TO BE THEIR MASTER!
THERE HE IS! I'VE FOUND HIM!! X-MEN, ATTACK!!
WRONG, YOU FLYING FOOL! IT IS I, MAGNETO, WHO HAVE FOUND YOU!
SEE HOW EASILY I CAN STOP YOUR FLIGHT BY MAGNETICALLY HURLING EVERY NEARBY OBJECT WHICH IS NOT BOLTED DOWN!
21.

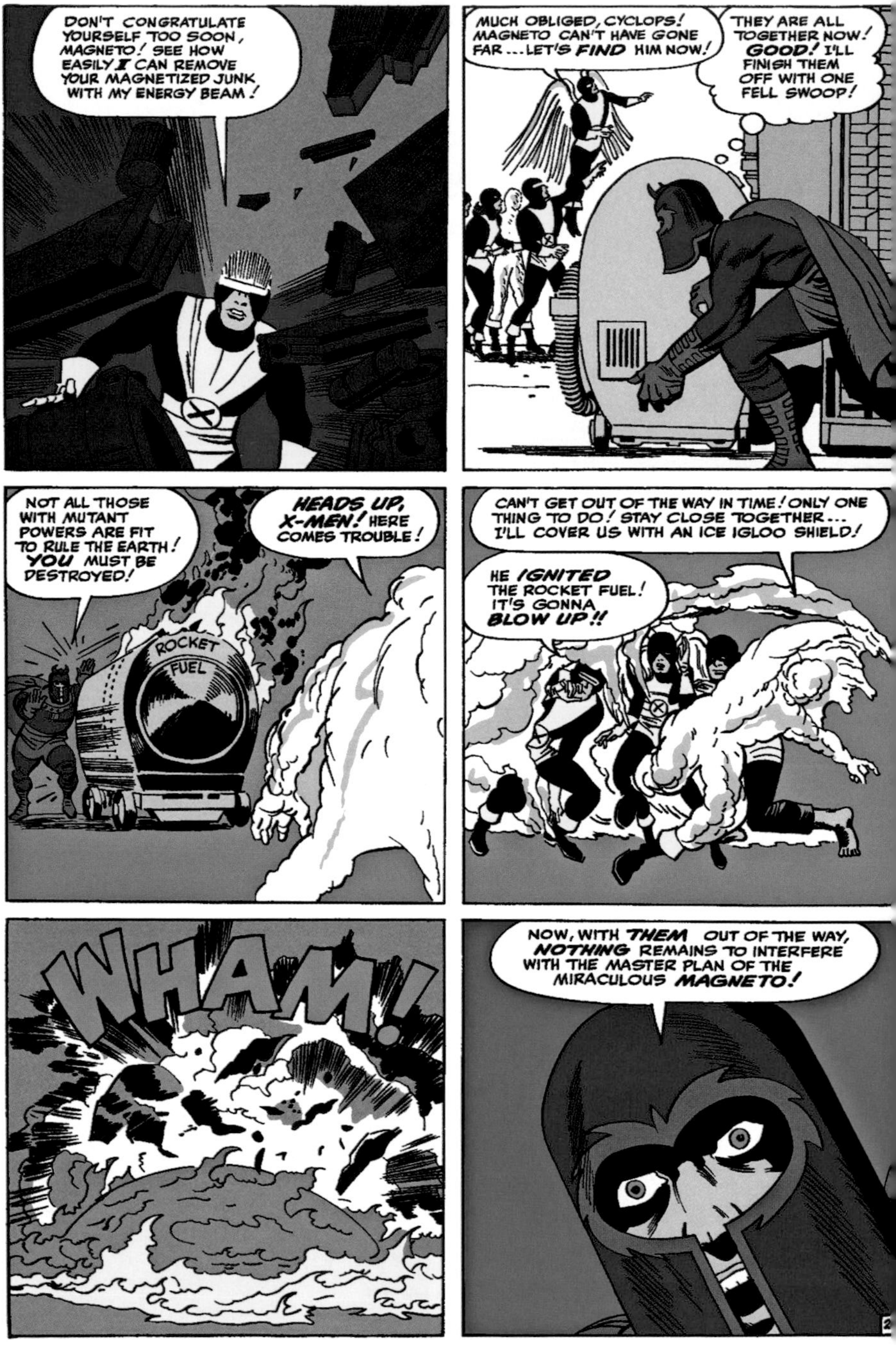
DON'T CONGRATULATE YOURSELF TOO SOON, MAGNETO! SEE HOW EASILY I CAN REMOVE YOUR MAGNETIZED JUNK WITH MY ENERGY BEAM!
MUCH OBLIGED, CYCLOPS! MAGNETO CAN'T HAVE GONE FAR... LET'S FIND HIM NOW!
THEY ARE ALL TOGETHER NOW! GOOD! I'LL FINISH THEM OFF WITH ONE FELL SWOOP!
NOT ALL THOSE WITH MUTANT POWERS ARE FIT TO RULE THE EARTH! YOU MUST BE DESTROYED!
HEADS UP, X-MEN! HERE COMES TROUBLE!
ROCKET FUEL
CAN'T GET OUT OF THE WAY IN TIME! ONLY ONE THING TO DO! STAY CLOSE TOGETHER... I'LL COVER US WITH AN ICE IGLOO SHIELD!
HE IGNITED THE ROCKET FUEL! IT'S GONNA BLOW UP!!
WHAM!
NOW, WITH THEM OUT OF THE WAY, NOTHING REMAINS TO INTERFERE WITH THE MASTER PLAN OF THE MIRACULOUS MAGNETO!

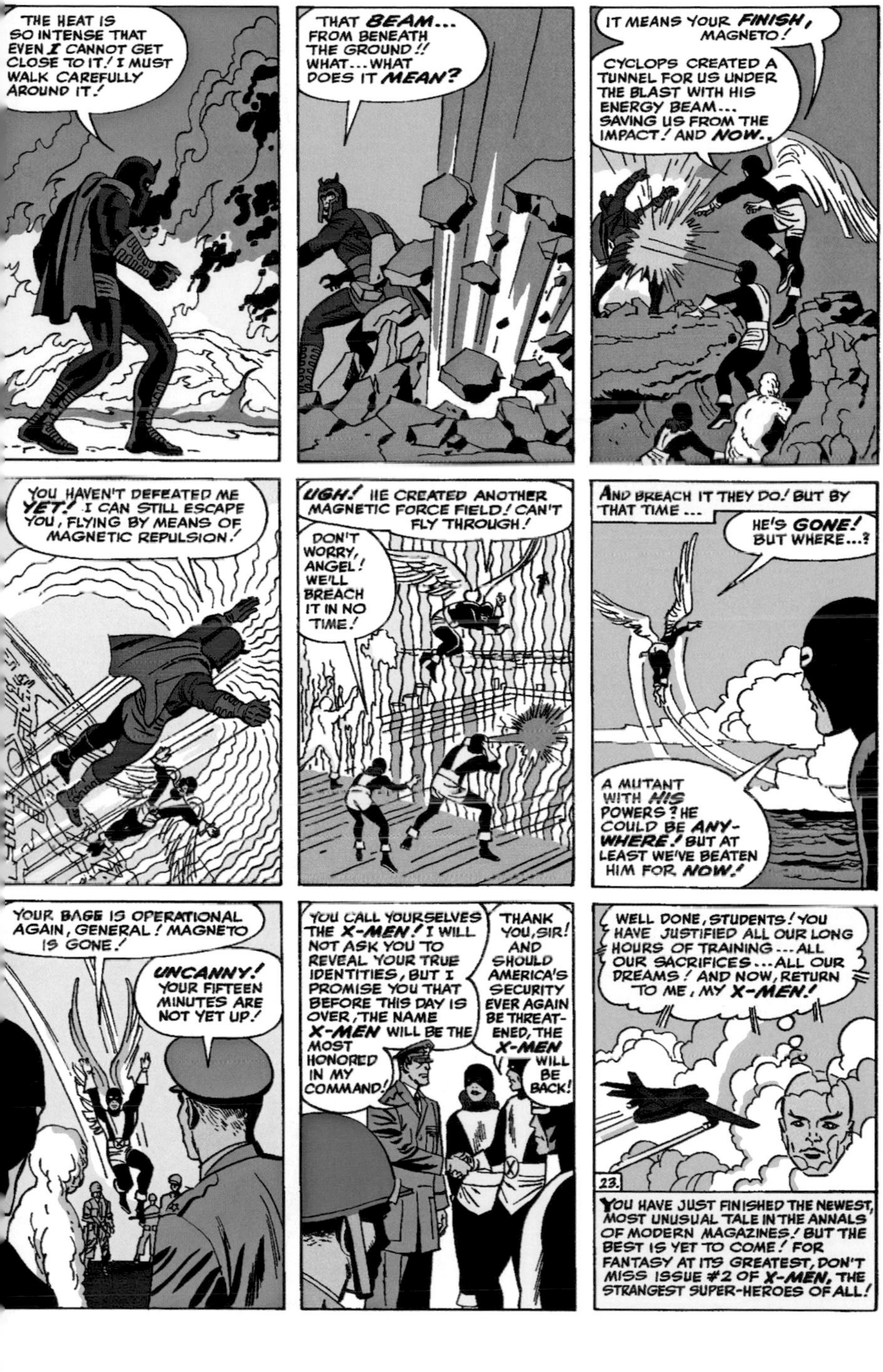
THE HEAT IS SO INTENSE THAT EVEN I CANNOT GET CLOSE TO IT! I MUST WALK CAREFULLY AROUND IT!
THAT BEAM... FROM BENEATH THE GROUND!! WHAT... WHAT DOES IT MEAN?
IT MEANS YOUR FINISH, MAGNETO!
CYCLOPS CREATED A TUNNEL FOR US UNDER THE BLAST WITH HIS ENERGY BEAM... SAVING US FROM THE IMPACT! AND NOW..
YOU HAVEN'T DEFEATED ME YET! I CAN STILL ESCAPE YOU, FLYING BY MEANS OF MAGNETIC REPULSION!
UGH! HE CREATED ANOTHER MAGNETIC FORCE FIELD! CAN'T FLY THROUGH!
DON'T WORRY, ANGEL! WE'LL BREACH IT IN NO TIME!
AND BREACH IT THEY DO! BUT BY THAT TIME ...
HE'S GONE! BUT WHERE...?
A MUTANT WITH HIS POWERS? HE COULD BE ANYWHERE! BUT AT LEAST WE'VE BEATEN HIM FOR NOW!
YOUR BASE IS OPERATIONAL AGAIN, GENERAL! MAGNETO IS GONE!
UNCANNY! YOUR FIFTEEN MINUTES ARE NOT YET UP!
YOU CALL YOURSELVES THE X-MEN! I WILL NOT ASK YOU TO REVEAL YOUR TRUE IDENTITIES, BUT I PROMISE YOU THAT BEFORE THIS DAY IS OVER, THE NAME X-MEN WILL BE THE MOST HONORED IN MY COMMAND!
THANK YOU, SIR! AND SHOULD AMERICA'S SECURITY EVER AGAIN BE THREATENED, THE X-MEN WILL BE BACK!
WELL DONE, STUDENTS! YOU HAVE JUSTIFIED ALL OUR LONG HOURS OF TRAINING... ALL OUR SACRIFICES... ALL OUR DREAMS! AND NOW, RETURN TO ME, MY X-MEN!
23.
YOU HAVE JUST FINISHED THE NEWEST, MOST UNUSUAL TALE IN THE ANNALS OF MODERN MAGAZINES! BUT THE BEST IS YET TO COME! FOR FANTASY AT ITS GREATEST, DON'T MISS ISSUE #2 OF X-MEN, THE STRANGEST SUPER-HEROES OF ALL!

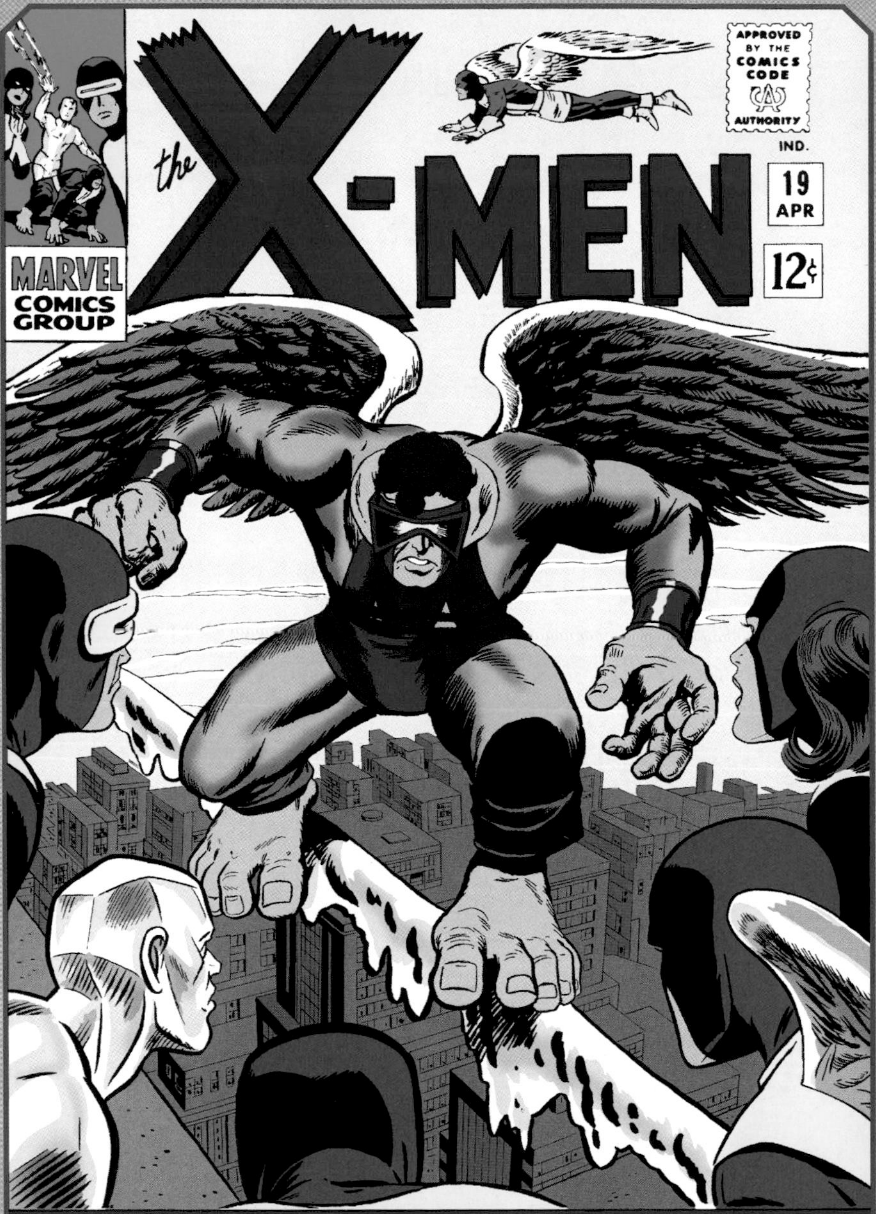

APPROVED BY THE COMICS CODE AUTHORITY
IND.
the X-MEN
19 APR
12¢
MARVEL COMICS GROUP
IS THE MIMIC ANOTHER MUTANT?--OR, SOMETHING FAR WORSE??

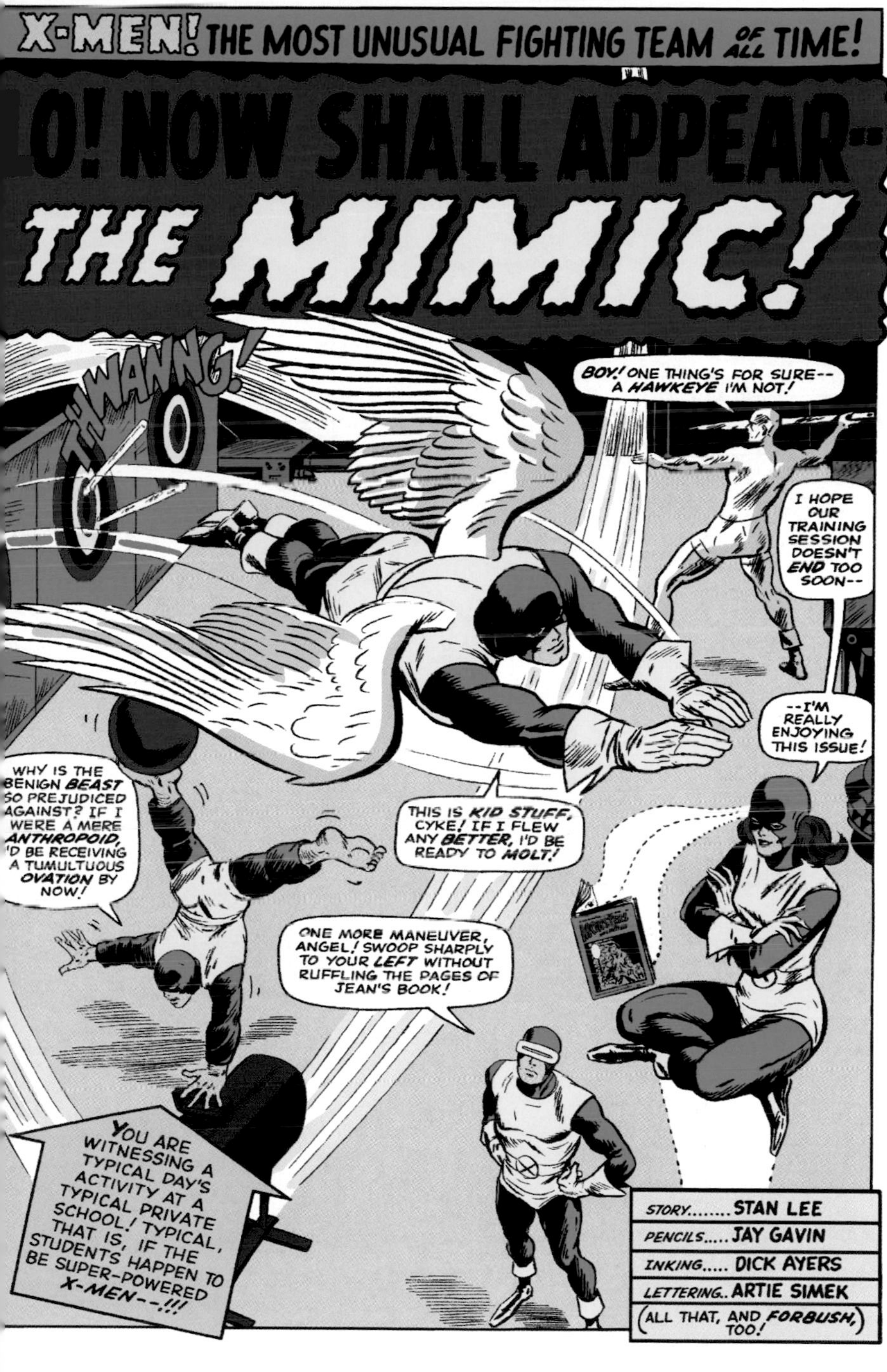
X-MEN! THE MOST UNUSUAL FIGHTING TEAM OF ALL TIME!
LO! NOW SHALL APPEAR-- THE MIMIC!
THWANNG!
BOY! ONE THING'S FOR SURE-- A HAWKEYE I'M NOT!
I HOPE OUR TRAINING SESSION DOESN'T END TOO SOON--
--I'M REALLY ENJOYING THIS ISSUE!
WHY IS THE BENIGN BEAST SO PREJUDICED AGAINST? IF I WERE A MERE ANTHROPOID, I'D BE RECEIVING A TUMULTUOUS OVATION BY NOW!
THIS IS KID STUFF, CYKE! IF I FLEW ANY BETTER, I'D BE READY TO MOLT!
ONE MORE MANEUVER, ANGEL! SWOOP SHARPLY TO YOUR LEFT WITHOUT RUFFLING THE PAGES OF JEAN'S BOOK!
YOU ARE WITNESSING A TYPICAL DAY'S ACTIVITY AT A TYPICAL PRIVATE SCHOOL! TYPICAL, THAT IS, IF THE STUDENTS HAPPEN TO BE SUPER-POWERED X-MEN--!!!
STORY........ STAN LEE
PENCILS..... JAY GAVIN
INKING..... DICK AYERS
LETTERING.. ARTIE SIMEK
(ALL THAT, AND FORBUSH, TOO!)

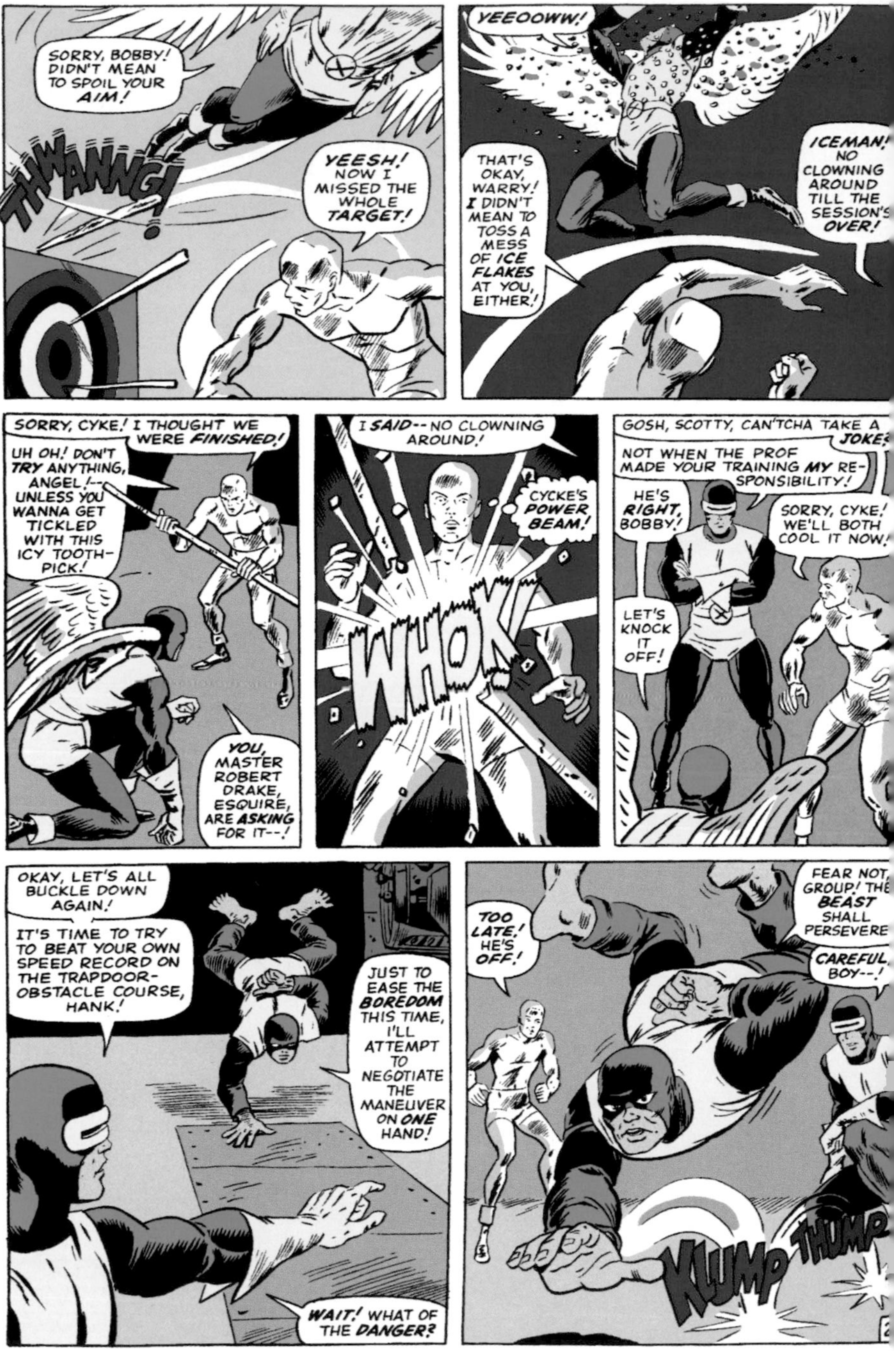
SORRY, BOBBY! DIDN'T MEAN TO SPOIL YOUR AIM!
THWANNG!
YEESH! NOW I MISSED THE WHOLE TARGET!
YEEEOOWW!
THAT'S OKAY, WARRY! I DIDN'T MEAN TO TOSS A MESS OF ICE FLAKES AT YOU, EITHER!
ICEMAN! NO CLOWNING AROUND TILL THE SESSION'S OVER!
SORRY, CYKE! I THOUGHT WE WERE FINISHED!
UH OH! DON'T TRY ANYTHING, ANGEL!-- UNLESS YOU WANNA GET TICKLED WITH THIS ICY TOOTH-PICK!
YOU, MASTER ROBERT DRAKE, ESQUIRE, ARE ASKING FOR IT--!
I SAID--NO CLOWNING AROUND!
CYCKE'S POWER BEAM!
WHOK!
GOSH, SCOTTY, CAN'TCHA TAKE A JOKE?
NOT WHEN THE PROF MADE YOUR TRAINING MY RE-SPONSIBILITY!
HE'S RIGHT, BOBBY!
SORRY, CYKE! WE'LL BOTH COOL IT NOW!
LET'S KNOCK IT OFF!
OKAY, LET'S ALL BUCKLE DOWN AGAIN!
IT'S TIME TO TRY TO BEAT YOUR OWN SPEED RECORD ON THE TRAPDOOR-OBSTACLE COURSE, HANK!
JUST TO EASE THE BOREDOM THIS TIME, I'LL ATTEMPT TO NEGOTIATE THE MANEUVER ON ONE HAND!
WAIT! WHAT OF THE DANGER?
TOO LATE! HE'S OFF!
FEAR NOT, GROUP! THE BEAST SHALL PERSEVERE
CAREFUL, BOY--!
KLUMP
THUMP

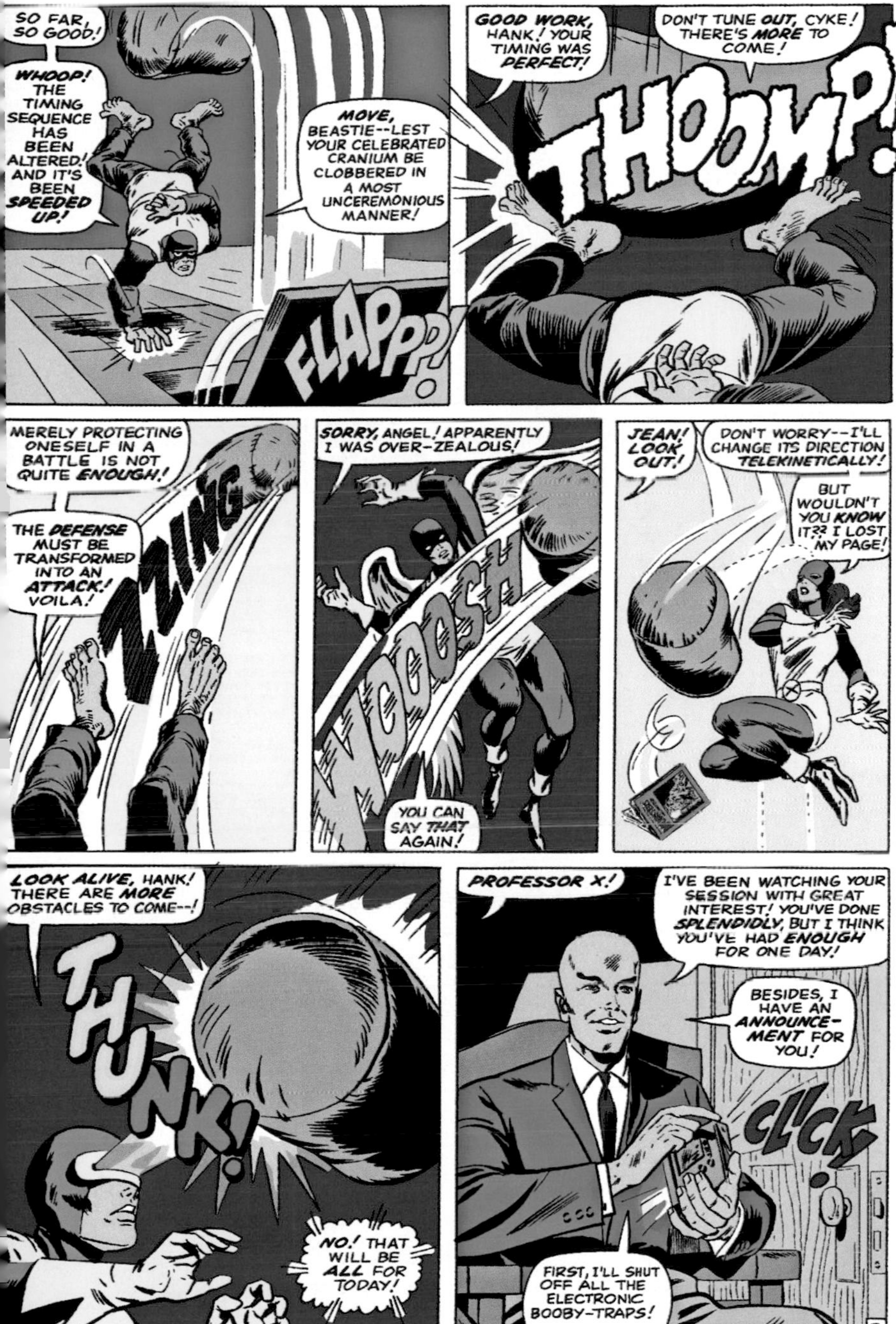
SO FAR, SO GOOD!
WHOOP! THE TIMING SEQUENCE HAS BEEN ALTERED! AND IT'S BEEN SPEEDED UP!
MOVE, BEASTIE--LEST YOUR CELEBRATED CRANIUM BE CLOBBERED IN A MOST UNCEREMONIOUS MANNER!
FLAPPP!
GOOD WORK, HANK! YOUR TIMING WAS PERFECT!
DON'T TUNE OUT, CYKE! THERE'S MORE TO COME!
THOOMP!
MERELY PROTECTING ONESELF IN A BATTLE IS NOT QUITE ENOUGH!
THE DEFENSE MUST BE TRANSFORMED INTO AN ATTACK! VOILA!
ZZING
SORRY, ANGEL! APPARENTLY I WAS OVER-ZEALOUS!
WHOOOSH
YOU CAN SAY THAT AGAIN!
JEAN! LOOK OUT!
DON'T WORRY--I'LL CHANGE ITS DIRECTION TELEKINETICALLY!
BUT WOULDN'T YOU KNOW IT?? I LOST MY PAGE!
LOOK ALIVE, HANK! THERE ARE MORE OBSTACLES TO COME--!
THUNK!
NO! THAT WILL BE ALL FOR TODAY!
PROFESSOR X!
I'VE BEEN WATCHING YOUR SESSION WITH GREAT INTEREST! YOU'VE DONE SPLENDIDLY, BUT I THINK YOU'VE HAD ENOUGH FOR ONE DAY!
BESIDES, I HAVE AN ANNOUNCEMENT FOR YOU!
CLICK!
FIRST, I'LL SHUT OFF ALL THE ELECTRONIC BOOBY-TRAPS!
3

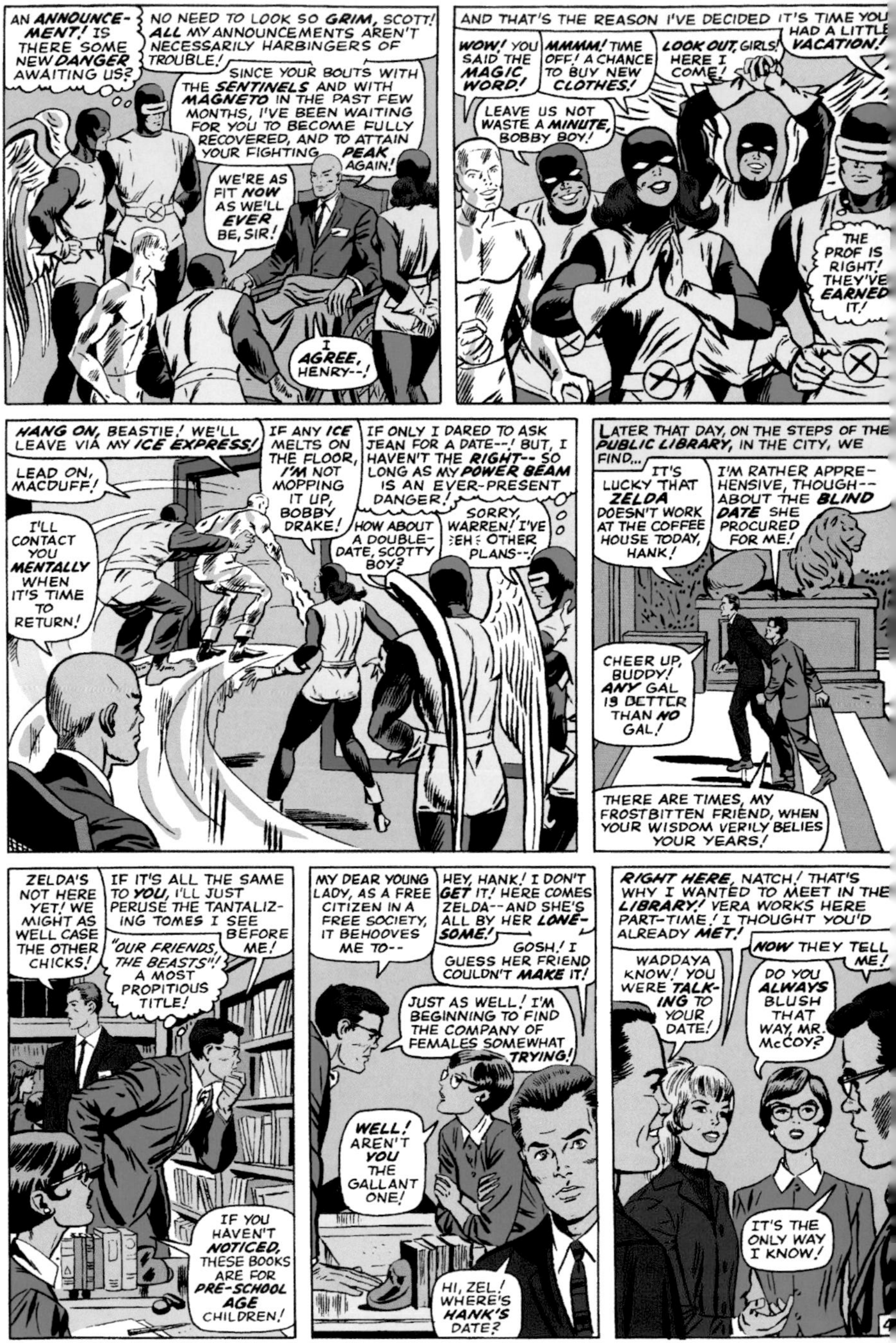

AN ANNOUNCEMENT! IS THERE SOME NEW DANGER AWAITING US?
NO NEED TO LOOK SO GRIM, SCOTT! ALL MY ANNOUNCEMENTS AREN'T NECESSARILY HARBINGERS OF TROUBLE!
SINCE YOUR BOUTS WITH THE SENTINELS AND WITH MAGNETO IN THE PAST FEW MONTHS, I'VE BEEN WAITING FOR YOU TO BECOME FULLY RECOVERED, AND TO ATTAIN YOUR FIGHTING PEAK AGAIN!
WE'RE AS FIT NOW AS WE'LL EVER BE, SIR!
I AGREE, HENRY--!
AND THAT'S THE REASON I'VE DECIDED IT'S TIME YOU HAD A LITTLE VACATION!
WOW! YOU SAID THE MAGIC WORD!
MMMM! TIME OFF! A CHANCE TO BUY NEW CLOTHES!
LOOK OUT, GIRLS! HERE I COME!
LEAVE US NOT WASTE A MINUTE, BOBBY BOY!
THE PROF IS RIGHT! THEY'VE EARNED IT!
HANG ON, BEASTIE! WE'LL LEAVE VIA MY ICE EXPRESS!
LEAD ON, MACDUFF!
IF ANY ICE MELTS ON THE FLOOR, I'M NOT MOPPING IT UP, BOBBY DRAKE!
IF ONLY I DARED TO ASK JEAN FOR A DATE--! BUT, I HAVEN'T THE RIGHT-- SO LONG AS MY POWER BEAM IS AN EVER-PRESENT DANGER!
HOW ABOUT A DOUBLE-DATE, SCOTTY BOY?
SORRY, WARREN! I'VE --EH-- OTHER PLANS--!
I'LL CONTACT YOU MENTALLY WHEN IT'S TIME TO RETURN!
LATER THAT DAY, ON THE STEPS OF THE PUBLIC LIBRARY, IN THE CITY, WE FIND...
IT'S LUCKY THAT ZELDA DOESN'T WORK AT THE COFFEE HOUSE TODAY, HANK!
I'M RATHER APPREHENSIVE, THOUGH-- ABOUT THE BLIND DATE SHE PROCURED FOR ME!
CHEER UP, BUDDY! ANY GAL IS BETTER THAN NO GAL!
THERE ARE TIMES, MY FROSTBITTEN FRIEND, WHEN YOUR WISDOM VERILY BELIES YOUR YEARS!
ZELDA'S NOT HERE YET! WE MIGHT AS WELL CASE THE OTHER CHICKS!
IF IT'S ALL THE SAME TO YOU, I'LL JUST PERUSE THE TANTALIZING TOMES I SEE BEFORE ME!
"OUR FRIENDS, THE BEASTS"! A MOST PROPITIOUS TITLE!
IF YOU HAVEN'T NOTICED, THESE BOOKS ARE FOR PRE-SCHOOL AGE CHILDREN!
MY DEAR YOUNG LADY, AS A FREE CITIZEN IN A FREE SOCIETY, IT BEHOOVES ME TO--
HEY, HANK! I DON'T GET IT! HERE COMES ZELDA--AND SHE'S ALL BY HER LONESOME!
GOSH! I GUESS HER FRIEND COULDN'T MAKE IT!
JUST AS WELL! I'M BEGINNING TO FIND THE COMPANY OF FEMALES SOMEWHAT TRYING!
WELL! AREN'T YOU THE GALLANT ONE!
HI, ZEL! WHERE'S HANK'S DATE?
RIGHT HERE, NATCH! THAT'S WHY I WANTED TO MEET IN THE LIBRARY! VERA WORKS HERE PART-TIME! I THOUGHT YOU'D ALREADY MET!
WADDAYA KNOW! YOU WERE TALKING TO YOUR DATE!
NOW THEY TELL ME!
DO YOU ALWAYS BLUSH THAT WAY, MR. McCOY?
IT'S THE ONLY WAY I KNOW!

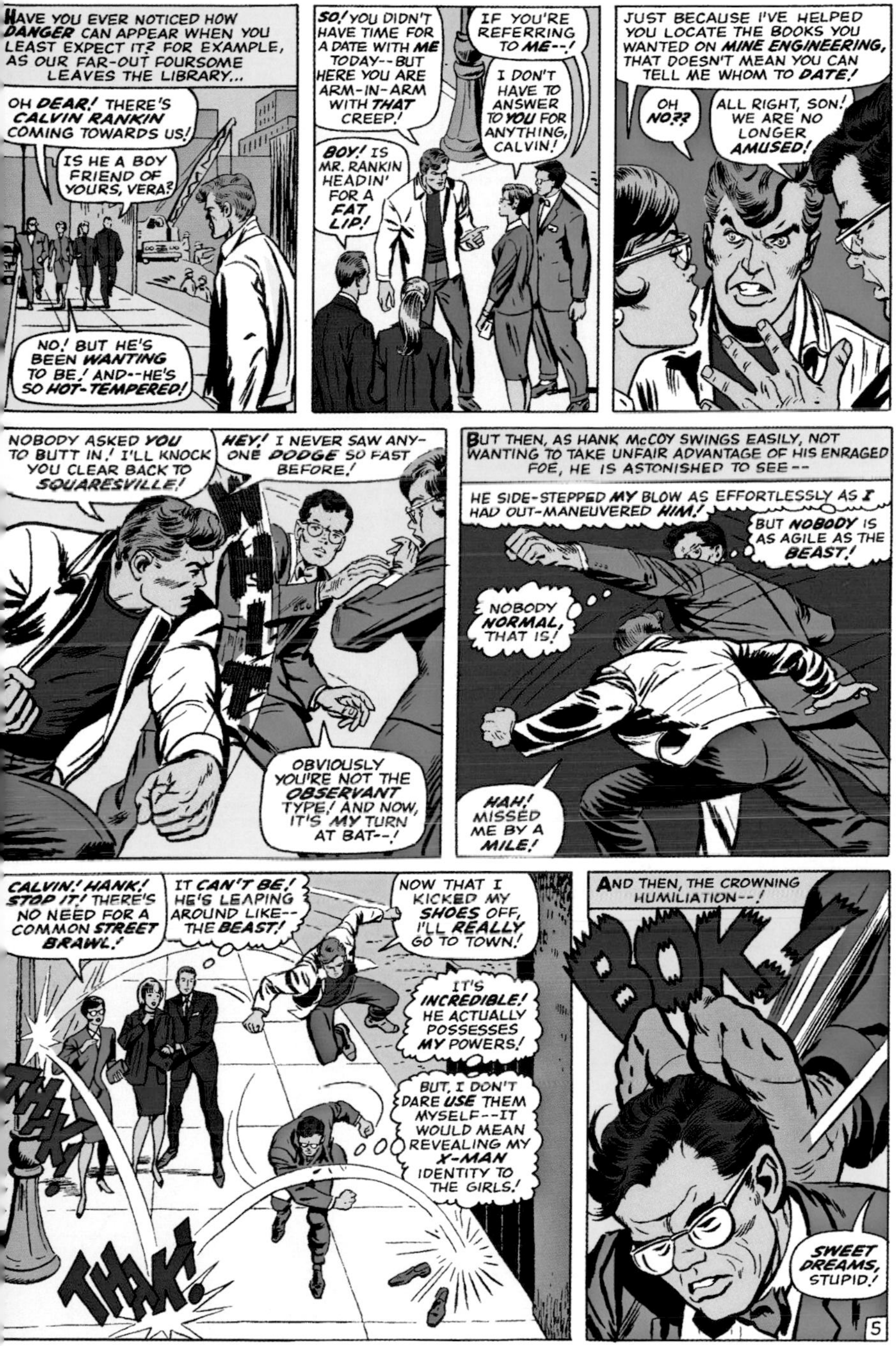
HAVE YOU EVER NOTICED HOW DANGER CAN APPEAR WHEN YOU LEAST EXPECT IT? FOR EXAMPLE, AS OUR FAR-OUT FOURSOME LEAVES THE LIBRARY...
OH DEAR! THERE'S CALVIN RANKIN COMING TOWARDS US!
IS HE A BOY FRIEND OF YOURS, VERA?
NO! BUT HE'S BEEN WANTING TO BE! AND--HE'S SO HOT-TEMPERED!
SO! YOU DIDN'T HAVE TIME FOR A DATE WITH ME TODAY--BUT HERE YOU ARE ARM-IN-ARM WITH THAT CREEP!
IF YOU'RE REFERRING TO ME--!
I DON'T HAVE TO ANSWER TO YOU FOR ANYTHING, CALVIN!
BOY! IS MR. RANKIN HEADIN' FOR A FAT LIP!
JUST BECAUSE I'VE HELPED YOU LOCATE THE BOOKS YOU WANTED ON MINE ENGINEERING, THAT DOESN'T MEAN YOU CAN TELL ME WHOM TO DATE!
OH NO??
ALL RIGHT, SON! WE ARE NO LONGER AMUSED!
NOBODY ASKED YOU TO BUTT IN! I'LL KNOCK YOU CLEAR BACK TO SQUARESVILLE!
HEY! I NEVER SAW ANY-ONE DODGE SO FAST BEFORE!
OBVIOUSLY YOU'RE NOT THE OBSERVANT TYPE! AND NOW, IT'S MY TURN AT BAT--!
BUT THEN, AS HANK McCOY SWINGS EASILY, NOT WANTING TO TAKE UNFAIR ADVANTAGE OF HIS ENRAGED FOE, HE IS ASTONISHED TO SEE--
HE SIDE-STEPPED MY BLOW AS EFFORTLESSLY AS I HAD OUT-MANEUVERED HIM!
BUT NOBODY IS AS AGILE AS THE BEAST!
NOBODY NORMAL, THAT IS!
HAH! MISSED ME BY A MILE!
CALVIN! HANK! STOP IT! THERE'S NO NEED FOR A COMMON STREET BRAWL!
IT CAN'T BE! HE'S LEAPING AROUND LIKE-- THE BEAST!
NOW THAT I KICKED MY SHOES OFF, I'LL REALLY GO TO TOWN!
IT'S INCREDIBLE! HE ACTUALLY POSSESSES MY POWERS!
BUT, I DON'T DARE USE THEM MYSELF--IT WOULD MEAN REVEALING MY X-MAN IDENTITY TO THE GIRLS!
THAK!
THAK!
AND THEN, THE CROWNING HUMILIATION--!
BOK!
SWEET DREAMS, STUPID!
5

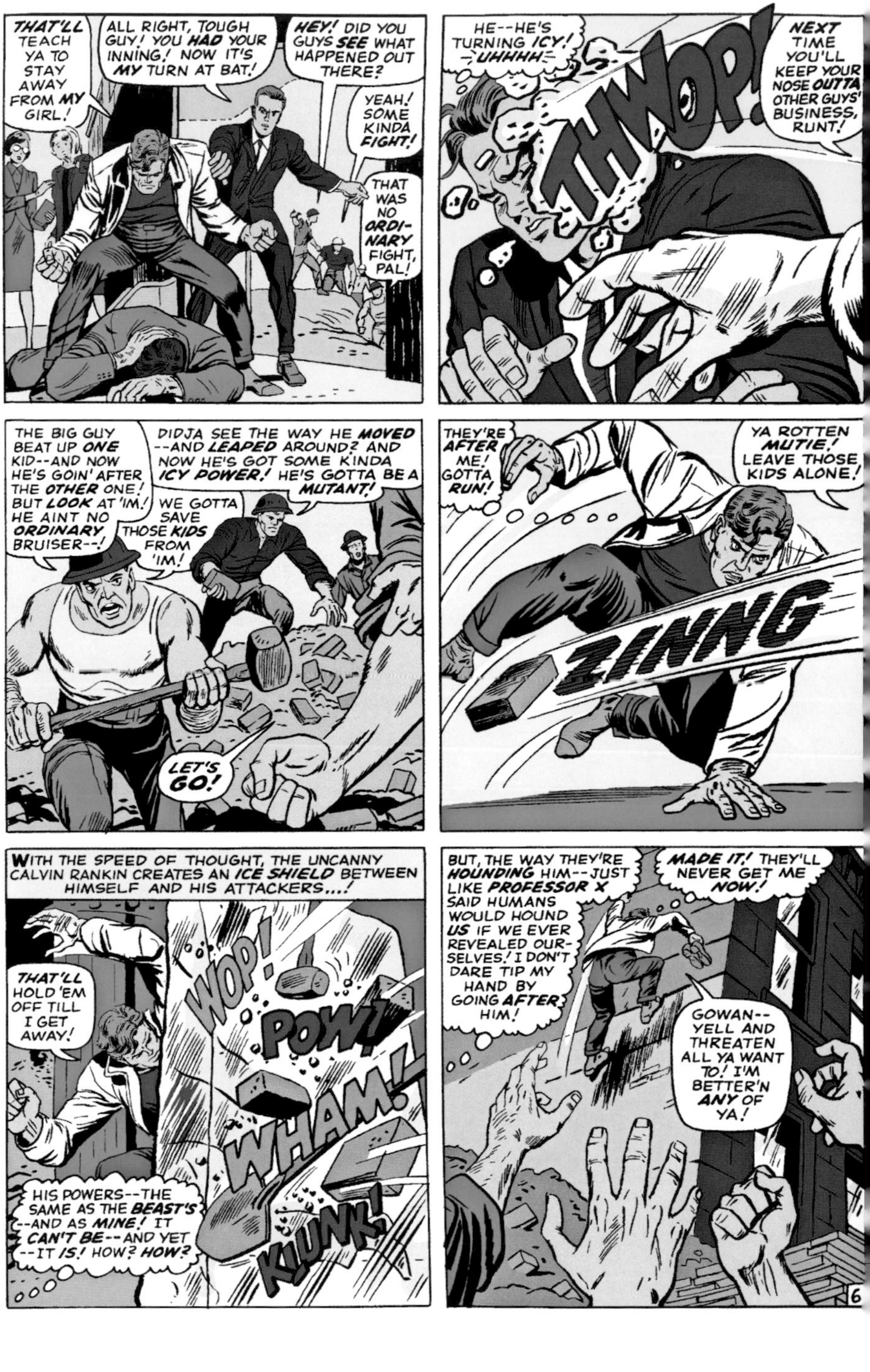
THAT'LL TEACH YA TO STAY AWAY FROM MY GIRL!
ALL RIGHT, TOUGH GUY! YOU HAD YOUR INNING! NOW IT'S MY TURN AT BAT!
HEY! DID YOU GUYS SEE WHAT HAPPENED OUT THERE?
YEAH! SOME KINDA FIGHT!
THAT WAS NO ORDINARY FIGHT, PAL!
HE--HE'S TURNING ICY! UHHHH
THWOP!
NEXT TIME YOU'LL KEEP YOUR NOSE OUTTA OTHER GUYS' BUSINESS, RUNT!
THE BIG GUY BEAT UP ONE KID--AND NOW HE'S GOIN' AFTER THE OTHER ONE! BUT LOOK AT 'IM! HE AINT NO ORDINARY BRUISER--!
DIDJA SEE THE WAY HE MOVED--AND LEAPED AROUND? AND NOW HE'S GOT SOME KINDA ICY POWER! HE'S GOTTA BE A MUTANT!
WE GOTTA SAVE THOSE KIDS FROM 'IM!
LET'S GO!
THEY'RE AFTER ME! GOTTA RUN!
YA ROTTEN MUTIE! LEAVE THOSE KIDS ALONE!
ZINNG
WITH THE SPEED OF THOUGHT, THE UNCANNY CALVIN RANKIN CREATES AN ICE SHIELD BETWEEN HIMSELF AND HIS ATTACKERS...!
THAT'LL HOLD 'EM OFF TILL I GET AWAY!
WOP!
POW!
WHAM!
KLUNK!
HIS POWERS--THE SAME AS THE BEAST'S--AND AS MINE! IT CAN'T BE--AND YET--IT IS! HOW? HOW?
BUT, THE WAY THEY'RE HOUNDING HIM--JUST LIKE PROFESSOR X SAID HUMANS WOULD HOUND US IF WE EVER REVEALED OURSELVES! I DON'T DARE TIP MY HAND BY GOING AFTER HIM!
MADE IT! THEY'LL NEVER GET ME NOW!
GOWAN--YELL AND THREATEN ALL YA WANT TO! I'M BETTER'N ANY OF YA!
6

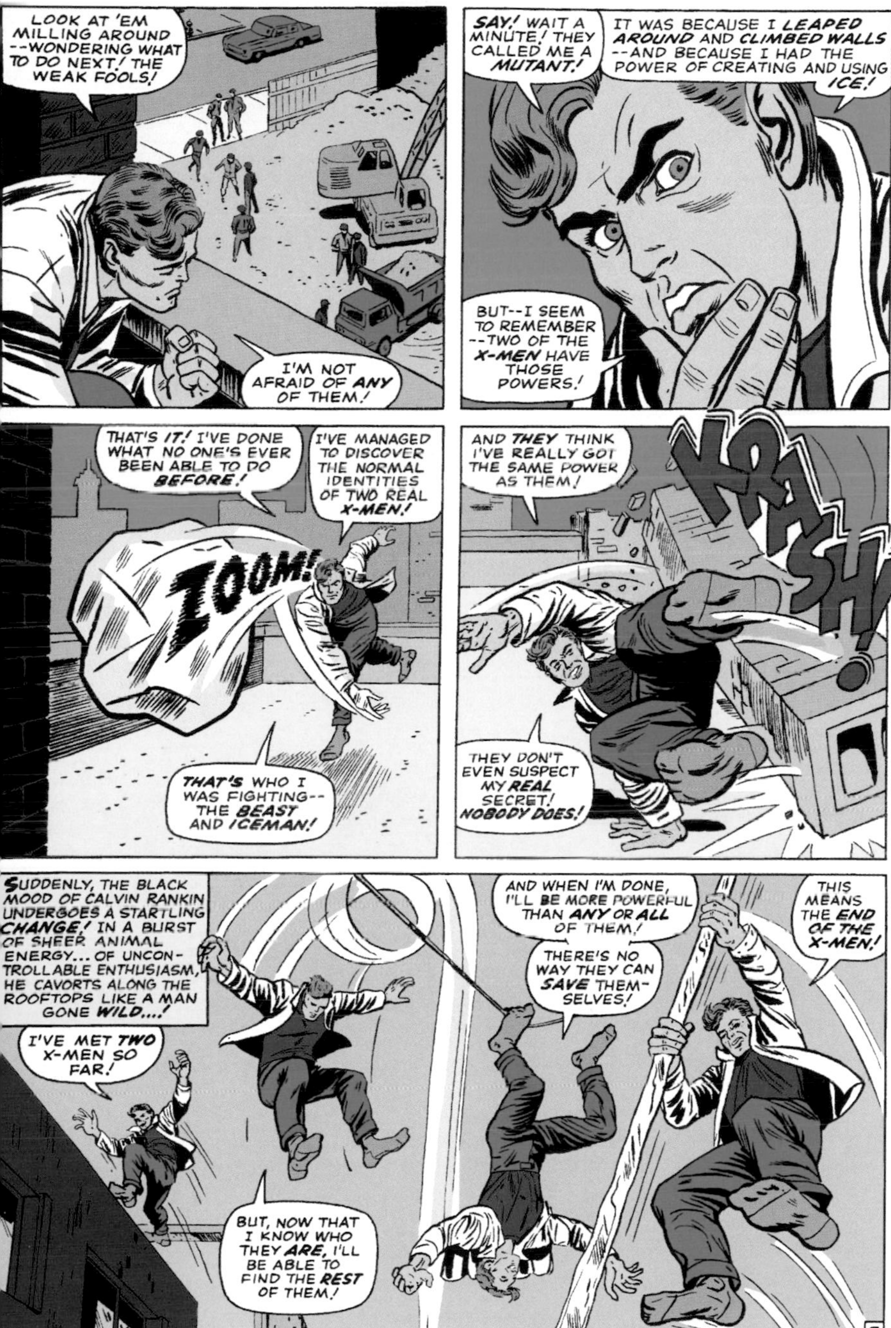

LOOK AT 'EM MILLING AROUND --WONDERING WHAT TO DO NEXT! THE WEAK FOOLS!
I'M NOT AFRAID OF ANY OF THEM!
SAY! WAIT A MINUTE! THEY CALLED ME A MUTANT!
IT WAS BECAUSE I LEAPED AROUND AND CLIMBED WALLS --AND BECAUSE I HAD THE POWER OF CREATING AND USING ICE!
BUT--I SEEM TO REMEMBER --TWO OF THE X-MEN HAVE THOSE POWERS!
THAT'S IT! I'VE DONE WHAT NO ONE'S EVER BEEN ABLE TO DO BEFORE!
I'VE MANAGED TO DISCOVER THE NORMAL IDENTITIES OF TWO REAL X-MEN!
ZOOM!
THAT'S WHO I WAS FIGHTING-- THE BEAST AND ICEMAN!
AND THEY THINK I'VE REALLY GOT THE SAME POWER AS THEM!
KRASH!
THEY DON'T EVEN SUSPECT MY REAL SECRET! NOBODY DOES!
SUDDENLY, THE BLACK MOOD OF CALVIN RANKIN UNDERGOES A STARTLING CHANGE! IN A BURST OF SHEER ANIMAL ENERGY... OF UNCONTROLLABLE ENTHUSIASM, HE CAVORTS ALONG THE ROOFTOPS LIKE A MAN GONE WILD...!
I'VE MET TWO X-MEN SO FAR!
BUT, NOW THAT I KNOW WHO THEY ARE, I'LL BE ABLE TO FIND THE REST OF THEM!
AND WHEN I'M DONE, I'LL BE MORE POWERFUL THAN ANY OR ALL OF THEM!
THERE'S NO WAY THEY CAN SAVE THEMSELVES!
THIS MEANS THE END OF THE X-MEN!

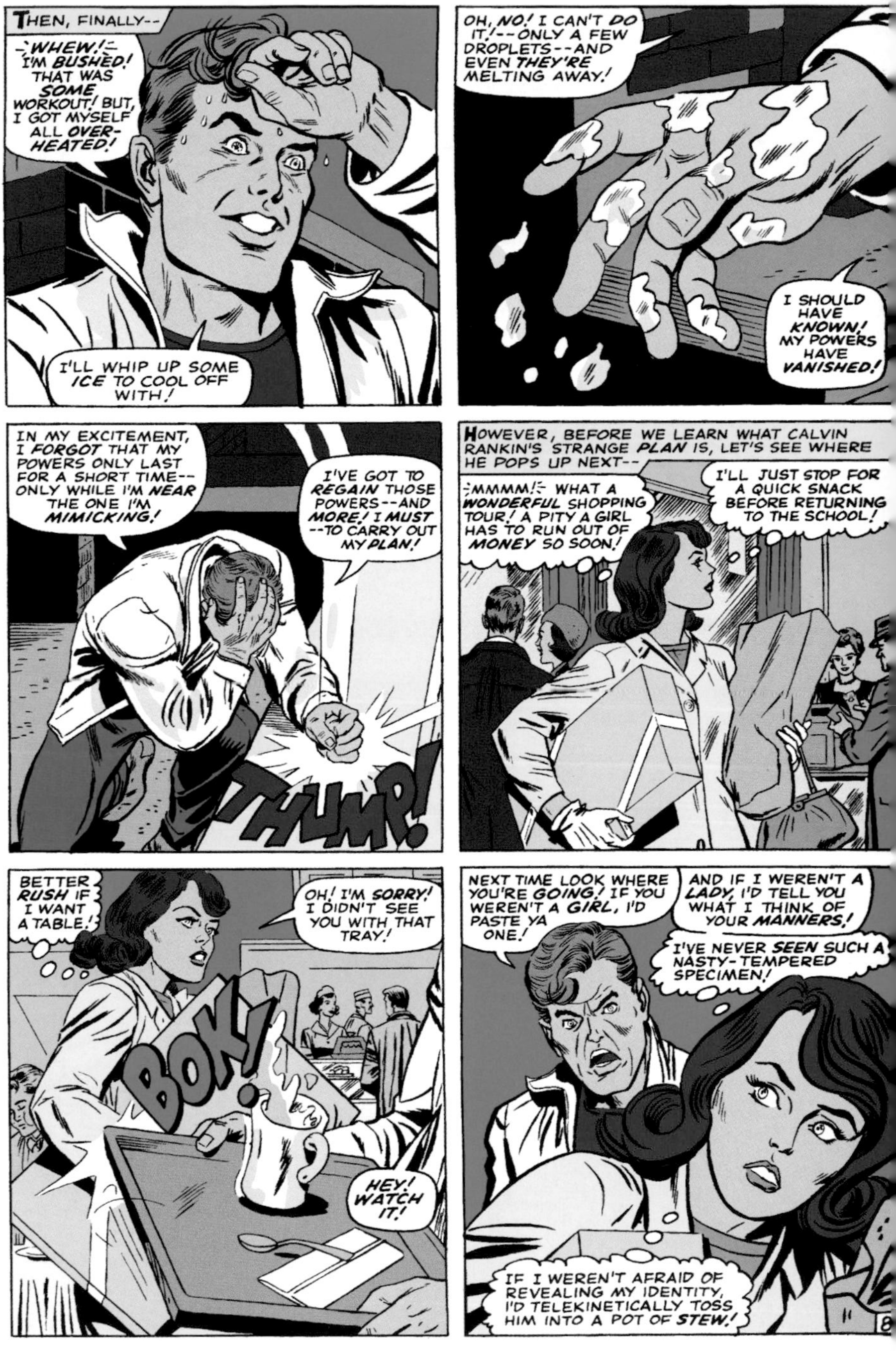
THEN, FINALLY--
-WHEW!- I'M BUSHED! THAT WAS SOME WORKOUT! BUT, I GOT MYSELF ALL OVER-HEATED!
I'LL WHIP UP SOME ICE TO COOL OFF WITH!
OH, NO! I CAN'T DO IT!--ONLY A FEW DROPLETS--AND EVEN THEY'RE MELTING AWAY!
I SHOULD HAVE KNOWN! MY POWERS HAVE VANISHED!
IN MY EXCITEMENT, I FORGOT THAT MY POWERS ONLY LAST FOR A SHORT TIME--ONLY WHILE I'M NEAR THE ONE I'M MIMICKING!
I'VE GOT TO REGAIN THOSE POWERS--AND MORE! I MUST--TO CARRY OUT MY PLAN!
THUMP!
HOWEVER, BEFORE WE LEARN WHAT CALVIN RANKIN'S STRANGE PLAN IS, LET'S SEE WHERE HE POPS UP NEXT--
-MMMM!- WHAT A WONDERFUL SHOPPING TOUR! A PITY A GIRL HAS TO RUN OUT OF MONEY SO SOON!
I'LL JUST STOP FOR A QUICK SNACK BEFORE RETURNING TO THE SCHOOL!
BETTER RUSH IF I WANT A TABLE!
OH! I'M SORRY! I DIDN'T SEE YOU WITH THAT TRAY!
BOK!
HEY! WATCH IT!
NEXT TIME LOOK WHERE YOU'RE GOING! IF YOU WEREN'T A GIRL, I'D PASTE YA ONE!
AND IF I WEREN'T A LADY, I'D TELL YOU WHAT I THINK OF YOUR MANNERS!
I'VE NEVER SEEN SUCH A NASTY-TEMPERED SPECIMEN!
IF I WEREN'T AFRAID OF REVEALING MY IDENTITY, I'D TELEKINETICALLY TOSS HIM INTO A POT OF STEW!
8

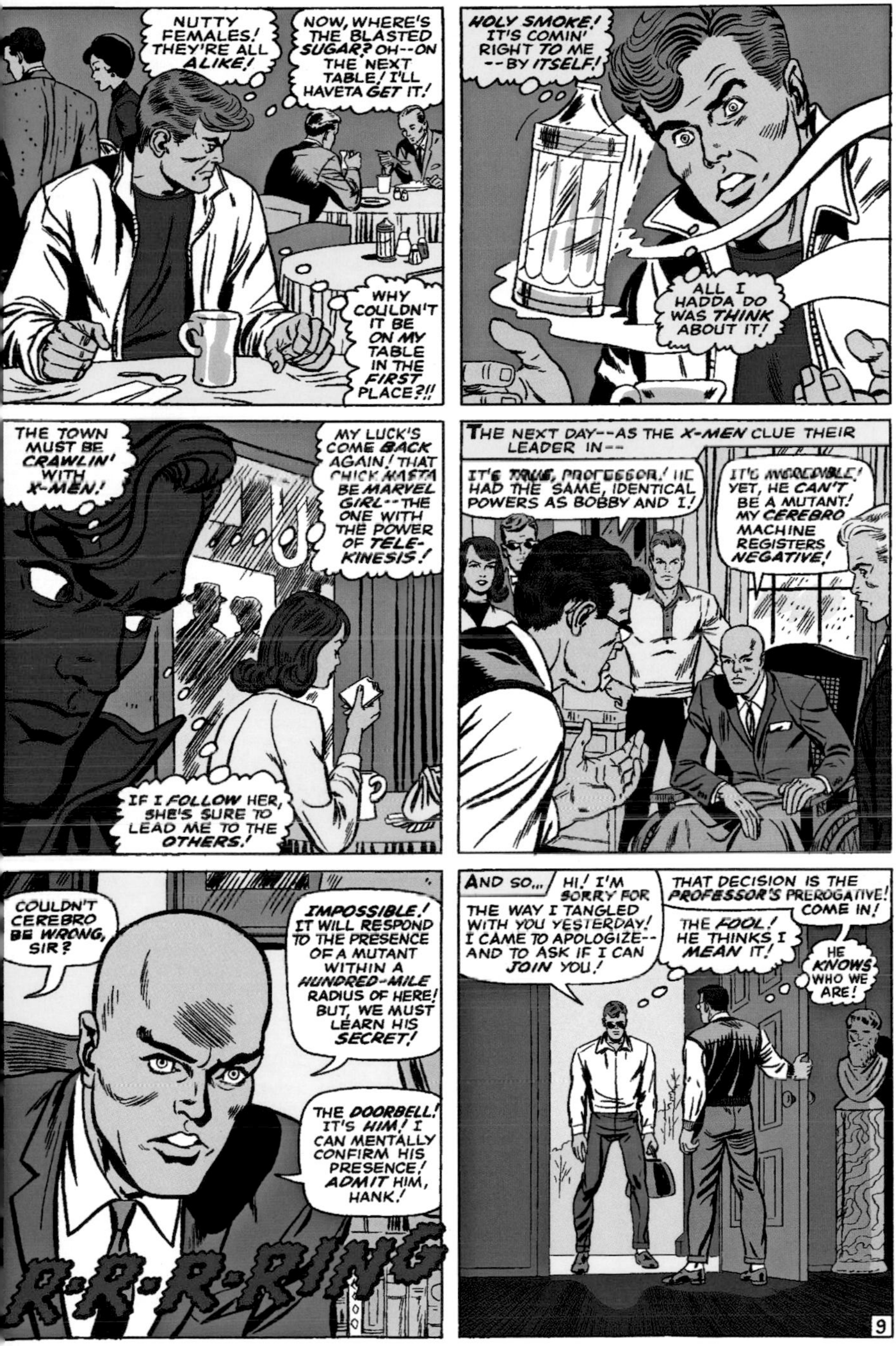
NUTTY FEMALES! THEY'RE ALL ALIKE!
NOW, WHERE'S THE BLASTED SUGAR? OH--ON THE NEXT TABLE! I'LL HAVETA GET IT!
WHY COULDN'T IT BE ON MY TABLE IN THE FIRST PLACE?!!
HOLY SMOKE! IT'S COMIN' RIGHT TO ME --BY ITSELF!
ALL I HADDA DO WAS THINK ABOUT IT!
THE TOWN MUST BE CRAWLIN' WITH X-MEN!
MY LUCK'S COME BACK AGAIN! THAT CHICK HASTA BE MARVEL GIRL--THE ONE WITH THE POWER OF TELE-KINESIS!
IF I FOLLOW HER, SHE'S SURE TO LEAD ME TO THE OTHERS!
THE NEXT DAY--AS THE X-MEN CLUE THEIR LEADER IN--
IT'S TRUE, PROFESSOR! HE HAD THE SAME, IDENTICAL POWERS AS BOBBY AND I!
IT'S INCREDIBLE! YET, HE CAN'T BE A MUTANT! MY CEREBRO MACHINE REGISTERS NEGATIVE!
COULDN'T CEREBRO BE WRONG, SIR?
IMPOSSIBLE! IT WILL RESPOND TO THE PRESENCE OF A MUTANT WITHIN A HUNDRED-MILE RADIUS OF HERE! BUT, WE MUST LEARN HIS SECRET!
THE DOORBELL! IT'S HIM! I CAN MENTALLY CONFIRM HIS PRESENCE! ADMIT HIM, HANK!
R-R-R-RING
AND SO...
HI! I'M SORRY FOR THE WAY I TANGLED WITH YOU YESTERDAY! I CAME TO APOLOGIZE--AND TO ASK IF I CAN JOIN YOU!
THAT DECISION IS THE PROFESSOR'S PREROGATIVE! COME IN!
THE FOOL! HE THINKS I MEAN IT!
HE KNOWS WHO WE ARE!

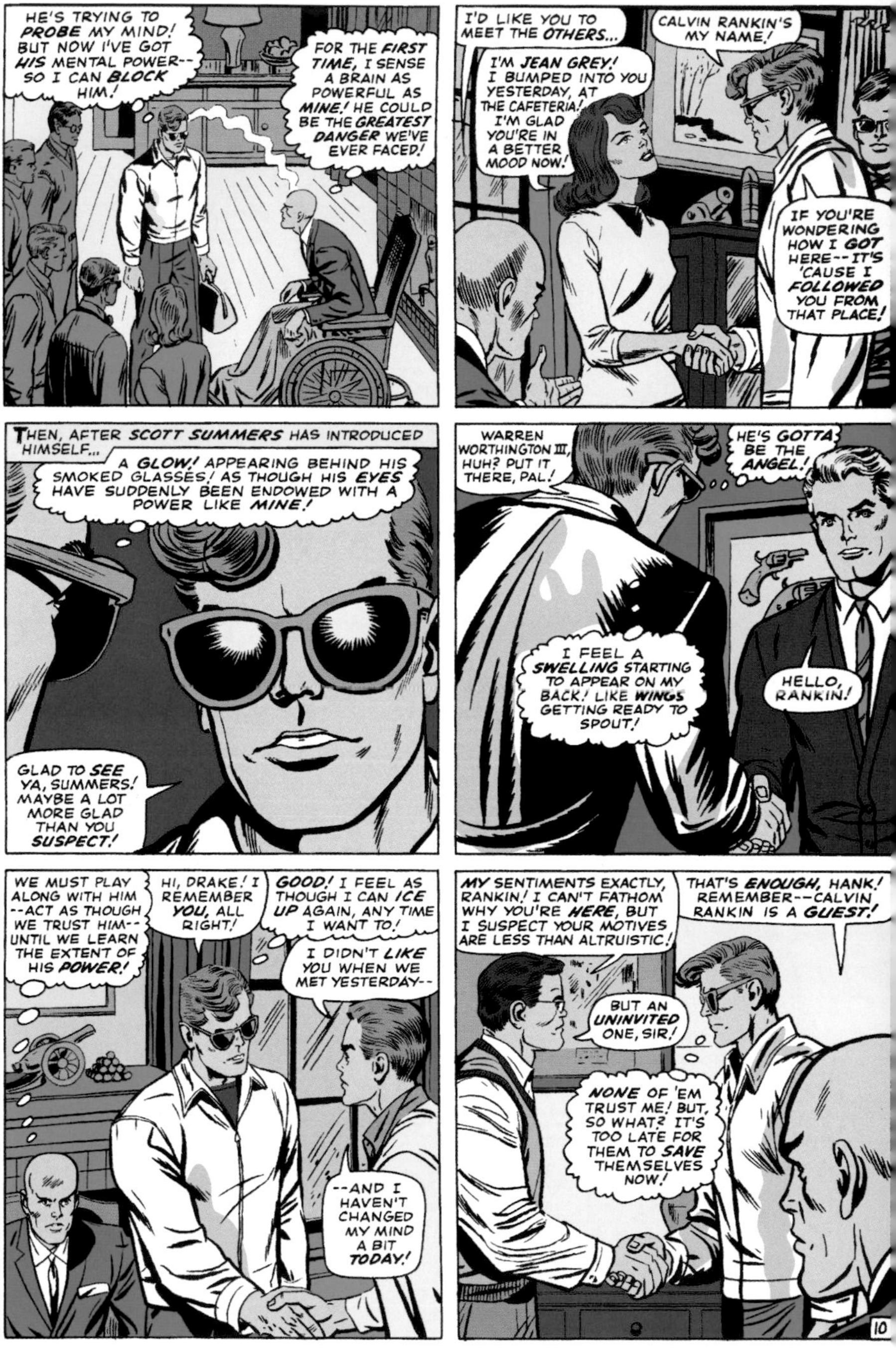
HE'S TRYING TO PROBE MY MIND! BUT NOW I'VE GOT HIS MENTAL POWER-- SO I CAN BLOCK HIM!
FOR THE FIRST TIME, I SENSE A BRAIN AS POWERFUL AS MINE! HE COULD BE THE GREATEST DANGER WE'VE EVER FACED!
I'D LIKE YOU TO MEET THE OTHERS...
CALVIN RANKIN'S MY NAME!
I'M JEAN GREY! I BUMPED INTO YOU YESTERDAY, AT THE CAFETERIA! I'M GLAD YOU'RE IN A BETTER MOOD NOW!
IF YOU'RE WONDERING HOW I GOT HERE--IT'S 'CAUSE I FOLLOWED YOU FROM THAT PLACE!
THEN, AFTER SCOTT SUMMERS HAS INTRODUCED HIMSELF...
A GLOW! APPEARING BEHIND HIS SMOKED GLASSES! AS THOUGH HIS EYES HAVE SUDDENLY BEEN ENDOWED WITH A POWER LIKE MINE!
GLAD TO SEE YA, SUMMERS! MAYBE A LOT MORE GLAD THAN YOU SUSPECT!
WARREN WORTHINGTON III, HUH? PUT IT THERE, PAL!
HE'S GOTTA BE THE ANGEL!
I FEEL A SWELLING STARTING TO APPEAR ON MY BACK! LIKE WINGS GETTING READY TO SPOUT!
HELLO, RANKIN!
WE MUST PLAY ALONG WITH HIM --ACT AS THOUGH WE TRUST HIM-- UNTIL WE LEARN THE EXTENT OF HIS POWER!
HI, DRAKE! I REMEMBER YOU, ALL RIGHT!
GOOD! I FEEL AS THOUGH I CAN ICE UP AGAIN, ANY TIME I WANT TO!
I DIDN'T LIKE YOU WHEN WE MET YESTERDAY--
--AND I HAVEN'T CHANGED MY MIND A BIT TODAY!
MY SENTIMENTS EXACTLY, RANKIN! I CAN'T FATHOM WHY YOU'RE HERE, BUT I SUSPECT YOUR MOTIVES ARE LESS THAN ALTRUISTIC!
THAT'S ENOUGH, HANK! REMEMBER--CALVIN RANKIN IS A GUEST!
BUT AN UNINVITED ONE, SIR!
NONE OF 'EM TRUST ME! BUT, SO WHAT? IT'S TOO LATE FOR THEM TO SAVE THEMSELVES NOW!
10

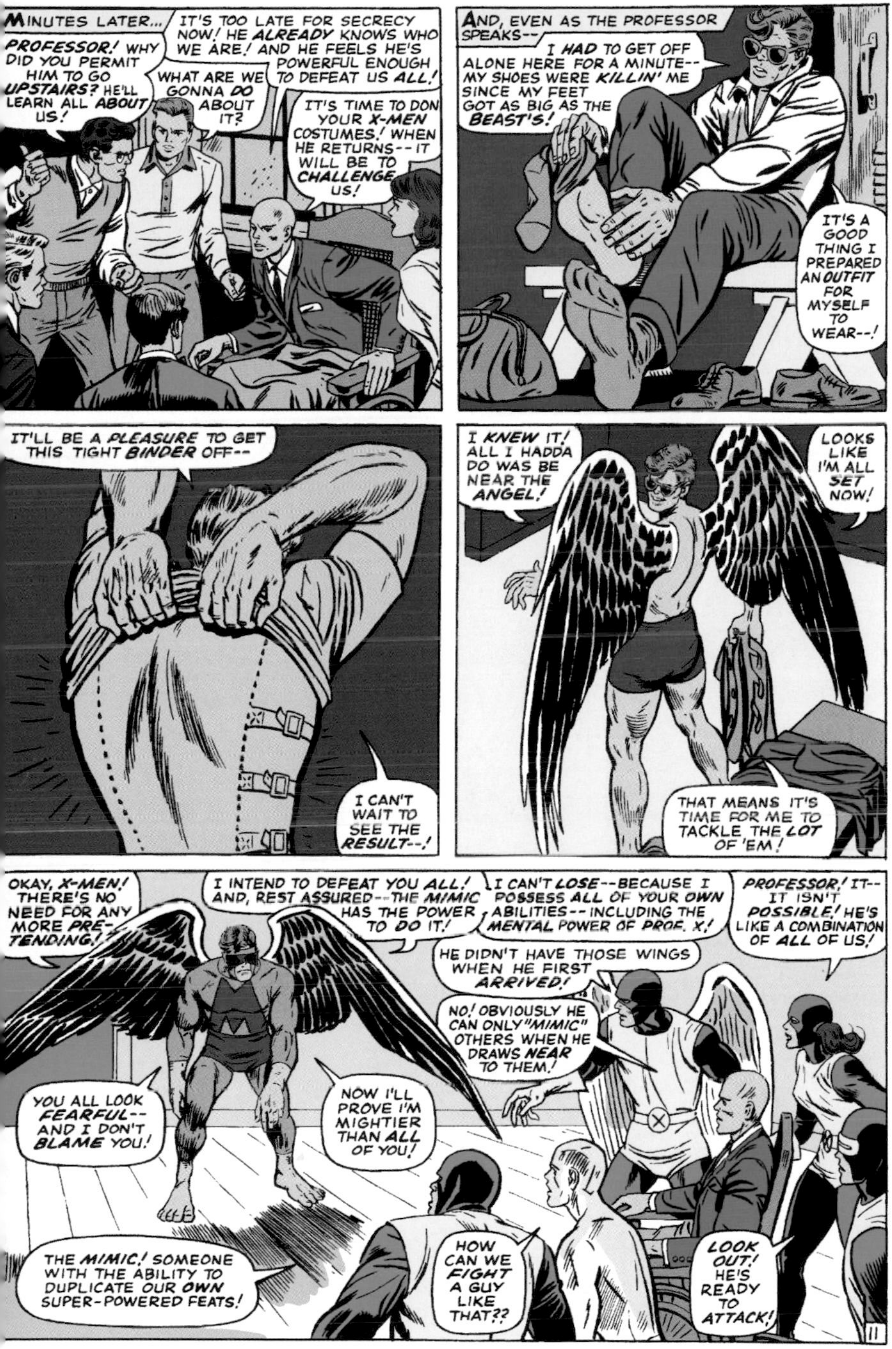
MINUTES LATER...
PROFESSOR! WHY DID YOU PERMIT HIM TO GO UPSTAIRS? HE'LL LEARN ALL ABOUT US!
IT'S TOO LATE FOR SECRECY NOW! HE ALREADY KNOWS WHO WE ARE! AND HE FEELS HE'S POWERFUL ENOUGH TO DEFEAT US ALL!
WHAT ARE WE GONNA DO ABOUT IT?
IT'S TIME TO DON YOUR X-MEN COSTUMES! WHEN HE RETURNS-- IT WILL BE TO CHALLENGE US!
AND, EVEN AS THE PROFESSOR SPEAKS--
I HAD TO GET OFF ALONE HERE FOR A MINUTE-- MY SHOES WERE KILLIN' ME SINCE MY FEET GOT AS BIG AS THE BEAST'S!
IT'S A GOOD THING I PREPARED AN OUTFIT FOR MYSELF TO WEAR--!
IT'LL BE A PLEASURE TO GET THIS TIGHT BINDER OFF--
I CAN'T WAIT TO SEE THE RESULT--!
I KNEW IT! ALL I HADDA DO WAS BE NEAR THE ANGEL!
LOOKS LIKE I'M ALL SET NOW!
THAT MEANS IT'S TIME FOR ME TO TACKLE THE LOT OF 'EM!
OKAY, X-MEN! THERE'S NO NEED FOR ANY MORE PRE-TENDING!
I INTEND TO DEFEAT YOU ALL! AND, REST ASSURED--THE MIMIC HAS THE POWER TO DO IT!
I CAN'T LOSE--BECAUSE I POSSESS ALL OF YOUR OWN ABILITIES--INCLUDING THE MENTAL POWER OF PROF. X!
PROFESSOR! IT-- IT ISN'T POSSIBLE! HE'S LIKE A COMBINATION OF ALL OF US!
HE DIDN'T HAVE THOSE WINGS WHEN HE FIRST ARRIVED!
NO! OBVIOUSLY HE CAN ONLY "MIMIC" OTHERS WHEN HE DRAWS NEAR TO THEM!
YOU ALL LOOK FEARFUL-- AND I DON'T BLAME YOU!
NOW I'LL PROVE I'M MIGHTIER THAN ALL OF YOU!
THE MIMIC! SOMEONE WITH THE ABILITY TO DUPLICATE OUR OWN SUPER-POWERED FEATS!
HOW CAN WE FIGHT A GUY LIKE THAT??
LOOK OUT! HE'S READY TO ATTACK!
11

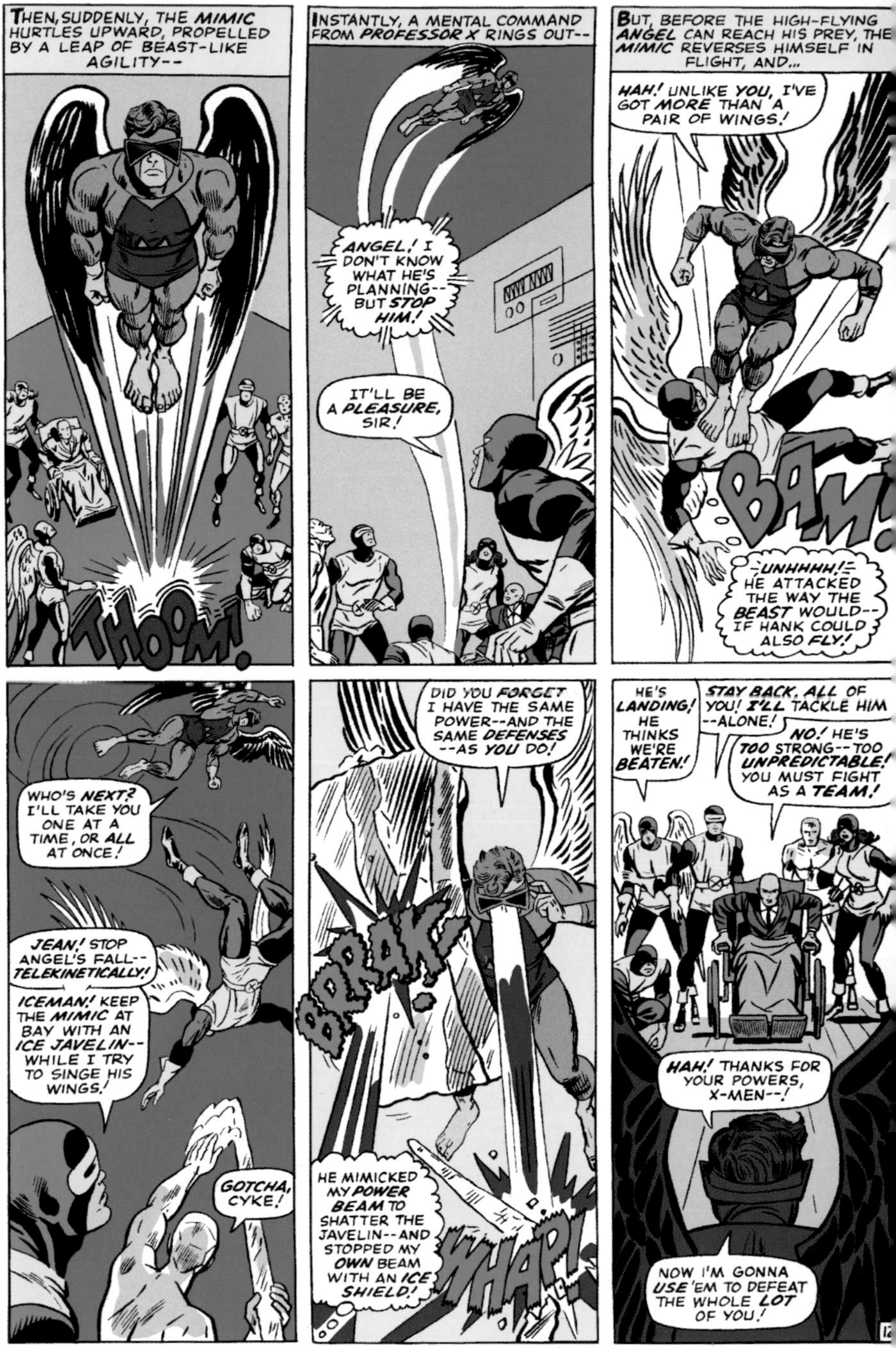
THEN, SUDDENLY, THE MIMIC HURTLES UPWARD, PROPELLED BY A LEAP OF BEAST-LIKE AGILITY--
THOOM!
INSTANTLY, A MENTAL COMMAND FROM PROFESSOR X RINGS OUT--
ANGEL! I DON'T KNOW WHAT HE'S PLANNING--BUT STOP HIM!
IT'LL BE A PLEASURE, SIR!
BUT, BEFORE THE HIGH-FLYING ANGEL CAN REACH HIS PREY, THE MIMIC REVERSES HIMSELF IN FLIGHT, AND...
HAH! UNLIKE YOU, I'VE GOT MORE THAN A PAIR OF WINGS!
BAM!
UNHHHH! HE ATTACKED THE WAY THE BEAST WOULD--IF HANK COULD ALSO FLY!
WHO'S NEXT? I'LL TAKE YOU ONE AT A TIME, OR ALL AT ONCE!
JEAN! STOP ANGEL'S FALL--TELEKINETICALLY!
ICEMAN! KEEP THE MIMIC AT BAY WITH AN ICE JAVELIN--WHILE I TRY TO SINGE HIS WINGS!
GOTCHA, CYKE!
DID YOU FORGET I HAVE THE SAME POWER--AND THE SAME DEFENSES--AS YOU DO!
BRRAK!
WHAP!
HE MIMICKED MY POWER BEAM TO SHATTER THE JAVELIN--AND STOPPED MY OWN BEAM WITH AN ICE SHIELD!
HE'S LANDING! HE THINKS WE'RE BEATEN!
STAY BACK, ALL OF YOU! I'LL TACKLE HIM--ALONE!
NO! HE'S TOO STRONG--TOO UNPREDICTABLE! YOU MUST FIGHT AS A TEAM!
HAH! THANKS FOR YOUR POWERS, X-MEN--!
NOW I'M GONNA USE 'EM TO DEFEAT THE WHOLE LOT OF YOU!

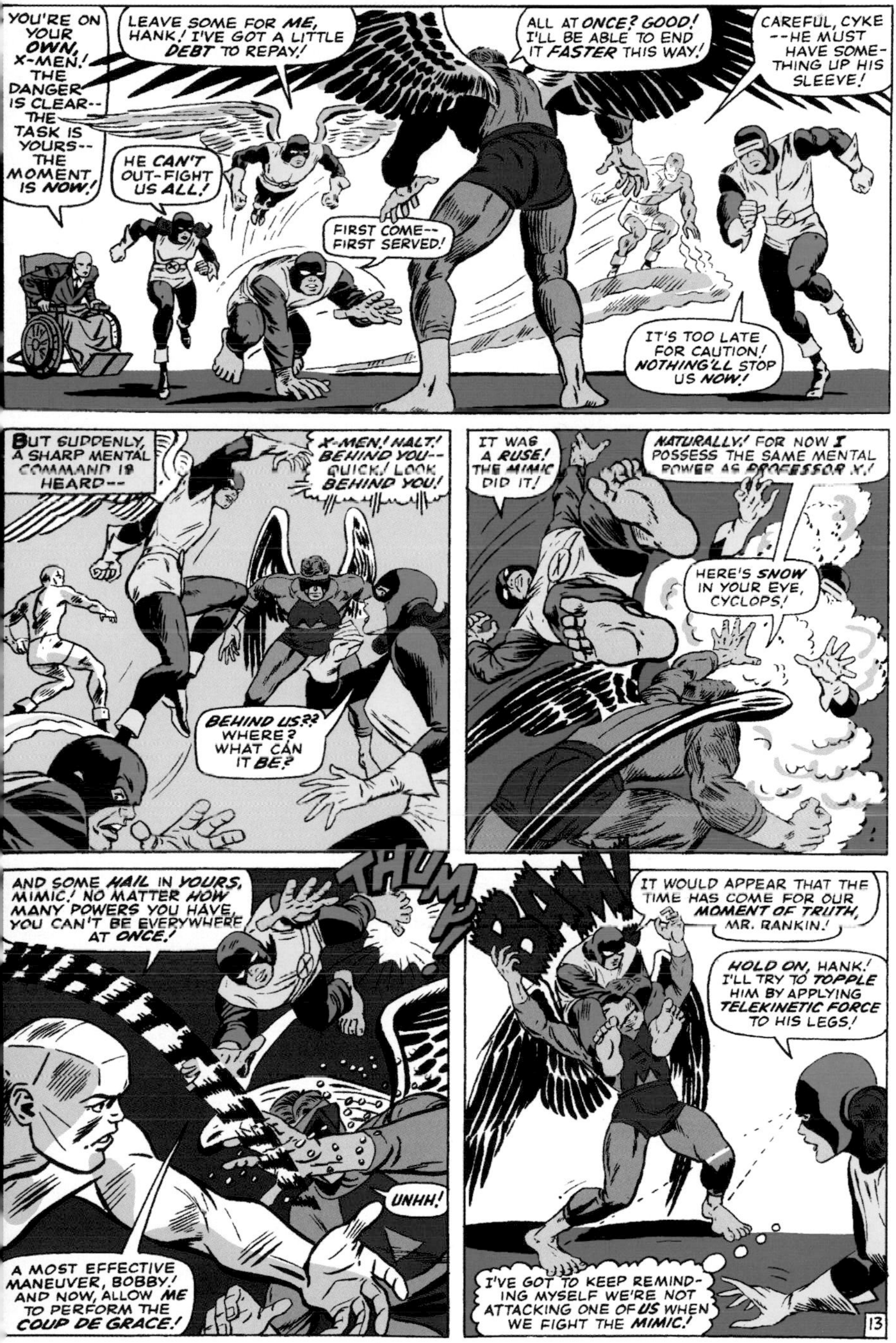

YOU'RE ON YOUR OWN, X-MEN! THE DANGER IS CLEAR-- THE TASK IS YOURS-- THE MOMENT IS NOW!
LEAVE SOME FOR ME, HANK! I'VE GOT A LITTLE DEBT TO REPAY!
HE CAN'T OUT-FIGHT US ALL!
FIRST COME-- FIRST SERVED!
ALL AT ONCE? GOOD! I'LL BE ABLE TO END IT FASTER THIS WAY!
CAREFUL, CYKE --HE MUST HAVE SOME-THING UP HIS SLEEVE!
IT'S TOO LATE FOR CAUTION! NOTHING'LL STOP US NOW!
BUT SUDDENLY, A SHARP MENTAL COMMAND IS HEARD--
X-MEN! HALT! BEHIND YOU-- QUICK! LOOK BEHIND YOU!
BEHIND US?? WHERE? WHAT CAN IT BE?
IT WAS A RUSE! THE MIMIC DID IT!
NATURALLY! FOR NOW I POSSESS THE SAME MENTAL POWER AS PROFESSOR X.!
HERE'S SNOW IN YOUR EYE, CYCLOPS!
AND SOME HAIL IN YOURS, MIMIC! NO MATTER HOW MANY POWERS YOU HAVE, YOU CAN'T BE EVERYWHERE AT ONCE!
THUMP!
UNHH!
A MOST EFFECTIVE MANEUVER, BOBBY! AND NOW, ALLOW ME TO PERFORM THE COUP DE GRACE!
BAM!
IT WOULD APPEAR THAT THE TIME HAS COME FOR OUR MOMENT OF TRUTH, MR. RANKIN!
HOLD ON, HANK! I'LL TRY TO TOPPLE HIM BY APPLYING TELEKINETIC FORCE TO HIS LEGS!
I'VE GOT TO KEEP REMIND-ING MYSELF WE'RE NOT ATTACKING ONE OF US WHEN WE FIGHT THE MIMIC!
13

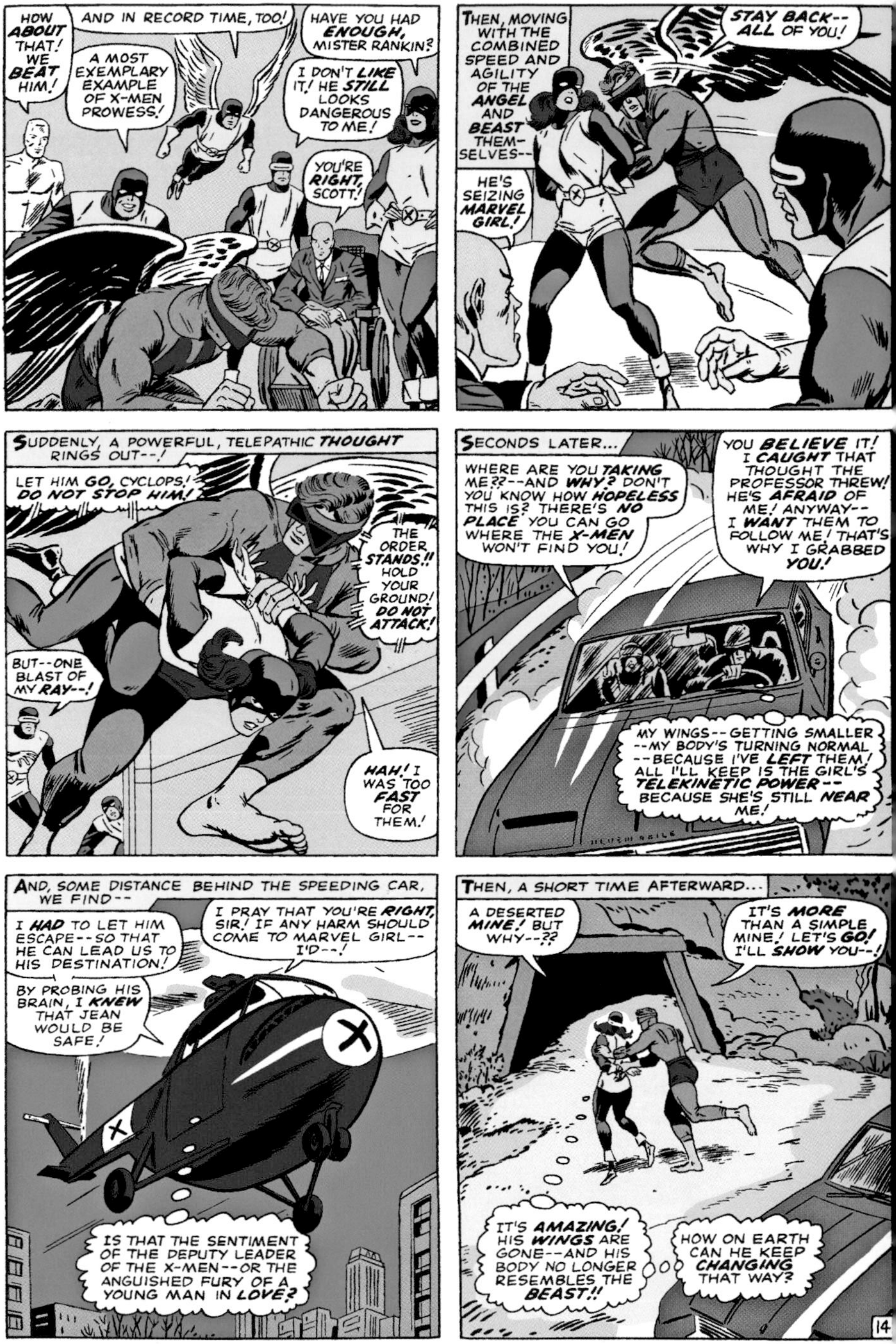

HOW ABOUT THAT! WE BEAT HIM!
AND IN RECORD TIME, TOO!
A MOST EXEMPLARY EXAMPLE OF X-MEN PROWESS!
HAVE YOU HAD ENOUGH, MISTER RANKIN?
I DON'T LIKE IT! HE STILL LOOKS DANGEROUS TO ME!
YOU'RE RIGHT, SCOTT!
THEN, MOVING WITH THE COMBINED SPEED AND AGILITY OF THE ANGEL AND BEAST THEMSELVES--
STAY BACK-- ALL OF YOU!
HE'S SEIZING MARVEL GIRL!
SUDDENLY, A POWERFUL, TELEPATHIC THOUGHT RINGS OUT--!
LET HIM GO, CYCLOPS! DO NOT STOP HIM!
THE ORDER STANDS!! HOLD YOUR GROUND! DO NOT ATTACK!
BUT--ONE BLAST OF MY RAY--!
HAH! I WAS TOO FAST FOR THEM!
SECONDS LATER...
WHERE ARE YOU TAKING ME??--AND WHY? DON'T YOU KNOW HOW HOPELESS THIS IS? THERE'S NO PLACE YOU CAN GO WHERE THE X-MEN WON'T FIND YOU!
YOU BELIEVE IT! I CAUGHT THAT THOUGHT THE PROFESSOR THREW! HE'S AFRAID OF ME! ANYWAY-- I WANT THEM TO FOLLOW ME! THAT'S WHY I GRABBED YOU!
MY WINGS--GETTING SMALLER --MY BODY'S TURNING NORMAL --BECAUSE I'VE LEFT THEM! ALL I'LL KEEP IS THE GIRL'S TELEKINETIC POWER-- BECAUSE SHE'S STILL NEAR ME!
AND, SOME DISTANCE BEHIND THE SPEEDING CAR, WE FIND--
I HAD TO LET HIM ESCAPE--SO THAT HE CAN LEAD US TO HIS DESTINATION!
BY PROBING HIS BRAIN, I KNEW THAT JEAN WOULD BE SAFE!
I PRAY THAT YOU'RE RIGHT, SIR! IF ANY HARM SHOULD COME TO MARVEL GIRL-- I'D--!
IS THAT THE SENTIMENT OF THE DEPUTY LEADER OF THE X-MEN--OR THE ANGUISHED FURY OF A YOUNG MAN IN LOVE?
THEN, A SHORT TIME AFTERWARD...
A DESERTED MINE! BUT WHY--??
IT'S MORE THAN A SIMPLE MINE! LET'S GO! I'LL SHOW YOU--!
IT'S AMAZING! HIS WINGS ARE GONE--AND HIS BODY NO LONGER RESEMBLES THE BEAST!!
HOW ON EARTH CAN HE KEEP CHANGING THAT WAY?
14

SOON, DEEP WITHIN THE MINE, JEAN GREY IS ASTONISHED TO FIND--

LIVING QUARTERS!! IT'S A PLACE FOR SOMEONE TO LIVE--IN COMFORT --AND IN SECRET! BUT, FOR WHAT PURPOSE??

WHILE WE WAIT FOR THE X-MEN TO FIND ME, I'LL TELL YOU A LITTLE STORY --!

THEN, PERHAPS YOU'LL FINALLY UNDERSTAND THE SECRET OF THE MIMIC!

"IT'S THE STORY OF A YOUNG BOY WHOSE FATHER WAS A SCIENTIST, WORKING ON A STRANGE, DANGEROUS EXPERIMENT... MORE DANGEROUS THAN ANY OF THEM DREAMED!"

DAD--?

I'VE TOLD YOU TO STAY OUT WHEN I'M WORKING!! THIS ROOM IS OFF LIMITS TO YOU!

"BUT, THE BOY WAS YOUNG--FOOLISH--AND DEFIANT! ONE DAY, WHEN HIS FATHER WAS OUT ON AN ERRAND, HE TRIED TO SATISFY HIS YOUTHFUL CURIOSITY-- AND THEN--"

OH! I KNOCKED OVER A BEAKER--!

GAS!! FILLING THE AIR ALL AROUND ME!! CAN'T STOP BREATHING IT IN--!

"COUGHING, GASPING, HIS EYES SMARTING, HE CAREFULLY CLEANED UP THE LAB AND THEN LEFT! BUT, IN THE MONTHS AND YEARS THAT FOLLOWED, STRANGE THINGS BEGAN TO HAPPEN, MORE AND MORE FREQUENTLY--!"

I DON'T GET IT! BLACKIE'S THE SCHOOL BOXING CHAMP --AND I'M A DUD! BUT, I'M FIGHTING AS GOOD AS HE IS!!

LATELY, WHENEVER I'M NEAR ANYONE, I SEEM ABLE TO DO WHATEVER HE CAN DO!

POW!

"IT WAS THAT WAY ALL THRU SCHOOL! HE WAS AS GOOD AS THE BEST ATHLETES--SO LONG AS HE WAS NEAR TO THEM! THERE WAS NOTHING HE DIDN'T EXCEL AT! AND, AS HIS ABILITY GREW, SO DID HIS ARROGANCE--AND HIS CONCEIT!"

THAT'S YOUR FIFTH HOMER-- IN FIVE TIMES AT BAT!!

NATURALLY! IT'S NOT HARD WHEN YOU'RE PLAYING AGAINST A BUNCH OF NO-TALENT MISFITS!!

THWAK!

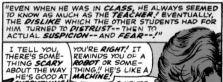

"EVEN WHEN HE WAS IN CLASS, HE ALWAYS SEEMED TO KNOW AS MUCH AS THE TEACHER! EVENTUALLY, THE DISLIKE WHICH THE OTHER STUDENTS HAD FOR HIM TURNED TO DISTRUST--THEN TO ACTUAL SUSPICION--AND FEAR--!"

I TELL YOU, THERE'S SOMETHING SCARY ABOUT THE WAY HE'S GOOD AT EVERYTHING!

YOU'RE RIGHT! IT REMINDS YOU OF A ROBOT OR SOMETHING! HE'S LIKE A MACHINE!

I NEVER HEARD OF ANYONE BEING TOPS AT EVERY SPORT--AND GETTING STRAIGHT A'S IN EVERY SUBJECT--WITHOUT EVEN TRYING!

I SHOULD WORRY WHAT THEY THINK OF ME! I'M BETTER'N ALL OF THEM! THEY'RE JUST JEALOUS OF ME, THAT'S WHAT!

15

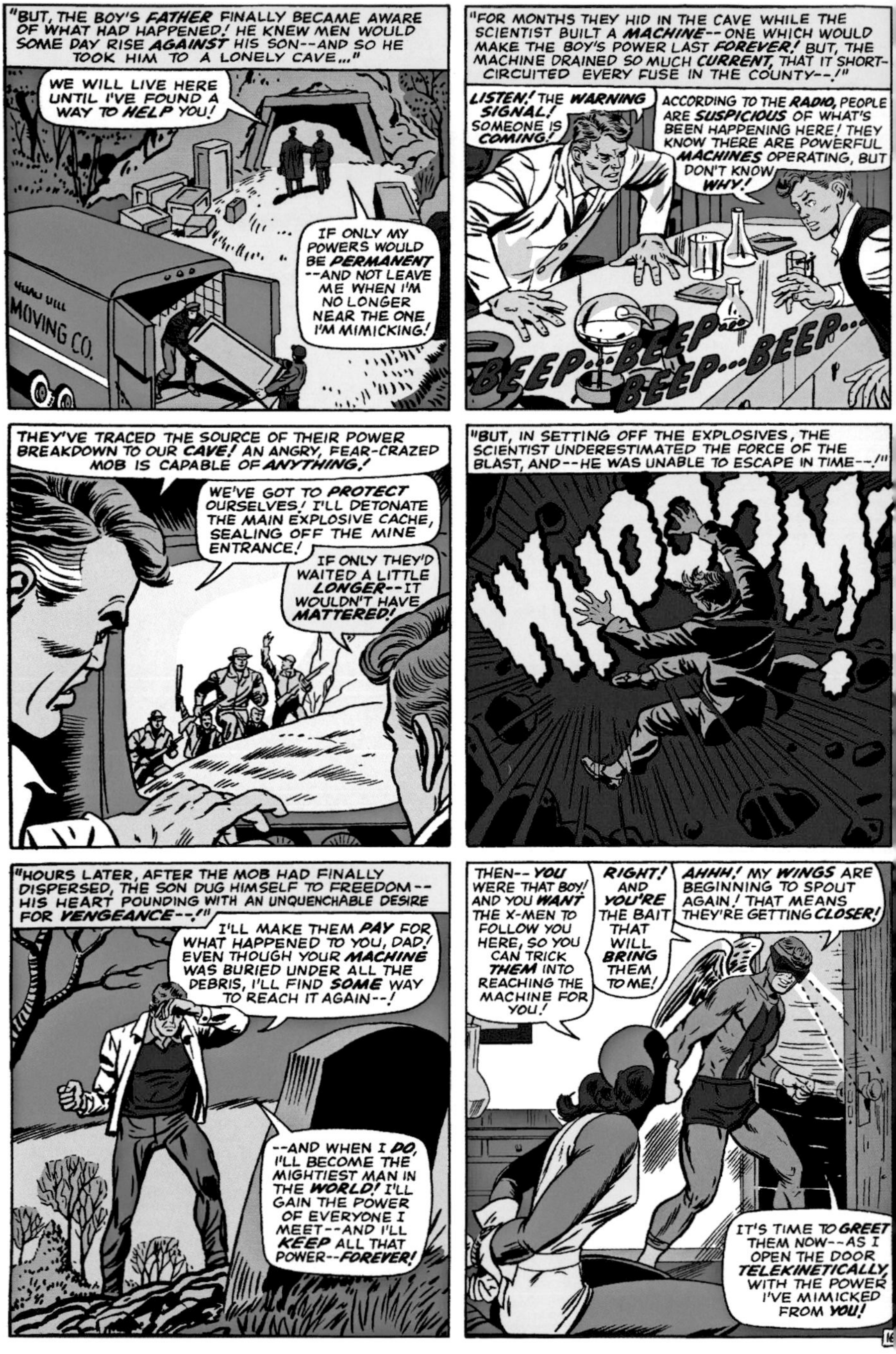
"BUT, THE BOY'S FATHER FINALLY BECAME AWARE OF WHAT HAD HAPPENED! HE KNEW MEN WOULD SOME DAY RISE AGAINST HIS SON--AND SO HE TOOK HIM TO A LONELY CAVE..."
WE WILL LIVE HERE UNTIL I'VE FOUND A WAY TO HELP YOU!
IF ONLY MY POWERS WOULD BE PERMANENT --AND NOT LEAVE ME WHEN I'M NO LONGER NEAR THE ONE I'M MIMICKING!
MOVING CO.
"FOR MONTHS THEY HID IN THE CAVE WHILE THE SCIENTIST BUILT A MACHINE--ONE WHICH WOULD MAKE THE BOY'S POWER LAST FOREVER! BUT, THE MACHINE DRAINED SO MUCH CURRENT, THAT IT SHORT-CIRCUITED EVERY FUSE IN THE COUNTY--!"
LISTEN! THE WARNING SIGNAL! SOMEONE IS COMING!
ACCORDING TO THE RADIO, PEOPLE ARE SUSPICIOUS OF WHAT'S BEEN HAPPENING HERE! THEY KNOW THERE ARE POWERFUL MACHINES OPERATING, BUT DON'T KNOW WHY!
BEEP...BEEP...BEEP...BEEP...
THEY'VE TRACED THE SOURCE OF THEIR POWER BREAKDOWN TO OUR CAVE! AN ANGRY, FEAR-CRAZED MOB IS CAPABLE OF ANYTHING!
WE'VE GOT TO PROTECT OURSELVES! I'LL DETONATE THE MAIN EXPLOSIVE CACHE, SEALING OFF THE MINE ENTRANCE!
IF ONLY THEY'D WAITED A LITTLE LONGER--IT WOULDN'T HAVE MATTERED!
"BUT, IN SETTING OFF THE EXPLOSIVES, THE SCIENTIST UNDERESTIMATED THE FORCE OF THE BLAST, AND--HE WAS UNABLE TO ESCAPE IN TIME--!"
WHOOM!
"HOURS LATER, AFTER THE MOB HAD FINALLY DISPERSED, THE SON DUG HIMSELF TO FREEDOM--HIS HEART POUNDING WITH AN UNQUENCHABLE DESIRE FOR VENGEANCE--!"
I'LL MAKE THEM PAY FOR WHAT HAPPENED TO YOU, DAD! EVEN THOUGH YOUR MACHINE WAS BURIED UNDER ALL THE DEBRIS, I'LL FIND SOME WAY TO REACH IT AGAIN--!
--AND WHEN I DO, I'LL BECOME THE MIGHTIEST MAN IN THE WORLD! I'LL GAIN THE POWER OF EVERYONE I MEET--AND I'LL KEEP ALL THAT POWER--FOREVER!
THEN--YOU WERE THAT BOY! AND YOU WANT THE X-MEN TO FOLLOW YOU HERE, SO YOU CAN TRICK THEM INTO REACHING THE MACHINE FOR YOU!
RIGHT! AND YOU'RE THE BAIT THAT WILL BRING THEM TO ME!
AHHH! MY WINGS ARE BEGINNING TO SPOUT AGAIN! THAT MEANS THEY'RE GETTING CLOSER!
IT'S TIME TO GREET THEM NOW--AS I OPEN THE DOOR TELEKINETICALLY, WITH THE POWER I'VE MIMICKED FROM YOU!

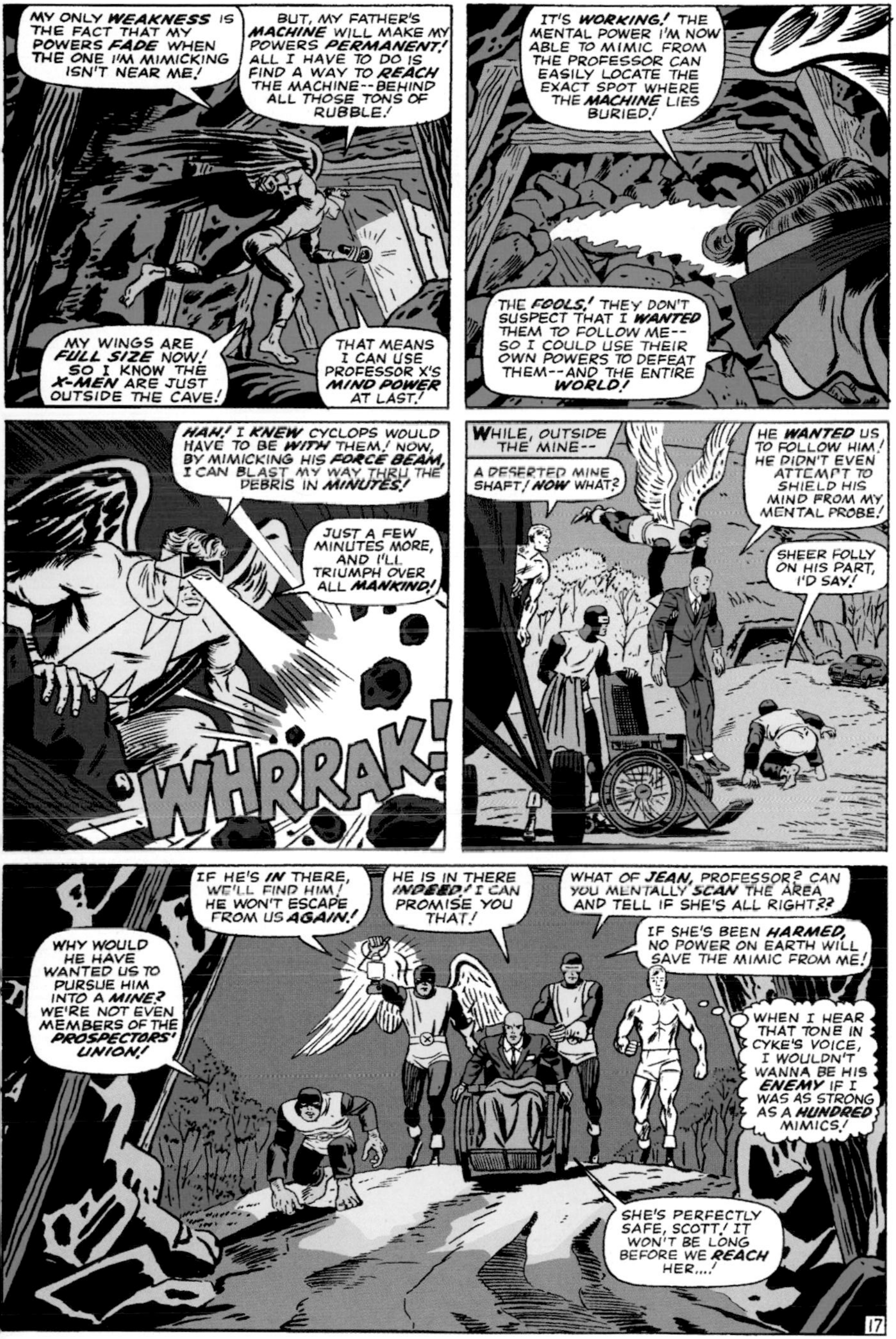
MY ONLY WEAKNESS IS THE FACT THAT MY POWERS FADE WHEN THE ONE I'M MIMICKING ISN'T NEAR ME!
BUT, MY FATHER'S MACHINE WILL MAKE MY POWERS PERMANENT! ALL I HAVE TO DO IS FIND A WAY TO REACH THE MACHINE--BEHIND ALL THOSE TONS OF RUBBLE!
MY WINGS ARE FULL SIZE NOW! SO I KNOW THE X-MEN ARE JUST OUTSIDE THE CAVE!
THAT MEANS I CAN USE PROFESSOR X'S MIND POWER AT LAST!
IT'S WORKING! THE MENTAL POWER I'M NOW ABLE TO MIMIC FROM THE PROFESSOR CAN EASILY LOCATE THE EXACT SPOT WHERE THE MACHINE LIES BURIED!
THE FOOLS! THEY DON'T SUSPECT THAT I WANTED THEM TO FOLLOW ME--SO I COULD USE THEIR OWN POWERS TO DEFEAT THEM--AND THE ENTIRE WORLD!
HAH! I KNEW CYCLOPS WOULD HAVE TO BE WITH THEM! NOW, BY MIMICKING HIS FORCE BEAM, I CAN BLAST MY WAY THRU THE DEBRIS IN MINUTES!
JUST A FEW MINUTES MORE, AND I'LL TRIUMPH OVER ALL MANKIND!
WHRRAK!
WHILE, OUTSIDE THE MINE--
A DESERTED MINE SHAFT! NOW WHAT?
HE WANTED US TO FOLLOW HIM! HE DIDN'T EVEN ATTEMPT TO SHIELD HIS MIND FROM MY MENTAL PROBE!
SHEER FOLLY ON HIS PART, I'D SAY!
WHY WOULD HE HAVE WANTED US TO PURSUE HIM INTO A MINE? WE'RE NOT EVEN MEMBERS OF THE PROSPECTORS' UNION!
IF HE'S IN THERE, WE'LL FIND HIM! HE WON'T ESCAPE FROM US AGAIN!
HE IS IN THERE INDEED! I CAN PROMISE YOU THAT!
WHAT OF JEAN, PROFESSOR? CAN YOU MENTALLY SCAN THE AREA AND TELL IF SHE'S ALL RIGHT??
IF SHE'S BEEN HARMED, NO POWER ON EARTH WILL SAVE THE MIMIC FROM ME!
WHEN I HEAR THAT TONE IN CYKE'S VOICE, I WOULDN'T WANNA BE HIS ENEMY IF I WAS AS STRONG AS A HUNDRED MIMICS!
SHE'S PERFECTLY SAFE, SCOTT! IT WON'T BE LONG BEFORE WE REACH HER...!
17

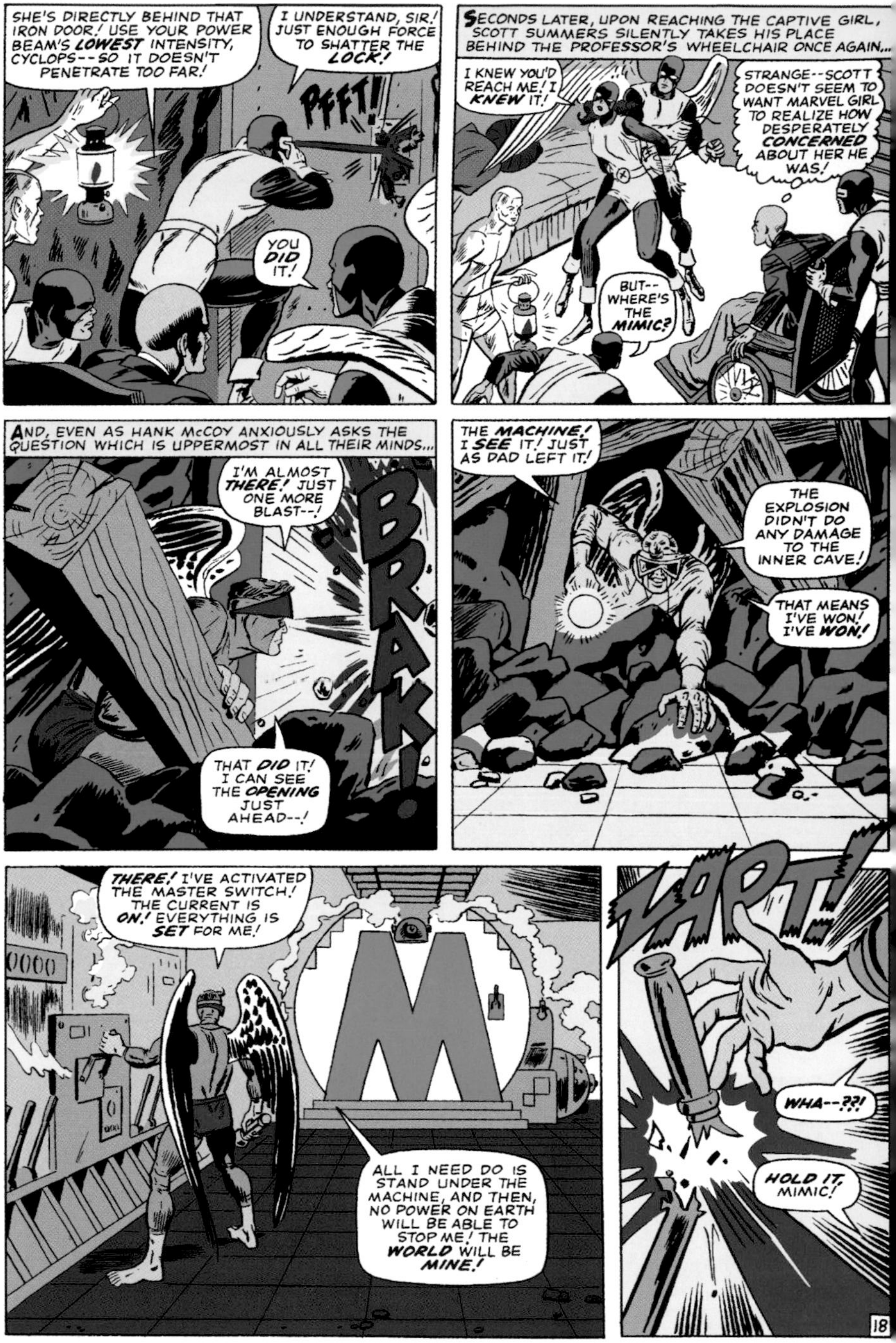

SHE'S DIRECTLY BEHIND THAT IRON DOOR! USE YOUR POWER BEAM'S LOWEST INTENSITY, CYCLOPS--SO IT DOESN'T PENETRATE TOO FAR!
I UNDERSTAND, SIR! JUST ENOUGH FORCE TO SHATTER THE LOCK!
PFFT!
YOU DID IT!
SECONDS LATER, UPON REACHING THE CAPTIVE GIRL, SCOTT SUMMERS SILENTLY TAKES HIS PLACE BEHIND THE PROFESSOR'S WHEELCHAIR ONCE AGAIN...
I KNEW YOU'D REACH ME! I KNEW IT!
STRANGE--SCOTT DOESN'T SEEM TO WANT MARVEL GIRL TO REALIZE HOW DESPERATELY CONCERNED ABOUT HER HE WAS!
BUT--WHERE'S THE MIMIC?
AND, EVEN AS HANK McCOY ANXIOUSLY ASKS THE QUESTION WHICH IS UPPERMOST IN ALL THEIR MINDS...
I'M ALMOST THERE! JUST ONE MORE BLAST--!
BRAK!
THAT DID IT! I CAN SEE THE OPENING JUST AHEAD--!
THE MACHINE! I SEE IT! JUST AS DAD LEFT IT!
THE EXPLOSION DIDN'T DO ANY DAMAGE TO THE INNER CAVE!
THAT MEANS I'VE WON! I'VE WON!
THERE! I'VE ACTIVATED THE MASTER SWITCH! THE CURRENT IS ON! EVERYTHING IS SET FOR ME!
ALL I NEED DO IS STAND UNDER THE MACHINE, AND THEN, NO POWER ON EARTH WILL BE ABLE TO STOP ME! THE WORLD WILL BE MINE!
ZAPT!
WHA--??!
HOLD IT, MIMIC!

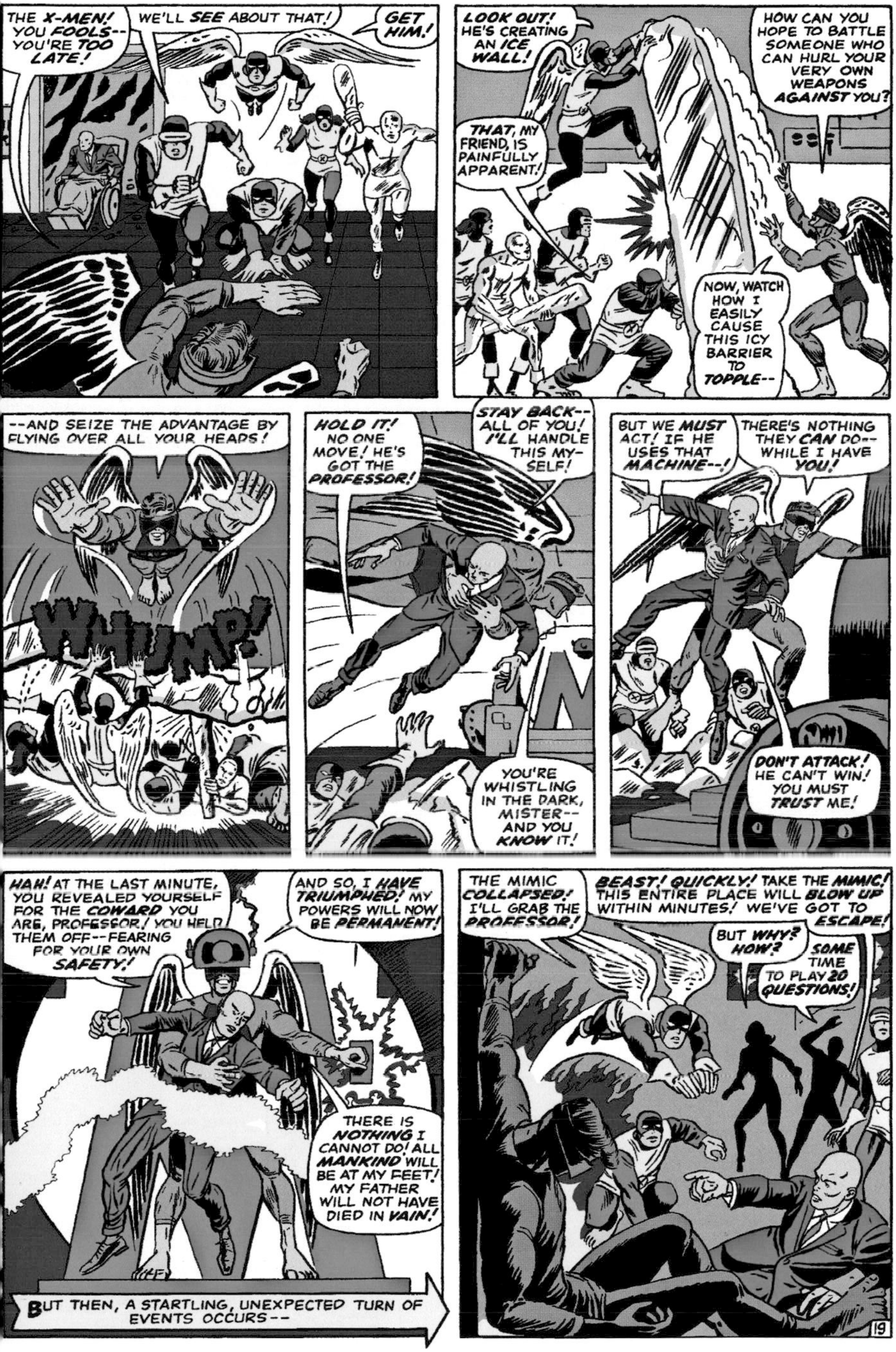
THE X-MEN! YOU FOOLS-- YOU'RE TOO LATE!
WE'LL SEE ABOUT THAT!
GET HIM!
LOOK OUT! HE'S CREATING AN ICE WALL!
HOW CAN YOU HOPE TO BATTLE SOMEONE WHO CAN HURL YOUR VERY OWN WEAPONS AGAINST YOU?
THAT, MY FRIEND, IS PAINFULLY APPARENT!
NOW, WATCH HOW I EASILY CAUSE THIS ICY BARRIER TO TOPPLE--
--AND SEIZE THE ADVANTAGE BY FLYING OVER ALL YOUR HEADS!
WHUMP!
HOLD IT! NO ONE MOVE! HE'S GOT THE PROFESSOR!
STAY BACK-- ALL OF YOU! I'LL HANDLE THIS MY-SELF!
YOU'RE WHISTLING IN THE DARK, MISTER-- AND YOU KNOW IT!
BUT WE MUST ACT! IF HE USES THAT MACHINE--!
THERE'S NOTHING THEY CAN DO-- WHILE I HAVE YOU!
DON'T ATTACK! HE CAN'T WIN! YOU MUST TRUST ME!
HAH! AT THE LAST MINUTE, YOU REVEALED YOURSELF FOR THE COWARD YOU ARE, PROFESSOR! YOU HELD THEM OFF--FEARING FOR YOUR OWN SAFETY!
AND SO, I HAVE TRIUMPHED! MY POWERS WILL NOW BE PERMANENT!
THERE IS NOTHING I CANNOT DO! ALL MANKIND WILL BE AT MY FEET! MY FATHER WILL NOT HAVE DIED IN VAIN!
BUT THEN, A STARTLING, UNEXPECTED TURN OF EVENTS OCCURS--
THE MIMIC COLLAPSED! I'LL GRAB THE PROFESSOR!
BEAST! QUICKLY! TAKE THE MIMIC! THIS ENTIRE PLACE WILL BLOW UP WITHIN MINUTES! WE'VE GOT TO ESCAPE!
BUT WHY? HOW?
SOME TIME TO PLAY 20 QUESTIONS!
19

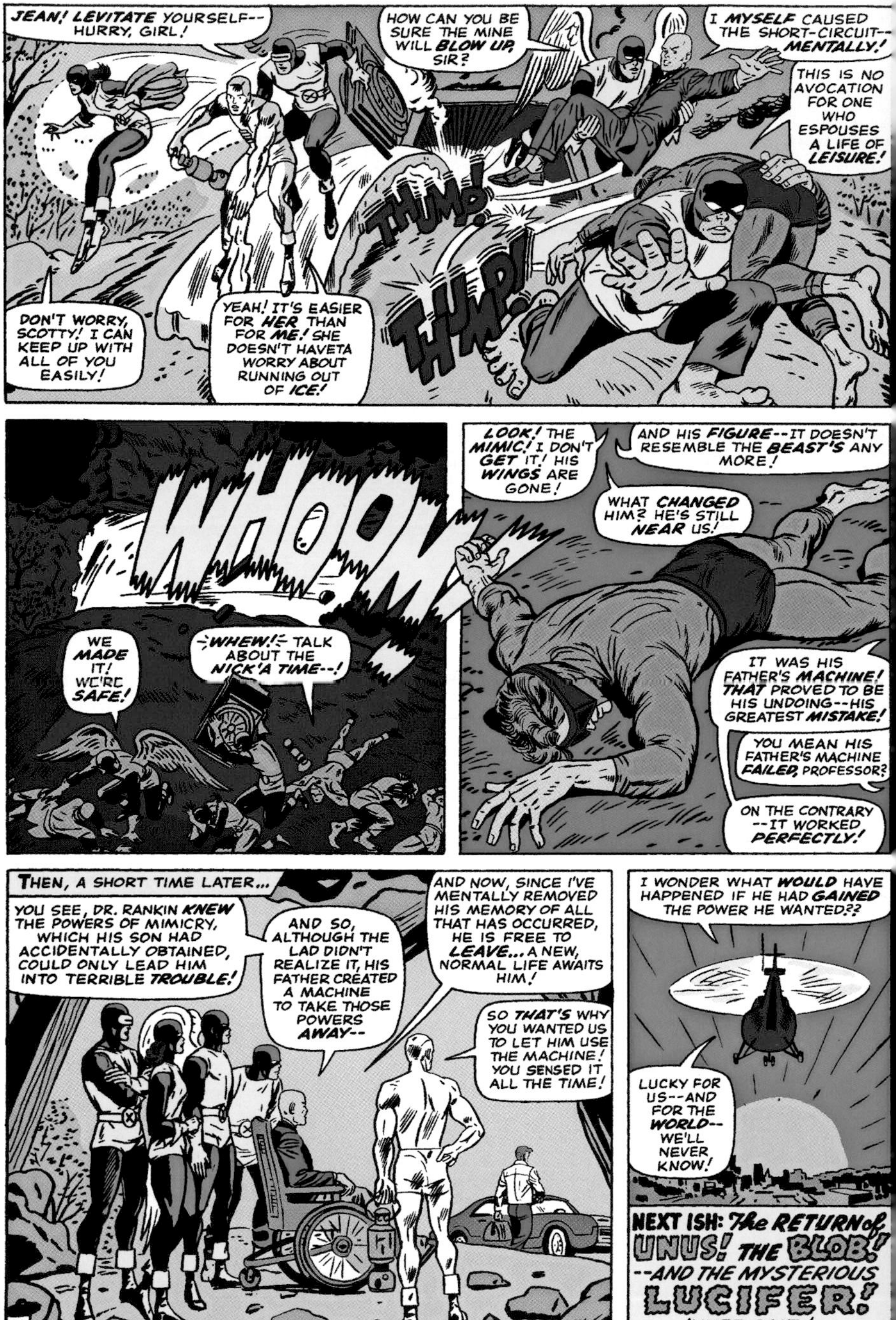

JEAN! LEVITATE YOURSELF-- HURRY, GIRL!
HOW CAN YOU BE SURE THE MINE WILL BLOW UP, SIR?
I MYSELF CAUSED THE SHORT-CIRCUIT-- MENTALLY!
THIS IS NO AVOCATION FOR ONE WHO ESPOUSES A LIFE OF LEISURE!
THUMP! THUMP!
DON'T WORRY, SCOTTY! I CAN KEEP UP WITH ALL OF YOU EASILY!
YEAH! IT'S EASIER FOR HER THAN FOR ME! SHE DOESN'T HAVETA WORRY ABOUT RUNNING OUT OF ICE!
WHOOM!
WE MADE IT! WE'RE SAFE!
-WHEW!- TALK ABOUT THE NICK'A TIME--!
LOOK! THE MIMIC! I DON'T GET IT! HIS WINGS ARE GONE!
AND HIS FIGURE--IT DOESN'T RESEMBLE THE BEAST'S ANY MORE!
WHAT CHANGED HIM? HE'S STILL NEAR US!
IT WAS HIS FATHER'S MACHINE! THAT PROVED TO BE HIS UNDOING--HIS GREATEST MISTAKE!
YOU MEAN HIS FATHER'S MACHINE FAILED, PROFESSOR?
ON THE CONTRARY --IT WORKED PERFECTLY!
THEN, A SHORT TIME LATER...
YOU SEE, DR. RANKIN KNEW THE POWERS OF MIMICRY, WHICH HIS SON HAD ACCIDENTALLY OBTAINED, COULD ONLY LEAD HIM INTO TERRIBLE TROUBLE!
AND SO, ALTHOUGH THE LAD DIDN'T REALIZE IT, HIS FATHER CREATED A MACHINE TO TAKE THOSE POWERS AWAY--
AND NOW, SINCE I'VE MENTALLY REMOVED HIS MEMORY OF ALL THAT HAS OCCURRED, HE IS FREE TO LEAVE... A NEW, NORMAL LIFE AWAITS HIM!
SO THAT'S WHY YOU WANTED US TO LET HIM USE THE MACHINE! YOU SENSED IT ALL THE TIME!
I WONDER WHAT WOULD HAVE HAPPENED IF HE HAD GAINED THE POWER HE WANTED??
LUCKY FOR US--AND FOR THE WORLD-- WE'LL NEVER KNOW!
NEXT ISH: The RETURN of UNUS! THE BLOB! --AND THE MYSTERIOUS LUCIFER!
'NUFF SAID!
20

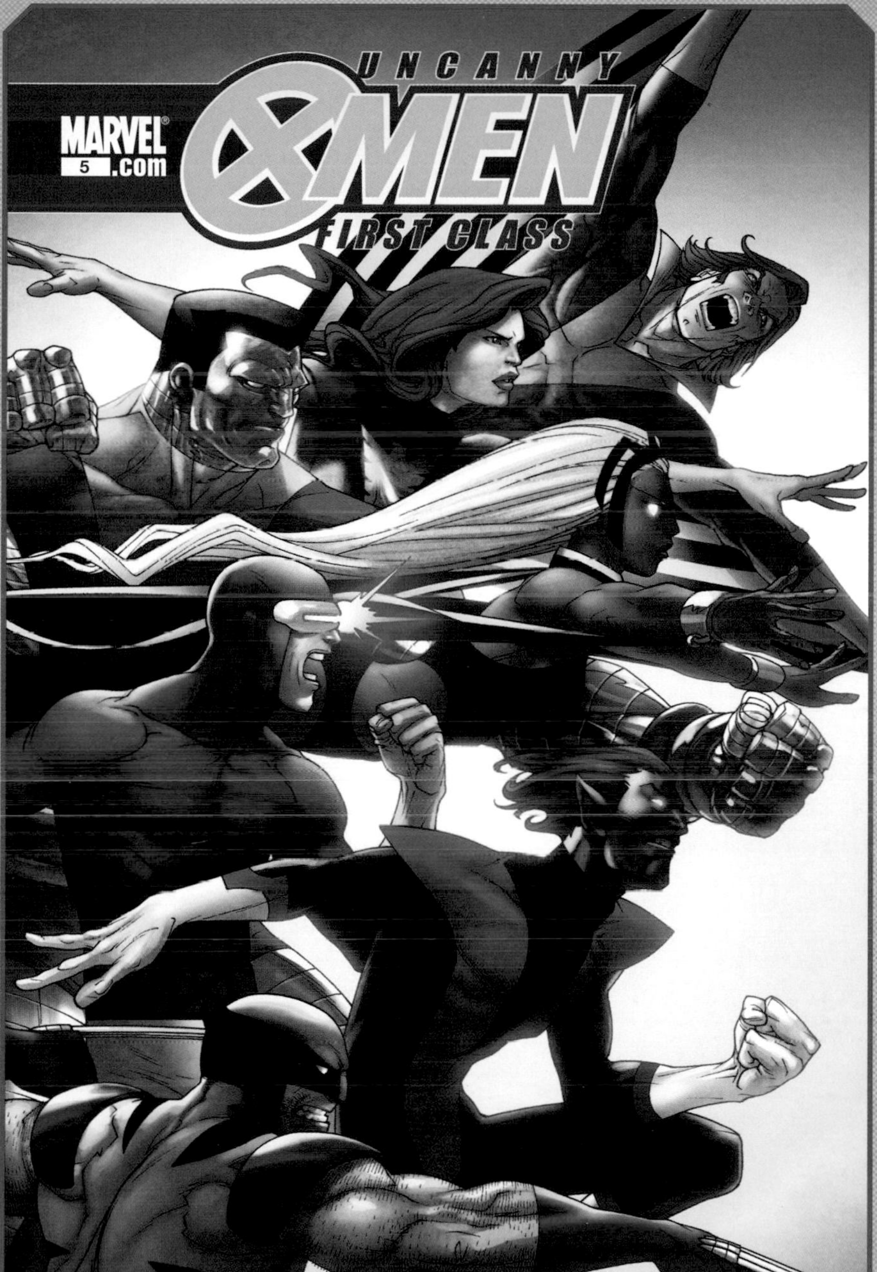
MARVEL
5 .com
UNCANNY
X-MEN
FIRST CLASS
ROGER CRUZ
JPR

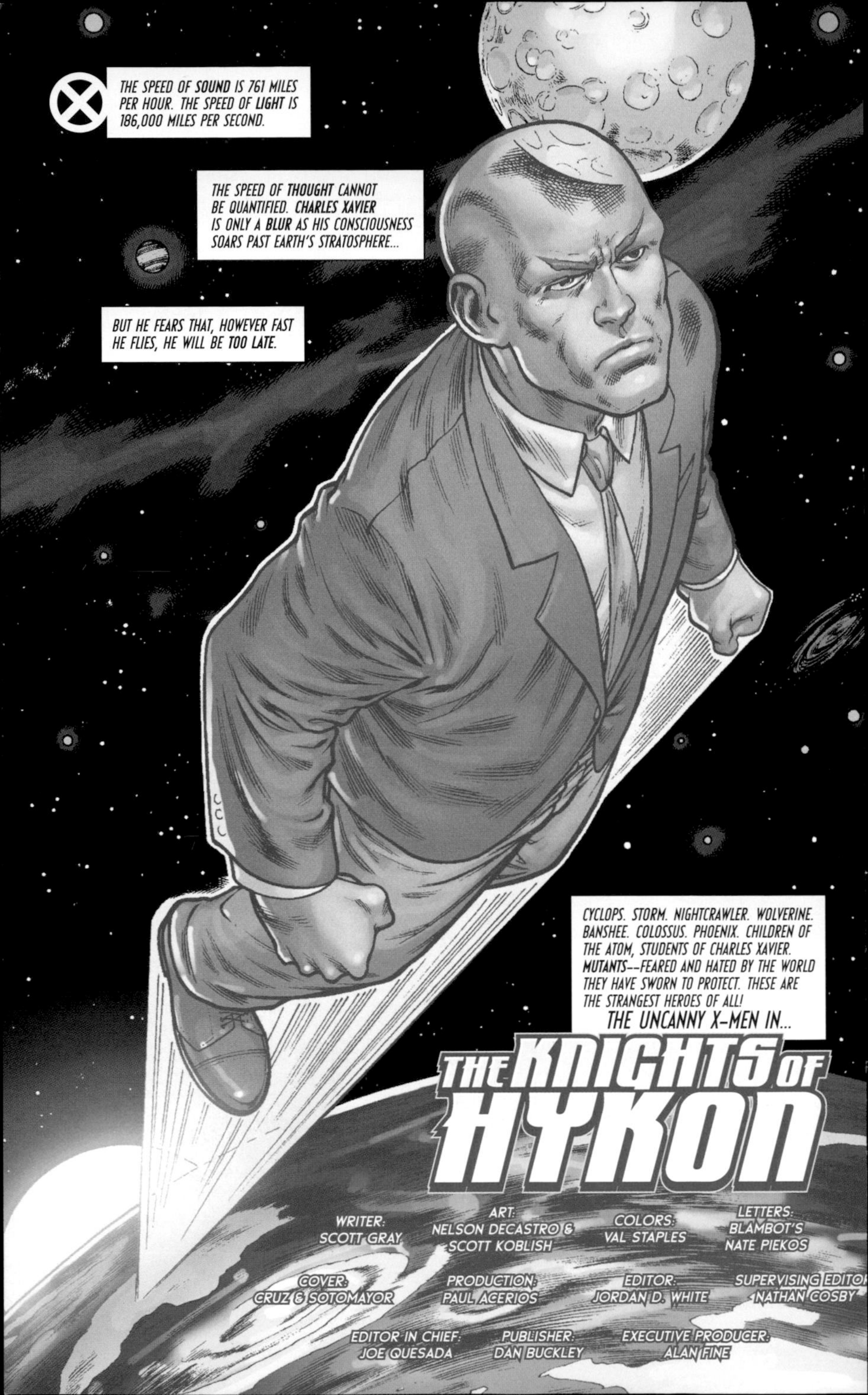
THE SPEED OF SOUND IS 761 MILES PER HOUR. THE SPEED OF LIGHT IS 186,000 MILES PER SECOND.
THE SPEED OF THOUGHT CANNOT BE QUANTIFIED. CHARLES XAVIER IS ONLY A BLUR AS HIS CONSCIOUSNESS SOARS PAST EARTH'S STRATOSPHERE...
BUT HE FEARS THAT, HOWEVER FAST HE FLIES, HE WILL BE TOO LATE.
CYCLOPS. STORM. NIGHTCRAWLER. WOLVERINE. BANSHEE. COLOSSUS. PHOENIX. CHILDREN OF THE ATOM, STUDENTS OF CHARLES XAVIER. MUTANTS--FEARED AND HATED BY THE WORLD THEY HAVE SWORN TO PROTECT. THESE ARE THE STRANGEST HEROES OF ALL!
THE UNCANNY X-MEN IN...
THE KNIGHTS OF HYKON
WRITER: SCOTT GRAY
ART: NELSON DECASTRO & SCOTT KOBLISH
COLORS: VAL STAPLES
LETTERS: BLAMBOT'S NATE PIEKOS
COVER: CRUZ & SOTOMAYOR
PRODUCTION: PAUL ACERIOS
EDITOR: JORDAN D. WHITE
SUPERVISING EDITOR: NATHAN COSBY
EDITOR IN CHIEF: JOE QUESADA
PUBLISHER: DAN BUCKLEY
EXECUTIVE PRODUCER: ALAN FINE

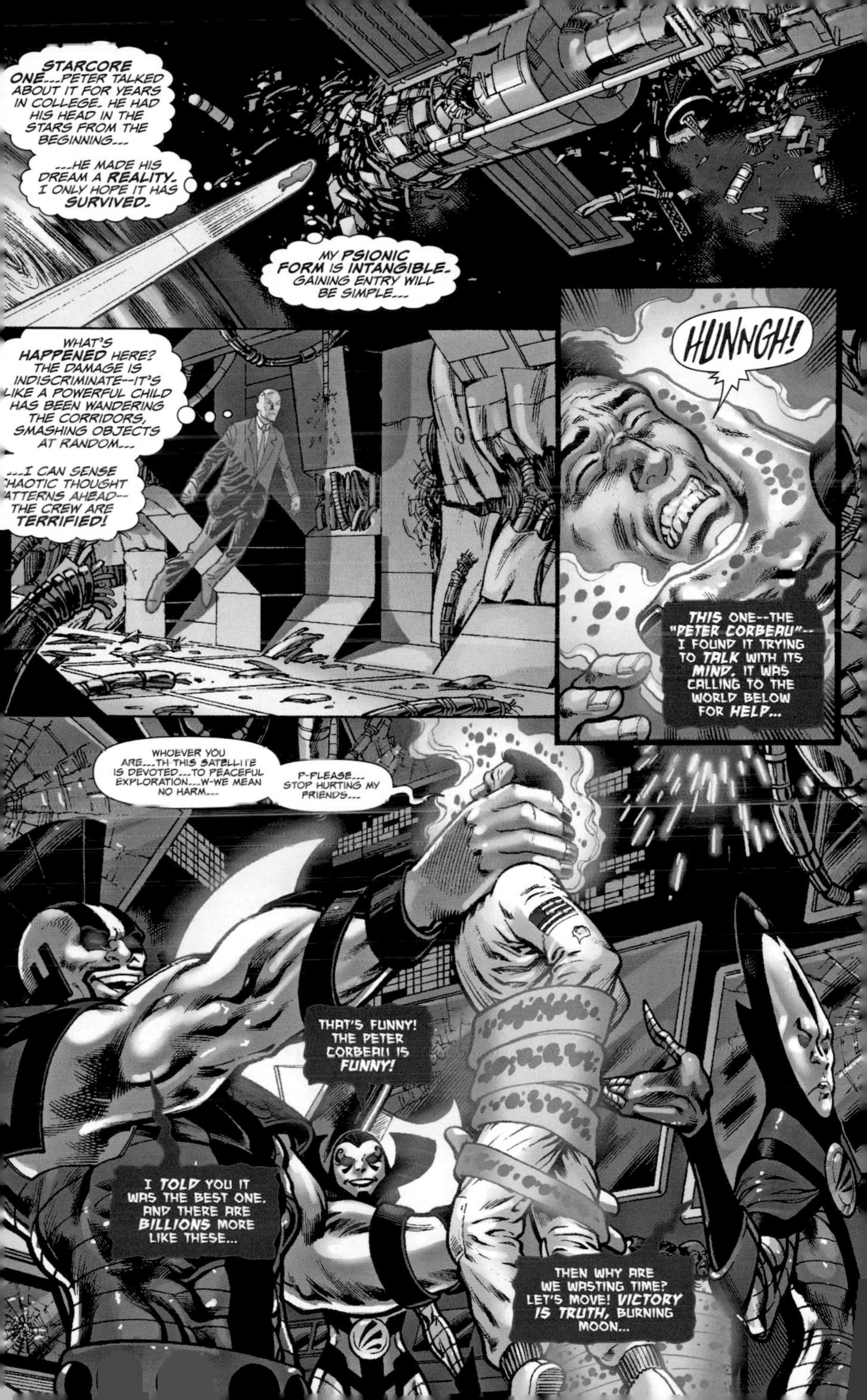
STARCORE ONE---PETER TALKED ABOUT IT FOR YEARS IN COLLEGE. HE HAD HIS HEAD IN THE STARS FROM THE BEGINNING---
---HE MADE HIS DREAM A REALITY. I ONLY HOPE IT HAS SURVIVED.
MY PSIONIC FORM IS INTANGIBLE. GAINING ENTRY WILL BE SIMPLE---
WHAT'S HAPPENED HERE? THE DAMAGE IS INDISCRIMINATE--IT'S LIKE A POWERFUL CHILD HAS BEEN WANDERING THE CORRIDORS, SMASHING OBJECTS AT RANDOM---
---I CAN SENSE CHAOTIC THOUGHT PATTERNS AHEAD--THE CREW ARE TERRIFIED!
HUNNGH!
THIS ONE--THE "PETER CORBEAU"--I FOUND IT TRYING TO TALK WITH ITS MIND. IT WAS CALLING TO THE WORLD BELOW FOR HELP...
WHOEVER YOU ARE---TH THIS SATELLITE IS DEVOTED---TO PEACEFUL EXPLORATION---W-WE MEAN NO HARM---
P-PLEASE--- STOP HURTING MY FRIENDS---
THAT'S FUNNY! THE PETER CORBEAU IS FUNNY!
I TOLD YOU IT WAS THE BEST ONE. AND THERE ARE BILLIONS MORE LIKE THESE...
THEN WHY ARE WE WASTING TIME? LET'S MOVE! VICTORY IS TRUTH, BURNING MOON...

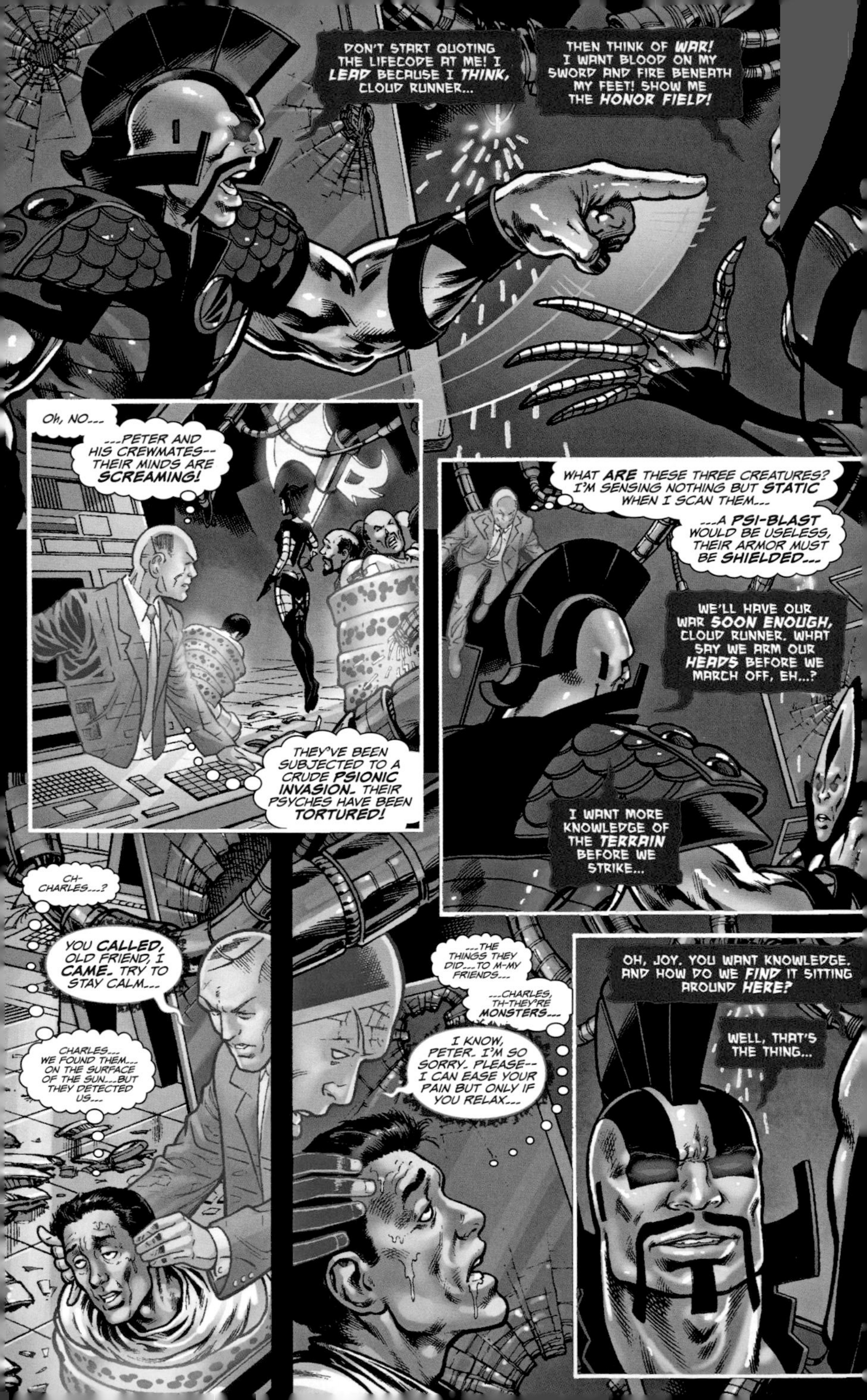
DON'T START QUOTING THE LIFECODE AT ME! I LEAD BECAUSE I THINK, CLOUD RUNNER...
THEN THINK OF WAR! I WANT BLOOD ON MY SWORD AND FIRE BENEATH MY FEET! SHOW ME THE HONOR FIELD!
OH, NO...
...PETER AND HIS CREWMATES-- THEIR MINDS ARE SCREAMING!
THEY'VE BEEN SUBJECTED TO A CRUDE PSIONIC INVASION. THEIR PSYCHES HAVE BEEN TORTURED!
WHAT ARE THESE THREE CREATURES? I'M SENSING NOTHING BUT STATIC WHEN I SCAN THEM...
...A PSI-BLAST WOULD BE USELESS, THEIR ARMOR MUST BE SHIELDED...
WE'LL HAVE OUR WAR SOON ENOUGH, CLOUD RUNNER. WHAT SAY WE ARM OUR HEADS BEFORE WE MARCH OFF, EH...?
I WANT MORE KNOWLEDGE OF THE TERRAIN BEFORE WE STRIKE...
CH- CHARLES...?
YOU CALLED, OLD FRIEND, I CAME. TRY TO STAY CALM...
CHARLES... WE FOUND THEM... ON THE SURFACE OF THE SUN... BUT THEY DETECTED US...
...THE THINGS THEY DID... TO M-MY FRIENDS...
...CHARLES, TH-THEY'RE MONSTERS...
I KNOW, PETER. I'M SO SORRY. PLEASE-- I CAN EASE YOUR PAIN BUT ONLY IF YOU RELAX...
OH, JOY. YOU WANT KNOWLEDGE. AND HOW DO WE FIND IT SITTING AROUND HERE?
WELL, THAT'S THE THING...

...IT JUST FOUND *US*!

AAAKK!

ZZRAKK

DID YOU THINK I COULDN'T *SEE* YOU, LITTLE THING? I AM *BURNING MOON*--I SEE THE *DUST* GATHERING ON THE *CORPSE OF TIME*...

HE'S -- *HOLDING MY PSIONIC FORM*! THAT'S *IMPOSSIBLE*!

ZZRASH

ALL THINGS ARE POSSIBLE FOR *LEGENDS*, FOOL.

WE ARE *THE KNIGHTS OF HYKON*.

HNGHH!

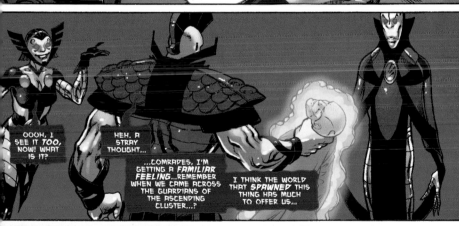

OOOH, I SEE IT *TOO*, NOW! WHAT IS IT?

HEH. A STRAY THOUGHT...

...COMRADES, I'M GETTING A *FAMILIAR FEELING*...REMEMBER WHEN WE CAME ACROSS THE *GUARDIANS OF THE ASCENDING CLUSTER*...?

I THINK THE WORLD THAT *SPAWNED* THIS THING HAS MUCH TO OFFER US...

CLOUD RUNNER, GO AND MARK THE TERRITORY. IT'S *OURS* NOW, LET THE ENEMY KNOW THAT.

FINALLY!

OH, I WANTED TO DO THAT!

NO, SKY SONG, YOU'RE ON SCOUTING DUTY. I'LL SHOW YOU THE PATH THIS CREATURE TRAVELLED...

...TRACE IT BACK TO ITS ORIGIN...

"...I WANT TO SEE WHERE IT CAME FROM."

Y'KNOW, I DO A LOT OF THINGS REAL WELL, CREW...

...BUT *WAITIN'* AIN'T ONE OF THEM. WHY ARE WE LETTIN' SUMMERS AND CO. TREAT US LIKE A PACK O' GRUNTS?

PATIENCE, *BOYO*. I'M THINKIN' WE'LL GET OUR TURN AT THE WHEEL SOON ENOUGH...

EVEN SO, PROFESSOR XAVIER SUMMONED THE OTHERS OVER AN *HOUR* AGO. IT WOULD BE POLITE TO KEEP US *INFORMED*...

THEY WILL CALL US WHEN WE ARE *NEEDED*, KURT...

YOU'RE A REGULAR TIN SOLDIER, AIN'TCHA, PETEY? I'LL BET CHARLEY GIVES YOU AN EXTRA GOLD STAR ON YER REPORT CARD THIS MONTH...

THANK YOU, *TOVARISCH*, BUT THE PROFESSOR DOES NOT...

...WAIT. THIS IS SARCASM?

IF HIS LIPS ARE MOVING, PETER, THEN YES...

E-FLAMIN'-*NUFF!* YOU BOYS WANNA PLAY IN THE NURSERY WHILE THE GROWN-UPS TALK, *FINE*--I'M GETTIN' SOME *AIR*...

WE WER[E] ASKED T[O] STAY INSI[DE] WOLVERI[NE]

IF I CATCH A *CHILL* I'LL SCREAM FOR *HELP*, IRISH...

THAT MAN'S A *POWDER KEG* TO BE SURE. ONE DAY HE'S GOIN' TO *BLOW*, AN' HEAVEN HELP ANYONE STANDIN' IN HIS WAY...

ACH, I HATE TO ADMIT IT, BUT I KNOW HOW HE FEELS.

EASY NOW, LAD, DON'T LET YER IMAGINATIO[N] CARRY YOU AWAY. ALL *I'M* SENSIN' IS A CAFFEINE OVERLOAD...

...I'LL JUST POKE ME HEAD AROUND THE DOOR AN' SEE WHAT'S WHAT...

THERE IS A... *WRONGNESS* ABROAD TONIGHT, SEAN. CAN'T YOU SENSE IT? WE ARE ON THE EDGE OF SOMETHING *HUGE*. SOMETHING *TERRIBLE*...

DIDN'T WANT TO SAY ANYTHIN' TO KURT, BUT *MY SKIN'S BEEN CRAWLIN'* ALL NIGHT TOO.

FEELS LIKE THAT TIME IN PRAGUE, WHEN I GOT INSIDE THAT GUN-RUNNIN' RING. THE JOB *LOOKED* LIKE IT WAS GOIN' SMOOTH...

...BUT SOMEHOW I KNEW MY LUCK HAD *RUN OUT*.

Ah, C'MON, CASSIDY, *STOP IT*. YER JUST BEIN' *STUPID* NOW.

WE'RE THE X-MEN...

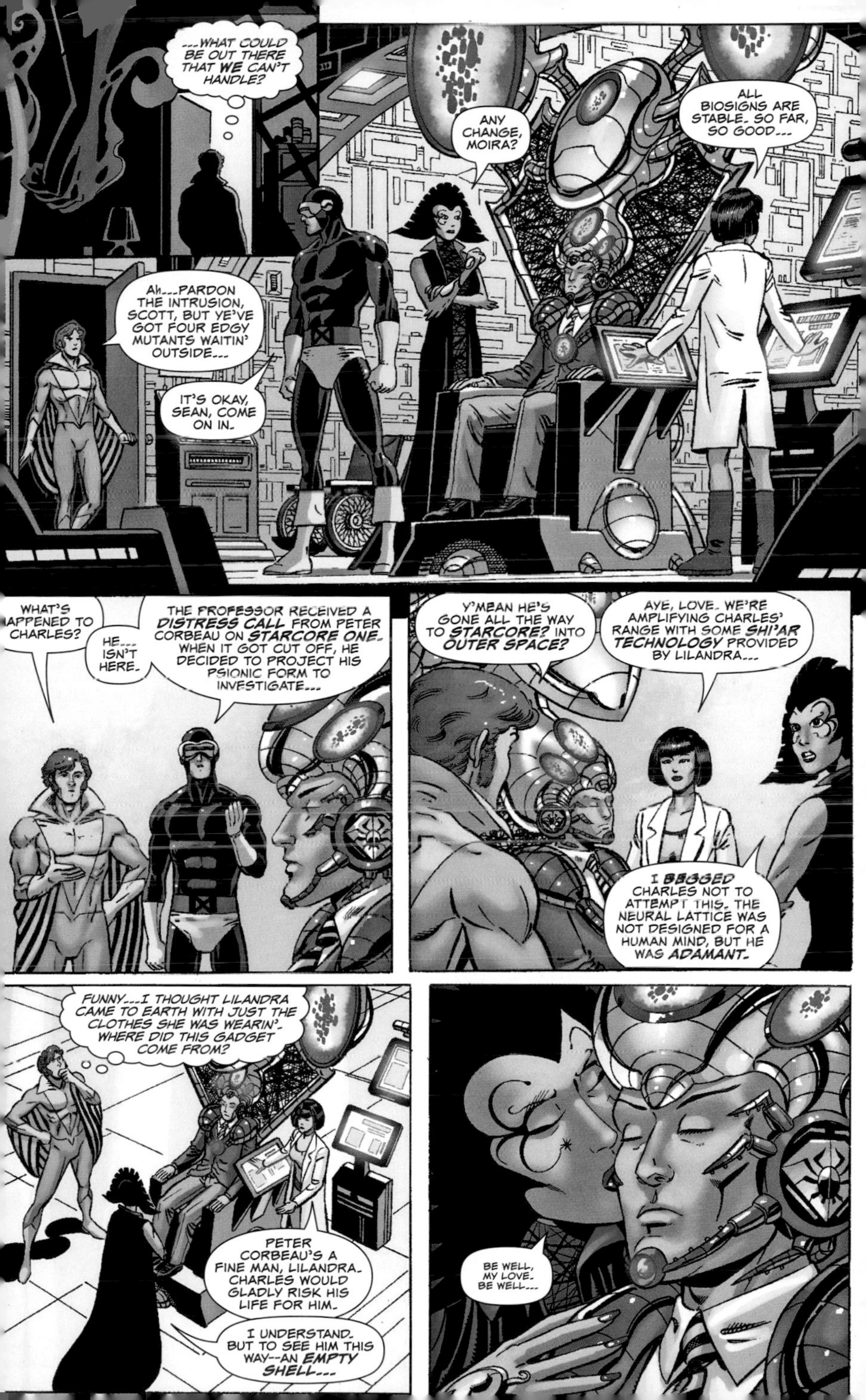

...WHAT COULD BE OUT THERE THAT WE CAN'T HANDLE?
ANY CHANGE, MOIRA?
ALL BIOSIGNS ARE STABLE. SO FAR, SO GOOD...
Ah...PARDON THE INTRUSION, SCOTT, BUT YE'VE GOT FOUR EDGY MUTANTS WAITIN' OUTSIDE...
IT'S OKAY, SEAN, COME ON IN.
WHAT'S 'APPENED TO CHARLES?
HE... ISN'T HERE.
THE PROFESSOR RECEIVED A DISTRESS CALL FROM PETER CORBEAU ON STARCORE ONE. WHEN IT GOT CUT OFF, HE DECIDED TO PROJECT HIS PSIONIC FORM TO INVESTIGATE...
Y'MEAN HE'S GONE ALL THE WAY TO STARCORE? INTO OUTER SPACE?
AYE, LOVE. WE'RE AMPLIFYING CHARLES' RANGE WITH SOME SHI'AR TECHNOLOGY PROVIDED BY LILANDRA...
I BEGGED CHARLES NOT TO ATTEMPT THIS. THE NEURAL LATTICE WAS NOT DESIGNED FOR A HUMAN MIND, BUT HE WAS ADAMANT.
FUNNY...I THOUGHT LILANDRA CAME TO EARTH WITH JUST THE CLOTHES SHE WAS WEARIN'. WHERE DID THIS GADGET COME FROM?
PETER CORBEAU'S A FINE MAN, LILANDRA. CHARLES WOULD GLADLY RISK HIS LIFE FOR HIM.
I UNDERSTAND. BUT TO SEE HIM THIS WAY--AN EMPTY SHELL...
BE WELL, MY LOVE. BE WELL...

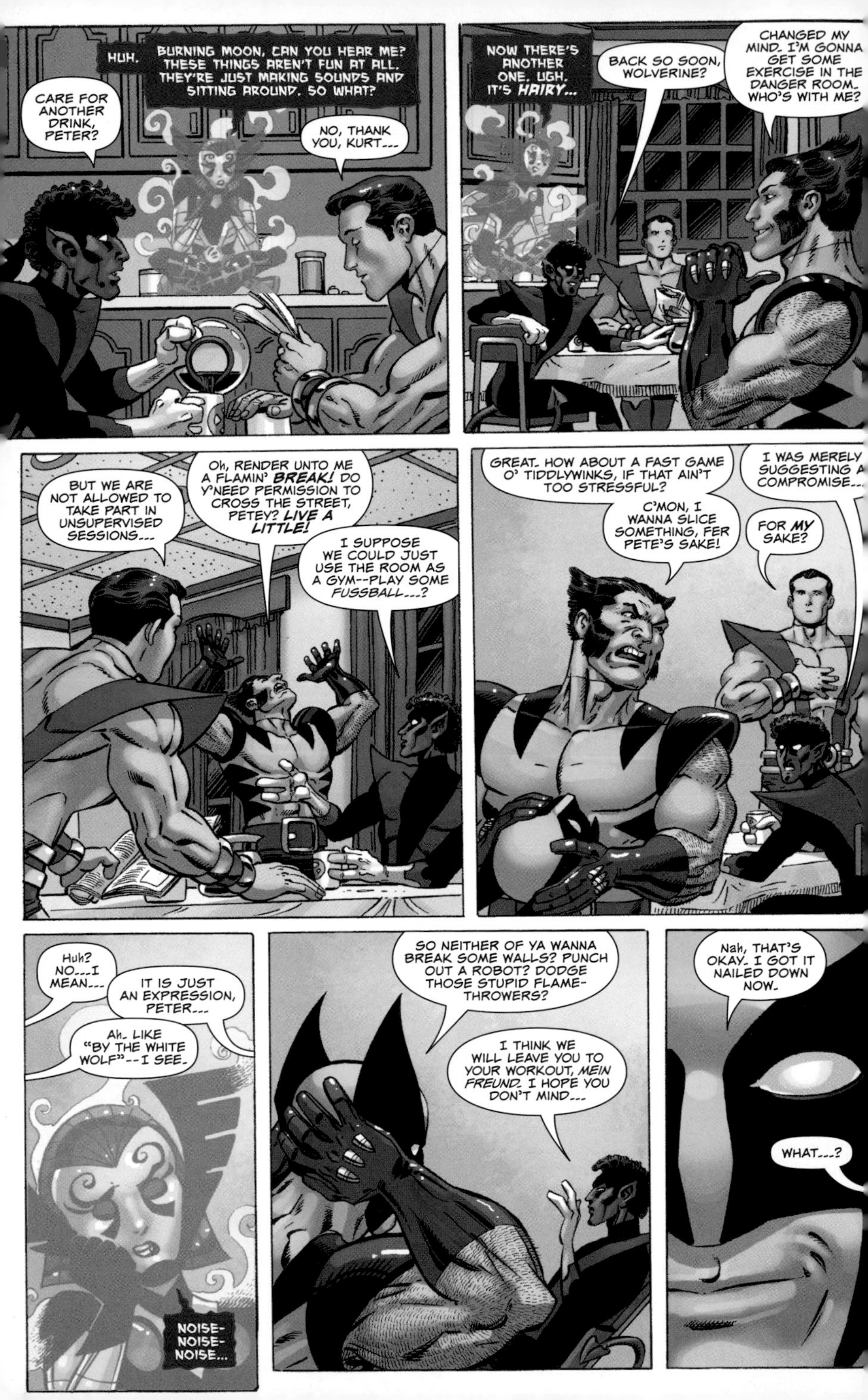
HUH.
BURNING MOON, CAN YOU HEAR ME? THESE THINGS AREN'T FUN AT ALL. THEY'RE JUST MAKING SOUNDS AND SITTING AROUND. SO WHAT?
CARE FOR ANOTHER DRINK, PETER?
NO, THANK YOU, KURT...
NOW THERE'S ANOTHER ONE. UGH. IT'S HAIRY...
BACK SO SOON, WOLVERINE?
CHANGED MY MIND. I'M GONNA GET SOME EXERCISE IN THE DANGER ROOM. WHO'S WITH ME?
BUT WE ARE NOT ALLOWED TO TAKE PART IN UNSUPERVISED SESSIONS...
Oh, RENDER UNTO ME A FLAMIN' BREAK! DO Y'NEED PERMISSION TO CROSS THE STREET, PETEY? LIVE A LITTLE!
I SUPPOSE WE COULD JUST USE THE ROOM AS A GYM--PLAY SOME FUSSBALL...?
GREAT. HOW ABOUT A FAST GAME O' TIDDLYWINKS, IF THAT AIN'T TOO STRESSFUL?
C'MON, I WANNA SLICE SOMETHING, FER PETE'S SAKE!
I WAS MERELY SUGGESTING A COMPROMISE...
FOR MY SAKE?
Huh? NO...I MEAN...
IT IS JUST AN EXPRESSION, PETER...
Ah. LIKE "BY THE WHITE WOLF"--I SEE.
NOISE-NOISE-NOISE...
SO NEITHER OF YA WANNA BREAK SOME WALLS? PUNCH OUT A ROBOT? DODGE THOSE STUPID FLAME-THROWERS?
I THINK WE WILL LEAVE YOU TO YOUR WORKOUT, MEIN FREUND. I HOPE YOU DON'T MIND...
Nah, THAT'S OKAY. I GOT IT NAILED DOWN NOW.
WHAT...?

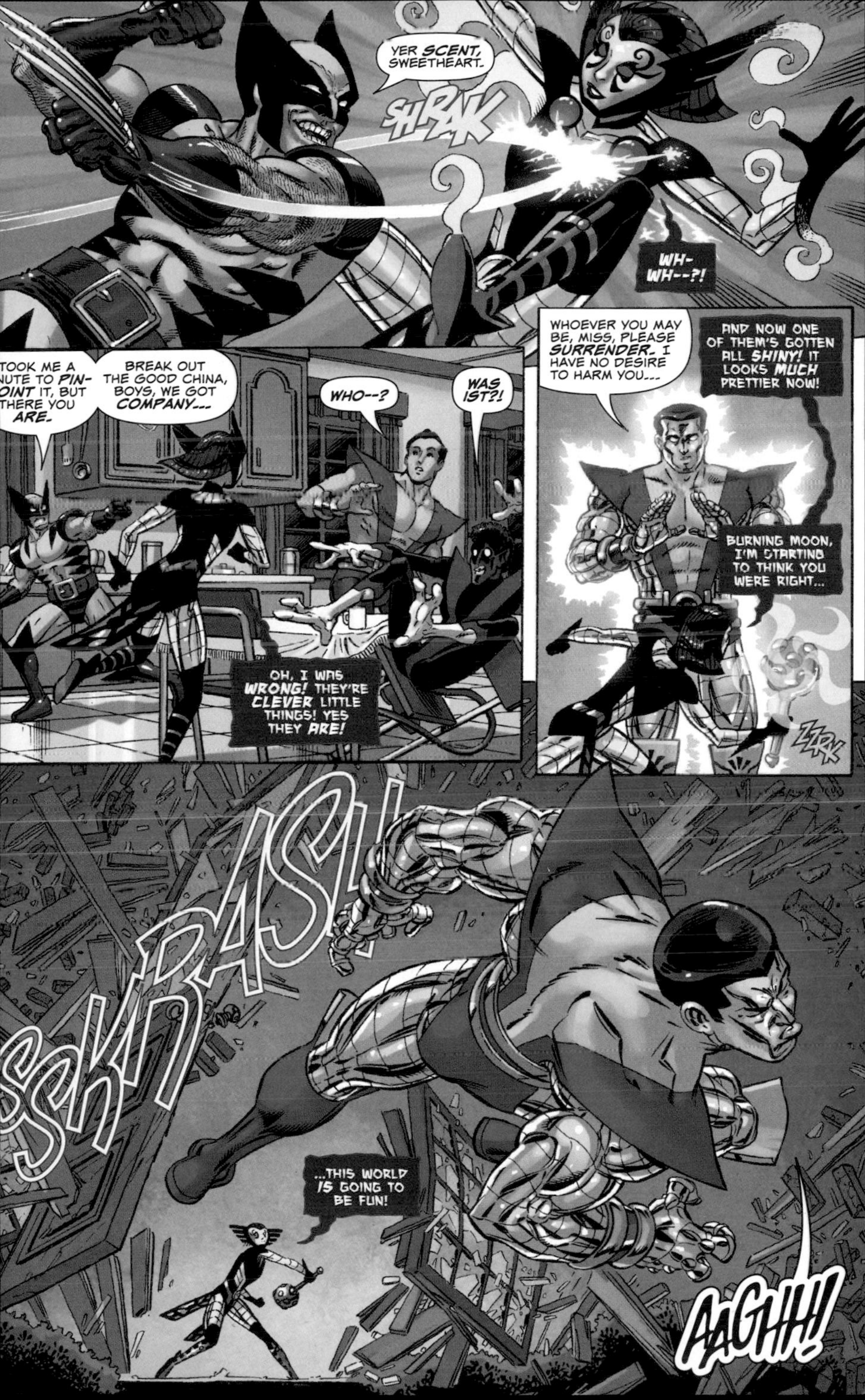
YER SCENT, SWEETHEART.
SHRAK
WH-WH--?!
TOOK ME A NUTE TO PINPOINT IT, BUT THERE YOU ARE.
BREAK OUT THE GOOD CHINA, BOYS, WE GOT COMPANY...
WHO--?
WAS IST?!
OH, I WAS WRONG! THEY'RE CLEVER LITTLE THINGS! YES THEY ARE!
WHOEVER YOU MAY BE, MISS, PLEASE SURRENDER. I HAVE NO DESIRE TO HARM YOU...
AND NOW ONE OF THEM'S GOTTEN ALL SHINY! IT LOOKS MUCH PRETTIER NOW!
BURNING MOON, I'M STARTING TO THINK YOU WERE RIGHT...
ZZRAK
SKRASH!
...THIS WORLD IS GOING TO BE FUN!
AAGHH!

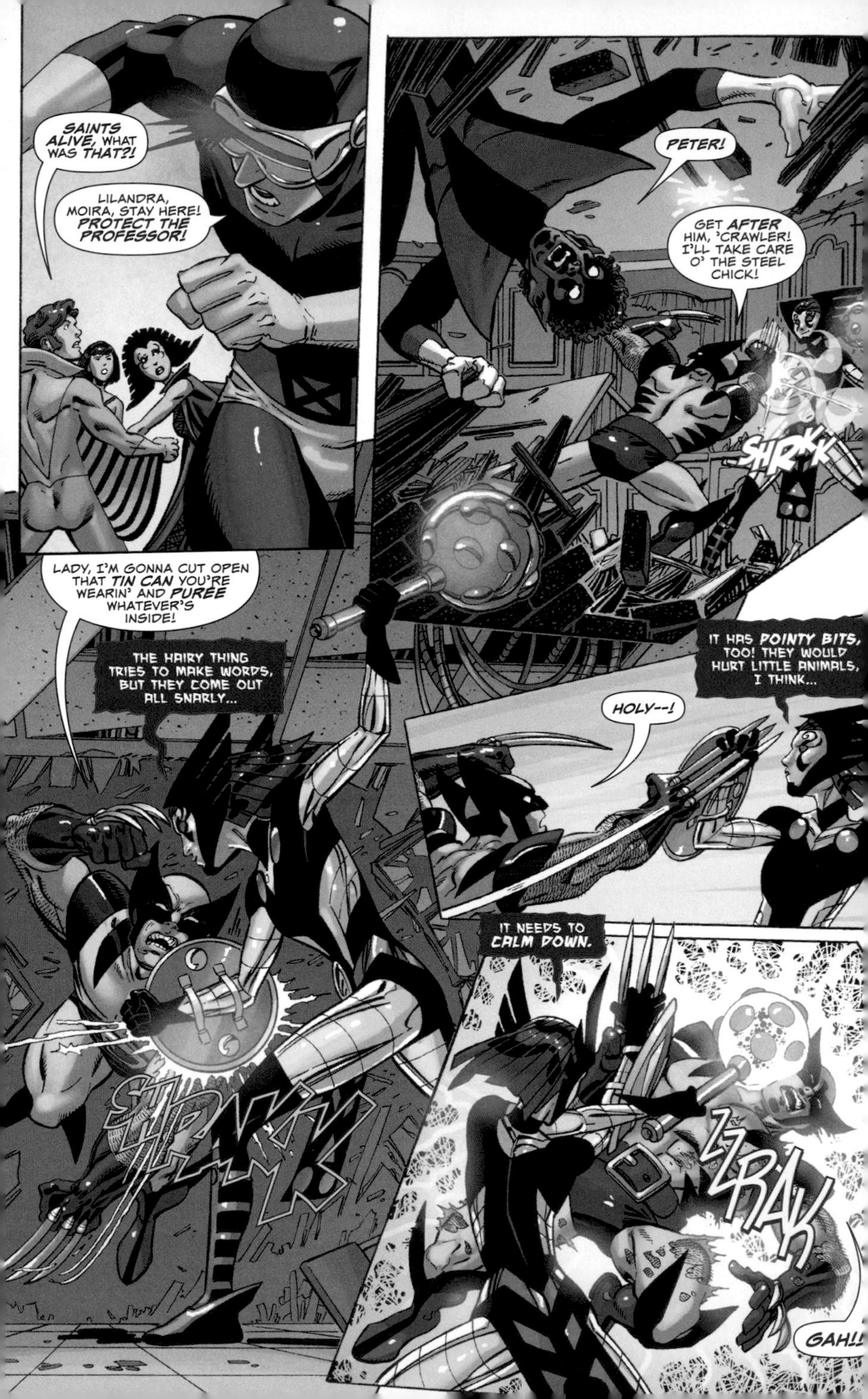
SAINTS ALIVE, WHAT WAS THAT?!
LILANDRA, MOIRA, STAY HERE! PROTECT THE PROFESSOR!
PETER!
GET AFTER HIM, 'CRAWLER! I'LL TAKE CARE O' THE STEEL CHICK!
SHRKK
LADY, I'M GONNA CUT OPEN THAT TIN CAN YOU'RE WEARIN' AND PUREE WHATEVER'S INSIDE!
THE HAIRY THING TRIES TO MAKE WORDS, BUT THEY COME OUT ALL SNARLY...
IT HAS POINTY BITS, TOO! THEY WOULD HURT LITTLE ANIMALS, I THINK...
HOLY--!
IT NEEDS TO CALM DOWN.
ZZRAK
GAH!!

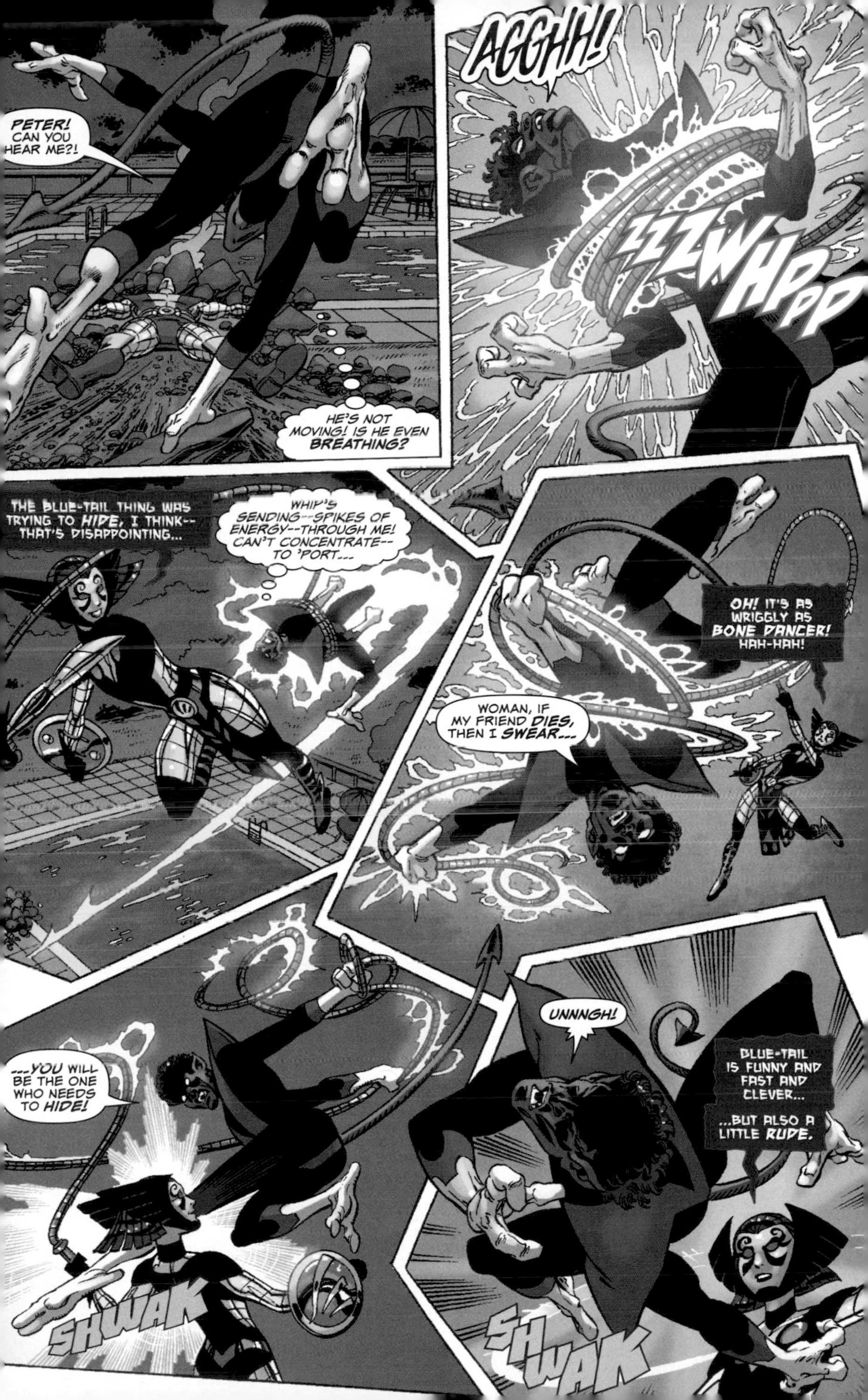
PETER! CAN YOU HEAR ME?!
HE'S NOT MOVING! IS HE EVEN BREATHING?
AGGHH!
ZZZWHPPP
THE BLUE-TAIL THING WAS TRYING TO HIDE, I THINK-- THAT'S DISAPPOINTING...
WHIP'S SENDING--SPIKES OF ENERGY--THROUGH ME! CAN'T CONCENTRATE-- TO 'PORT...
OH! IT'S AS WRIGGLY AS BONE DANCER! HAH-HAH!
WOMAN, IF MY FRIEND DIES, THEN I SWEAR...
...YOU WILL BE THE ONE WHO NEEDS TO HIDE!
SHWAK
UNNNGH!
BLUE-TAIL IS FUNNY AND FAST AND CLEVER...
...BUT ALSO A LITTLE RUDE.
SHWAK

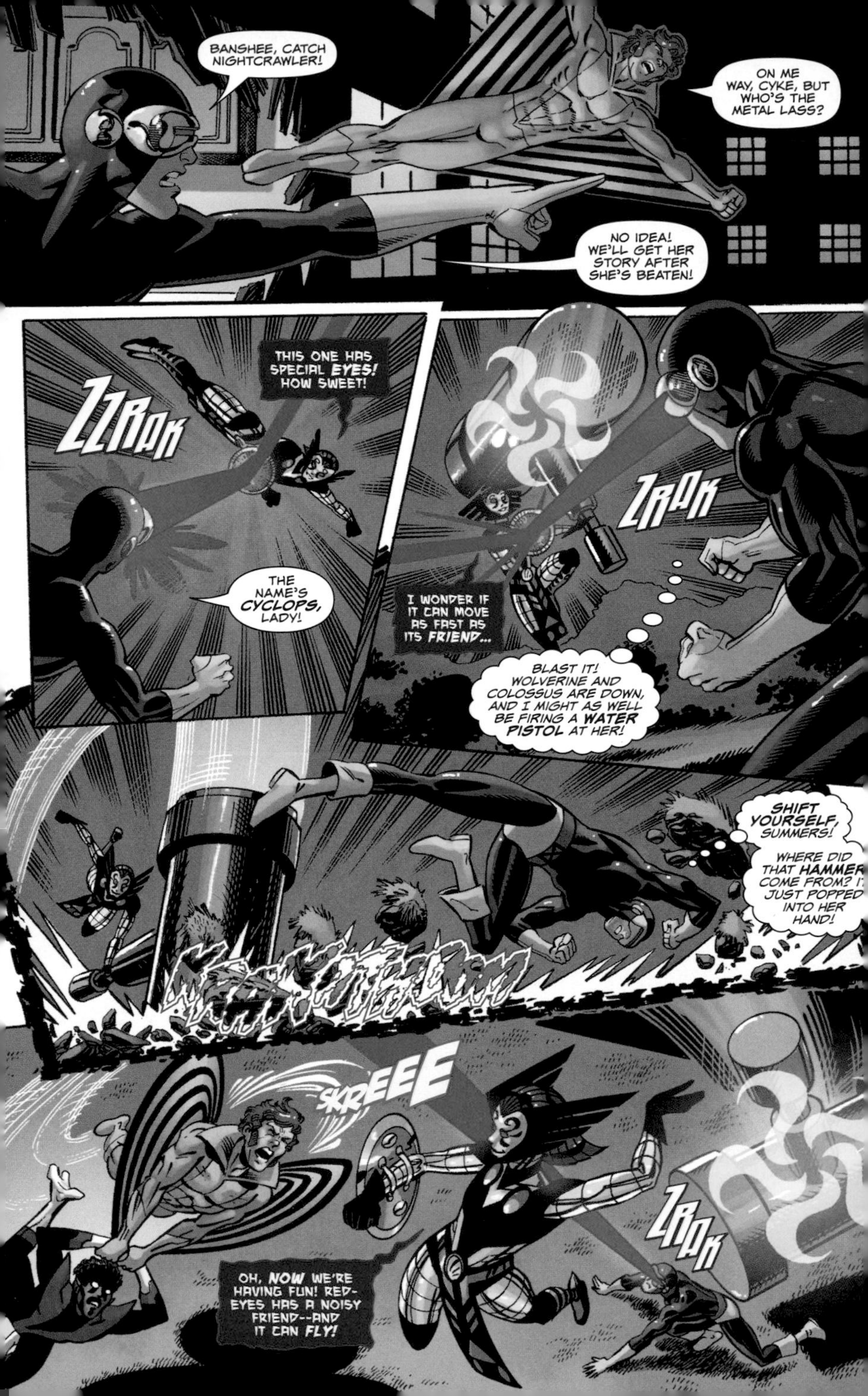
BANSHEE, CATCH NIGHTCRAWLER!
ON ME WAY, CYKE, BUT WHO'S THE METAL LASS?
NO IDEA! WE'LL GET HER STORY AFTER SHE'S BEATEN!
ZZRAK
THIS ONE HAS SPECIAL EYES! HOW SWEET!
THE NAME'S CYCLOPS, LADY!
ZRAK
I WONDER IF IT CAN MOVE AS FAST AS ITS FRIEND...
BLAST IT! WOLVERINE AND COLOSSUS ARE DOWN, AND I MIGHT AS WELL BE FIRING A WATER PISTOL AT HER!
SHIFT YOURSELF, SUMMERS!
WHERE DID THAT HAMMER COME FROM? IT JUST POPPED INTO HER HAND!
SKREEEE
ZRAK
OH, NOW WE'RE HAVING FUN! RED-EYES HAS A NOISY FRIEND--AND IT CAN FLY!

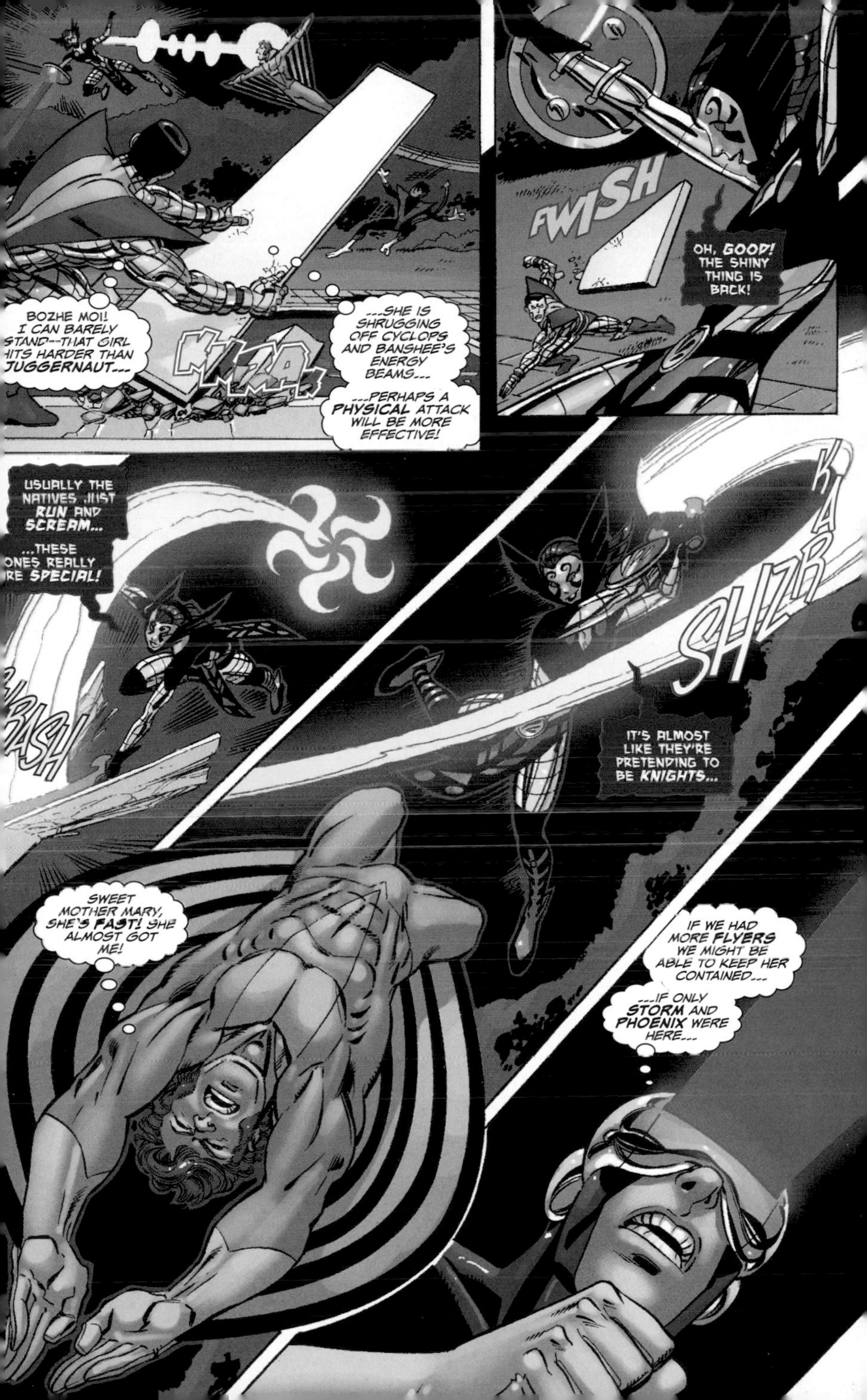
BOZHE MOI! I CAN BARELY STAND--THAT GIRL HITS HARDER THAN JUGGERNAUT---
KRA-
---SHE IS SHRUGGING OFF CYCLOPS AND BANSHEE'S ENERGY BEAMS---
---PERHAPS A PHYSICAL ATTACK WILL BE MORE EFFECTIVE!
FWISH
OH, GOOD! THE SHINY THING IS BACK!
USUALLY THE NATIVES JUST RUN AND SCREAM...
...THESE ONES REALLY ARE SPECIAL!
KA
SHIZR
IT'S ALMOST LIKE THEY'RE PRETENDING TO BE KNIGHTS...
SWEET MOTHER MARY, SHE'S FAST! SHE ALMOST GOT ME!
IF WE HAD MORE FLYERS WE MIGHT BE ABLE TO KEEP HER CONTAINED---
---IF ONLY STORM AND PHOENIX WERE HERE---

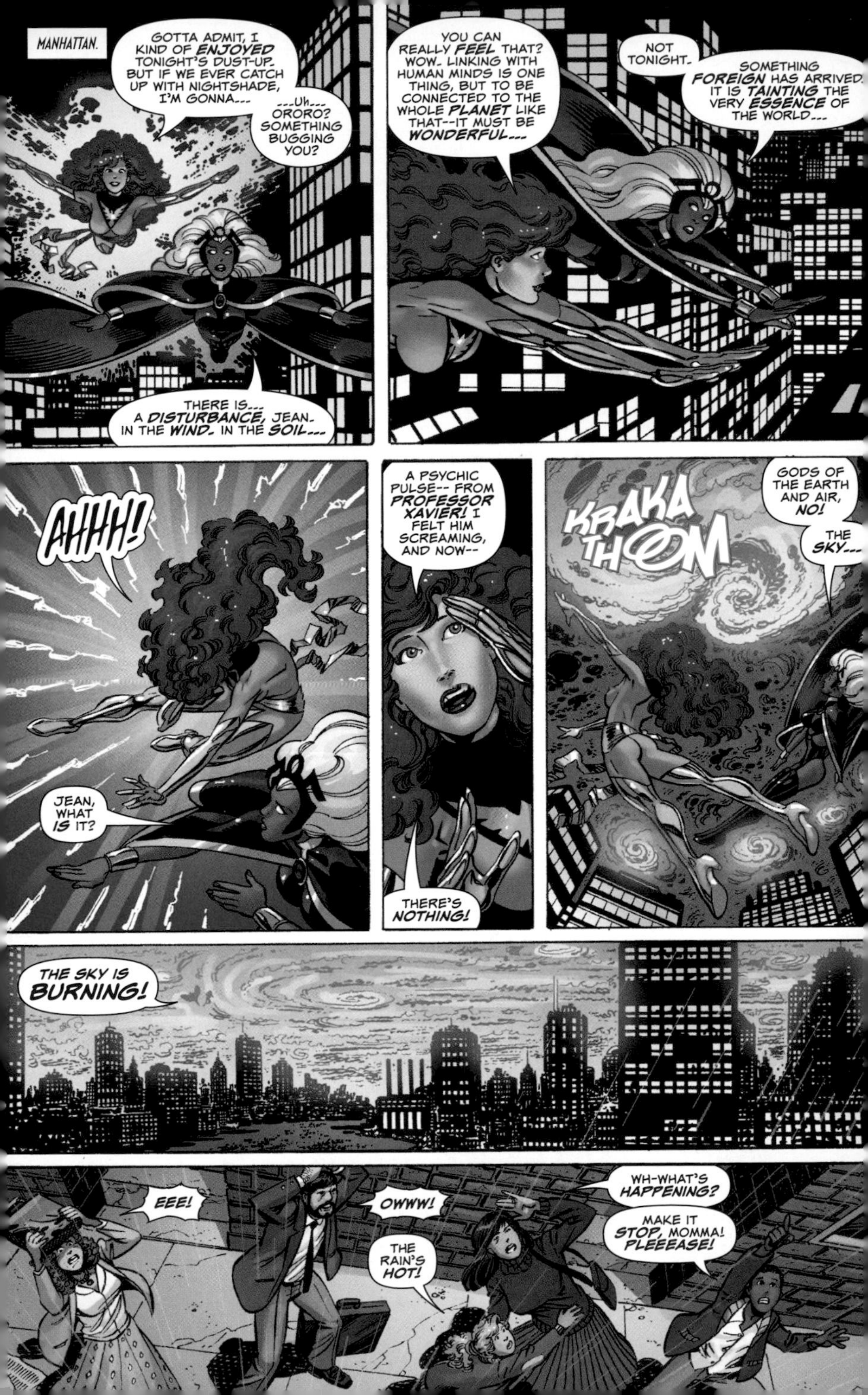
MANHATTAN.
GOTTA ADMIT, I KIND OF ENJOYED TONIGHT'S DUST-UP. BUT IF WE EVER CATCH UP WITH NIGHTSHADE, I'M GONNA...
...Uh... ORORO? SOMETHING BUGGING YOU?
THERE IS... A DISTURBANCE, JEAN. IN THE WIND. IN THE SOIL...
YOU CAN REALLY FEEL THAT? WOW. LINKING WITH HUMAN MINDS IS ONE THING, BUT TO BE CONNECTED TO THE WHOLE PLANET LIKE THAT--IT MUST BE WONDERFUL...
NOT TONIGHT.
SOMETHING FOREIGN HAS ARRIVED. IT IS TAINTING THE VERY ESSENCE OF THE WORLD...
AHHH!
JEAN, WHAT IS IT?
A PSYCHIC PULSE-- FROM PROFESSOR XAVIER! I FELT HIM SCREAMING, AND NOW--
THERE'S NOTHING!
KRAKA THOOM
GODS OF THE EARTH AND AIR, NO!
THE SKY...
THE SKY IS BURNING!
EEE!
OWWW!
WH-WHAT'S HAPPENING?
THE RAIN'S HOT!
MAKE IT STOP, MOMMA! PLEEEASE!

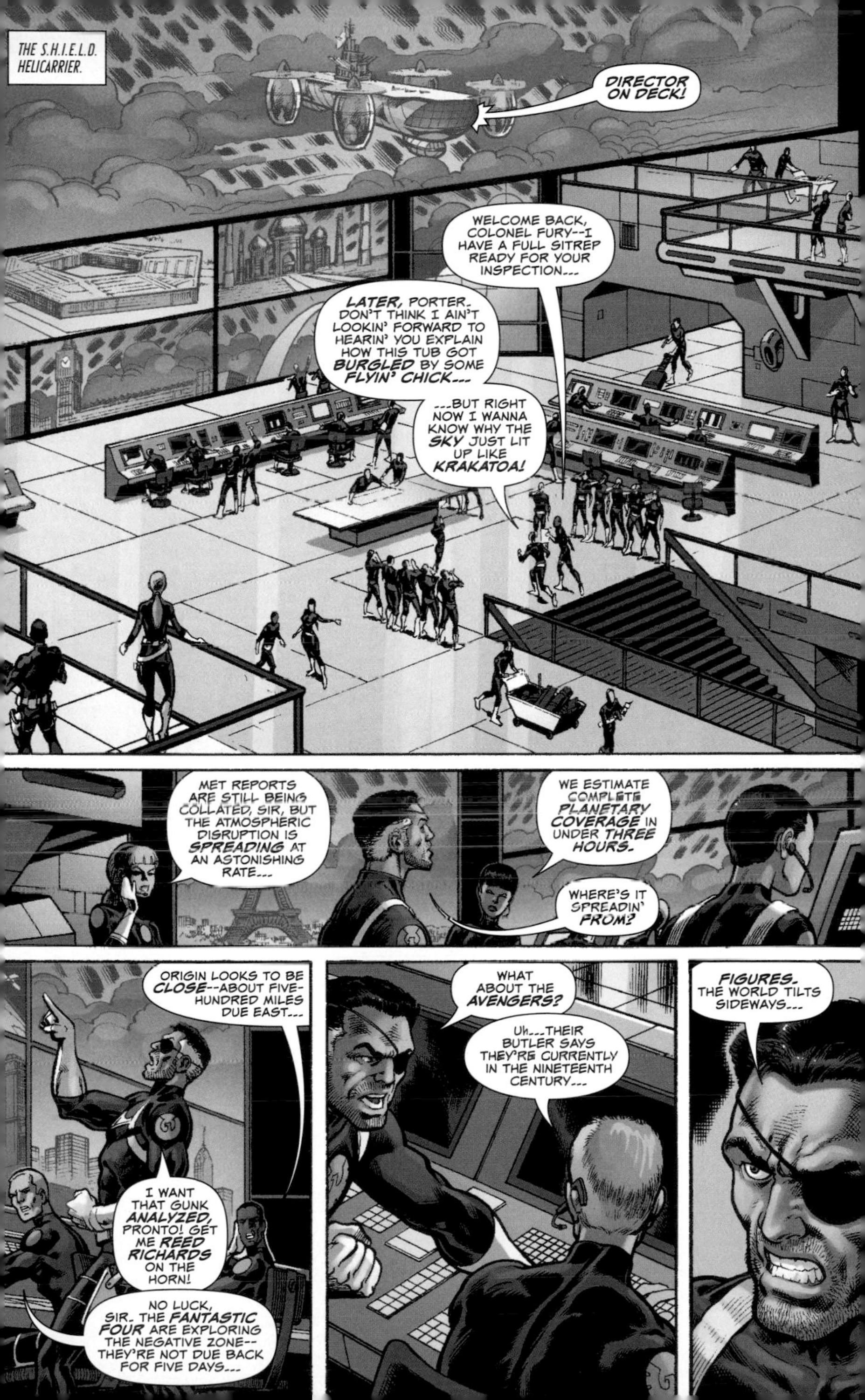
THE S.H.I.E.L.D. HELICARRIER.
DIRECTOR ON DECK!
WELCOME BACK, COLONEL FURY--I HAVE A FULL SITREP READY FOR YOUR INSPECTION...
LATER, PORTER. DON'T THINK I AIN'T LOOKIN' FORWARD TO HEARIN' YOU EXPLAIN HOW THIS TUB GOT BURGLED BY SOME FLYIN' CHICK...
...BUT RIGHT NOW I WANNA KNOW WHY THE SKY JUST LIT UP LIKE KRAKATOA!
MET REPORTS ARE STILL BEING COLLATED, SIR, BUT THE ATMOSPHERIC DISRUPTION IS SPREADING AT AN ASTONISHING RATE...
WE ESTIMATE COMPLETE PLANETARY COVERAGE IN UNDER THREE HOURS.
WHERE'S IT SPREADIN' FROM?
ORIGIN LOOKS TO BE CLOSE--ABOUT FIVE-HUNDRED MILES DUE EAST...
I WANT THAT GUNK ANALYZED, PRONTO! GET ME REED RICHARDS ON THE HORN!
NO LUCK, SIR. THE FANTASTIC FOUR ARE EXPLORING THE NEGATIVE ZONE--THEY'RE NOT DUE BACK FOR FIVE DAYS...
WHAT ABOUT THE AVENGERS?
Uh...THEIR BUTLER SAYS THEY'RE CURRENTLY IN THE NINETEENTH CENTURY...
FIGURES. THE WORLD TILTS SIDEWAYS...

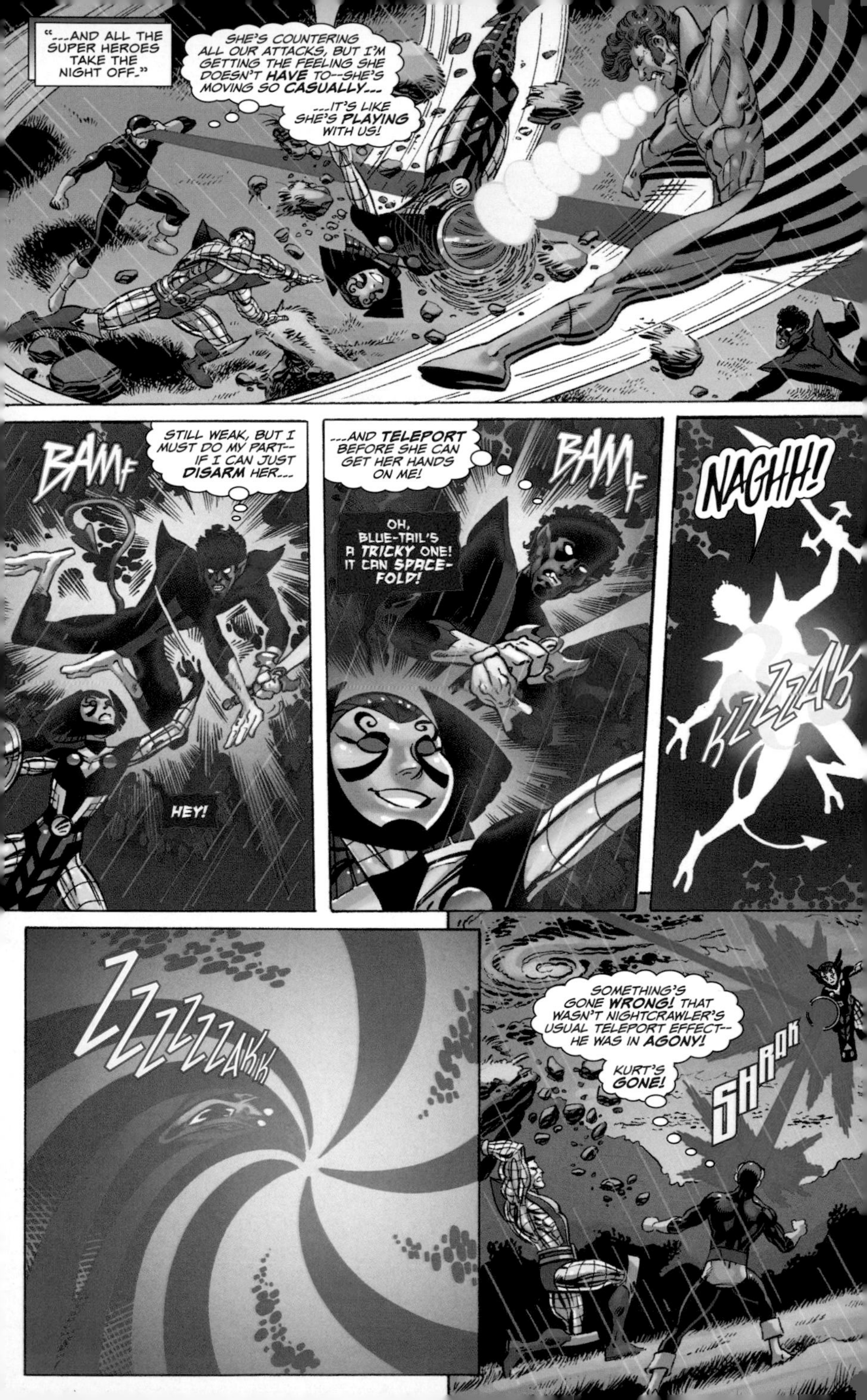
"...AND ALL THE SUPER HEROES TAKE THE NIGHT OFF."
SHE'S COUNTERING ALL OUR ATTACKS, BUT I'M GETTING THE FEELING SHE DOESN'T HAVE TO--SHE'S MOVING SO CASUALLY...
...IT'S LIKE SHE'S PLAYING WITH US!
BAMF
STILL WEAK, BUT I MUST DO MY PART-- IF I CAN JUST DISARM HER...
HEY!
...AND TELEPORT BEFORE SHE CAN GET HER HANDS ON ME!
BAMF
OH, BLUE-TAIL'S A TRICKY ONE! IT CAN SPACE-FOLD!
NAGHH!
KZZZZAK
ZZZZZZZAKK
SOMETHING'S GONE WRONG! THAT WASN'T NIGHTCRAWLER'S USUAL TELEPORT EFFECT-- HE WAS IN AGONY!
KURT'S GONE!
SHRAK

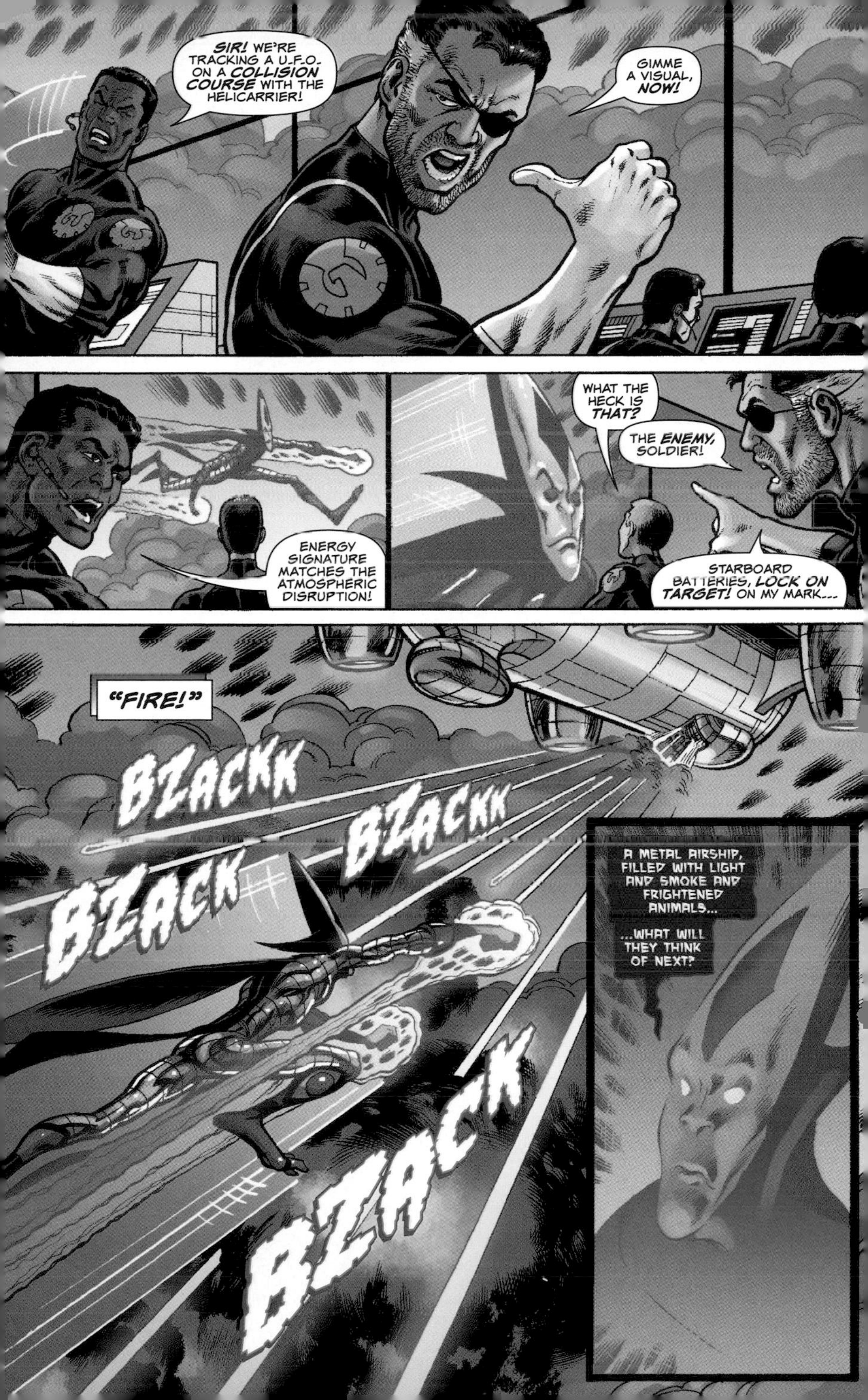
SIR! WE'RE TRACKING A U.F.O. ON A COLLISION COURSE WITH THE HELICARRIER!
GIMME A VISUAL, NOW!
ENERGY SIGNATURE MATCHES THE ATMOSPHERIC DISRUPTION!
WHAT THE HECK IS THAT?
THE ENEMY, SOLDIER!
STARBOARD BATTERIES, LOCK ON TARGET! ON MY MARK...
"FIRE!"
BZACKK
BZACKK
BZACK
A METAL AIRSHIP, FILLED WITH LIGHT AND SMOKE AND FRIGHTENED ANIMALS...
...WHAT WILL THEY THINK OF NEXT?
BZACK

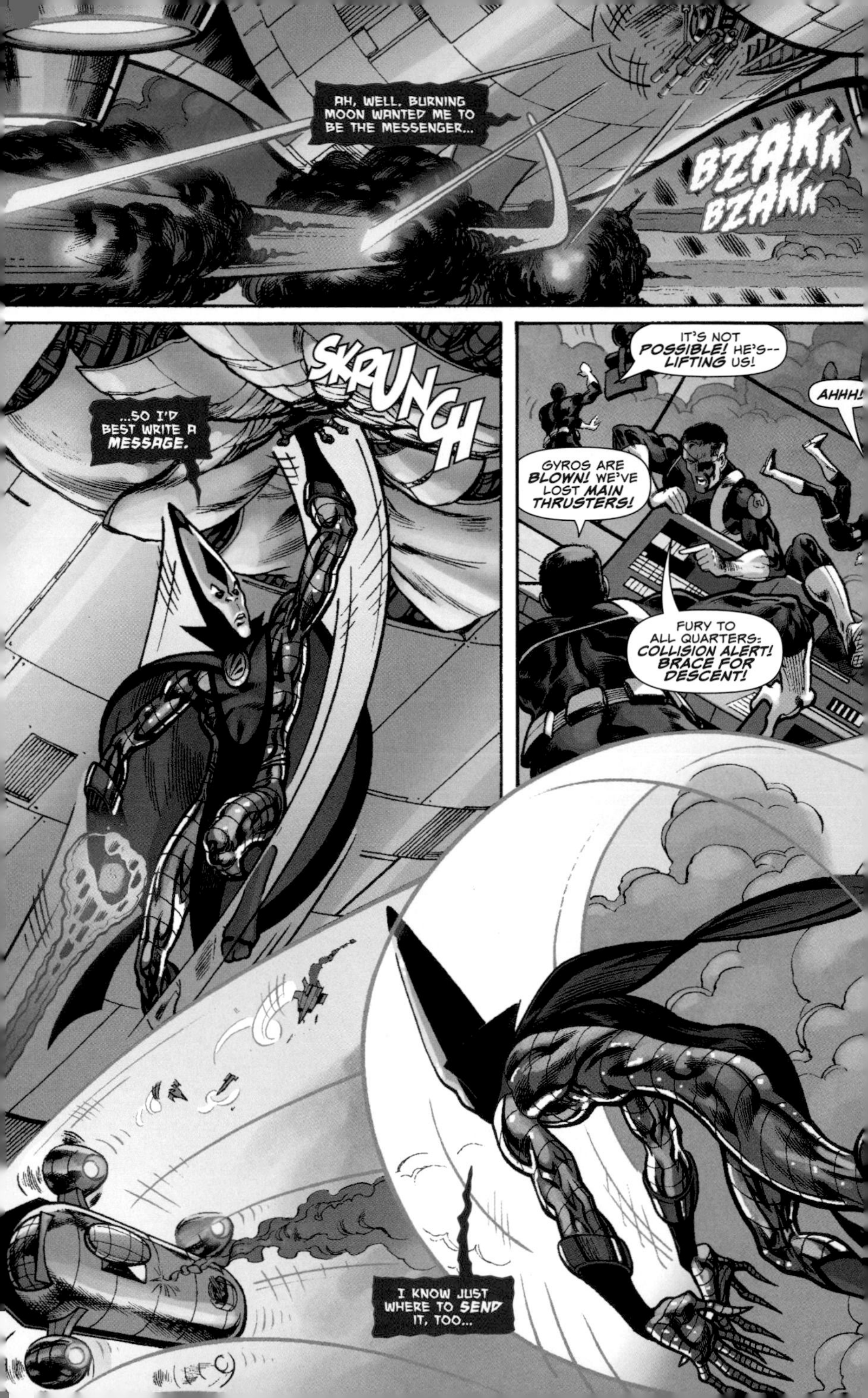
AH, WELL. BURNING MOON WANTED ME TO BE THE MESSENGER...
BZAKK BZAKK
...SO I'D BEST WRITE A MESSAGE.
SKRUNCH
IT'S NOT POSSIBLE! HE'S-- LIFTING US!
AHHH!
GYROS ARE BLOWN! WE'VE LOST MAIN THRUSTERS!
FURY TO ALL QUARTERS: COLLISION ALERT! BRACE FOR DESCENT!
I KNOW JUST WHERE TO SEND IT, TOO...

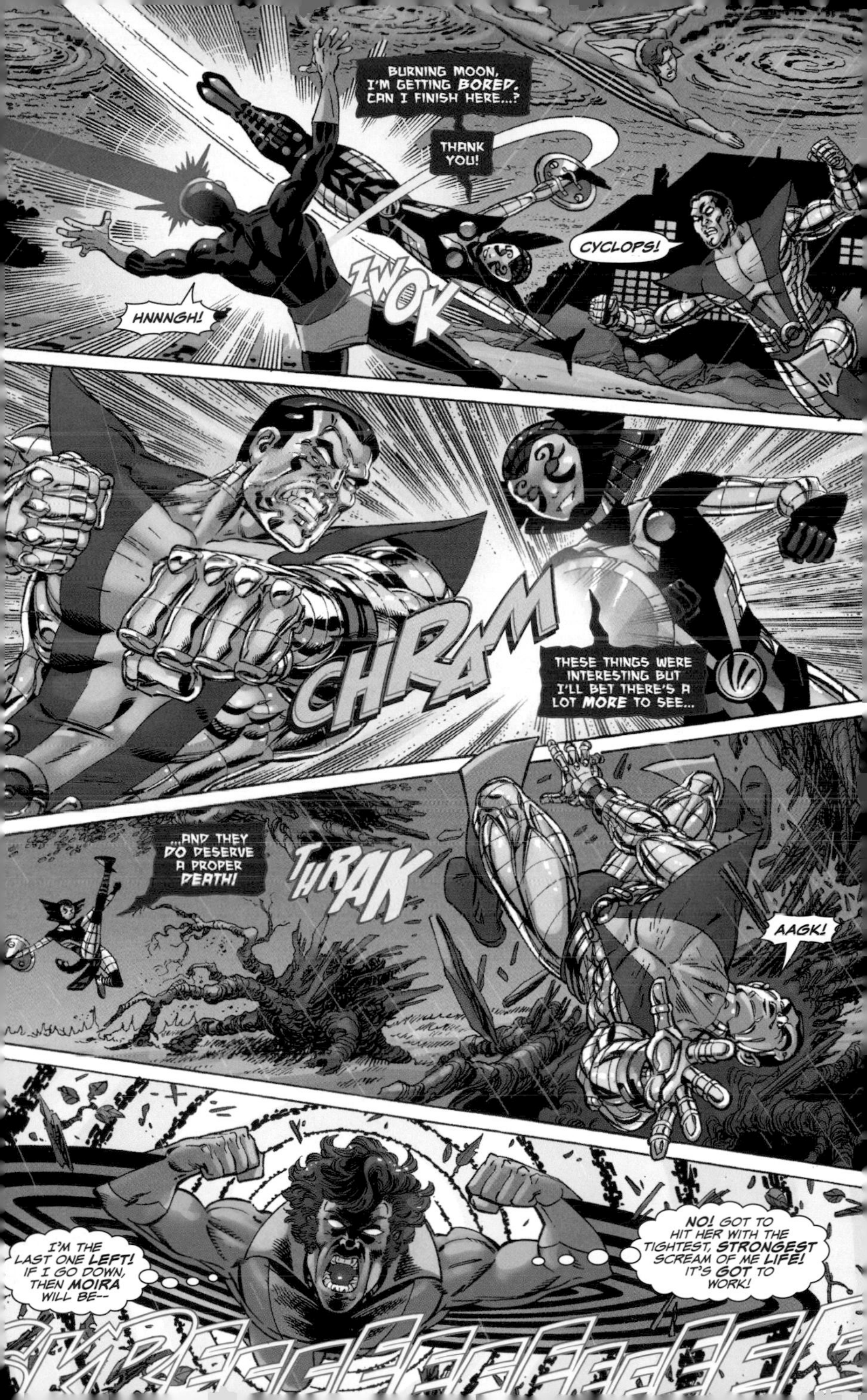
BURNING MOON, I'M GETTING BORED. CAN I FINISH HERE...?
THANK YOU!
CYCLOPS!
ZWOK
HNNNGH!
CHRAM
THESE THINGS WERE INTERESTING BUT I'LL BET THERE'S A LOT MORE TO SEE...
...AND THEY DO DESERVE A PROPER DEATH!
THRAK
AAGK!
I'M THE LAST ONE LEFT! IF I GO DOWN, THEN MOIRA WILL BE--
NO! GOT TO HIT HER WITH THE TIGHTEST, STRONGEST SCREAM OF ME LIFE! IT'S GOT TO WORK!

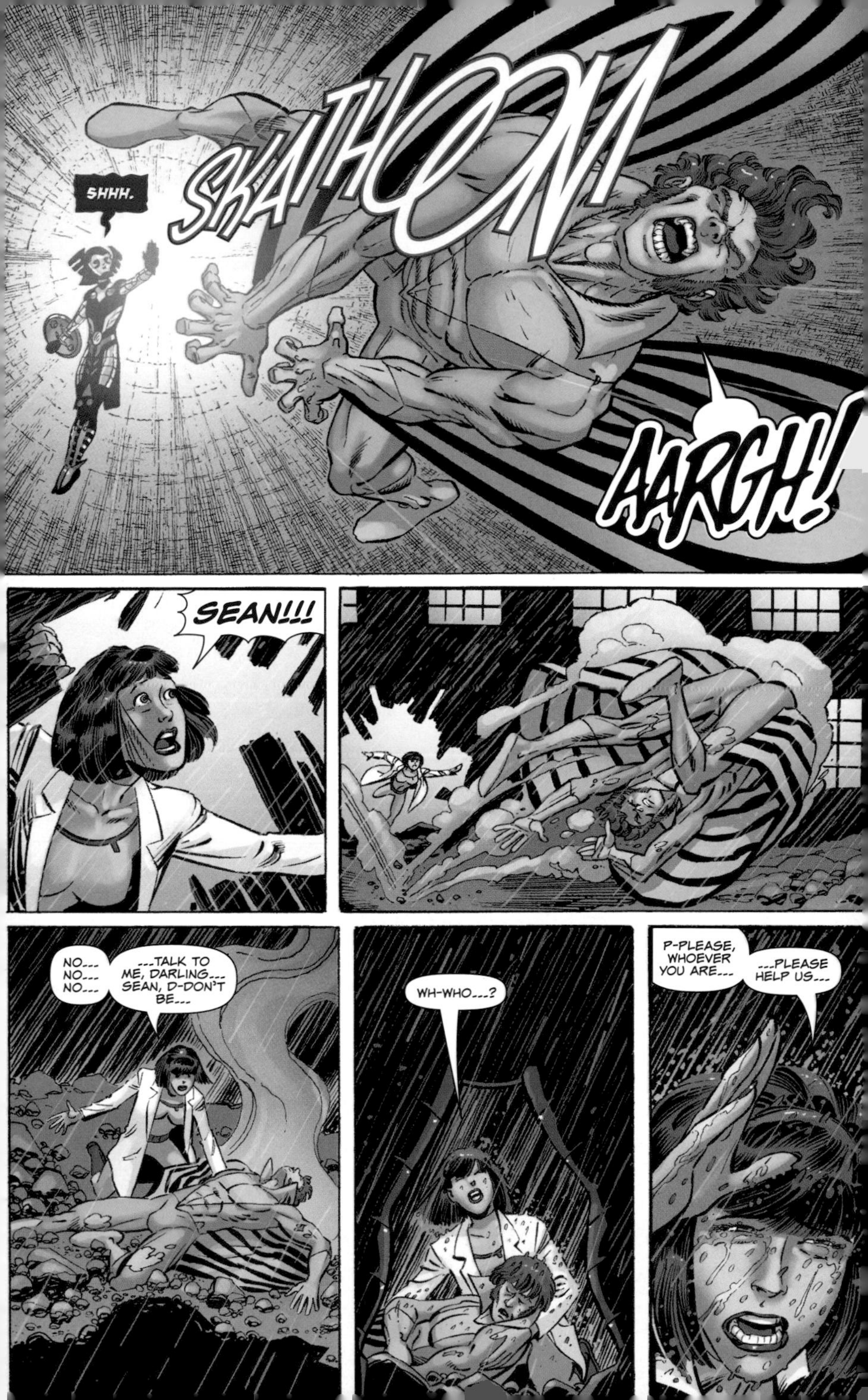
SHHH.
SKATHOOM
AARGH!
SEAN!!!
NO--- NO--- NO---
---TALK TO ME, DARLING--- SEAN, D-DON'T BE---
WH-WHO---?
P-PLEASE, WHOEVER YOU ARE---
---PLEASE HELP US---

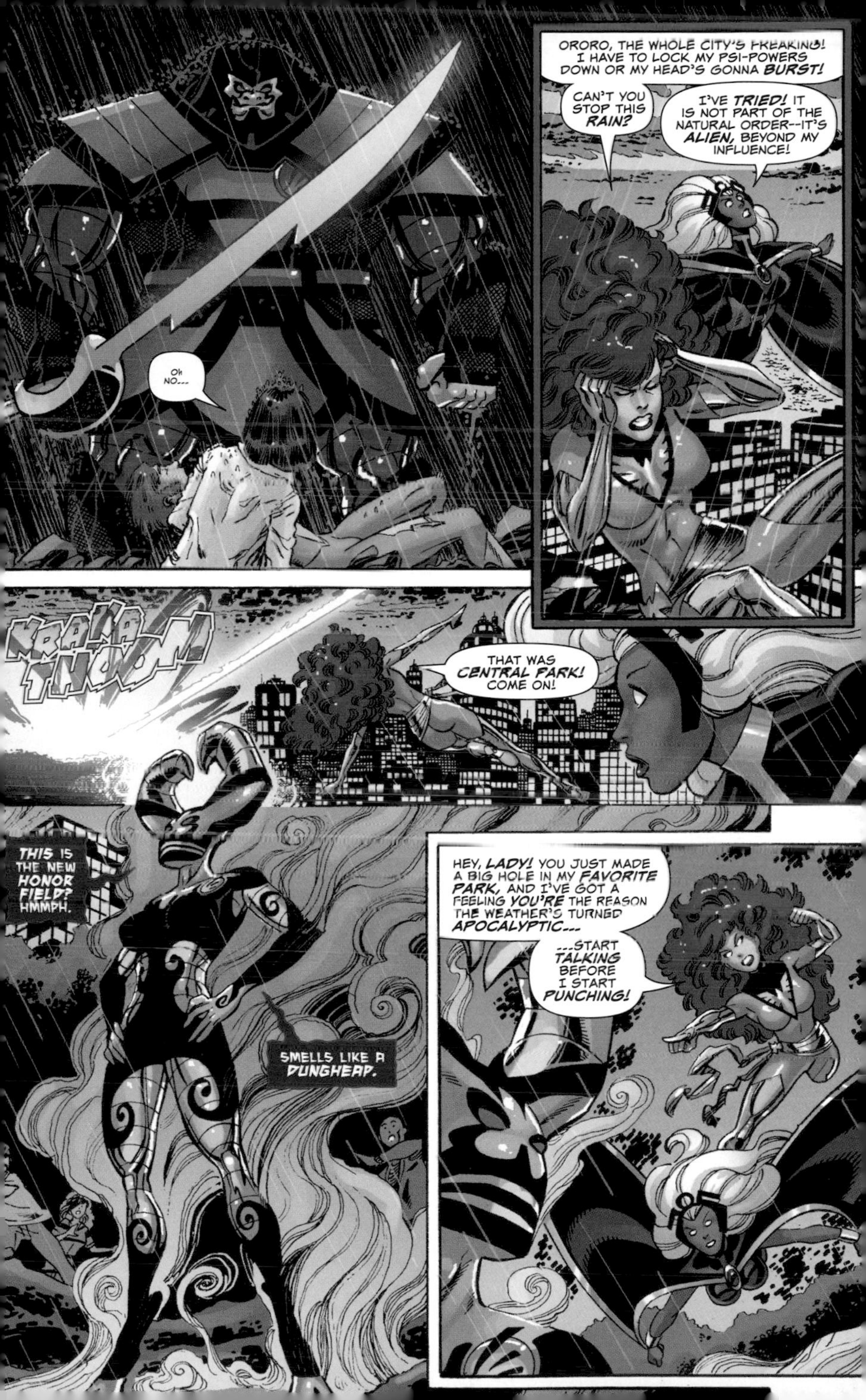
Oh NO---
ORORO, THE WHOLE CITY'S FREAKING! I HAVE TO LOCK MY PSI-POWERS DOWN OR MY HEAD'S GONNA BURST!
CAN'T YOU STOP THIS RAIN?
I'VE TRIED! IT IS NOT PART OF THE NATURAL ORDER--IT'S ALIEN, BEYOND MY INFLUENCE!
THAT WAS CENTRAL PARK! COME ON!
THIS IS THE NEW HONOR FIELD? HMMPH.
SMELLS LIKE A DUNGHEAP.
HEY, LADY! YOU JUST MADE A BIG HOLE IN MY FAVORITE PARK, AND I'VE GOT A FEELING YOU'RE THE REASON THE WEATHER'S TURNED APOCALYPTIC---
---START TALKING BEFORE I START PUNCHING!

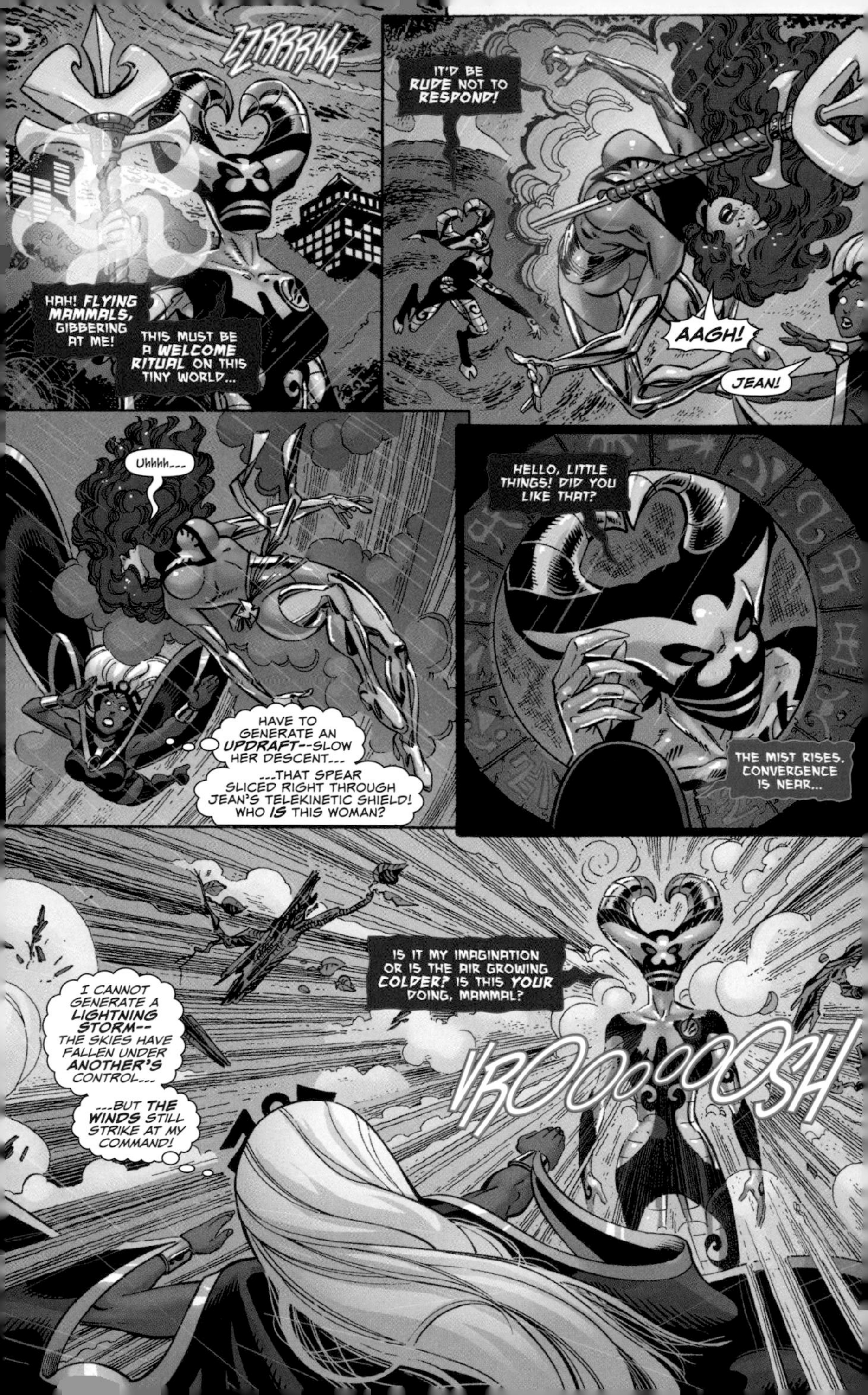
ZZRRRKK
HAH! FLYING MAMMALS, GIBBERING AT ME!
THIS MUST BE A WELCOME RITUAL ON THIS TINY WORLD...
IT'D BE RUDE NOT TO RESPOND!
AAGH!
JEAN!
Uhhhh...
HAVE TO GENERATE AN UPDRAFT--SLOW HER DESCENT...
...THAT SPEAR SLICED RIGHT THROUGH JEAN'S TELEKINETIC SHIELD! WHO IS THIS WOMAN?
HELLO, LITTLE THINGS! DID YOU LIKE THAT?
THE MIST RISES. CONVERGENCE IS NEAR...
IS IT MY IMAGINATION OR IS THE AIR GROWING COLDER? IS THIS YOUR DOING, MAMMAL?
I CANNOT GENERATE A LIGHTNING STORM-- THE SKIES HAVE FALLEN UNDER ANOTHER'S CONTROL...
...BUT THE WINDS STILL STRIKE AT MY COMMAND!
VROOOOOOSH

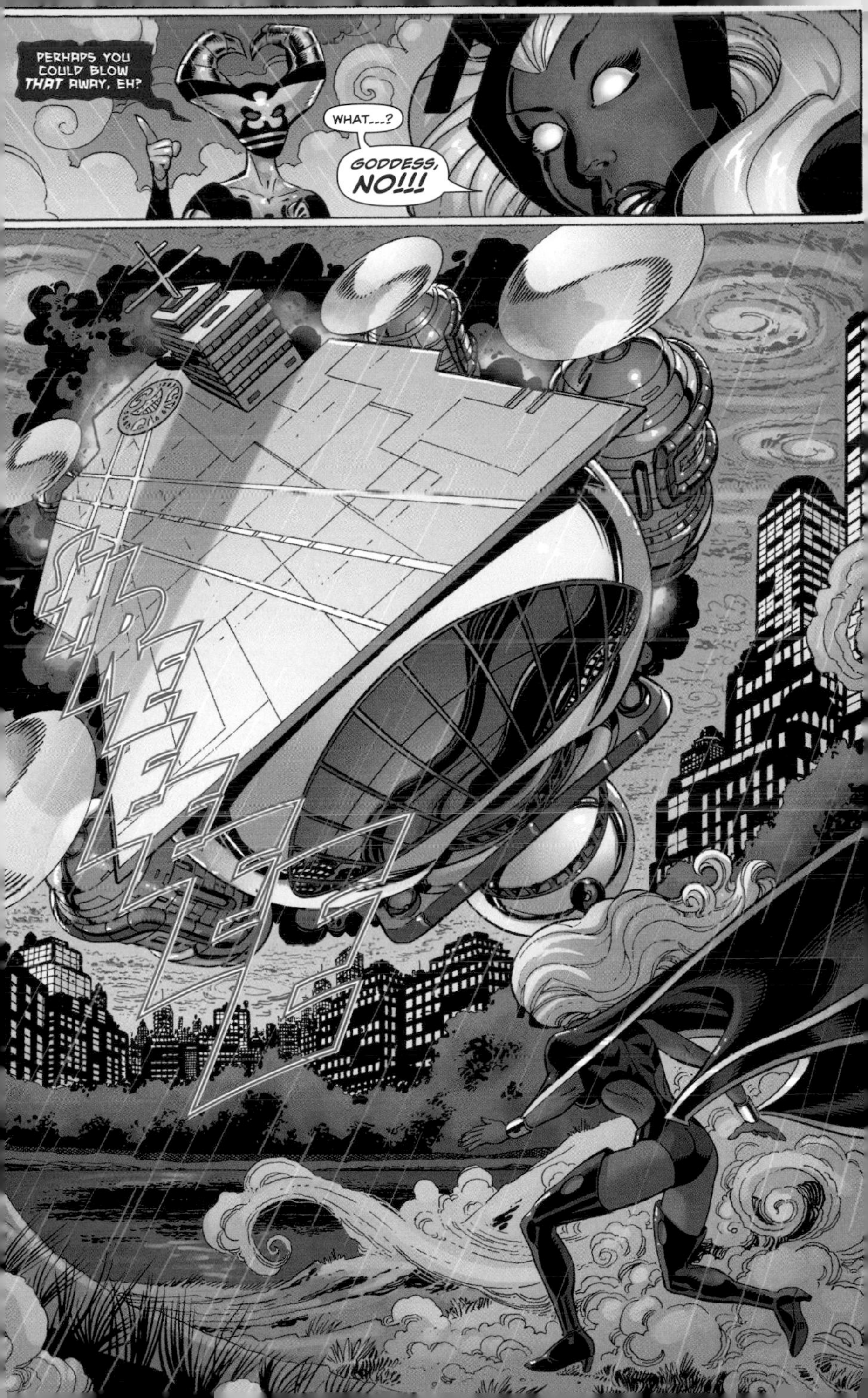
PERHAPS YOU COULD BLOW *THAT* AWAY, EH?
WHAT...?
GODDESS, **NO!!!**

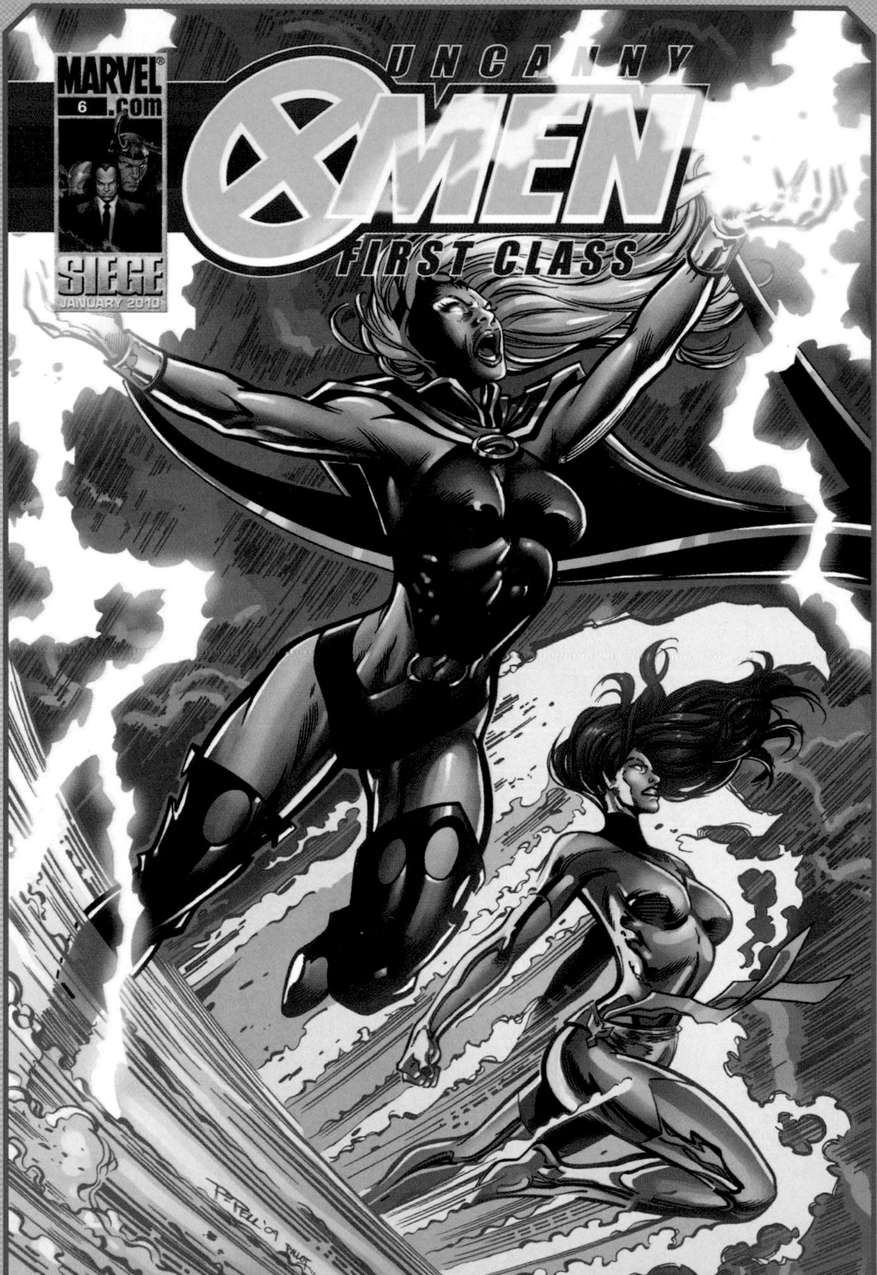

MARVEL
6
.com
SIEGE
JANUARY 2010
UNCANNY
X-MEN
FIRST CLASS

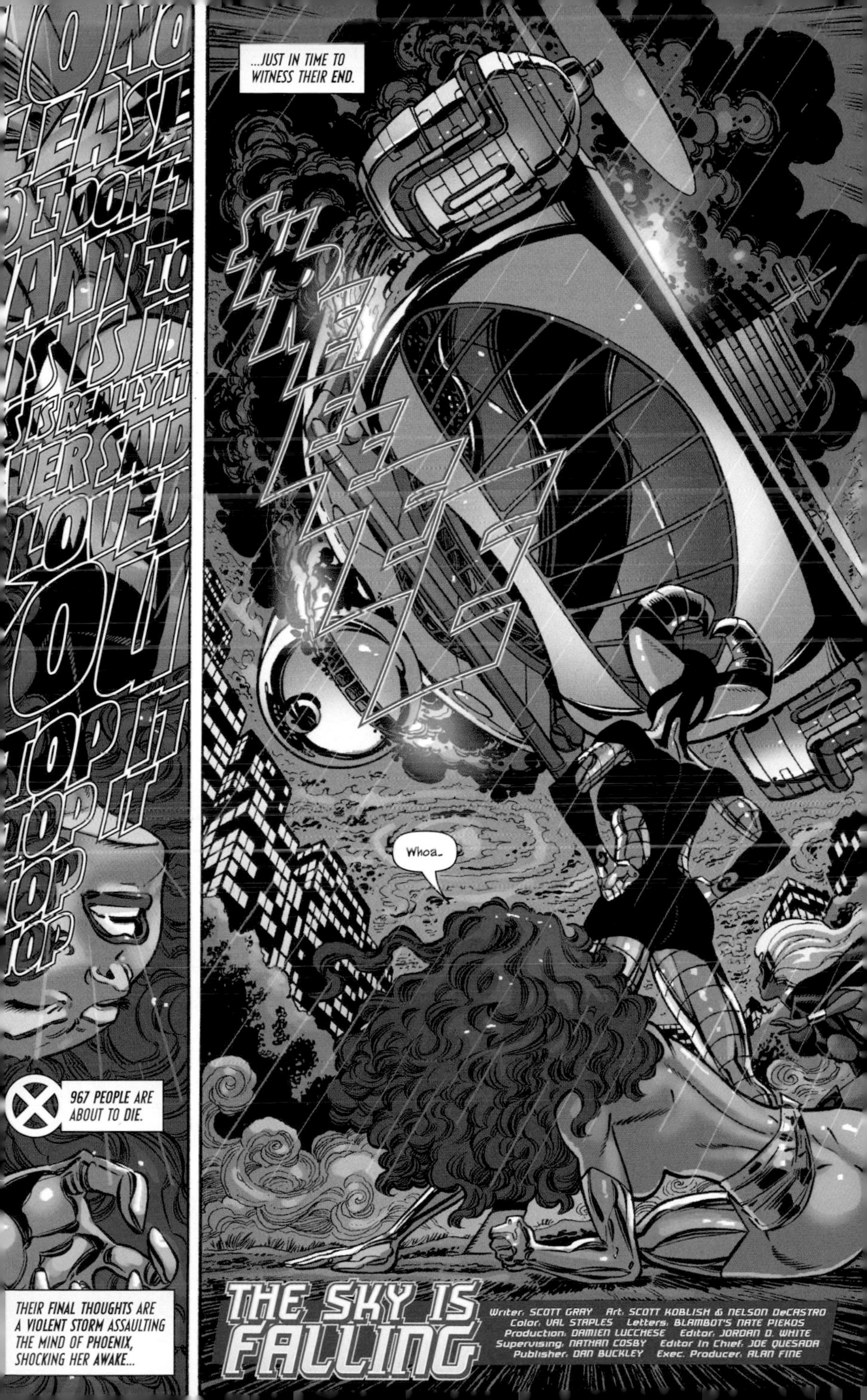
...JUST IN TIME TO WITNESS THEIR END.
Whoa_
967 PEOPLE ARE ABOUT TO DIE.
THEIR FINAL THOUGHTS ARE A VIOLENT STORM ASSAULTING THE MIND OF PHOENIX, SHOCKING HER AWAKE...
THE SKY IS FALLING
Writer: SCOTT GRAY Art: SCOTT KOBLISH & NELSON DeCASTRO
Color: VAL STAPLES Letters: BLAMBOT'S NATE PIEKOS
Production: DAMIEN LUCCHESE Editor: JORDAN D. WHITE
Supervising: NATHAN COSBY Editor In Chief: JOE QUESADA
Publisher: DAN BUCKLEY Exec. Producer: ALAN FINE

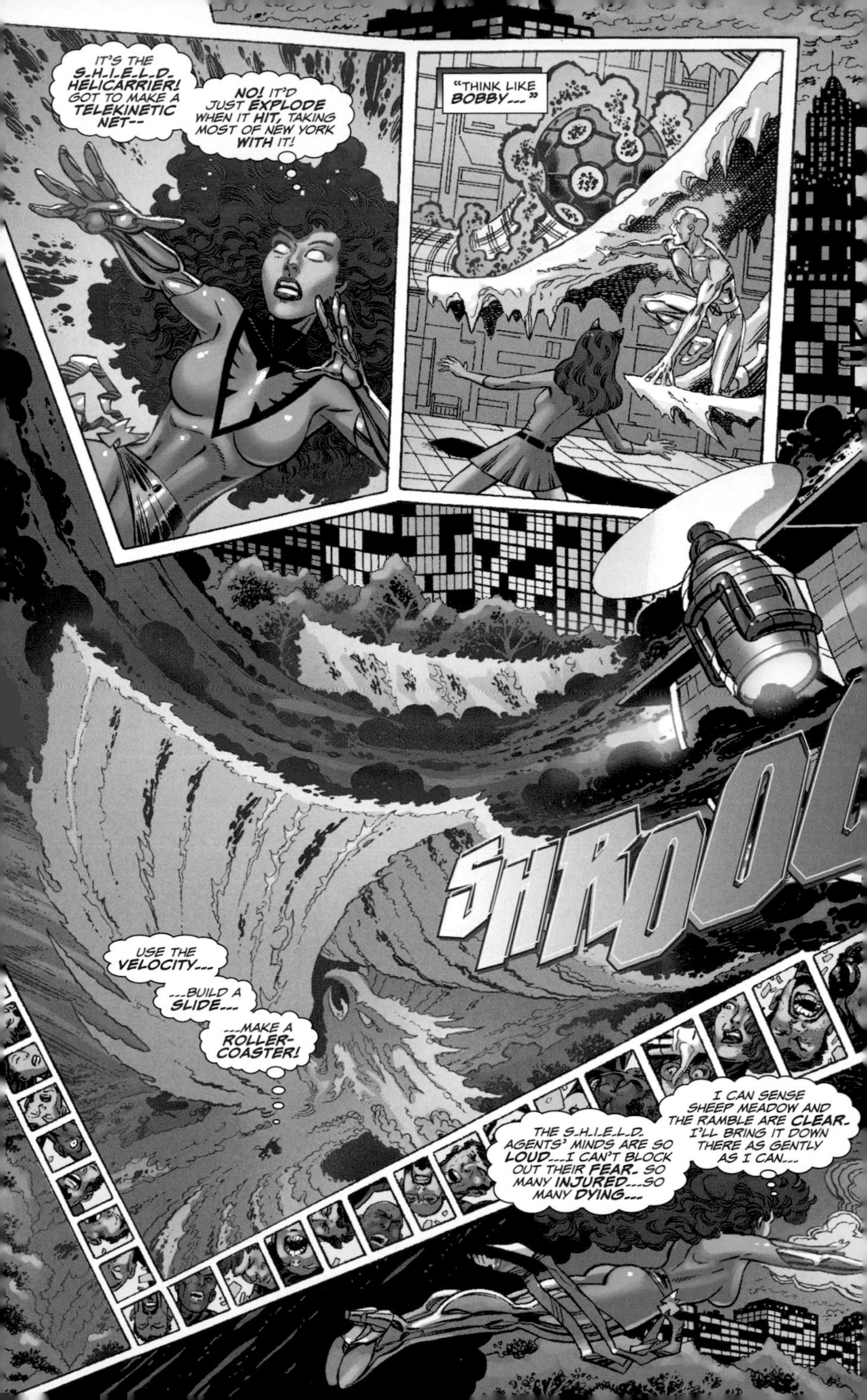
IT'S THE S.H.I.E.L.D. HELICARRIER! GOT TO MAKE A TELEKINETIC NET--
NO! IT'D JUST EXPLODE WHEN IT HIT, TAKING MOST OF NEW YORK WITH IT!
"THINK LIKE BOBBY---"
SHROO
USE THE VELOCITY---
---BUILD A SLIDE---
---MAKE A ROLLER-COASTER!
THE S.H.I.E.L.D. AGENTS' MINDS ARE SO LOUD---I CAN'T BLOCK OUT THEIR FEAR. SO MANY INJURED---SO MANY DYING---
I CAN SENSE SHEEP MEADOW AND THE RAMBLE ARE CLEAR. I'LL BRING IT DOWN THERE AS GENTLY AS I CAN---

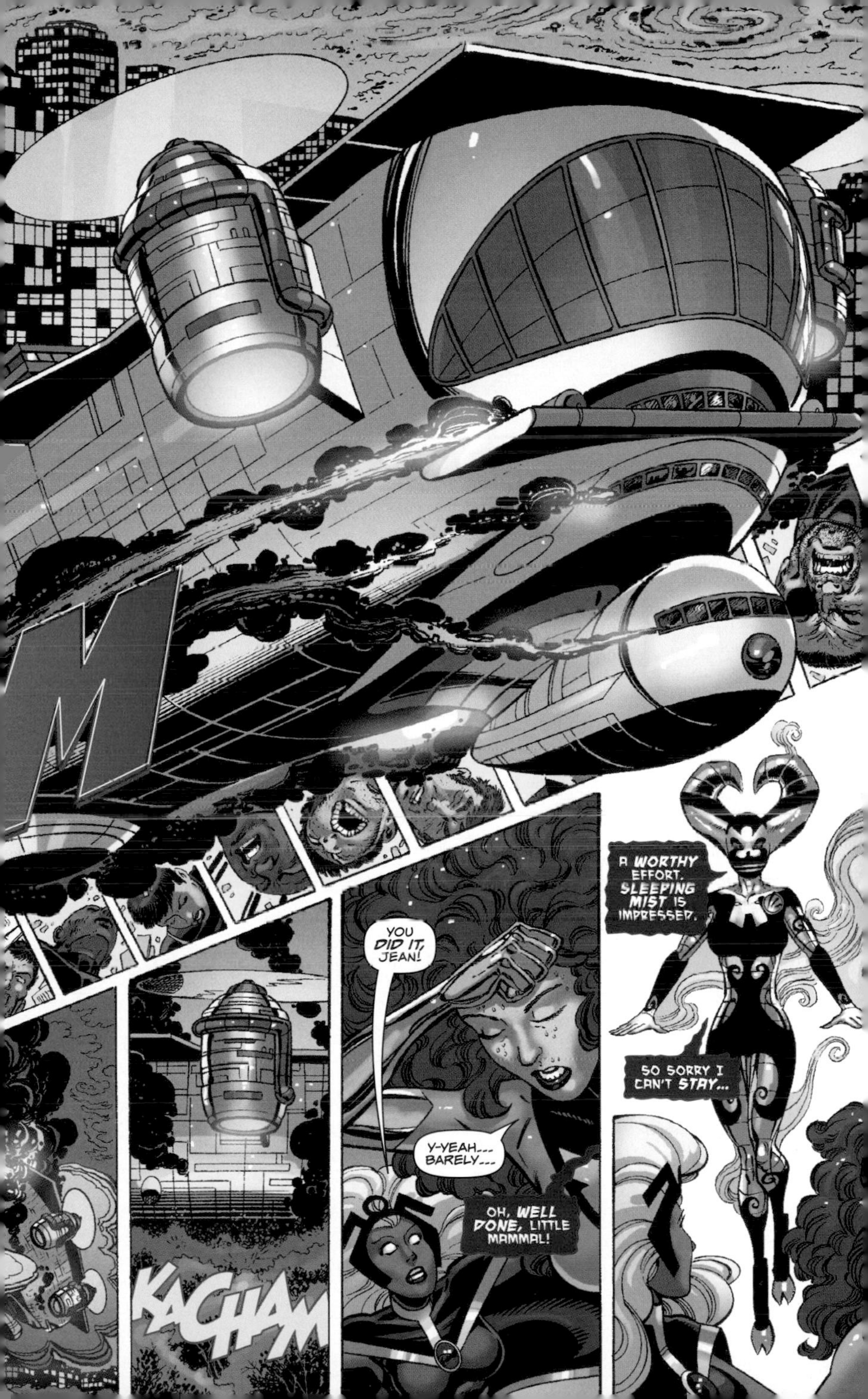
YOU DID IT, JEAN!
Y-YEAH... BARELY...
OH, WELL DONE, LITTLE MAMMAL!
A WORTHY EFFORT. SLEEPING MIST IS IMPRESSED.
SO SORRY I CAN'T STAY...
KACHAM

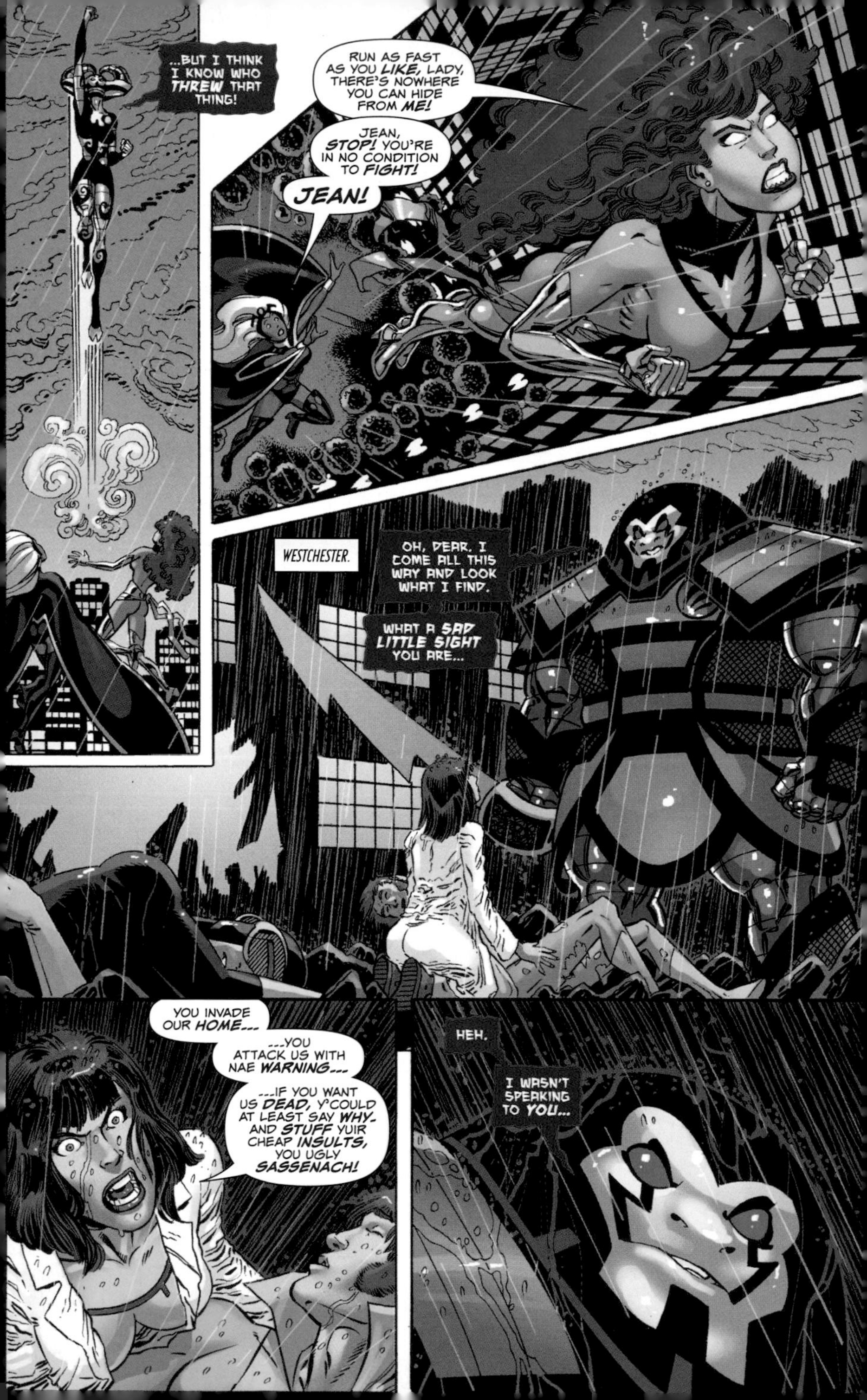

...BUT I THINK I KNOW WHO THREW THAT THING!
RUN AS FAST AS YOU LIKE, LADY, THERE'S NOWHERE YOU CAN HIDE FROM ME!
JEAN, STOP! YOU'RE IN NO CONDITION TO FIGHT!
JEAN!
WESTCHESTER.
OH, DEAR. I COME ALL THIS WAY AND LOOK WHAT I FIND.
WHAT A SAD LITTLE SIGHT YOU ARE...
YOU INVADE OUR HOME---
---YOU ATTACK US WITH NAE WARNING---
---IF YOU WANT US DEAD, Y'COULD AT LEAST SAY WHY-AND STUFF YUIR CHEAP INSULTS, YOU UGLY SASSENACH!
HEH.
I WASN'T SPEAKING TO YOU...

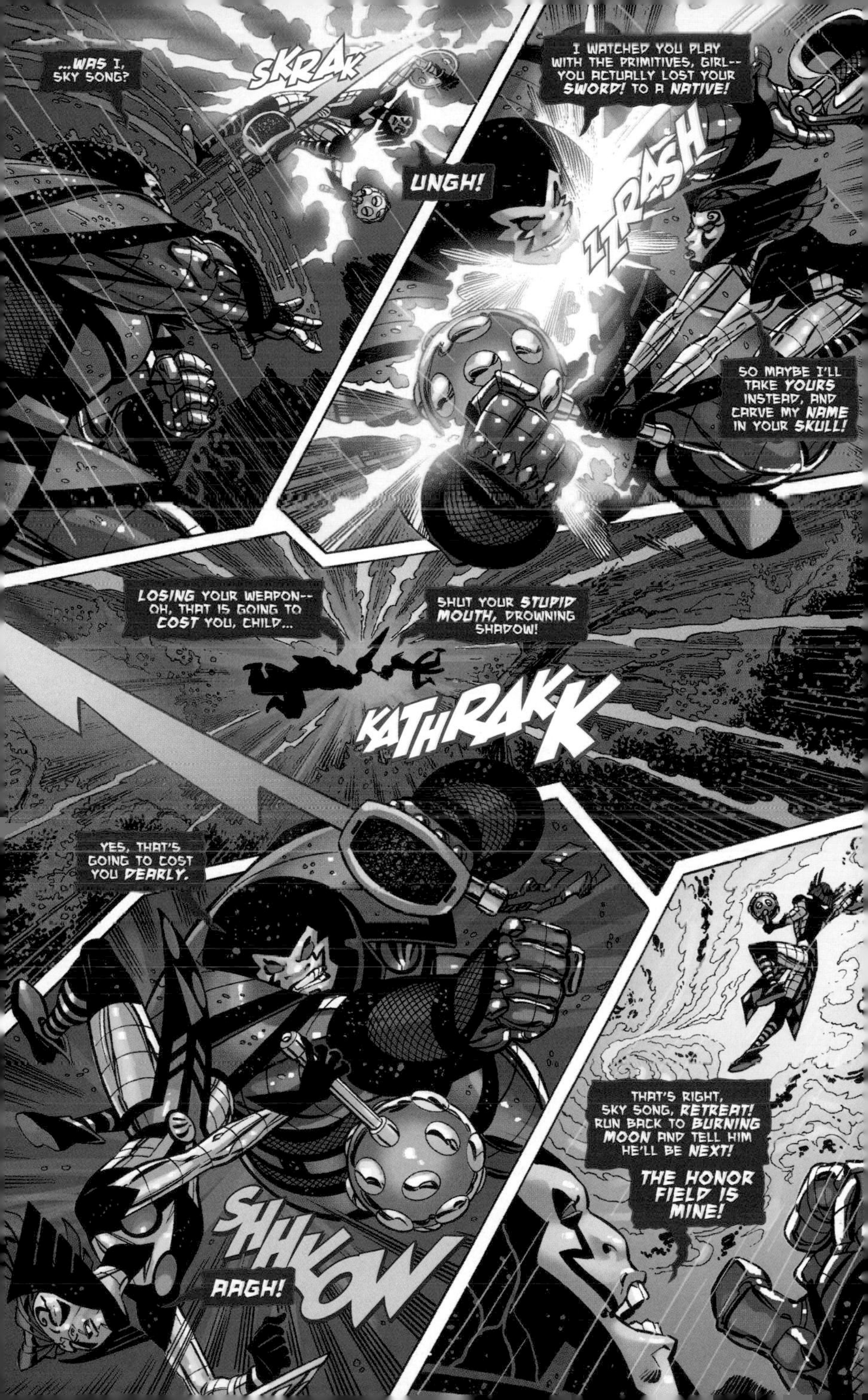
...WAS I, SKY SONG?
SKRAK
UNGH!
I WATCHED YOU PLAY WITH THE PRIMITIVES, GIRL-- YOU ACTUALLY LOST YOUR SWORD! TO A NATIVE!
ZZRASH
SO MAYBE I'LL TAKE YOURS INSTEAD, AND CARVE MY NAME IN YOUR SKULL!
LOSING YOUR WEAPON-- OH, THAT IS GOING TO COST YOU, CHILD...
SHUT YOUR STUPID MOUTH, DROWNING SHADOW!
KATHRAKK
YES, THAT'S GOING TO COST YOU DEARLY.
SHHVOW
AAGH!
THAT'S RIGHT, SKY SONG, RETREAT! RUN BACK TO BURNING MOON AND TELL HIM HE'LL BE NEXT!
THE HONOR FIELD IS MINE!

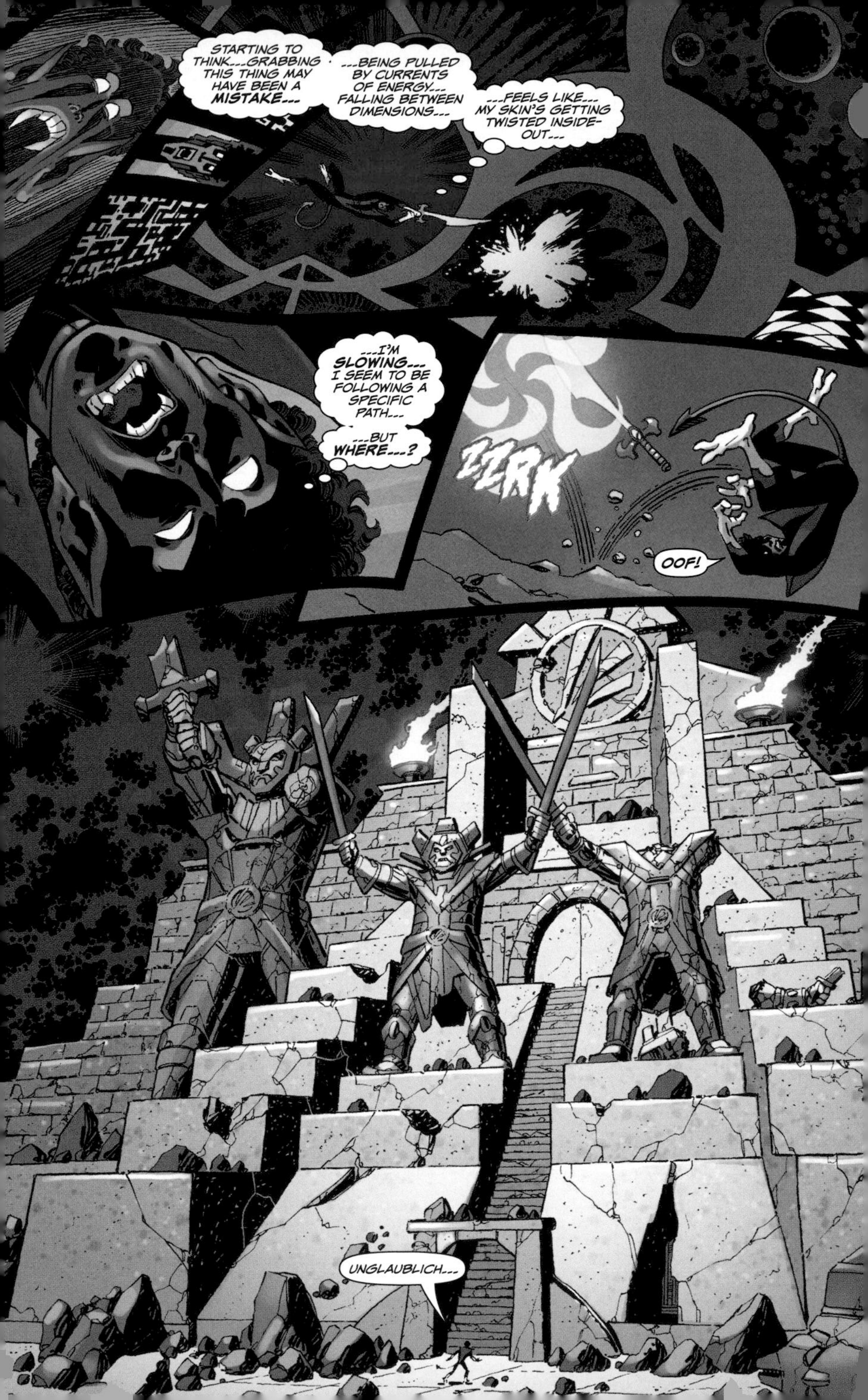

STARTING TO THINK---GRABBING THIS THING MAY HAVE BEEN A **MISTAKE**---
---BEING PULLED BY CURRENTS OF ENERGY--- FALLING BETWEEN DIMENSIONS---
---FEELS LIKE--- MY SKIN'S GETTING TWISTED INSIDE-OUT---
---I'M **SLOWING**--- I SEEM TO BE FOLLOWING A SPECIFIC PATH---
---BUT **WHERE**---?
ZZRK
OOF!
UNGLAUBLICH---

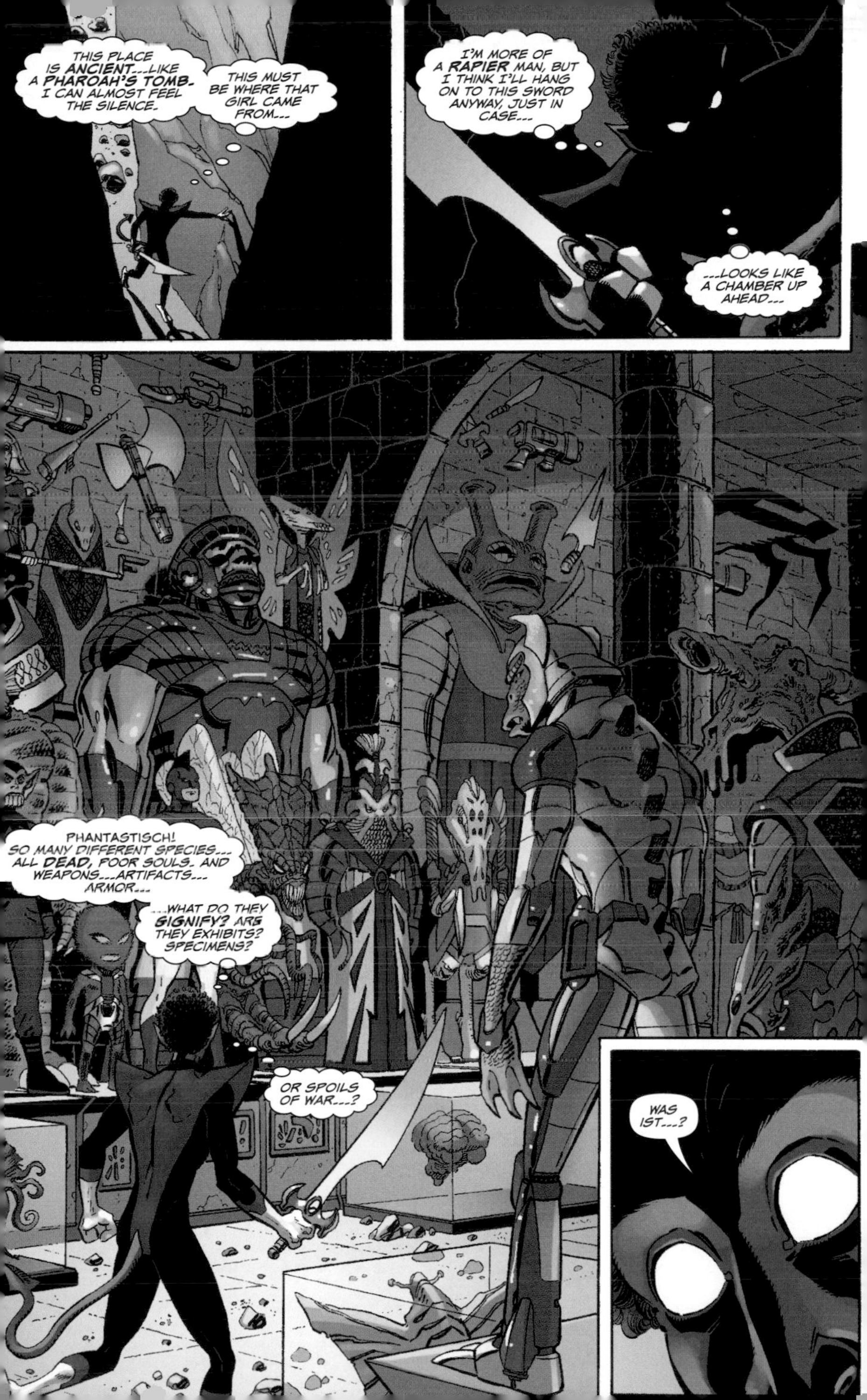
THIS PLACE IS ANCIENT...LIKE A PHAROAH'S TOMB- I CAN ALMOST FEEL THE SILENCE.
THIS MUST BE WHERE THAT GIRL CAME FROM...
I'M MORE OF A RAPIER MAN, BUT I THINK I'LL HANG ON TO THIS SWORD ANYWAY, JUST IN CASE...
...LOOKS LIKE A CHAMBER UP AHEAD...
PHANTASTISCH! SO MANY DIFFERENT SPECIES... ALL DEAD, POOR SOULS. AND WEAPONS...ARTIFACTS... ARMOR...
...WHAT DO THEY SIGNIFY? ARE THEY EXHIBITS? SPECIMENS?
OR SPOILS OF WAR...?
WAS IST...?

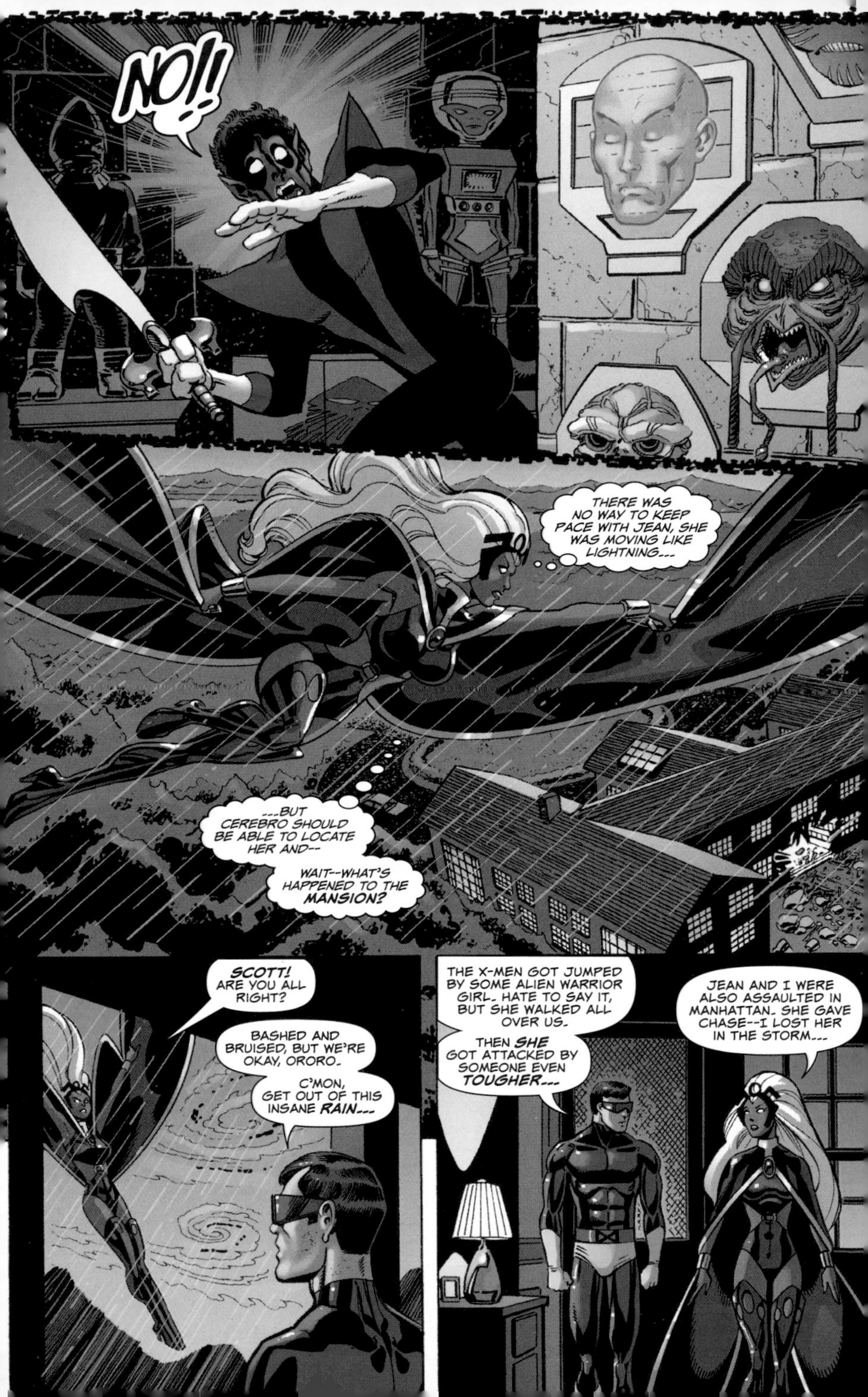
NO!!
THERE WAS NO WAY TO KEEP PACE WITH JEAN, SHE WAS MOVING LIKE LIGHTNING...
...BUT CEREBRO SHOULD BE ABLE TO LOCATE HER AND--
WAIT--WHAT'S HAPPENED TO THE MANSION?
SCOTT! ARE YOU ALL RIGHT?
BASHED AND BRUISED, BUT WE'RE OKAY, ORORO.
C'MON, GET OUT OF THIS INSANE RAIN...
THE X-MEN GOT JUMPED BY SOME ALIEN WARRIOR GIRL. HATE TO SAY IT, BUT SHE WALKED ALL OVER US.
THEN SHE GOT ATTACKED BY SOMEONE EVEN TOUGHER...
JEAN AND I WERE ALSO ASSAULTED IN MANHATTAN. SHE GAVE CHASE--I LOST HER IN THE STORM...

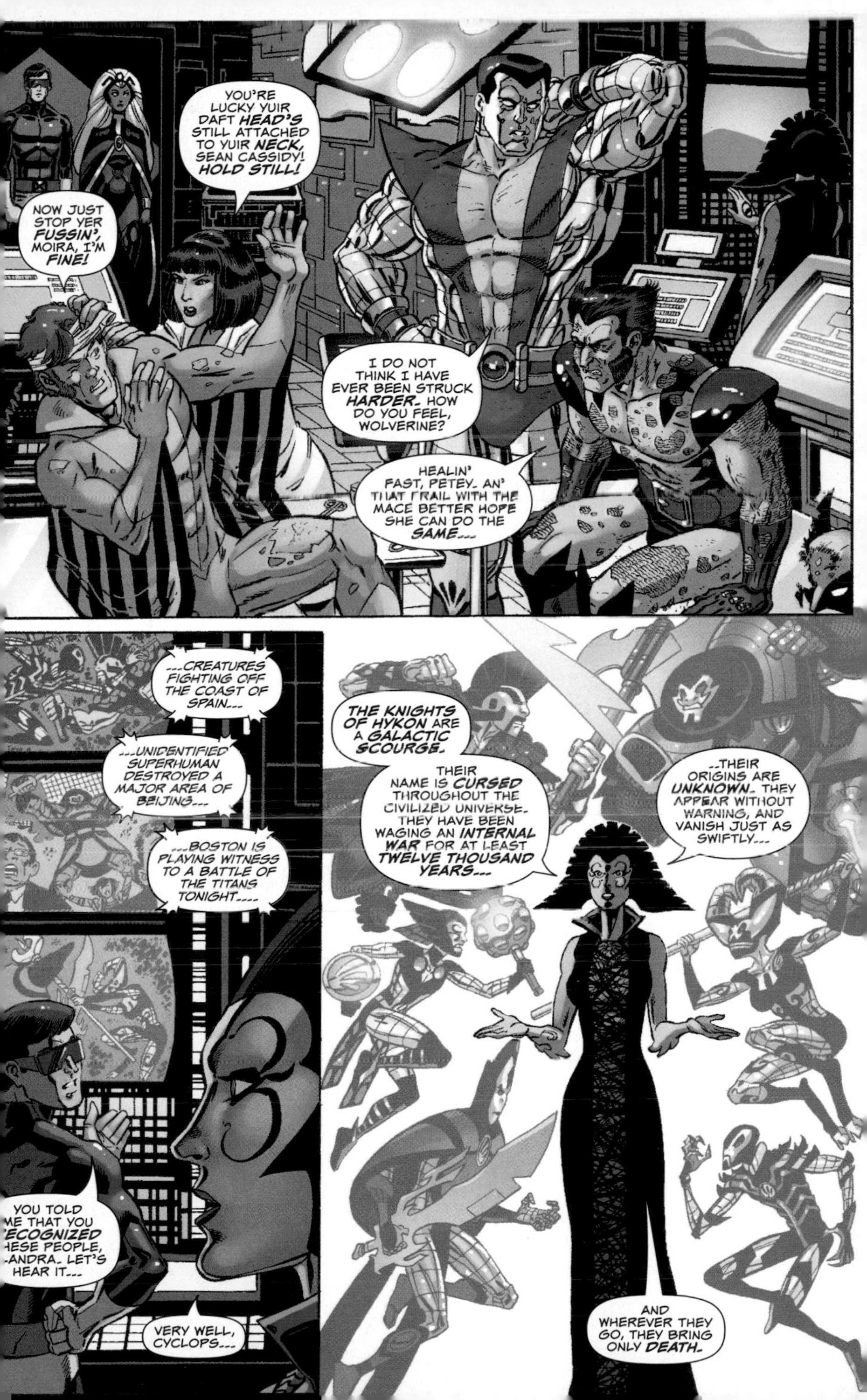

YOU'RE LUCKY YUIR DAFT HEAD'S STILL ATTACHED TO YUIR NECK, SEAN CASSIDY! HOLD STILL!
NOW JUST STOP YER FUSSIN', MOIRA, I'M FINE!
I DO NOT THINK I HAVE EVER BEEN STRUCK HARDER. HOW DO YOU FEEL, WOLVERINE?
HEALIN' FAST, PETEY. AN' THAT FRAIL WITH THE MACE BETTER HOPE SHE CAN DO THE SAME...
...CREATURES FIGHTING OFF THE COAST OF SPAIN...
...UNIDENTIFIED SUPERHUMAN DESTROYED A MAJOR AREA OF BEIJING...
...BOSTON IS PLAYING WITNESS TO A BATTLE OF THE TITANS TONIGHT....
YOU TOLD ME THAT YOU RECOGNIZED THESE PEOPLE, LANDRA. LET'S HEAR IT...
VERY WELL, CYCLOPS...
THE KNIGHTS OF HYKON ARE A GALACTIC SCOURGE.
THEIR NAME IS CURSED THROUGHOUT THE CIVILIZED UNIVERSE. THEY HAVE BEEN WAGING AN INTERNAL WAR FOR AT LEAST TWELVE THOUSAND YEARS...
..THEIR ORIGINS ARE UNKNOWN. THEY APPEAR WITHOUT WARNING, AND VANISH JUST AS SWIFTLY...
AND WHEREVER THEY GO, THEY BRING ONLY DEATH.

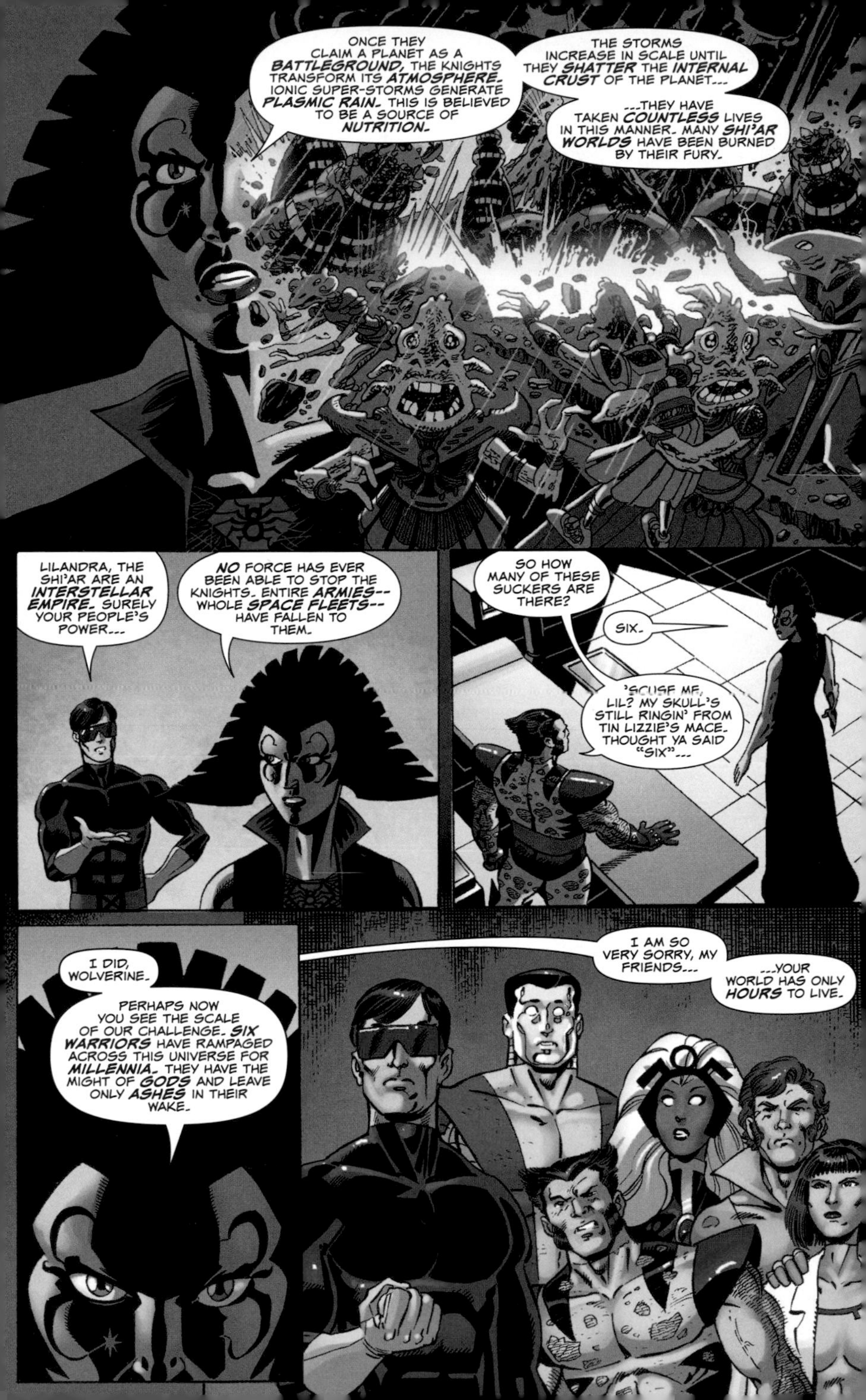
ONCE THEY CLAIM A PLANET AS A BATTLEGROUND, THE KNIGHTS TRANSFORM ITS ATMOSPHERE. IONIC SUPER-STORMS GENERATE PLASMIC RAIN. THIS IS BELIEVED TO BE A SOURCE OF NUTRITION.
THE STORMS INCREASE IN SCALE UNTIL THEY SHATTER THE INTERNAL CRUST OF THE PLANET...
...THEY HAVE TAKEN COUNTLESS LIVES IN THIS MANNER. MANY SHI'AR WORLDS HAVE BEEN BURNED BY THEIR FURY.
LILANDRA, THE SHI'AR ARE AN INTERSTELLAR EMPIRE. SURELY YOUR PEOPLE'S POWER...
NO FORCE HAS EVER BEEN ABLE TO STOP THE KNIGHTS. ENTIRE ARMIES--WHOLE SPACE FLEETS--HAVE FALLEN TO THEM.
SO HOW MANY OF THESE SUCKERS ARE THERE?
SIX.
'SCUSE ME, LIL? MY SKULL'S STILL RINGIN' FROM TIN LIZZIE'S MACE. THOUGHT YA SAID "SIX"...
I DID, WOLVERINE.
PERHAPS NOW YOU SEE THE SCALE OF OUR CHALLENGE. SIX WARRIORS HAVE RAMPAGED ACROSS THIS UNIVERSE FOR MILLENNIA. THEY HAVE THE MIGHT OF GODS AND LEAVE ONLY ASHES IN THEIR WAKE.
I AM SO VERY SORRY, MY FRIENDS...
...YOUR WORLD HAS ONLY HOURS TO LIVE.

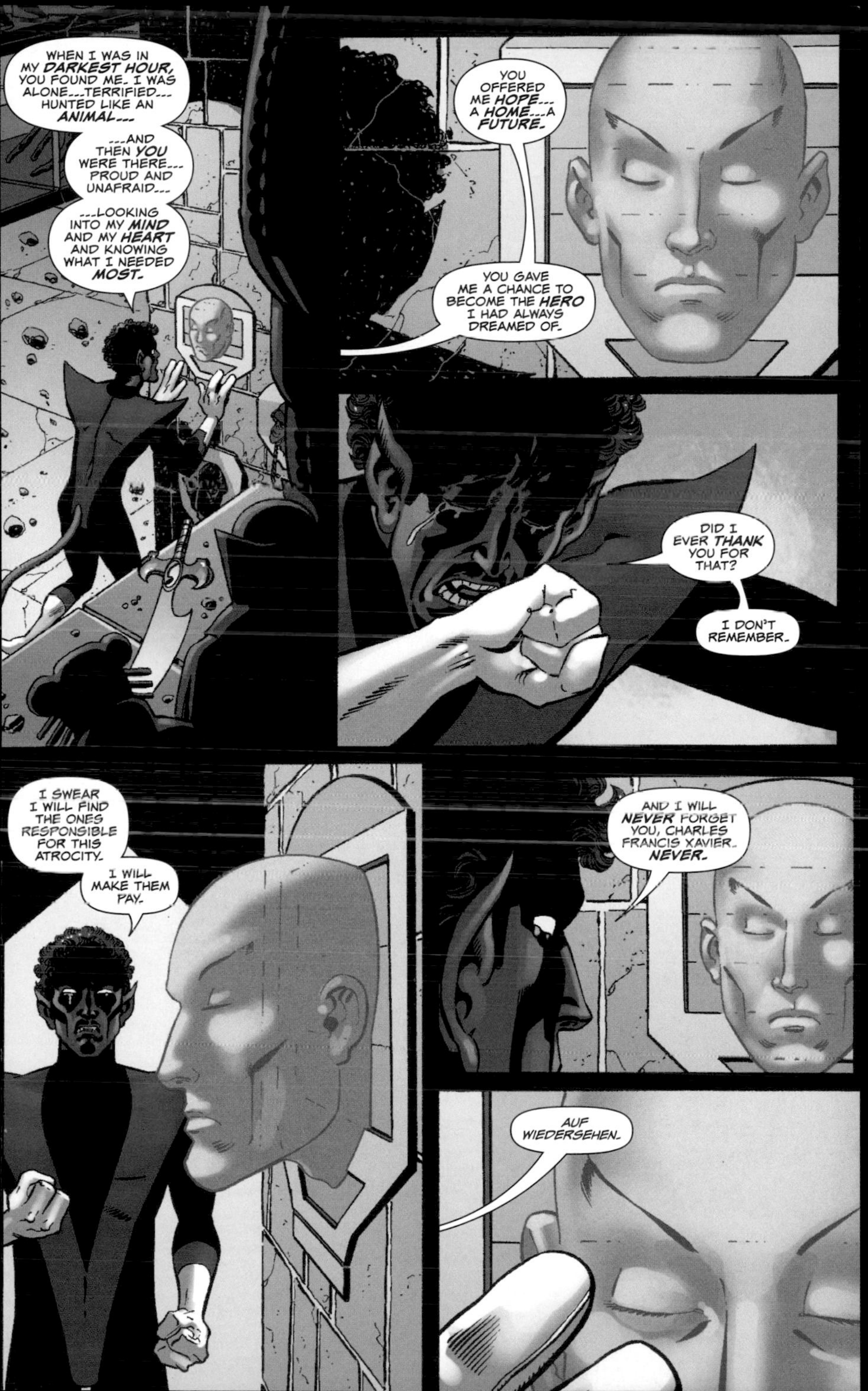
WHEN I WAS IN MY DARKEST HOUR, YOU FOUND ME. I WAS ALONE...TERRIFIED... HUNTED LIKE AN ANIMAL...
...AND THEN YOU WERE THERE... PROUD AND UNAFRAID...
...LOOKING INTO MY MIND AND MY HEART AND KNOWING WHAT I NEEDED MOST.
YOU OFFERED ME HOPE... A HOME...A FUTURE.
YOU GAVE ME A CHANCE TO BECOME THE HERO I HAD ALWAYS DREAMED OF.
DID I EVER THANK YOU FOR THAT?
I DON'T REMEMBER.
I SWEAR I WILL FIND THE ONES RESPONSIBLE FOR THIS ATROCITY.
I WILL MAKE THEM PAY.
AND I WILL NEVER FORGET YOU, CHARLES FRANCIS XAVIER. NEVER.
AUF WIEDERSEHEN.

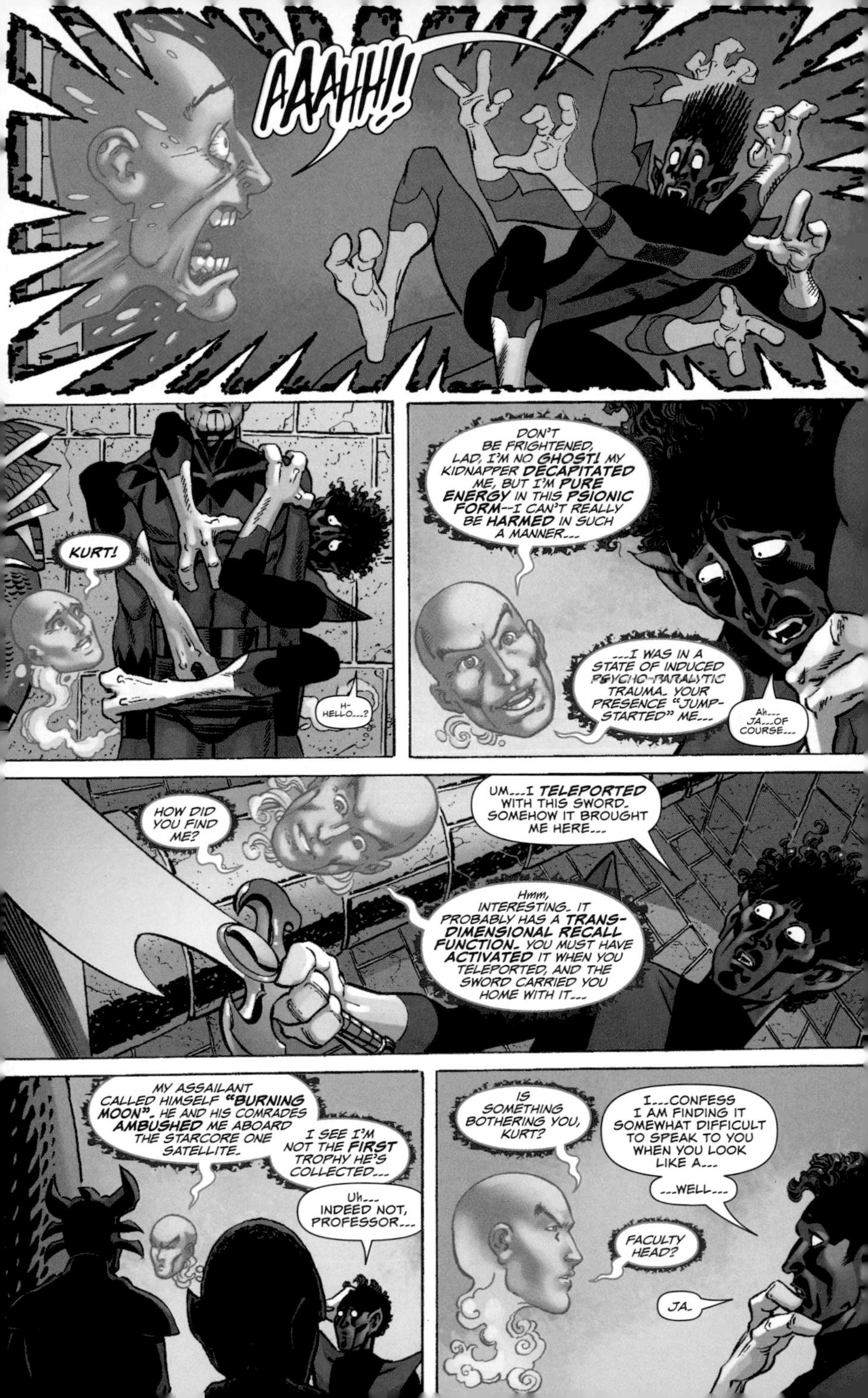
AAAHH!!
KURT!
H-HELLO...?
DON'T BE FRIGHTENED, LAD, I'M NO GHOST! MY KIDNAPPER DECAPITATED ME, BUT I'M PURE ENERGY IN THIS PSIONIC FORM--I CAN'T REALLY BE HARMED IN SUCH A MANNER...
...I WAS IN A STATE OF INDUCED PSYCHO-PARALYTIC TRAUMA. YOUR PRESENCE "JUMP-STARTED" ME...
Ah... JA...OF COURSE...
HOW DID YOU FIND ME?
UM...I TELEPORTED WITH THIS SWORD. SOMEHOW IT BROUGHT ME HERE...
Hmm, INTERESTING. IT PROBABLY HAS A TRANS-DIMENSIONAL RECALL FUNCTION. YOU MUST HAVE ACTIVATED IT WHEN YOU TELEPORTED, AND THE SWORD CARRIED YOU HOME WITH IT...
MY ASSAILANT CALLED HIMSELF "BURNING MOON". HE AND HIS COMRADES AMBUSHED ME ABOARD THE STARCORE ONE SATELLITE.
I SEE I'M NOT THE FIRST TROPHY HE'S COLLECTED...
Uh... INDEED NOT, PROFESSOR...
IS SOMETHING BOTHERING YOU, KURT?
I...CONFESS I AM FINDING IT SOMEWHAT DIFFICULT TO SPEAK TO YOU WHEN YOU LOOK LIKE A...
...WELL...
FACULTY HEAD?
JA.

EASILY FIXED. IT SIMPLY REQUIRES A LITTLE EXTRA THOUGHT...

THE SONG HAS FALLEN...

WHO...?

THIS WAY...

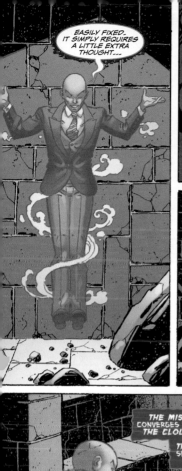

...THE SHADOW PREVAILS...

THE MIST CONVERGES WITH THE CLOUD.

THE BONE SEEKS THE MIST.

THE SONG RETURNS.

PEACE IS TORTURE...

...VICTORY IS TRUTH.

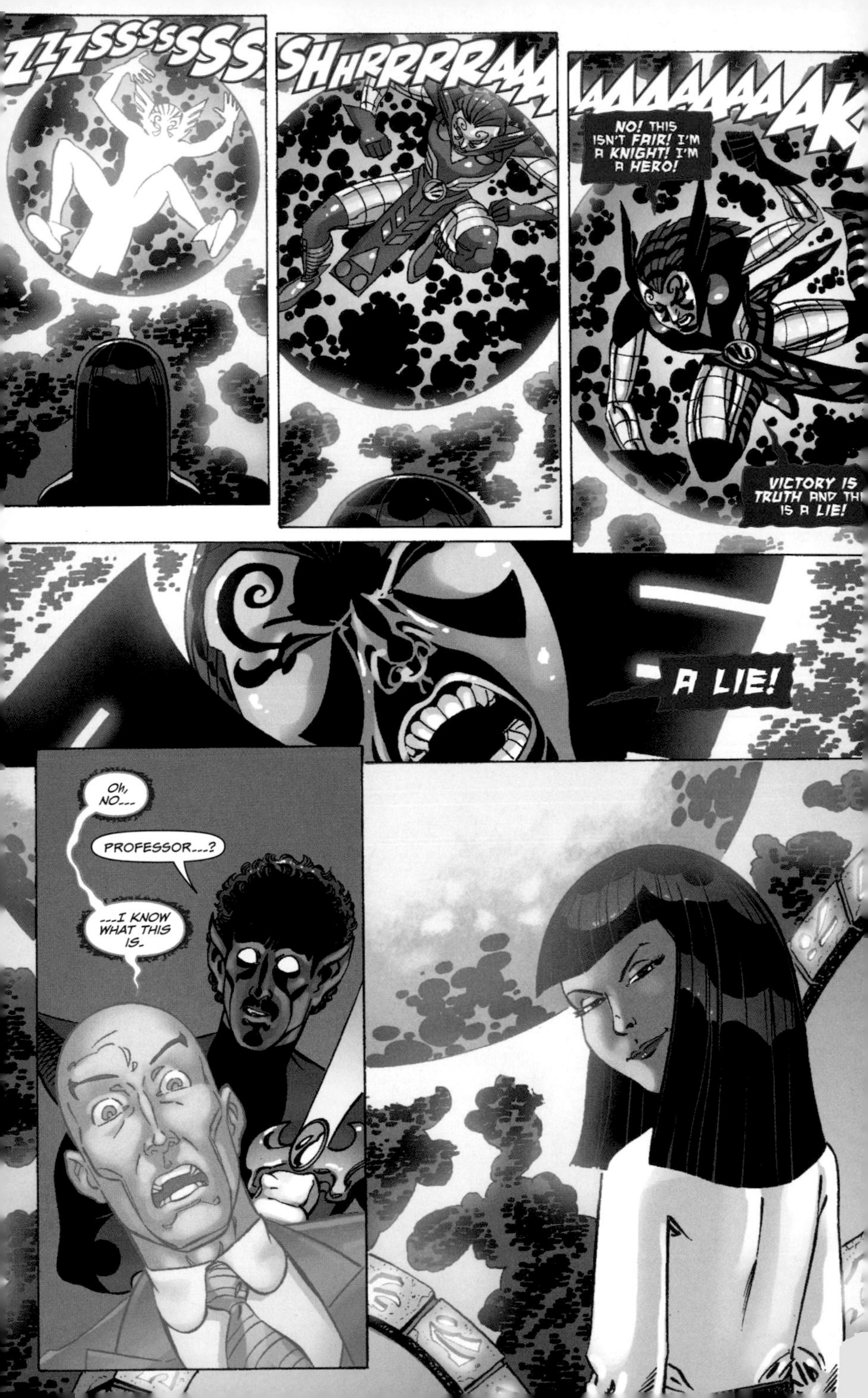

ZZZSSSSSSS
SHHRRRRAAAAAAAAAAAAK
NO! THIS ISN'T FAIR! I'M A KNIGHT! I'M A HERO!
VICTORY IS TRUTH AND THIS IS A LIE!
A LIE!
Oh, NO---
PROFESSOR---?
---I KNOW WHAT THIS IS.

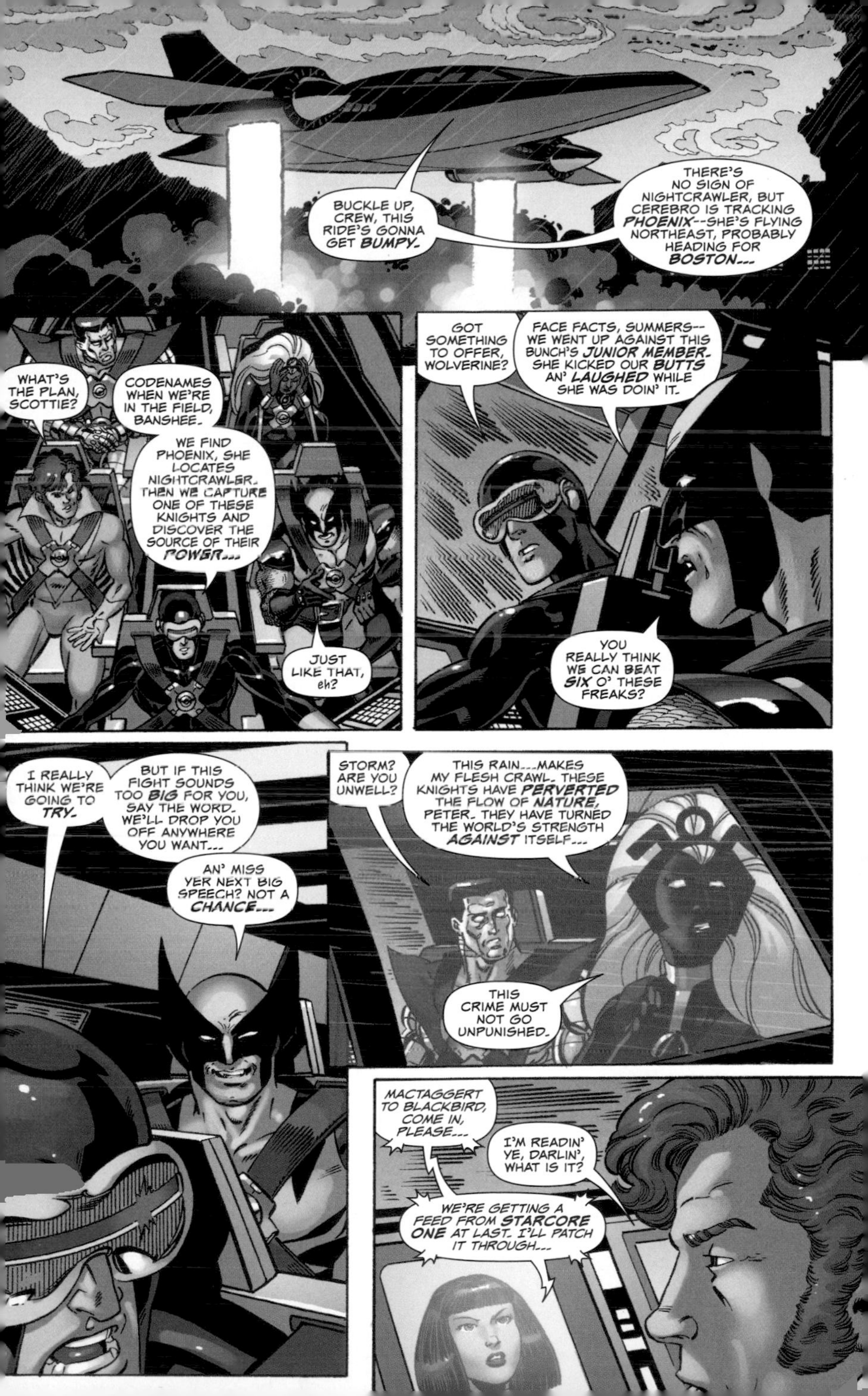
BUCKLE UP, CREW, THIS RIDE'S GONNA GET BUMPY.
THERE'S NO SIGN OF NIGHTCRAWLER, BUT CEREBRO IS TRACKING PHOENIX--SHE'S FLYING NORTHEAST, PROBABLY HEADING FOR BOSTON...
WHAT'S THE PLAN, SCOTTIE?
CODENAMES WHEN WE'RE IN THE FIELD, BANSHEE.
WE FIND PHOENIX, SHE LOCATES NIGHTCRAWLER. THEN WE CAPTURE ONE OF THESE KNIGHTS AND DISCOVER THE SOURCE OF THEIR POWER...
JUST LIKE THAT, eh?
GOT SOMETHING TO OFFER, WOLVERINE?
FACE FACTS, SUMMERS-- WE WENT UP AGAINST THIS BUNCH'S JUNIOR MEMBER. SHE KICKED OUR BUTTS AN' LAUGHED WHILE SHE WAS DOIN' IT.
YOU REALLY THINK WE CAN BEAT SIX O' THESE FREAKS?
I REALLY THINK WE'RE GOING TO TRY.
BUT IF THIS FIGHT SOUNDS TOO BIG FOR YOU, SAY THE WORD. WE'LL DROP YOU OFF ANYWHERE YOU WANT...
AN' MISS YER NEXT BIG SPEECH? NOT A CHANCE...
STORM? ARE YOU UNWELL?
THIS RAIN...MAKES MY FLESH CRAWL. THESE KNIGHTS HAVE PERVERTED THE FLOW OF NATURE, PETER. THEY HAVE TURNED THE WORLD'S STRENGTH AGAINST ITSELF...
THIS CRIME MUST NOT GO UNPUNISHED.
MACTAGGERT TO BLACKBIRD, COME IN, PLEASE...
I'M READIN' YE, DARLIN', WHAT IS IT?
WE'RE GETTING A FEED FROM STARCORE ONE AT LAST. I'LL PATCH IT THROUGH...

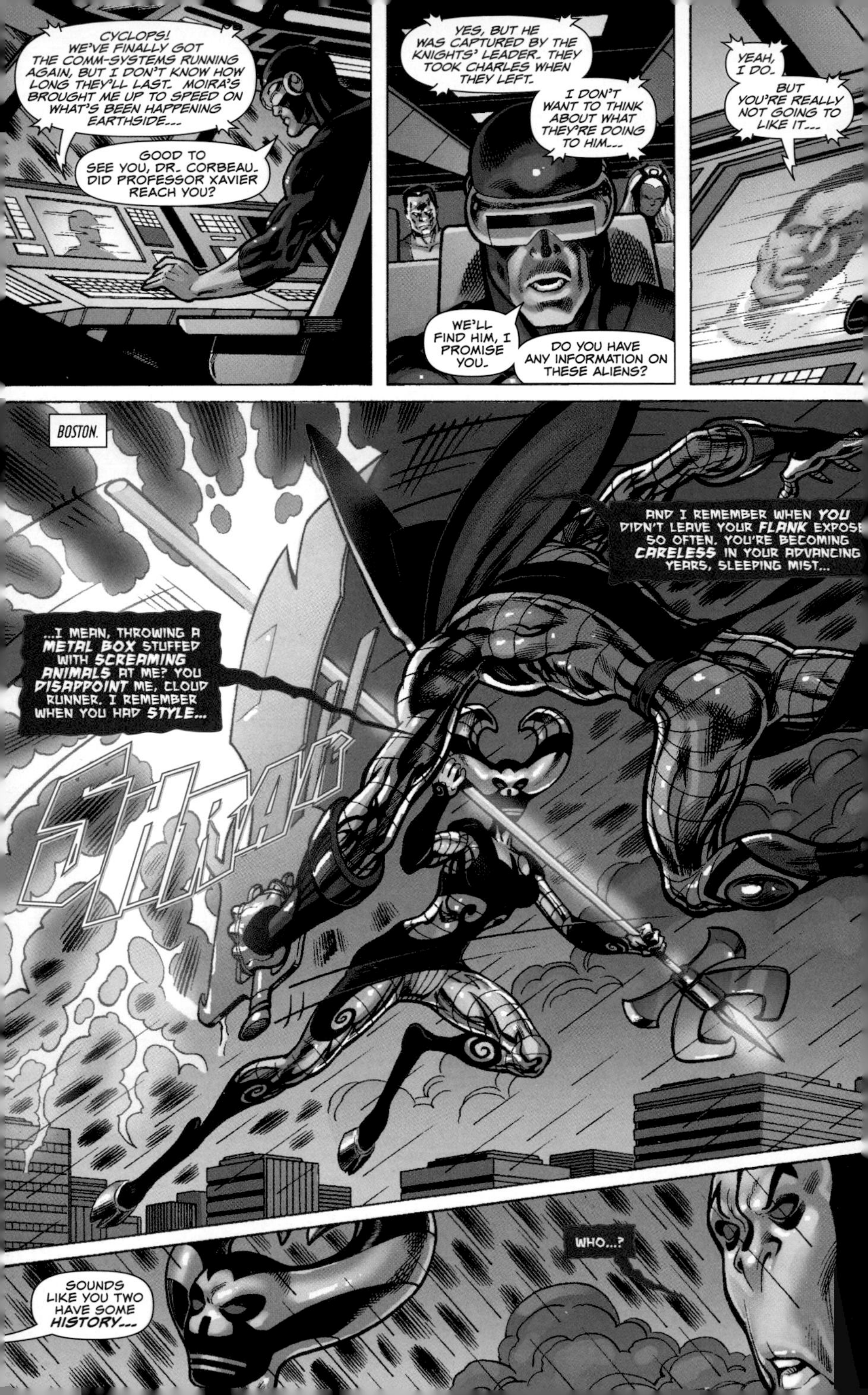
CYCLOPS! WE'VE FINALLY GOT THE COMM-SYSTEMS RUNNING AGAIN, BUT I DON'T KNOW HOW LONG THEY'LL LAST. MOIRA'S BROUGHT ME UP TO SPEED ON WHAT'S BEEN HAPPENING EARTHSIDE...
GOOD TO SEE YOU, DR. CORBEAU. DID PROFESSOR XAVIER REACH YOU?
YES, BUT HE WAS CAPTURED BY THE KNIGHTS' LEADER. THEY TOOK CHARLES WHEN THEY LEFT.
I DON'T WANT TO THINK ABOUT WHAT THEY'RE DOING TO HIM...
WE'LL FIND HIM, I PROMISE YOU.
DO YOU HAVE ANY INFORMATION ON THESE ALIENS?
YEAH, I DO.
BUT YOU'RE REALLY NOT GOING TO LIKE IT...
BOSTON.
...I MEAN, THROWING A METAL BOX STUFFED WITH SCREAMING ANIMALS AT ME? YOU DISAPPOINT ME, CLOUD RUNNER. I REMEMBER WHEN YOU HAD STYLE...
AND I REMEMBER WHEN YOU DIDN'T LEAVE YOUR FLANK EXPOSE SO OFTEN. YOU'RE BECOMING CARELESS IN YOUR ADVANCING YEARS, SLEEPING MIST...
SHRAK
WHO...?
SOUNDS LIKE YOU TWO HAVE SOME HISTORY...

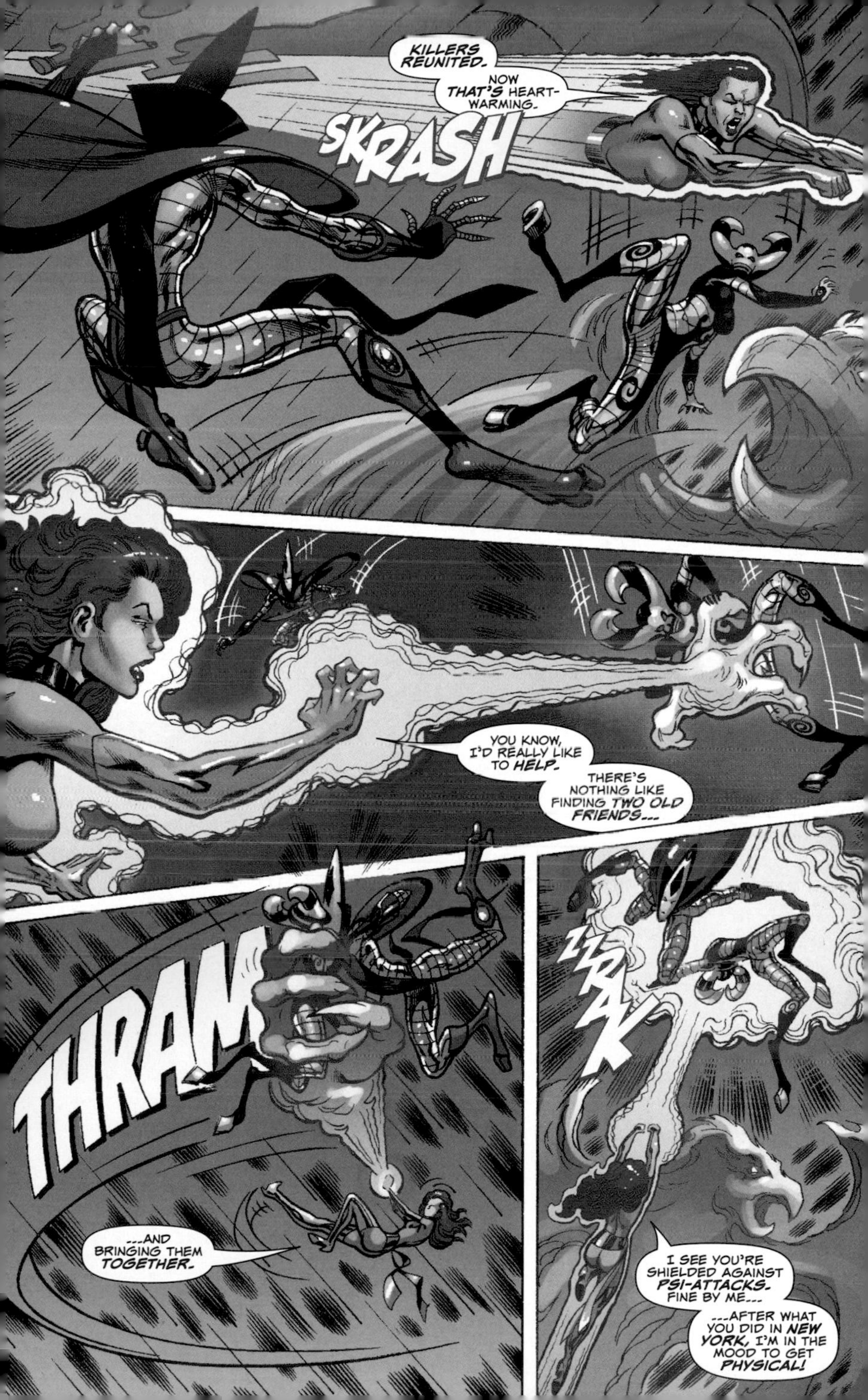

KILLERS REUNITED.
NOW THAT'S HEART-WARMING.
SKRASH
YOU KNOW, I'D REALLY LIKE TO HELP.
THERE'S NOTHING LIKE FINDING TWO OLD FRIENDS...
THRAM
...AND BRINGING THEM TOGETHER.
ZZRAK
I SEE YOU'RE SHIELDED AGAINST PSI-ATTACKS. FINE BY ME...
...AFTER WHAT YOU DID IN NEW YORK, I'M IN THE MOOD TO GET PHYSICAL!

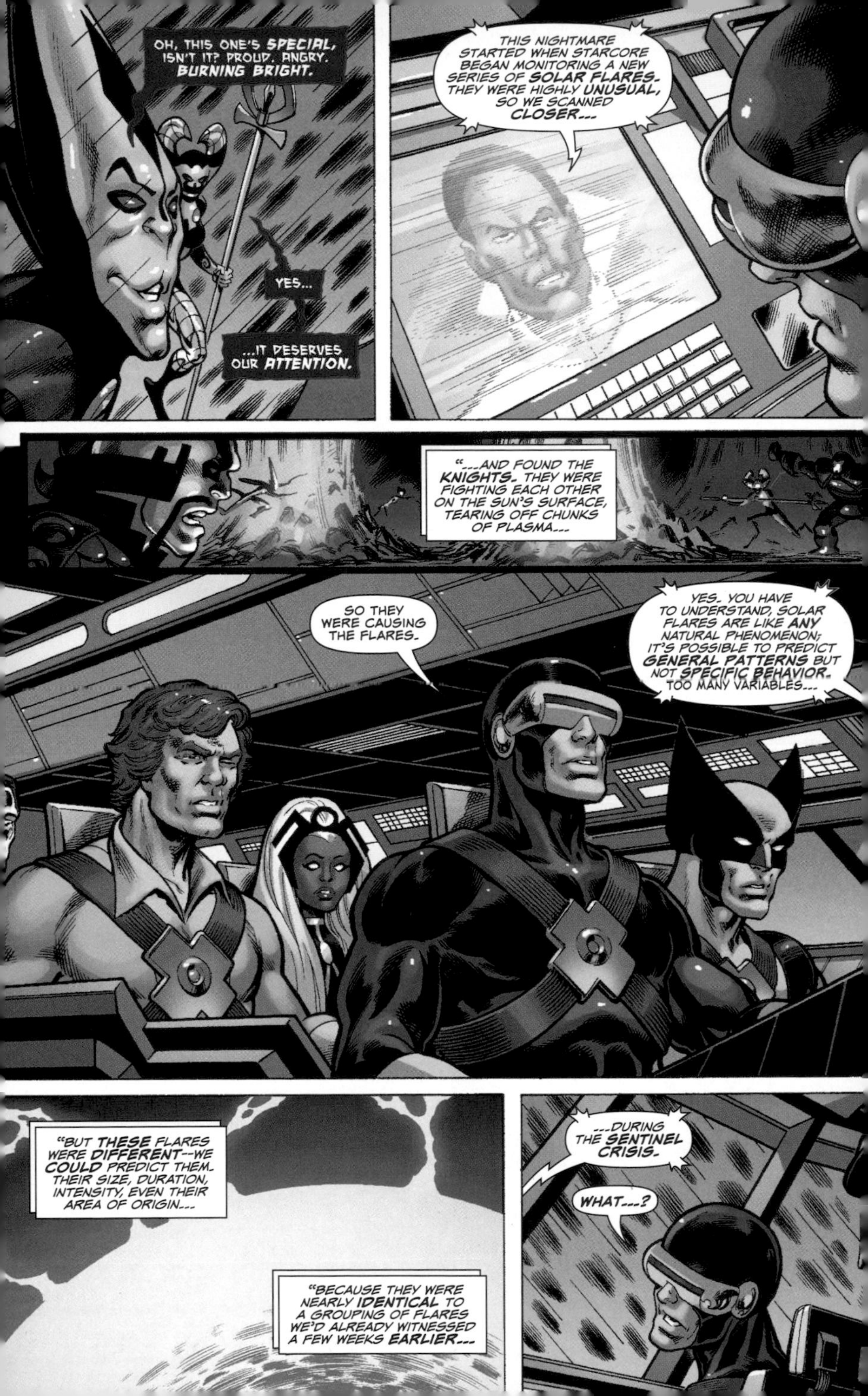

OH, THIS ONE'S SPECIAL, ISN'T IT? PROUD. ANGRY. BURNING BRIGHT.
YES...
...IT DESERVES OUR ATTENTION.
THIS NIGHTMARE STARTED WHEN STARCORE BEGAN MONITORING A NEW SERIES OF SOLAR FLARES. THEY WERE HIGHLY UNUSUAL, SO WE SCANNED CLOSER...
"...AND FOUND THE KNIGHTS. THEY WERE FIGHTING EACH OTHER ON THE SUN'S SURFACE, TEARING OFF CHUNKS OF PLASMA...
SO THEY WERE CAUSING THE FLARES.
YES. YOU HAVE TO UNDERSTAND, SOLAR FLARES ARE LIKE ANY NATURAL PHENOMENON; IT'S POSSIBLE TO PREDICT GENERAL PATTERNS BUT NOT SPECIFIC BEHAVIOR. TOO MANY VARIABLES...
"BUT THESE FLARES WERE DIFFERENT--WE COULD PREDICT THEM. THEIR SIZE, DURATION, INTENSITY, EVEN THEIR AREA OF ORIGIN...
"BECAUSE THEY WERE NEARLY IDENTICAL TO A GROUPING OF FLARES WE'D ALREADY WITNESSED A FEW WEEKS EARLIER...
...DURING THE SENTINEL CRISIS.
WHAT...?

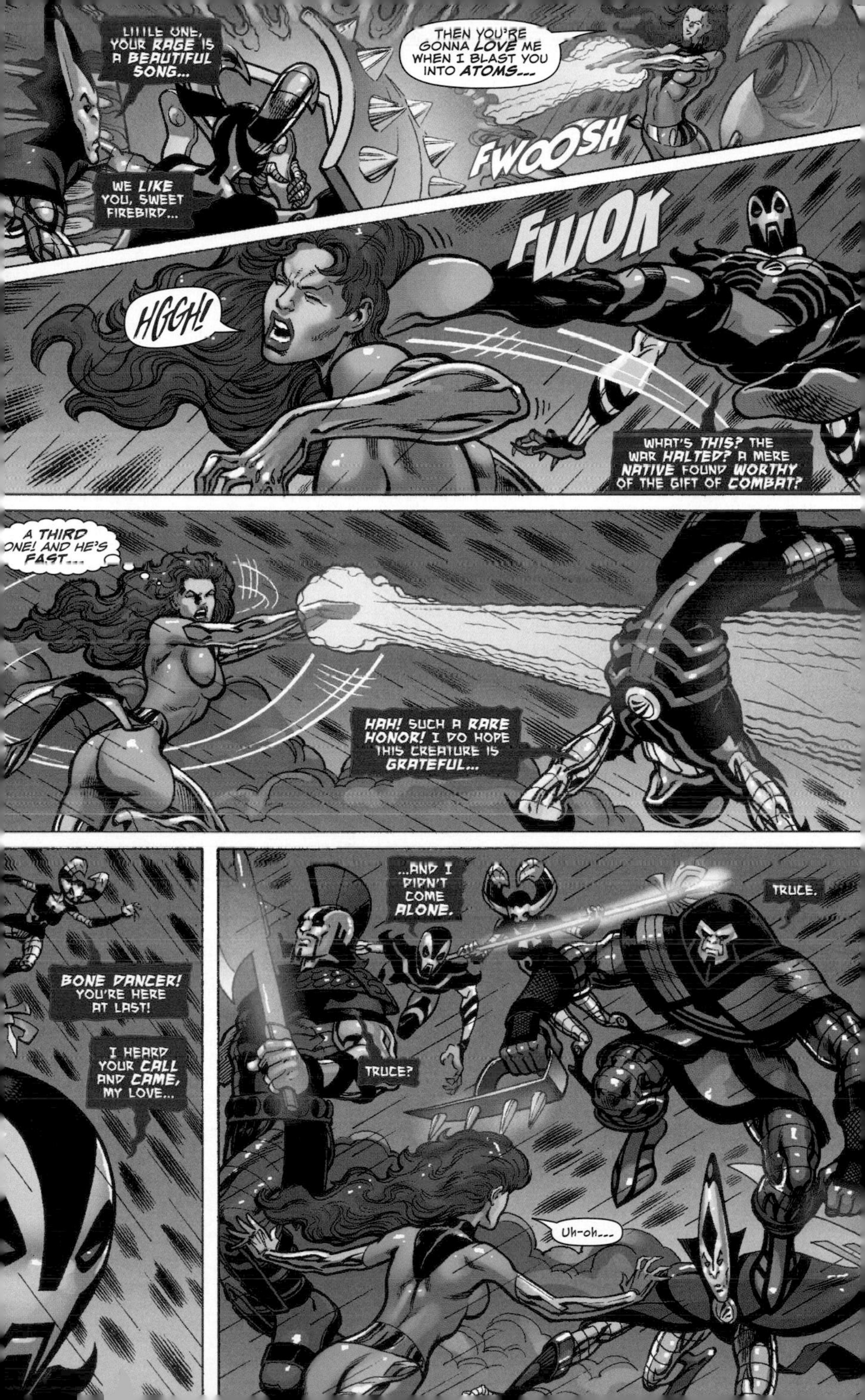
LITTLE ONE, YOUR RAGE IS A BEAUTIFUL SONG...
WE LIKE YOU, SWEET FIREBIRD...
THEN YOU'RE GONNA LOVE ME WHEN I BLAST YOU INTO ATOMS---
FWOOSH
FWOK
HGGH!
WHAT'S THIS? THE WAR HALTED? A MERE NATIVE FOUND WORTHY OF THE GIFT OF COMBAT?
A THIRD ONE! AND HE'S FAST...
HAH! SUCH A RARE HONOR! I DO HOPE THIS CREATURE IS GRATEFUL...
BONE DANCER! YOU'RE HERE AT LAST!
I HEARD YOUR CALL AND CAME, MY LOVE...
...AND I DIDN'T COME ALONE.
TRUCE.
TRUCE?
Uh-oh---

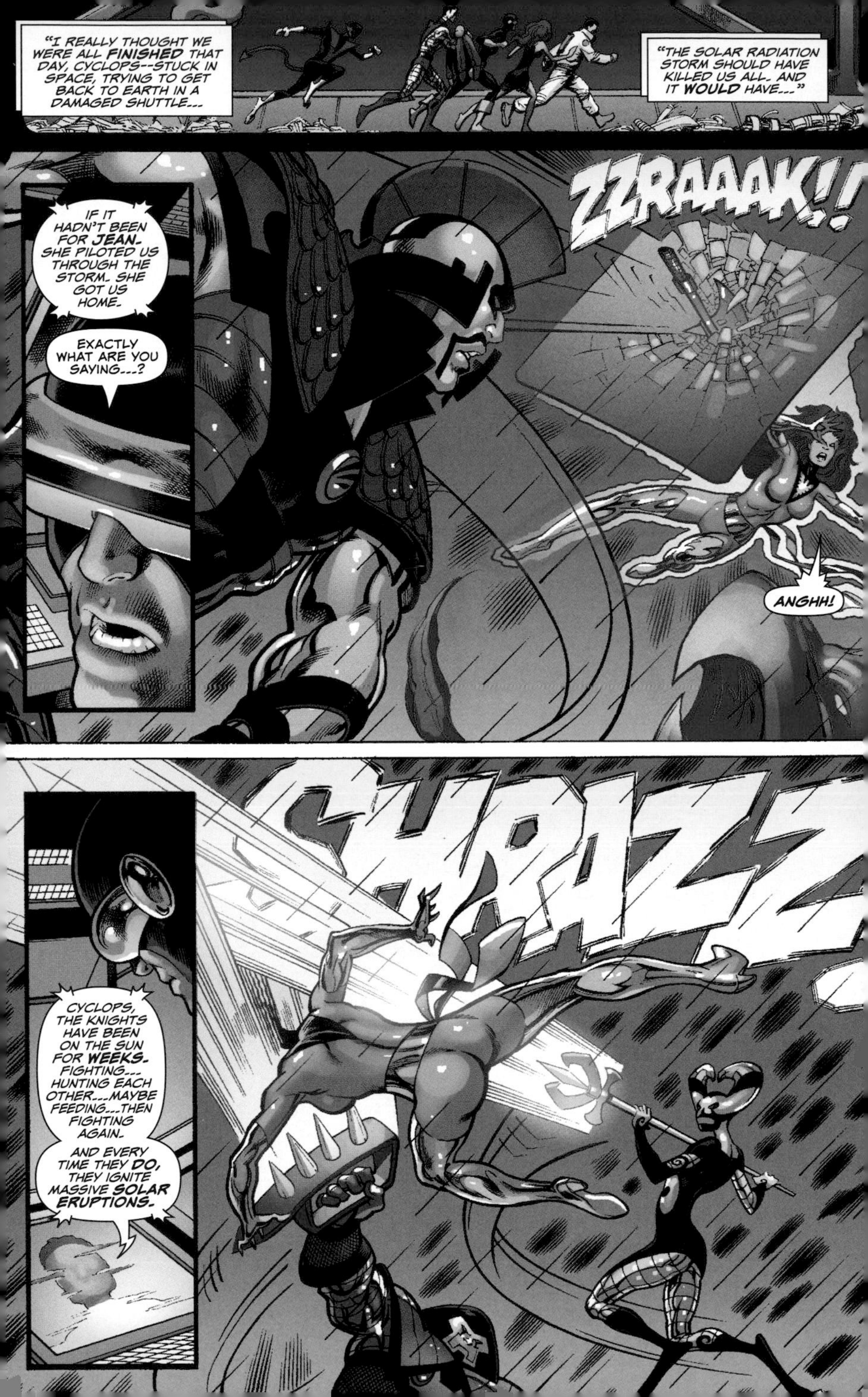
"I REALLY THOUGHT WE WERE ALL FINISHED THAT DAY, CYCLOPS--STUCK IN SPACE, TRYING TO GET BACK TO EARTH IN A DAMAGED SHUTTLE...
"THE SOLAR RADIATION STORM SHOULD HAVE KILLED US ALL. AND IT WOULD HAVE..."
IF IT HADN'T BEEN FOR JEAN. SHE PILOTED US THROUGH THE STORM. SHE GOT US HOME.
EXACTLY WHAT ARE YOU SAYING...?
ZZRAAAK!!
ANGHH!
CYCLOPS, THE KNIGHTS HAVE BEEN ON THE SUN FOR WEEKS. FIGHTING... HUNTING EACH OTHER... MAYBE FEEDING... THEN FIGHTING AGAIN.
AND EVERY TIME THEY DO, THEY IGNITE MASSIVE SOLAR ERUPTIONS.

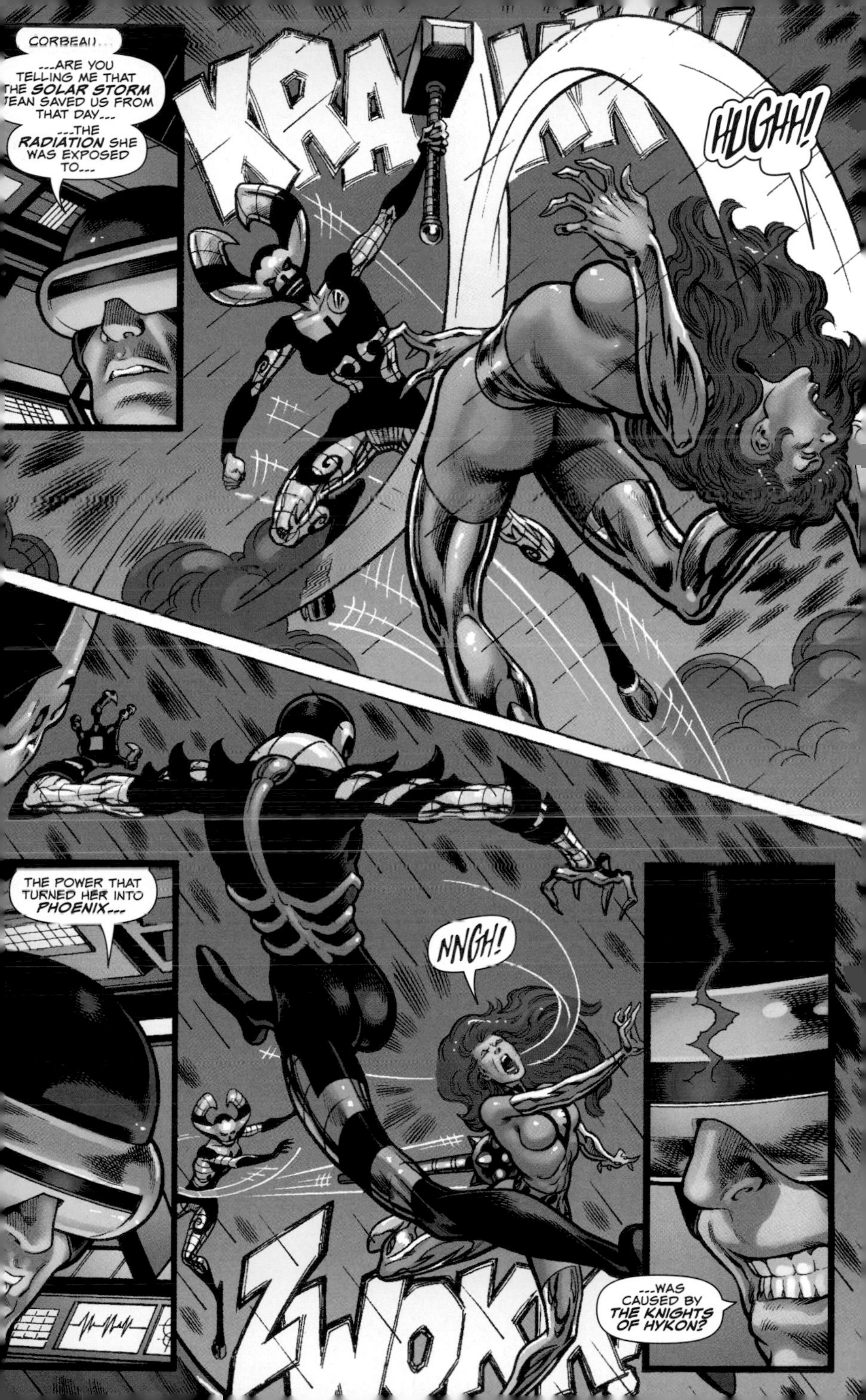

CORBEAU...
---ARE YOU TELLING ME THAT THE SOLAR STORM JEAN SAVED US FROM THAT DAY---
---THE RADIATION SHE WAS EXPOSED TO---
KRAAKK
HUGHH!
THE POWER THAT TURNED HER INTO PHOENIX---
NNGH!
---WAS CAUSED BY THE KNIGHTS OF HYKON?

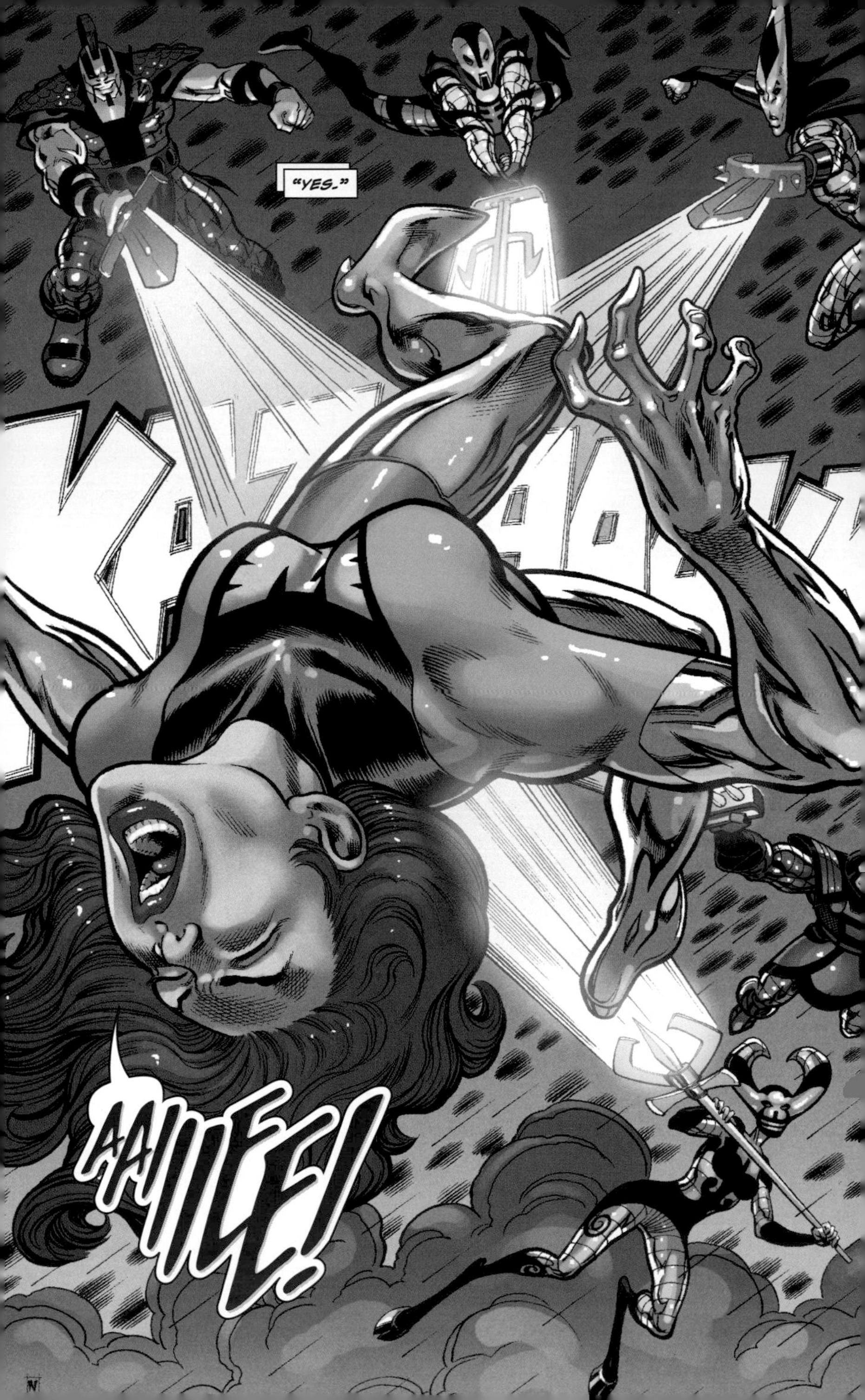
"YES-"
AAIIEE!

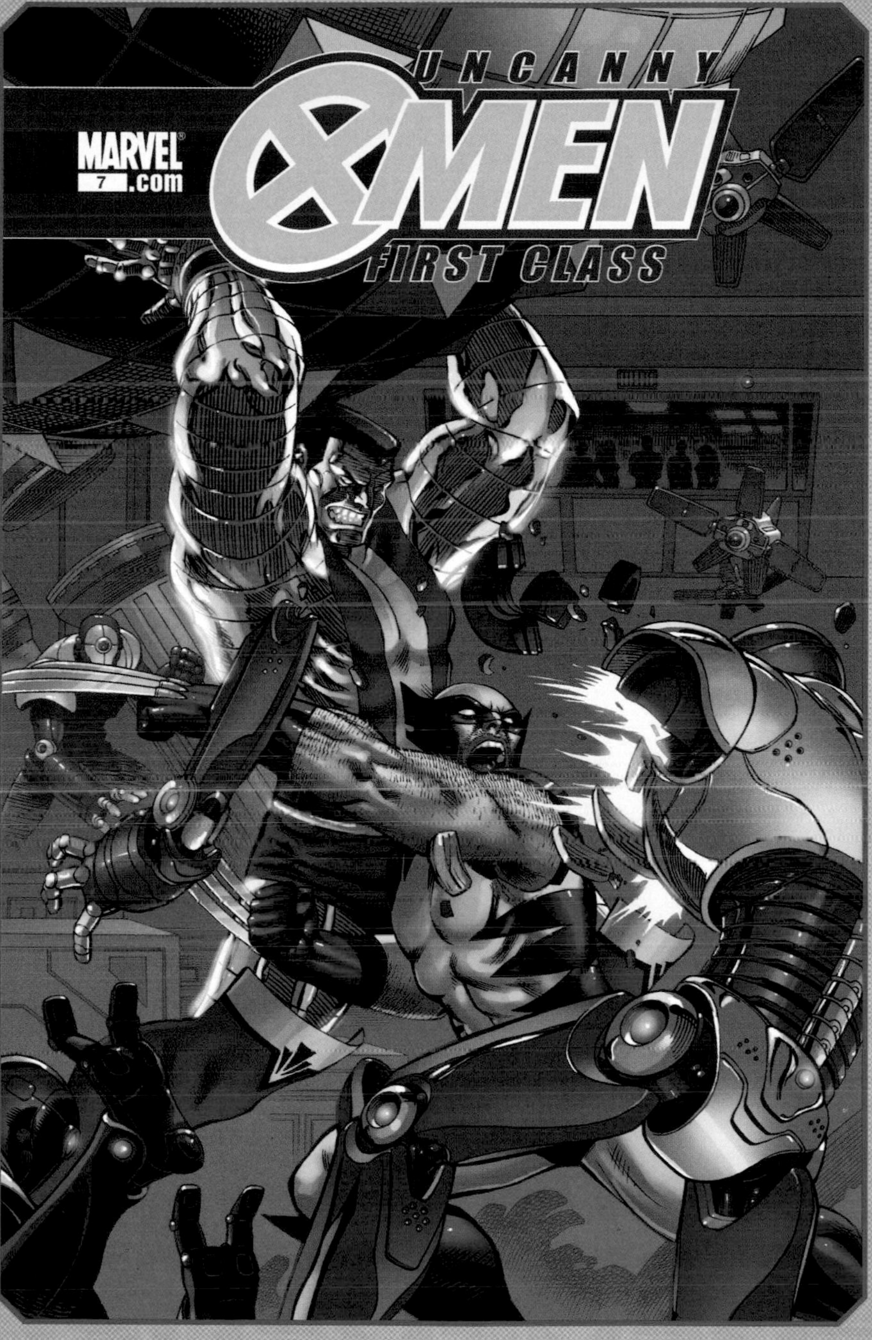
MARVEL
7 .com
UNCANNY
X-MEN
FIRST CLASS

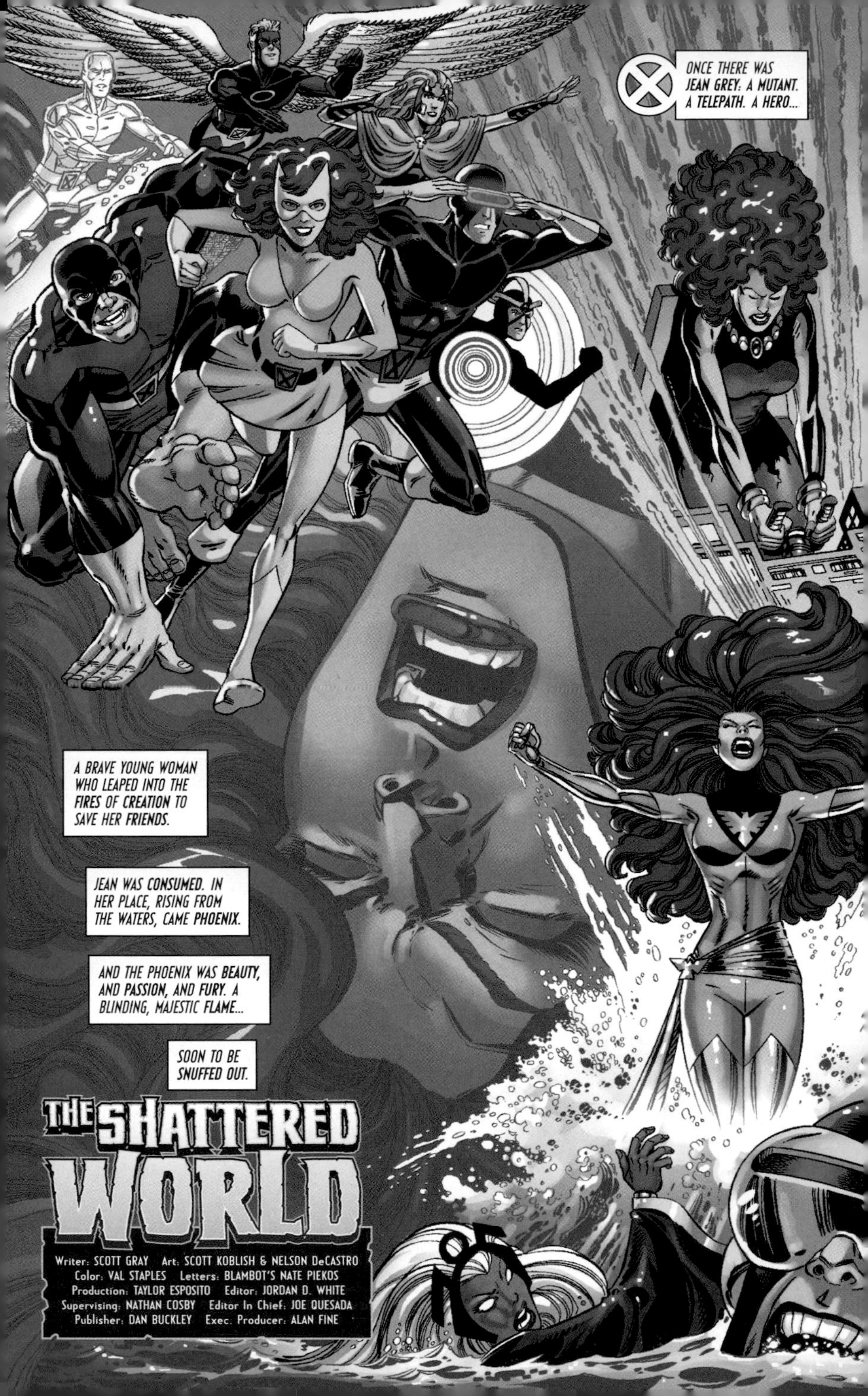
ONCE THERE WAS JEAN GREY: A MUTANT. A TELEPATH. A HERO...
A BRAVE YOUNG WOMAN WHO LEAPED INTO THE FIRES OF CREATION TO SAVE HER FRIENDS.
JEAN WAS CONSUMED. IN HER PLACE, RISING FROM THE WATERS, CAME PHOENIX.
AND THE PHOENIX WAS BEAUTY, AND PASSION, AND FURY. A BLINDING, MAJESTIC FLAME...
SOON TO BE SNUFFED OUT.
THE SHATTERED WORLD
Writer: SCOTT GRAY Art: SCOTT KOBLISH & NELSON DeCASTRO
Color: VAL STAPLES Letters: BLAMBOT'S NATE PIEKOS
Production: TAYLOR ESPOSITO Editor: JORDAN D. WHITE
Supervising: NATHAN COSBY Editor In Chief: JOE QUESADA
Publisher: DAN BUCKLEY Exec. Producer: ALAN FINE

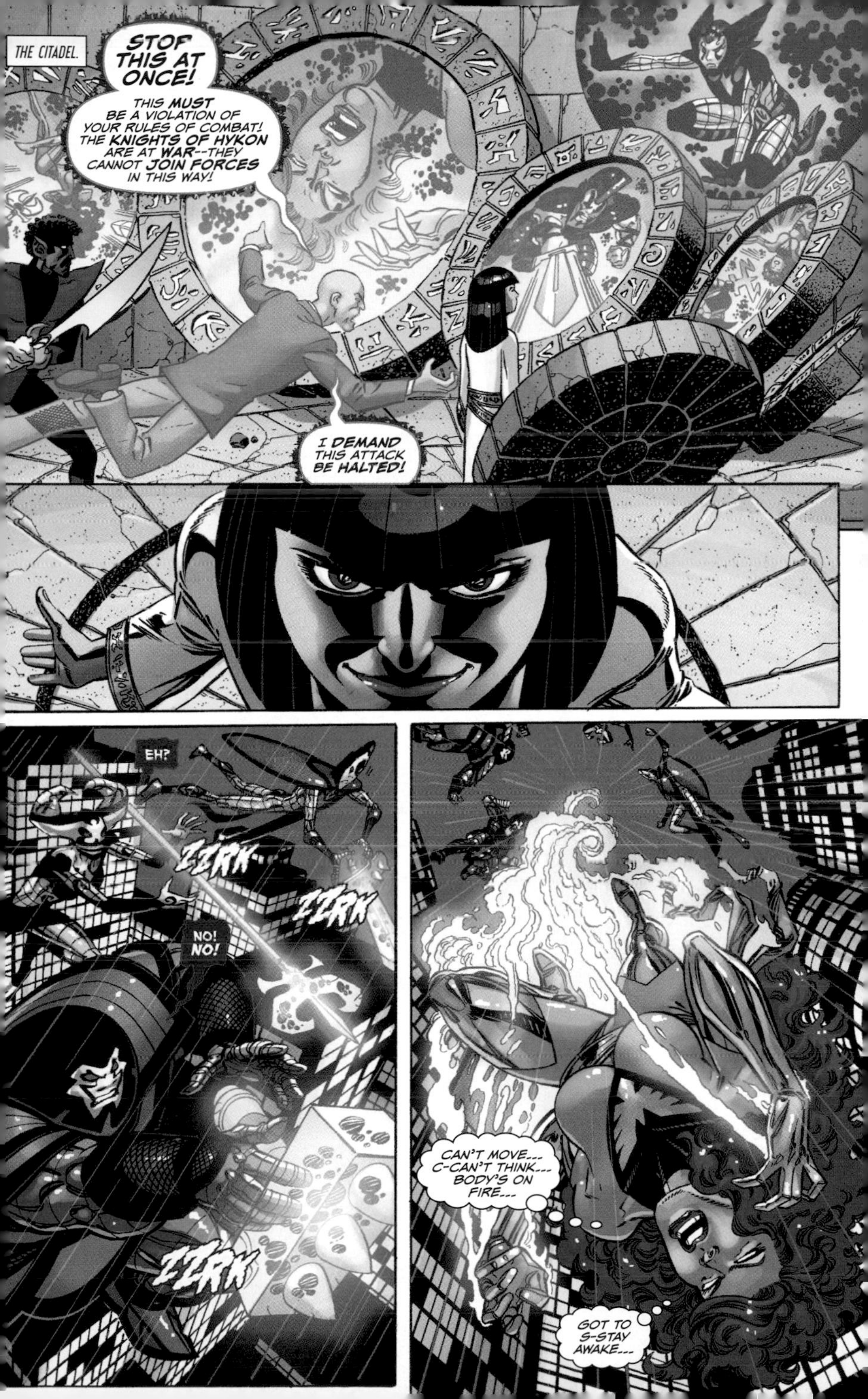
THE CITADEL.
STOP THIS AT ONCE!
THIS MUST BE A VIOLATION OF YOUR RULES OF COMBAT! THE KNIGHTS OF HYKON ARE AT WAR--THEY CANNOT JOIN FORCES IN THIS WAY!
I DEMAND THIS ATTACK BE HALTED!
EH?
ZZRK
ZZRK
NO! NO!
ZZRK
CAN'T MOVE... C-CAN'T THINK... BODY'S ON FIRE...
GOT TO S-STAY AWAKE...

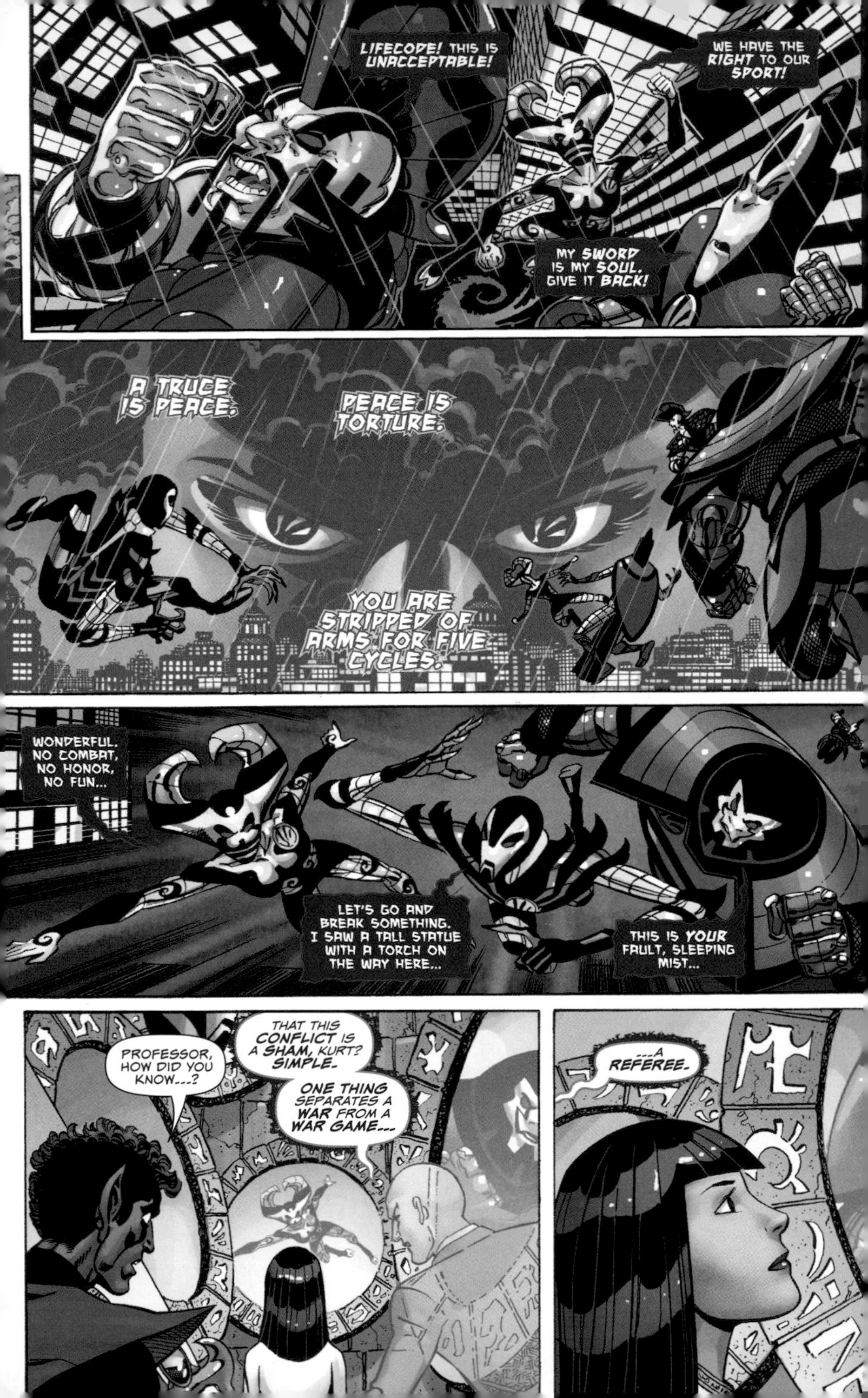
LIFECODE! THIS IS UNACCEPTABLE!
WE HAVE THE RIGHT TO OUR SPORT!
MY SWORD IS MY SOUL. GIVE IT BACK!
A TRUCE IS PEACE.
PEACE IS TORTURE.
YOU ARE STRIPPED OF ARMS FOR FIVE CYCLES.
WONDERFUL. NO COMBAT, NO HONOR, NO FUN...
LET'S GO AND BREAK SOMETHING. I SAW A TALL STATUE WITH A TORCH ON THE WAY HERE...
THIS IS YOUR FAULT, SLEEPING MIST...
PROFESSOR, HOW DID YOU KNOW...?
THAT THIS CONFLICT IS A SHAM, KURT? SIMPLE.
ONE THING SEPARATES A WAR FROM A WAR GAME...
...A REFEREE.

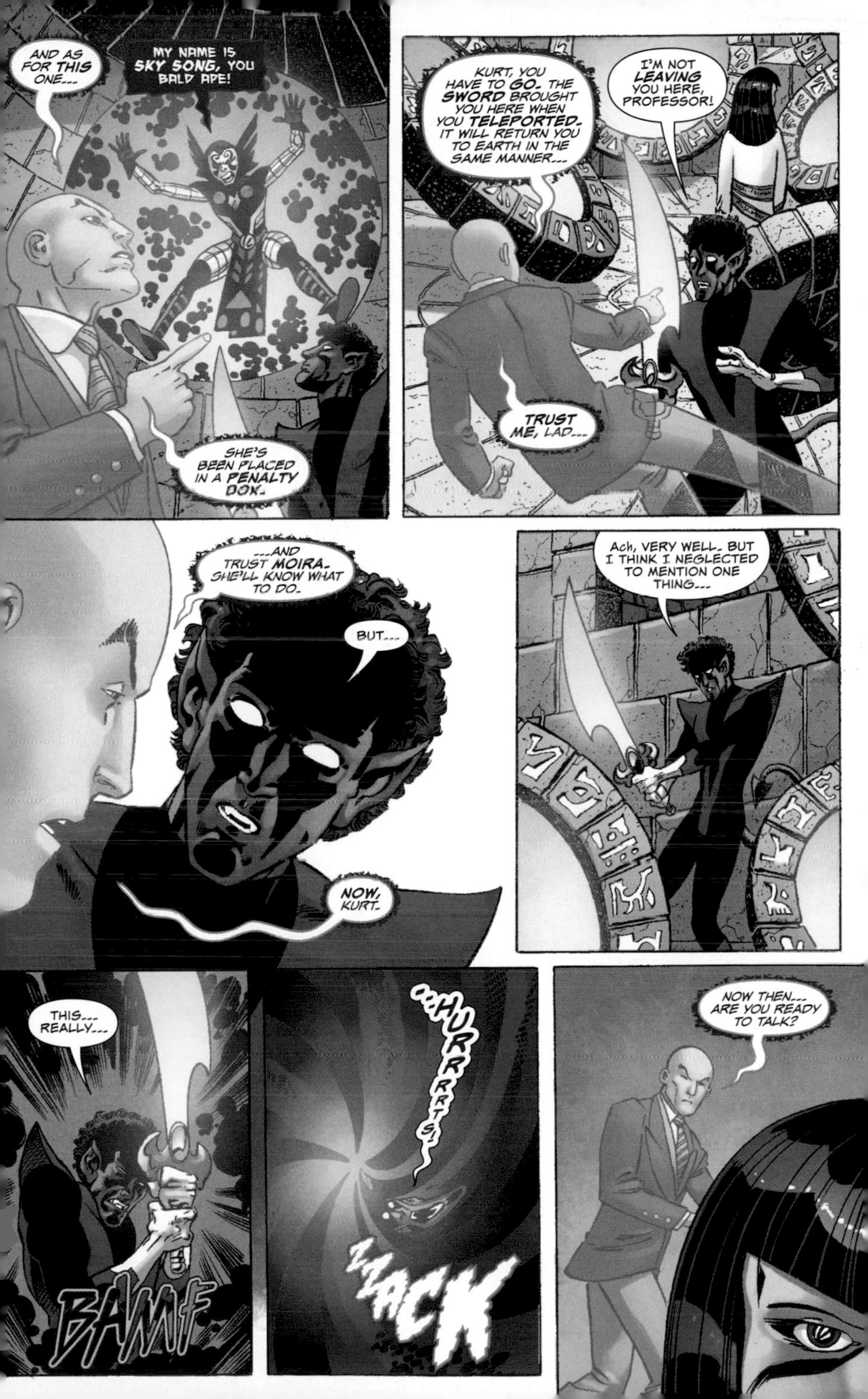

AND AS FOR THIS ONE...
MY NAME IS SKY SONG, YOU BALD APE!
SHE'S BEEN PLACED IN A PENALTY BOX.
KURT, YOU HAVE TO GO. THE SWORD BROUGHT YOU HERE WHEN YOU TELEPORTED. IT WILL RETURN YOU TO EARTH IN THE SAME MANNER...
I'M NOT LEAVING YOU HERE, PROFESSOR!
TRUST ME, LAD...
...AND TRUST MOIRA. SHE'LL KNOW WHAT TO DO.
BUT...
NOW, KURT.
Ach, VERY WELL. BUT I THINK I NEGLECTED TO MENTION ONE THING...
THIS... REALLY...
BAMF
...HURRRRTS!
ZZACK
NOW THEN... ARE YOU READY TO TALK?

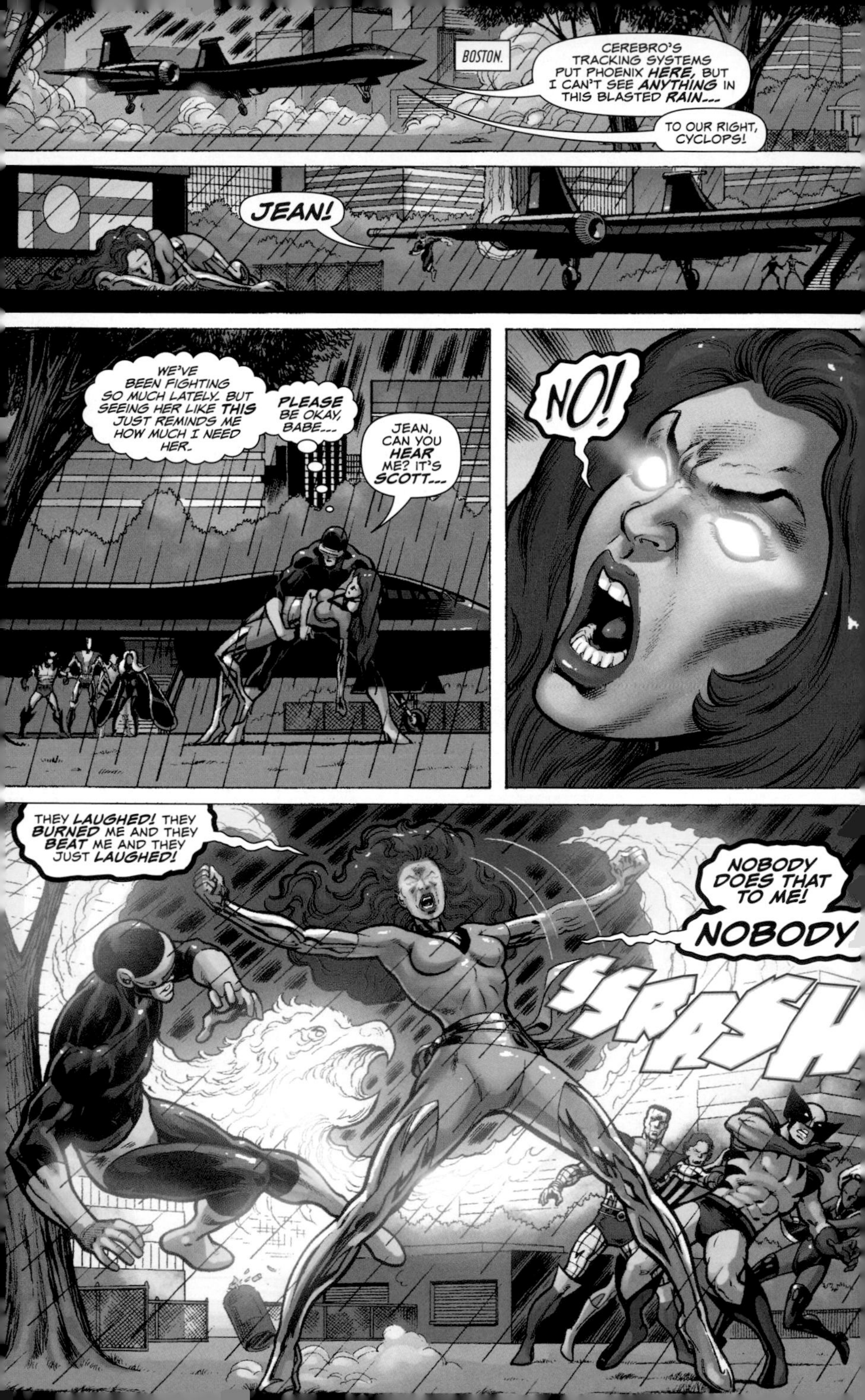
BOSTON.
CEREBRO'S TRACKING SYSTEMS PUT PHOENIX HERE, BUT I CAN'T SEE ANYTHING IN THIS BLASTED RAIN...
TO OUR RIGHT, CYCLOPS!
JEAN!
WE'VE BEEN FIGHTING SO MUCH LATELY. BUT SEEING HER LIKE THIS JUST REMINDS ME HOW MUCH I NEED HER.
PLEASE BE OKAY, BABE...
JEAN, CAN YOU HEAR ME? IT'S SCOTT...
NO!
THEY LAUGHED! THEY BURNED ME AND THEY BEAT ME AND THEY JUST LAUGHED!
NOBODY DOES THAT TO ME!
NOBODY
SSRASH

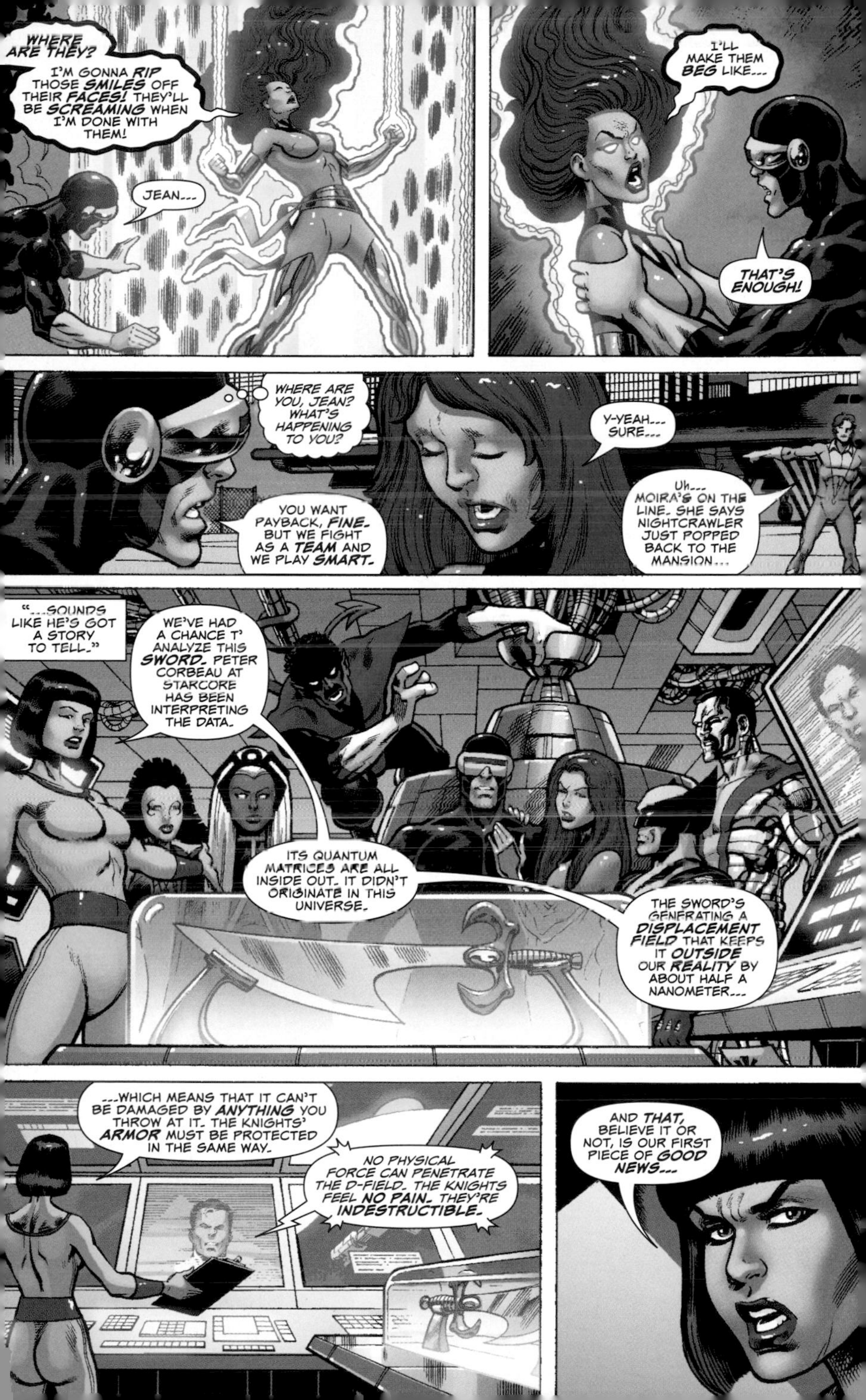

WHERE ARE THEY?
I'M GONNA RIP THOSE SMILES OFF THEIR FACES! THEY'LL BE SCREAMING WHEN I'M DONE WITH THEM!
JEAN...
I'LL MAKE THEM BEG LIKE...
THAT'S ENOUGH!
WHERE ARE YOU, JEAN? WHAT'S HAPPENING TO YOU?
YOU WANT PAYBACK, FINE. BUT WE FIGHT AS A TEAM AND WE PLAY SMART.
Y-YEAH... SURE...
Uh... MOIRA'S ON THE LINE. SHE SAYS NIGHTCRAWLER JUST POPPED BACK TO THE MANSION...
"...SOUNDS LIKE HE'S GOT A STORY TO TELL."
WE'VE HAD A CHANCE T' ANALYZE THIS SWORD. PETER CORBEAU AT STARCORE HAS BEEN INTERPRETING THE DATA.
ITS QUANTUM MATRICES ARE ALL INSIDE OUT. IT DIDN'T ORIGINATE IN THIS UNIVERSE.
THE SWORD'S GENERATING A DISPLACEMENT FIELD THAT KEEPS IT OUTSIDE OUR REALITY BY ABOUT HALF A NANOMETER...
...WHICH MEANS THAT IT CAN'T BE DAMAGED BY ANYTHING YOU THROW AT IT. THE KNIGHTS' ARMOR MUST BE PROTECTED IN THE SAME WAY.
NO PHYSICAL FORCE CAN PENETRATE THE D-FIELD. THE KNIGHTS FEEL NO PAIN. THEY'RE INDESTRUCTIBLE.
AND THAT, BELIEVE IT OR NOT, IS OUR FIRST PIECE OF GOOD NEWS...

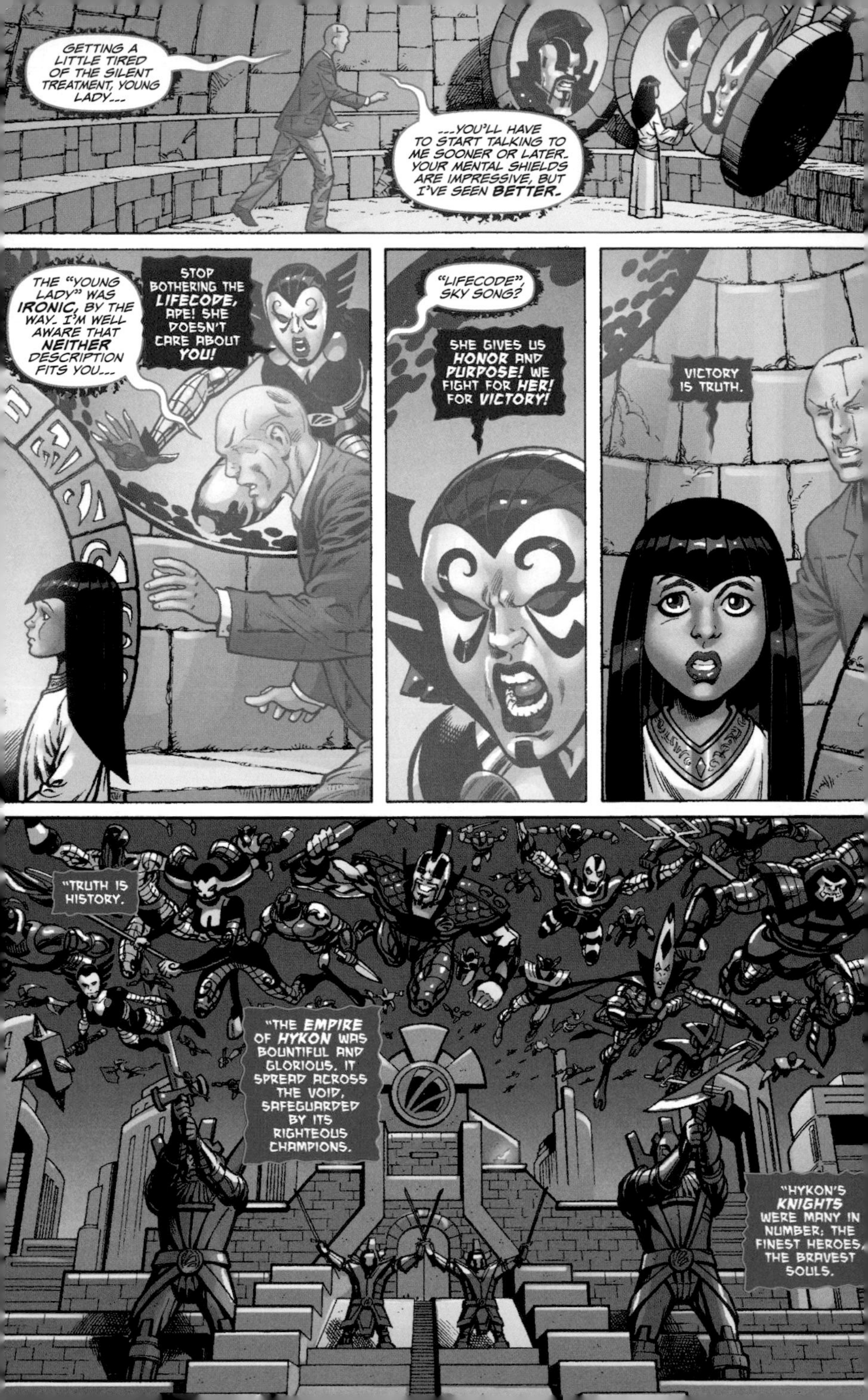
GETTING A LITTLE TIRED OF THE SILENT TREATMENT, YOUNG LADY...
...YOU'LL HAVE TO START TALKING TO ME SOONER OR LATER. YOUR MENTAL SHIELDS ARE IMPRESSIVE, BUT I'VE SEEN BETTER.
THE "YOUNG LADY" WAS IRONIC, BY THE WAY. I'M WELL AWARE THAT NEITHER DESCRIPTION FITS YOU...
STOP BOTHERING THE LIFECODE, APE! SHE DOESN'T CARE ABOUT YOU!
"LIFECODE", SKY SONG?
SHE GIVES US HONOR AND PURPOSE! WE FIGHT FOR HER! FOR VICTORY!
VICTORY IS TRUTH.
"TRUTH IS HISTORY.
"THE EMPIRE OF HYKON WAS BOUNTIFUL AND GLORIOUS. IT SPREAD ACROSS THE VOID, SAFEGUARDED BY ITS RIGHTEOUS CHAMPIONS.
"HYKON'S KNIGHTS WERE MANY IN NUMBER: THE FINEST HEROES, THE BRAVEST SOULS.

"AND THEN CAME THE DAY THE *LAST VILLAIN* WAS SLAIN.

"THE KNIGHTS *CHEERED*, FOR THEY HAD NEVER SEEN BEYOND THE NEXT SUNSET AND COULD NOT IMAGINE WHAT WAS TO COME.

"NO *CHALLENGES*. NO *VICTORIES*. NO *MEANING*.

"PEACE WAS TORTURE.

"THE HEROES GREW RESTLESS. *THE MOON* AND *THE SHADOW* WERE THE FIRST TO *FEUD*.

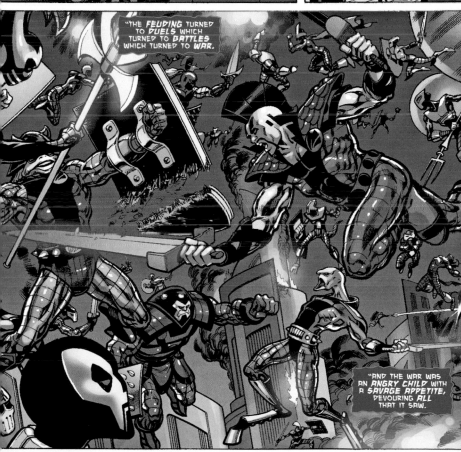

"THE *FEUDING* TURNED TO *DUELS* WHICH TURNED TO *BATTLES* WHICH TURNED TO *WAR*.

"AND THE WAR WAS AN *ANGRY CHILD* WITH A *SAVAGE APPETITE*, DEVOURING *ALL* THAT IT SAW.

"IT GREW BEYOND *IMAGINATION*, BEYOND *REASON*. DEATH UPON DEATH UPON DEATH.

"*PLANETS* AND *STARS* BECAME *WEAPONS*.

"*TIME* AND *SPACE SCREAMED*.

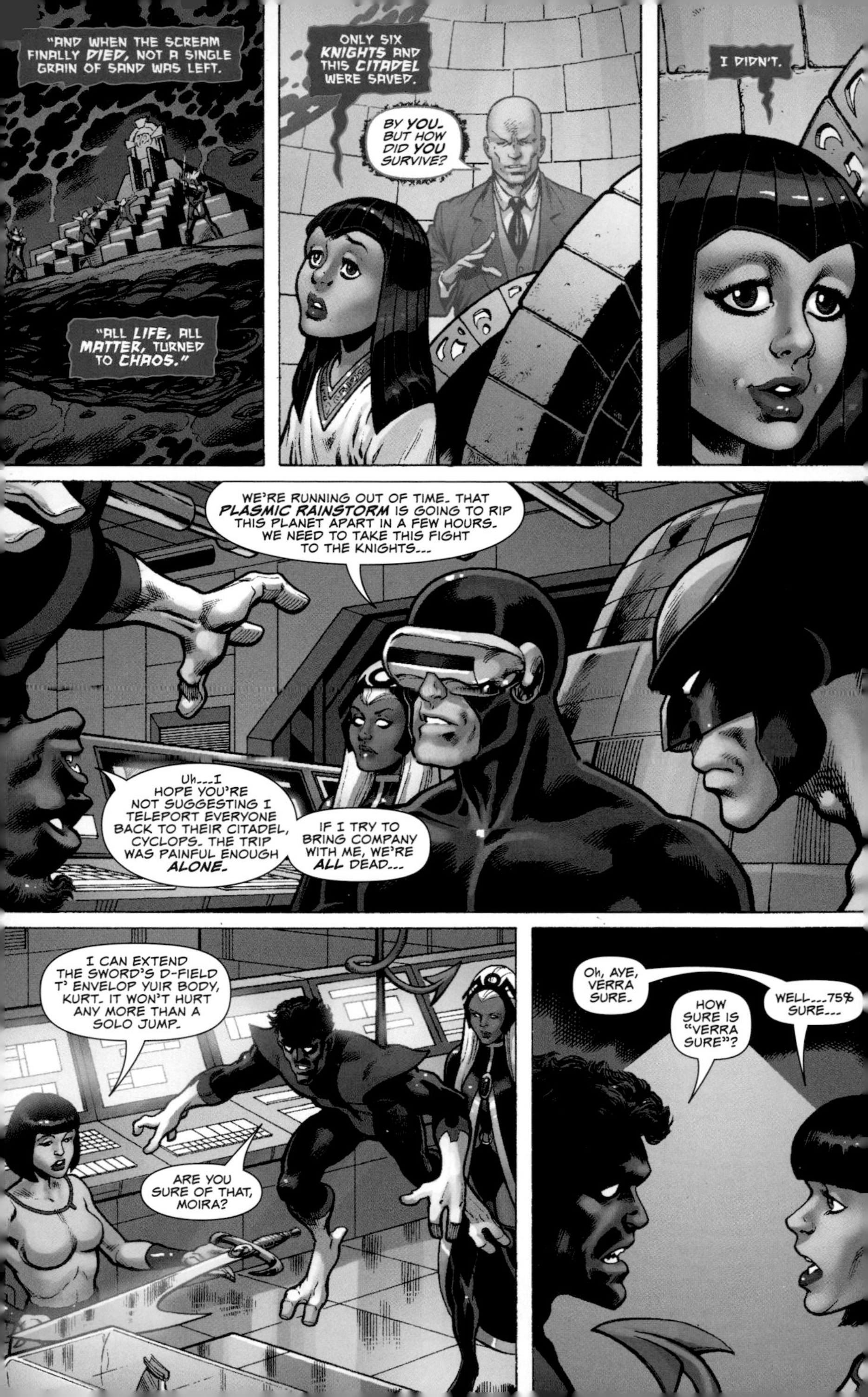
"AND WHEN THE SCREAM FINALLY DIED, NOT A SINGLE GRAIN OF SAND WAS LEFT.
"ALL LIFE, ALL MATTER, TURNED TO CHAOS."
ONLY SIX KNIGHTS AND THIS CITADEL WERE SAVED.
BY YOU. BUT HOW DID YOU SURVIVE?
I DIDN'T.
WE'RE RUNNING OUT OF TIME. THAT PLASMIC RAINSTORM IS GOING TO RIP THIS PLANET APART IN A FEW HOURS. WE NEED TO TAKE THIS FIGHT TO THE KNIGHTS...
Uh...I HOPE YOU'RE NOT SUGGESTING I TELEPORT EVERYONE BACK TO THEIR CITADEL, CYCLOPS. THE TRIP WAS PAINFUL ENOUGH ALONE.
IF I TRY TO BRING COMPANY WITH ME, WE'RE ALL DEAD...
I CAN EXTEND THE SWORD'S D-FIELD T' ENVELOP YUIR BODY, KURT. IT WON'T HURT ANY MORE THAN A SOLO JUMP.
ARE YOU SURE OF THAT, MOIRA?
Oh, AYE, VERRA SURE.
HOW SURE IS "VERRA SURE"?
WELL...75% SURE...

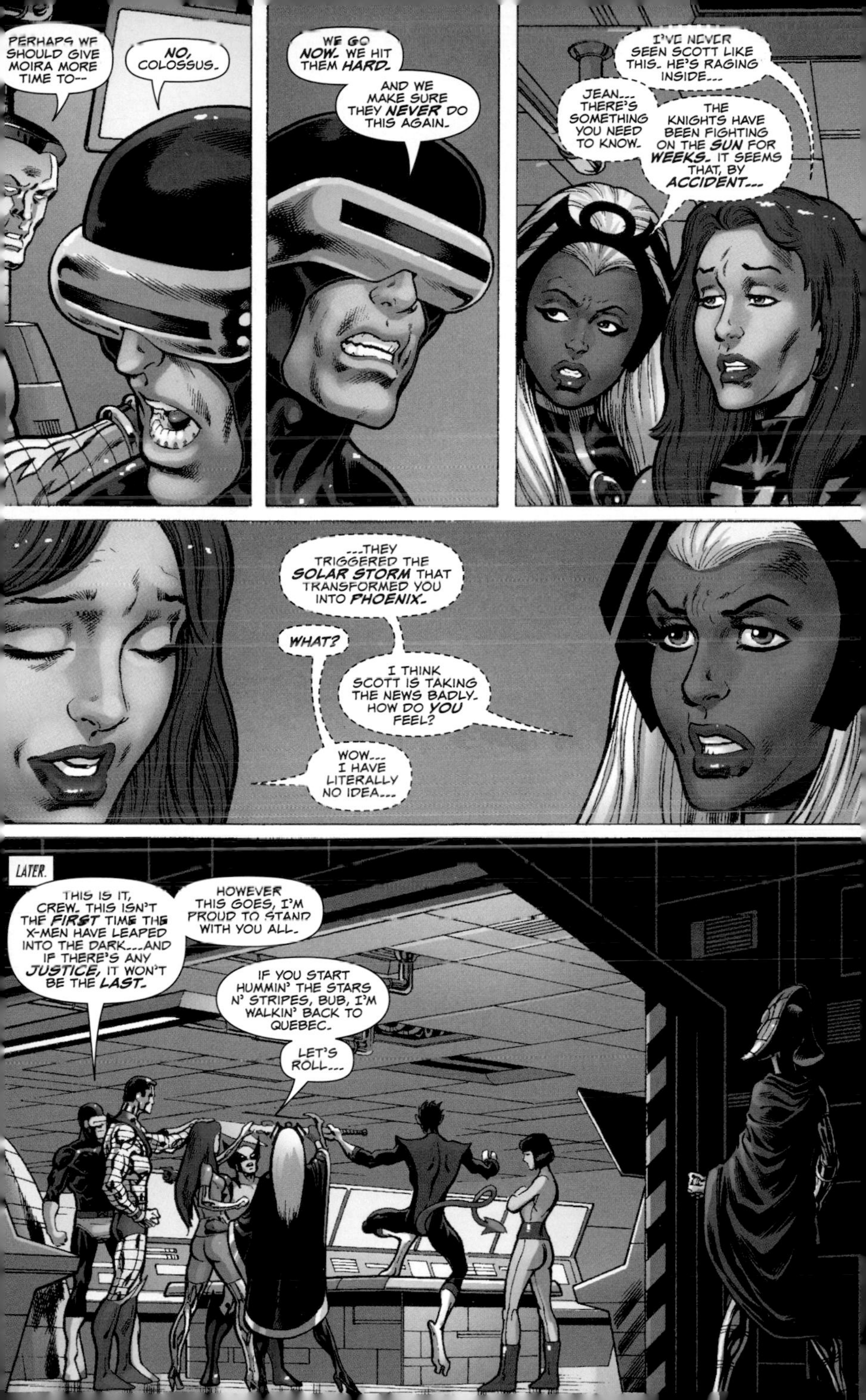

PERHAPS WE SHOULD GIVE MOIRA MORE TIME TO--
NO, COLOSSUS.
WE GO NOW. WE HIT THEM HARD.
AND WE MAKE SURE THEY NEVER DO THIS AGAIN.
I'VE NEVER SEEN SCOTT LIKE THIS. HE'S RAGING INSIDE...
JEAN... THERE'S SOMETHING YOU NEED TO KNOW.
THE KNIGHTS HAVE BEEN FIGHTING ON THE SUN FOR WEEKS. IT SEEMS THAT, BY ACCIDENT...
...THEY TRIGGERED THE SOLAR STORM THAT TRANSFORMED YOU INTO PHOENIX.
WHAT?
I THINK SCOTT IS TAKING THE NEWS BADLY. HOW DO YOU FEEL?
WOW... I HAVE LITERALLY NO IDEA...
LATER.
THIS IS IT, CREW. THIS ISN'T THE FIRST TIME THE X-MEN HAVE LEAPED INTO THE DARK...AND IF THERE'S ANY JUSTICE, IT WON'T BE THE LAST.
HOWEVER THIS GOES, I'M PROUD TO STAND WITH YOU ALL.
IF YOU START HUMMIN' THE STARS N' STRIPES, BUB, I'M WALKIN' BACK TO QUEBEC.
LET'S ROLL...

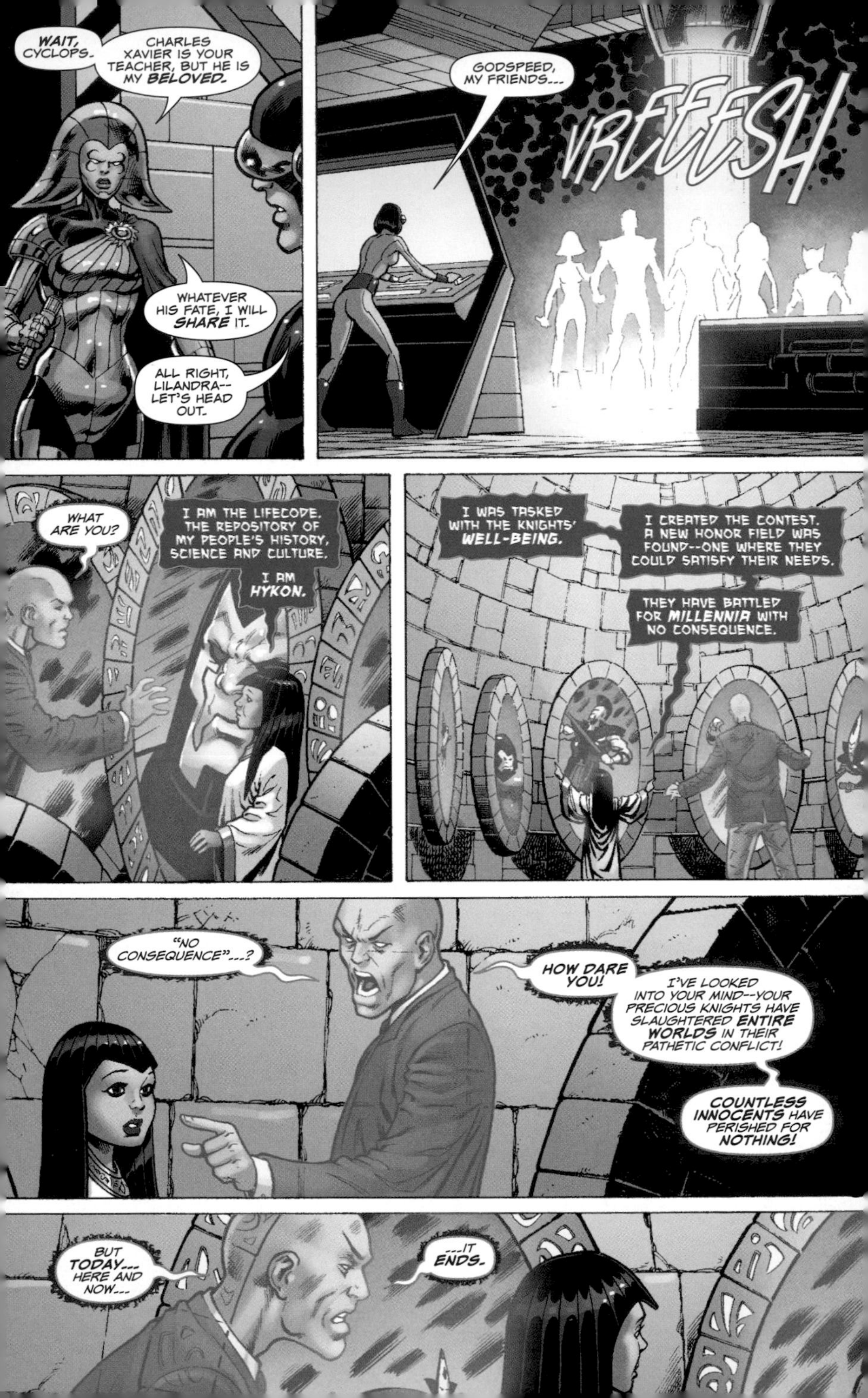
WAIT, CYCLOPS.
CHARLES XAVIER IS YOUR TEACHER, BUT HE IS MY BELOVED.
WHATEVER HIS FATE, I WILL SHARE IT.
ALL RIGHT, LILANDRA--LET'S HEAD OUT.
GODSPEED, MY FRIENDS...
VREEESH
WHAT ARE YOU?
I AM THE LIFECODE. THE REPOSITORY OF MY PEOPLE'S HISTORY, SCIENCE AND CULTURE.
I AM HYKON.
I WAS TASKED WITH THE KNIGHTS' WELL-BEING.
I CREATED THE CONTEST. A NEW HONOR FIELD WAS FOUND--ONE WHERE THEY COULD SATISFY THEIR NEEDS.
THEY HAVE BATTLED FOR MILLENNIA WITH NO CONSEQUENCE.
"NO CONSEQUENCE"...?
HOW DARE YOU!
I'VE LOOKED INTO YOUR MIND--YOUR PRECIOUS KNIGHTS HAVE SLAUGHTERED ENTIRE WORLDS IN THEIR PATHETIC CONFLICT!
COUNTLESS INNOCENTS HAVE PERISHED FOR NOTHING!
BUT TODAY... HERE AND NOW...
...IT ENDS.

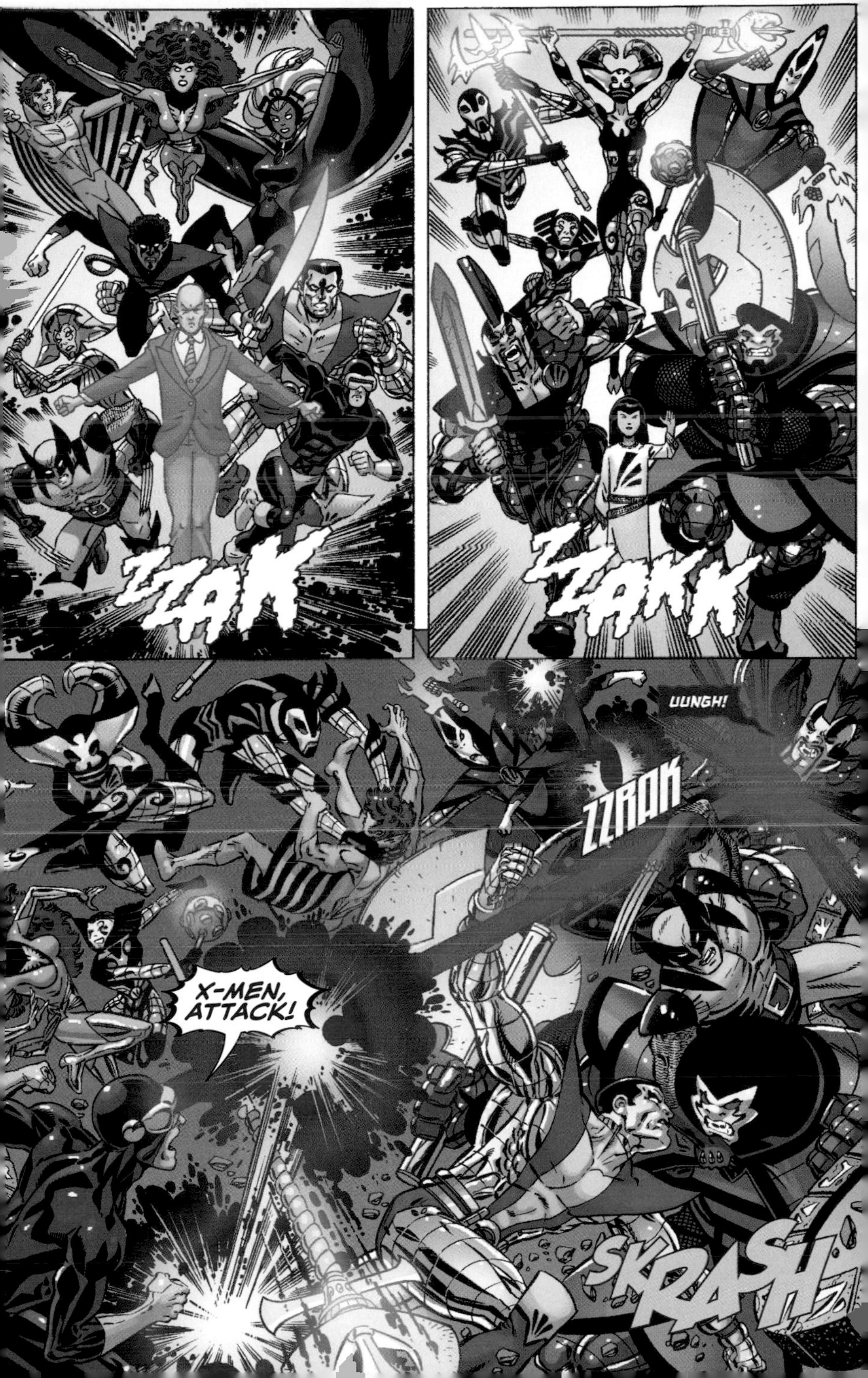
ZZAK
ZZAKK
UUNGH!
ZZRAK
X-MEN, ATTACK!
SKRASH

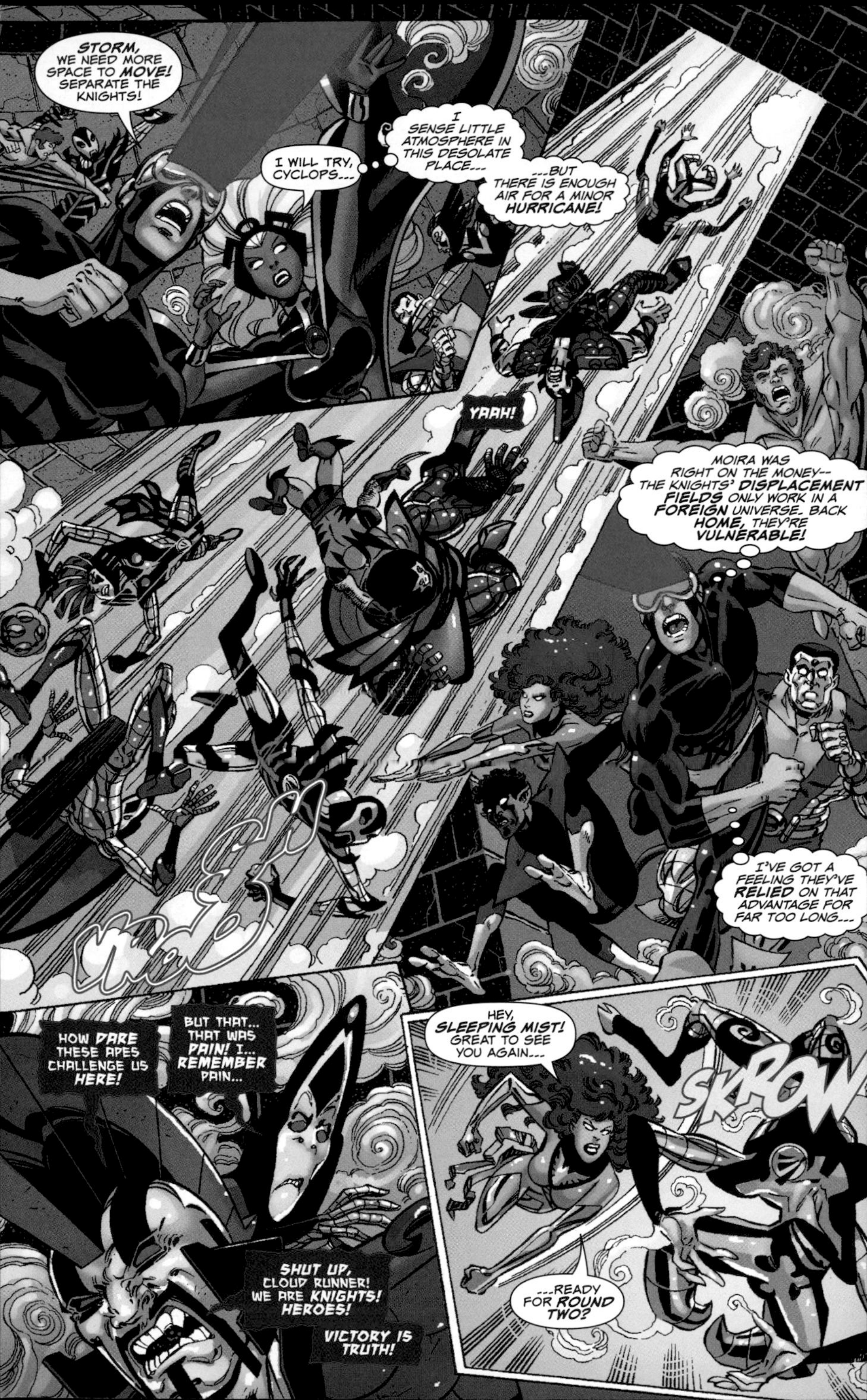

STORM, WE NEED MORE SPACE TO MOVE! SEPARATE THE KNIGHTS!
I WILL TRY, CYCLOPS...
I SENSE LITTLE ATMOSPHERE IN THIS DESOLATE PLACE...
...BUT THERE IS ENOUGH AIR FOR A MINOR HURRICANE!
YAAH!
MOIRA WAS RIGHT ON THE MONEY-- THE KNIGHTS' DISPLACEMENT FIELDS ONLY WORK IN A FOREIGN UNIVERSE. BACK HOME, THEY'RE VULNERABLE!
I'VE GOT A FEELING THEY'VE RELIED ON THAT ADVANTAGE FOR FAR TOO LONG...
HOW DARE THESE APES CHALLENGE US HERE!
BUT THAT... THAT WAS PAIN! I... REMEMBER PAIN...
SHUT UP, CLOUD RUNNER! WE ARE KNIGHTS! HEROES!
VICTORY IS TRUTH!
HEY, SLEEPING MIST! GREAT TO SEE YOU AGAIN...
...READY FOR ROUND TWO?
SKROW

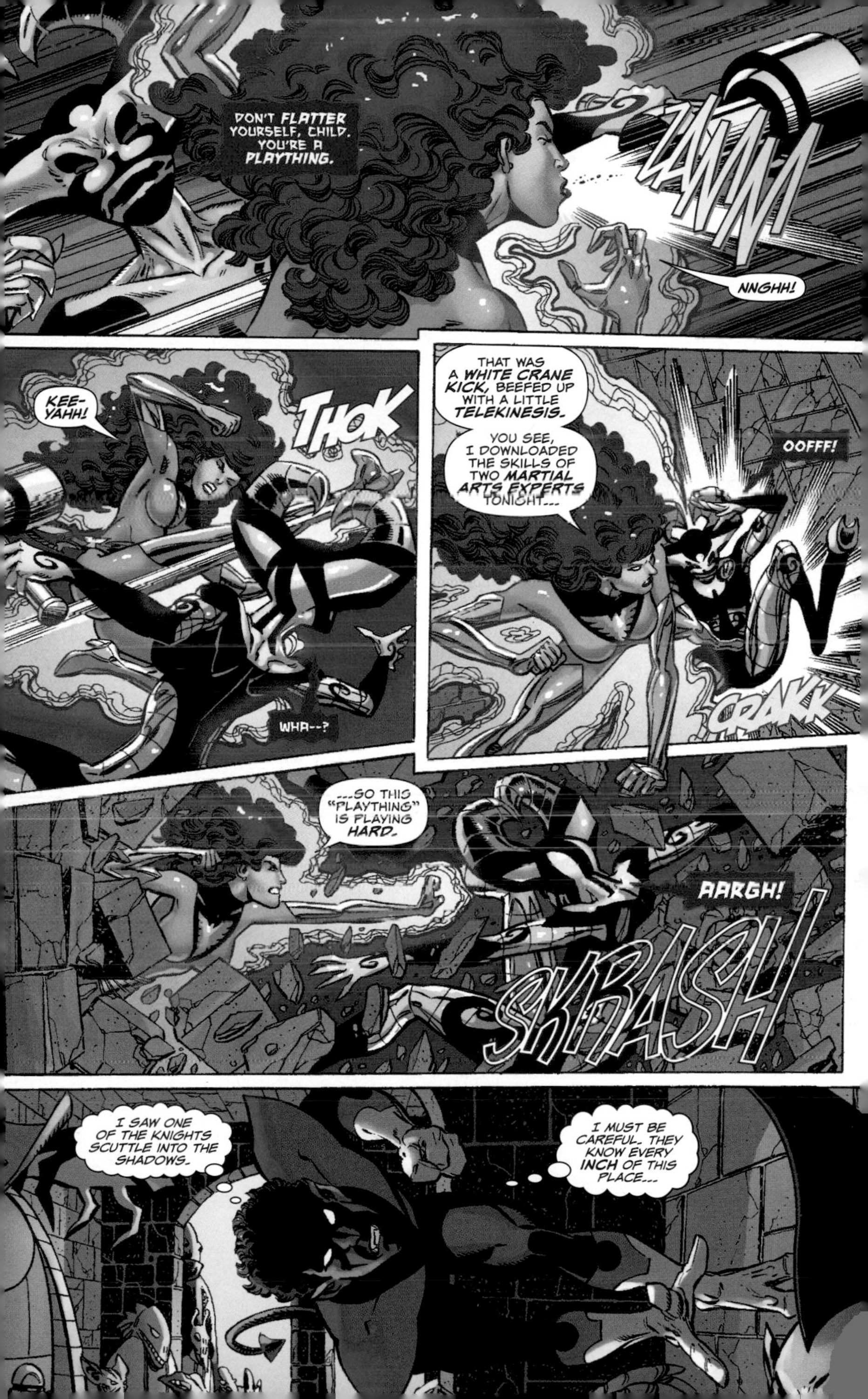
DON'T FLATTER YOURSELF, CHILD. YOU'RE A PLAYTHING.
ZAAAAK
NNGHH!
KEE-YAHH!
THOK
WHA--?
THAT WAS A WHITE CRANE KICK, BEEFED UP WITH A LITTLE TELEKINESIS.
YOU SEE, I DOWNLOADED THE SKILLS OF TWO MARTIAL ARTS EXPERTS TONIGHT---
OOFFF!
CRAKK
---SO THIS "PLAYTHING" IS PLAYING HARD.
AARGH!
SKRASH
I SAW ONE OF THE KNIGHTS SCUTTLE INTO THE SHADOWS.
I MUST BE CAREFUL. THEY KNOW EVERY INCH OF THIS PLACE---

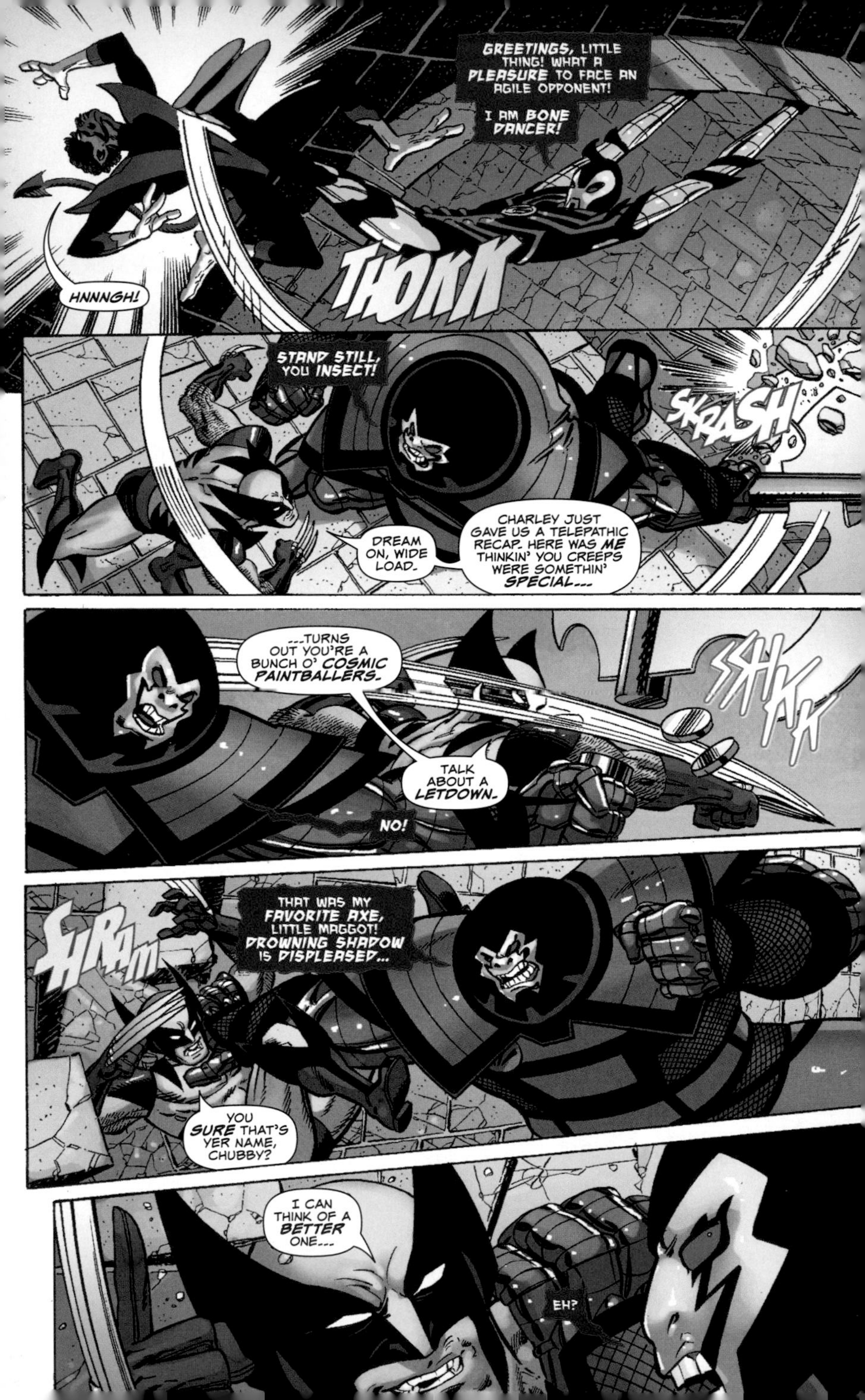
GREETINGS, LITTLE THING! WHAT A PLEASURE TO FACE AN AGILE OPPONENT!
I AM BONE DANCER!
HNNNGH!
THOKK
STAND STILL, YOU INSECT!
SKRASH
DREAM ON, WIDE LOAD.
CHARLEY JUST GAVE US A TELEPATHIC RECAP. HERE WAS ME THINKIN' YOU CREEPS WERE SOMETHIN' SPECIAL...
...TURNS OUT YOU'RE A BUNCH O' COSMIC PAINTBALLERS.
SSHKK
TALK ABOUT A LETDOWN.
NO!
SHRAM
THAT WAS MY FAVORITE AXE, LITTLE MAGGOT! DROWNING SHADOW IS DISPLEASED...
YOU SURE THAT'S YER NAME, CHUBBY?
I CAN THINK OF A BETTER ONE...
EH?

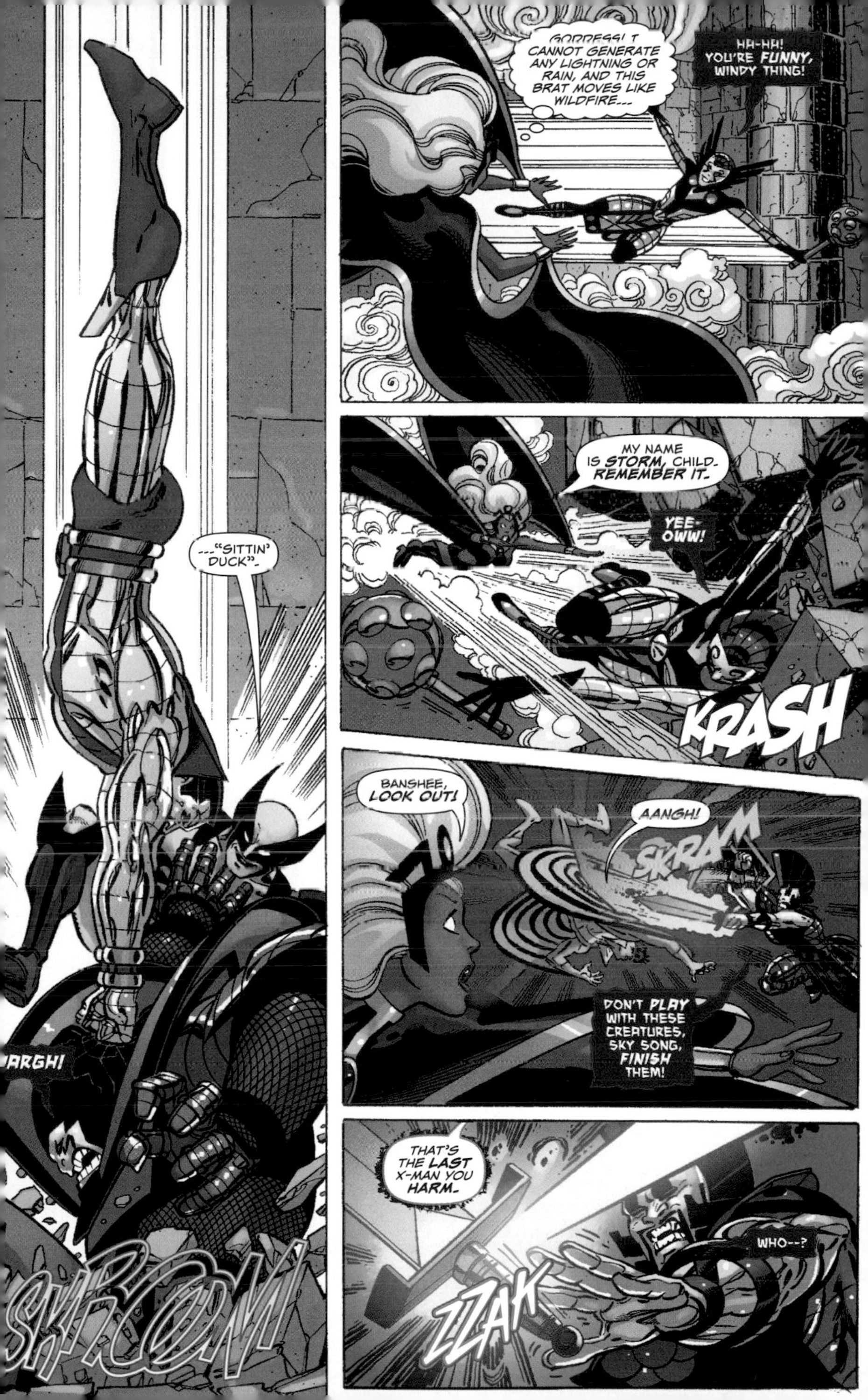

---"SITTIN' DUCK"-
ARGH!
GODDESS! I CANNOT GENERATE ANY LIGHTNING OR RAIN, AND THIS BRAT MOVES LIKE WILDFIRE---
HA-HA! YOU'RE FUNNY, WINDY THING!
MY NAME IS STORM, CHILD. REMEMBER IT.
YEE-OWW!
KRASH
BANSHEE, LOOK OUT!
AANGH!
SKRAM
DON'T PLAY WITH THESE CREATURES, SKY SONG, FINISH THEM!
THAT'S THE LAST X-MAN YOU HARM.
WHO--?
ZZAK

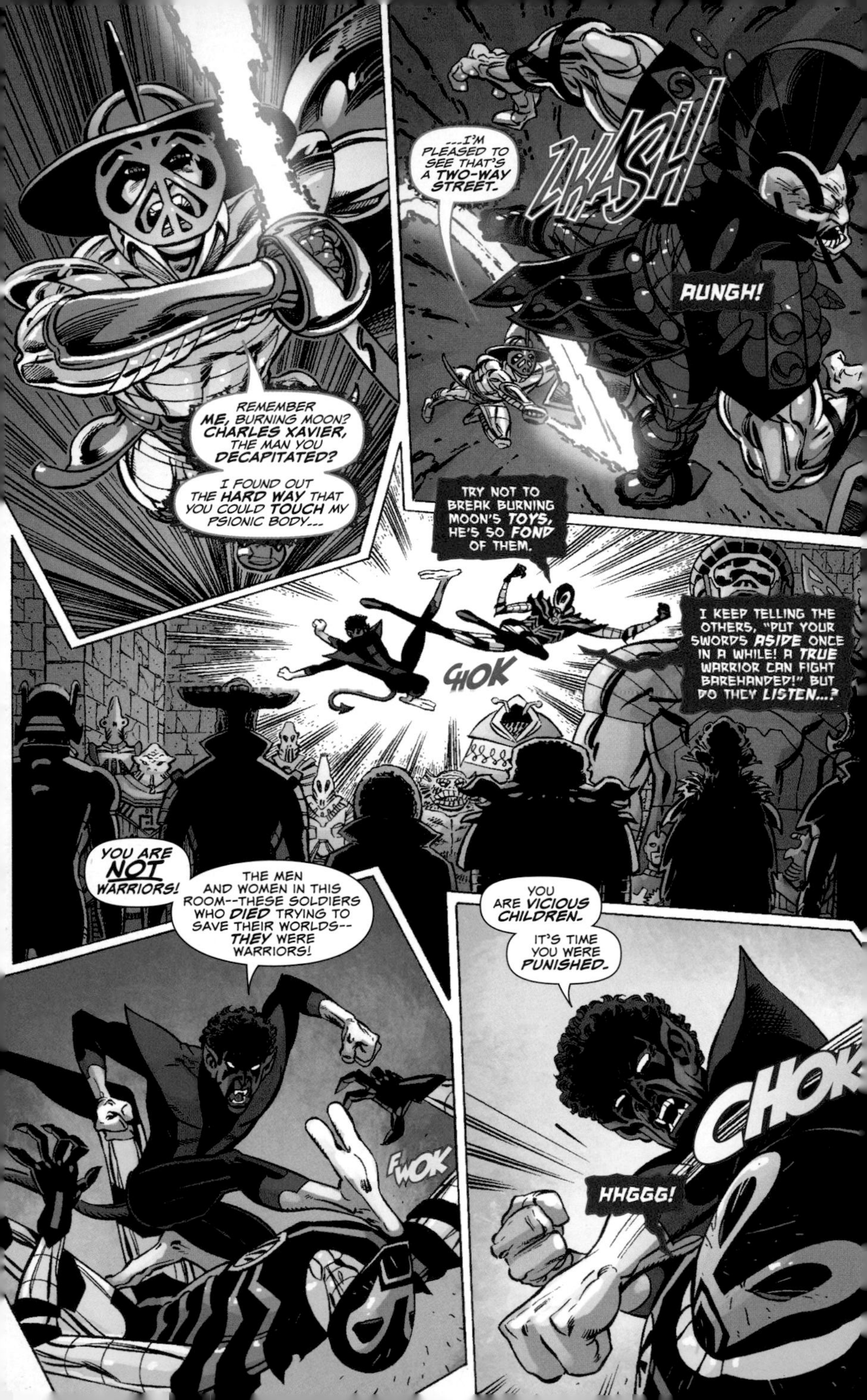

REMEMBER ME, BURNING MOON? CHARLES XAVIER, THE MAN YOU DECAPITATED?
I FOUND OUT THE HARD WAY THAT YOU COULD TOUCH MY PSIONIC BODY...
...I'M PLEASED TO SEE THAT'S A TWO-WAY STREET.
ZKASH
AUNGH!
TRY NOT TO BREAK BURNING MOON'S TOYS, HE'S SO FOND OF THEM.
CHOK
I KEEP TELLING THE OTHERS, "PUT YOUR SWORDS ASIDE ONCE IN A WHILE! A TRUE WARRIOR CAN FIGHT BAREHANDED!" BUT DO THEY LISTEN...?
YOU ARE NOT WARRIORS!
THE MEN AND WOMEN IN THIS ROOM--THESE SOLDIERS WHO DIED TRYING TO SAVE THEIR WORLDS--THEY WERE WARRIORS!
FWOK
YOU ARE VICIOUS CHILDREN.
IT'S TIME YOU WERE PUNISHED.
CHOK
HHGGG!

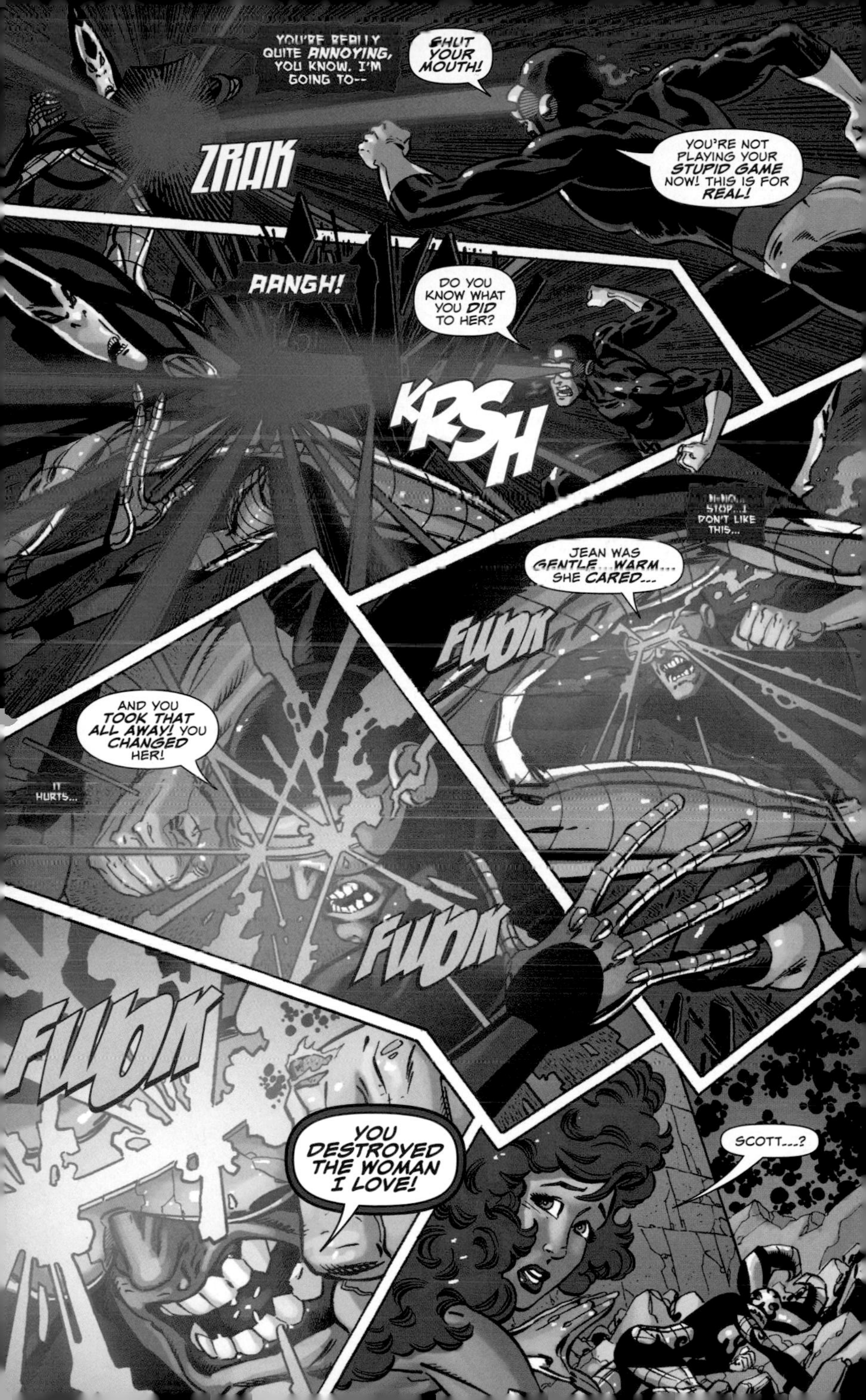

YOU'RE REALLY QUITE ANNOYING, YOU KNOW. I'M GOING TO--
SHUT YOUR MOUTH!
ZRAK
YOU'RE NOT PLAYING YOUR STUPID GAME NOW! THIS IS FOR REAL!
AANGH!
DO YOU KNOW WHAT YOU DID TO HER?
KRSH
STOP...I DON'T LIKE THIS...
JEAN WAS GENTLE...WARM... SHE CARED...
FWOM
AND YOU TOOK THAT ALL AWAY! YOU CHANGED HER!
IT HURTS...
FWOM
FWOM
YOU DESTROYED THE WOMAN I LOVE!
SCOTT...?

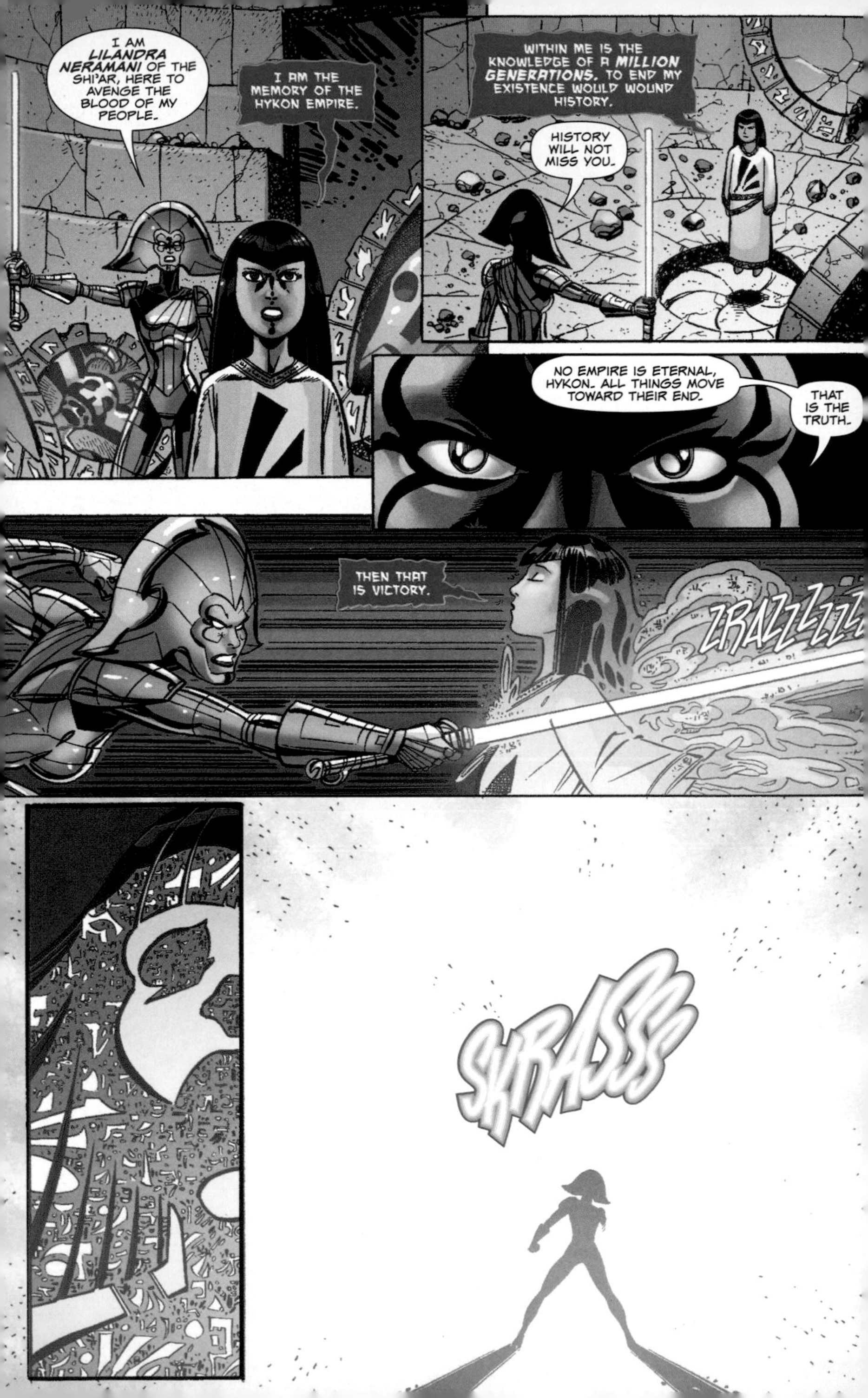

I AM LILANDRA NERAMANI OF THE SHI'AR, HERE TO AVENGE THE BLOOD OF MY PEOPLE.
I AM THE MEMORY OF THE HYKON EMPIRE.
WITHIN ME IS THE KNOWLEDGE OF A MILLION GENERATIONS. TO END MY EXISTENCE WOULD WOUND HISTORY.
HISTORY WILL NOT MISS YOU.
NO EMPIRE IS ETERNAL, HYKON. ALL THINGS MOVE TOWARD THEIR END.
THAT IS THE TRUTH.
THEN THAT IS VICTORY.
ZRAZZZZZZ
SKRASSS

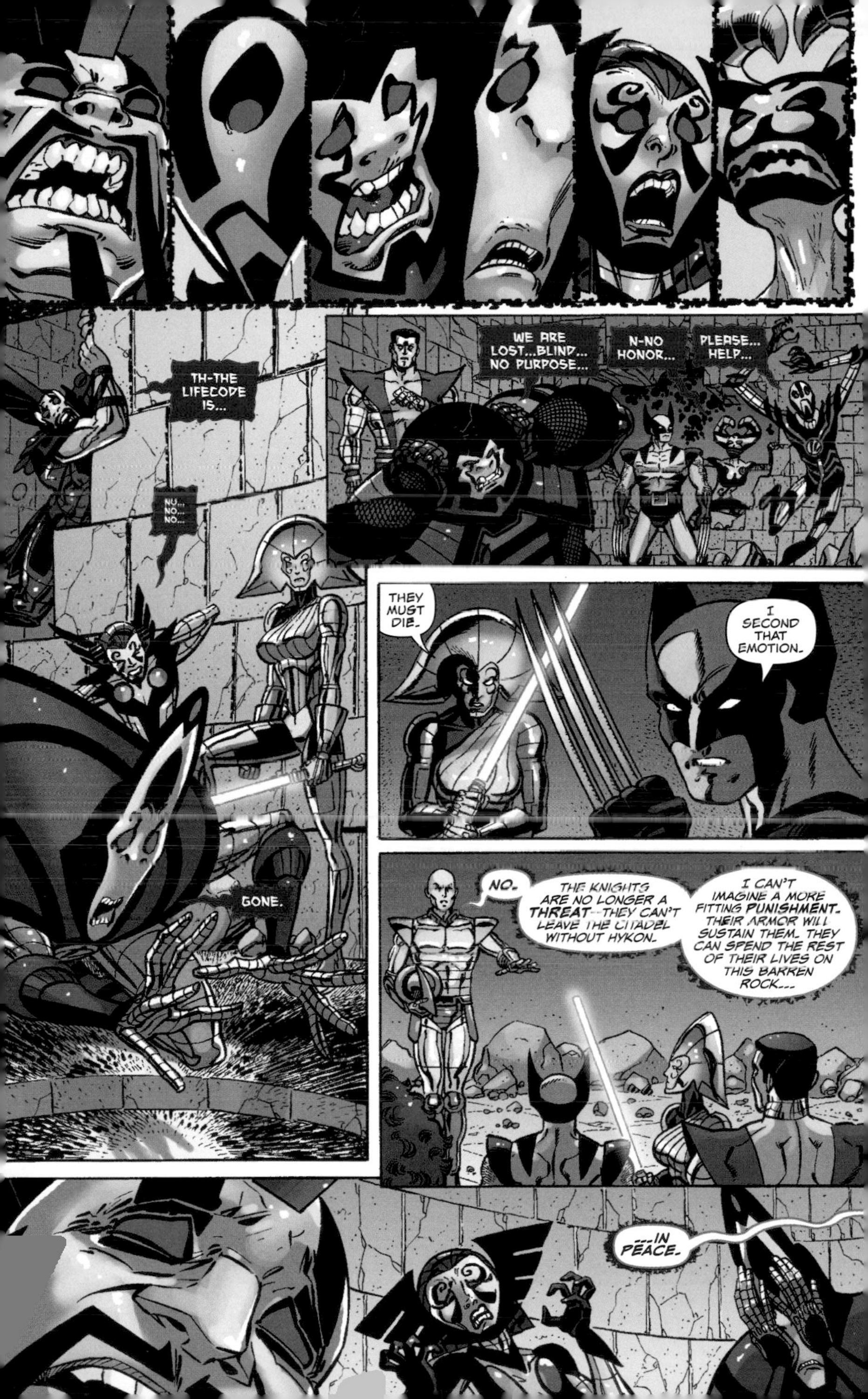

TH-THE LIFECODE IS...
NO... NO... NO...
GONE.
WE ARE LOST...BLIND... NO PURPOSE...
N-NO HONOR...
PLEASE... HELP...
THEY MUST DIE.
I SECOND THAT EMOTION.
NO.
THE KNIGHTS ARE NO LONGER A THREAT--THEY CAN'T LEAVE THE CITADEL WITHOUT HYKON.
I CAN'T IMAGINE A MORE FITTING PUNISHMENT. THEIR ARMOR WILL SUSTAIN THEM. THEY CAN SPEND THE REST OF THEIR LIVES ON THIS BARREN ROCK...
...IN PEACE.

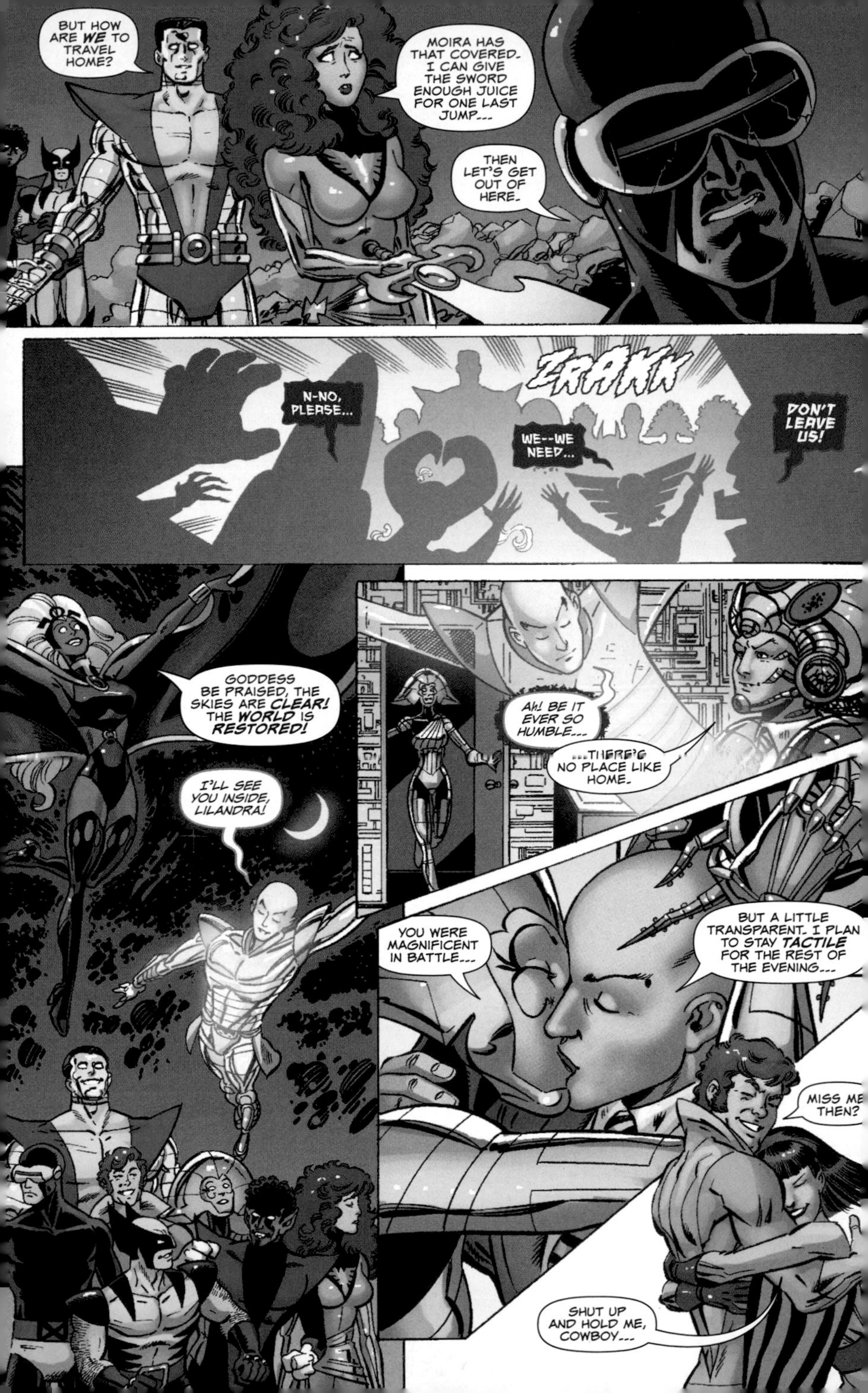

BUT HOW ARE WE TO TRAVEL HOME?
MOIRA HAS THAT COVERED. I CAN GIVE THE SWORD ENOUGH JUICE FOR ONE LAST JUMP...
THEN LET'S GET OUT OF HERE.
N-NO, PLEASE...
ZRAKK
WE--WE NEED...
DON'T LEAVE US!
GODDESS BE PRAISED, THE SKIES ARE CLEAR! THE WORLD IS RESTORED!
I'LL SEE YOU INSIDE, LILANDRA!
Ah! BE IT EVER SO HUMBLE...
...THERE'S NO PLACE LIKE HOME.
YOU WERE MAGNIFICENT IN BATTLE...
BUT A LITTLE TRANSPARENT. I PLAN TO STAY TACTILE FOR THE REST OF THE EVENING...
MISS ME THEN?
SHUT UP AND HOLD ME, COWBOY...

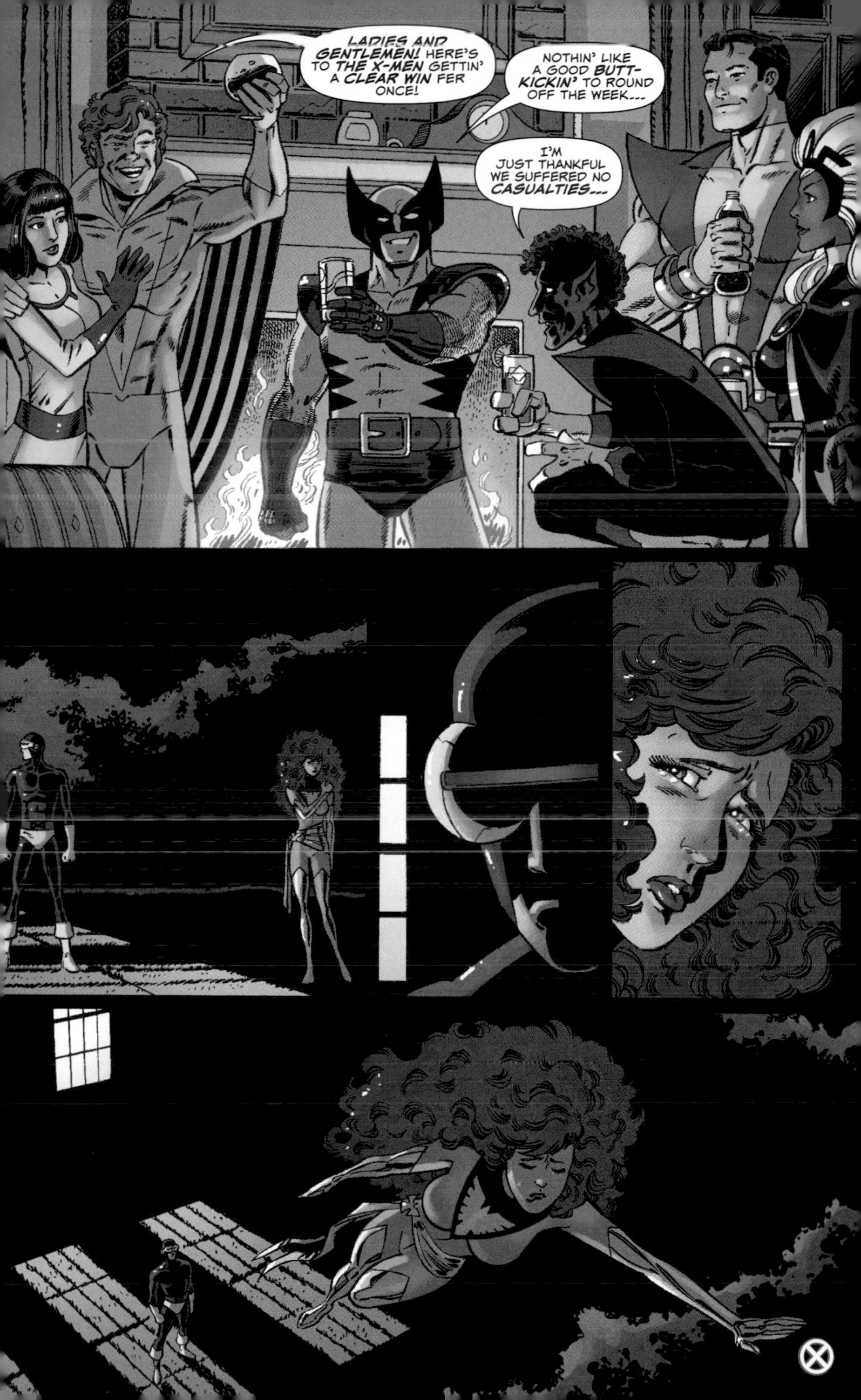
LADIES AND GENTLEMEN! HERE'S TO THE X-MEN GETTIN' A CLEAR WIN FER ONCE!
NOTHIN' LIKE A GOOD BUTT-KICKIN' TO ROUND OFF THE WEEK...
I'M JUST THANKFUL WE SUFFERED NO CASUALTIES...

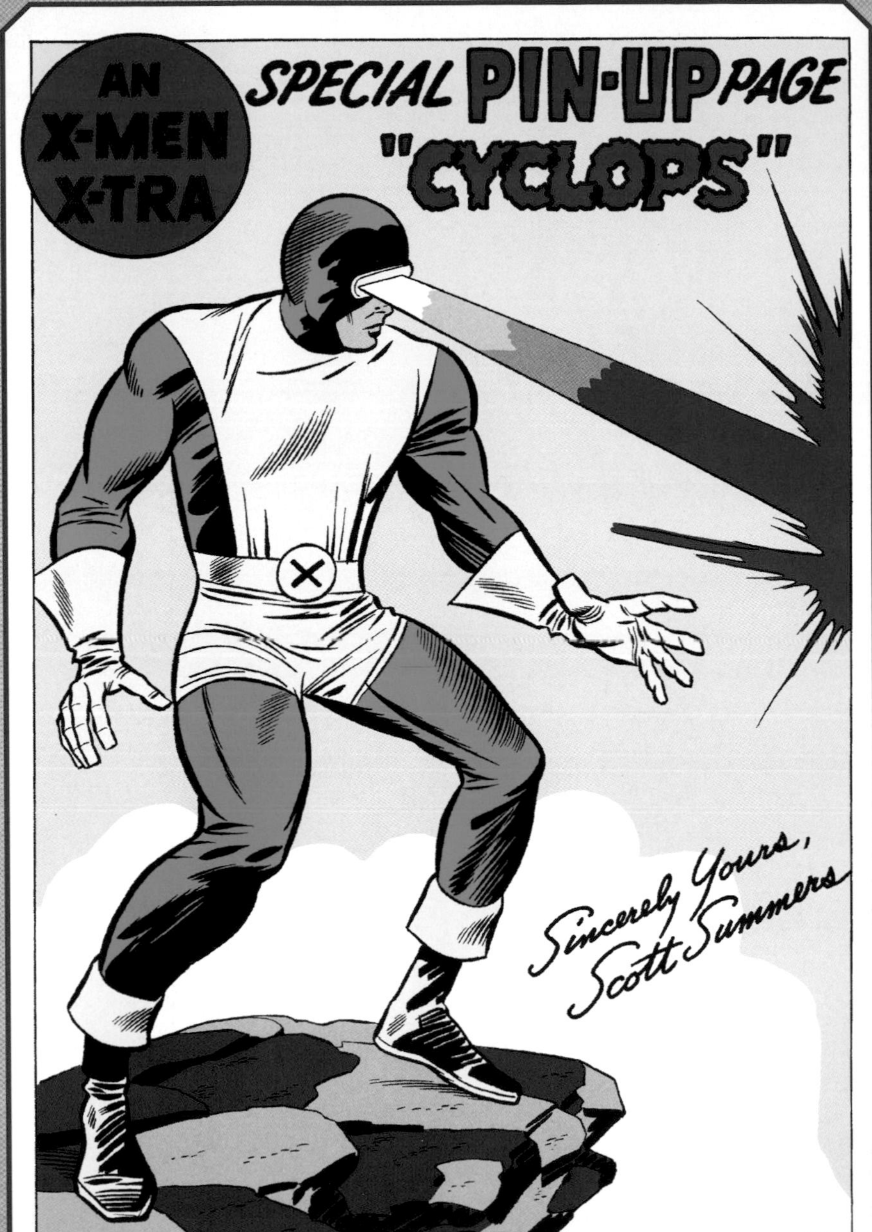
AN X-MEN X-TRA
SPECIAL PIN-UP PAGE
"CYCLOPS"
Sincerely Yours, Scott Summers
X-706

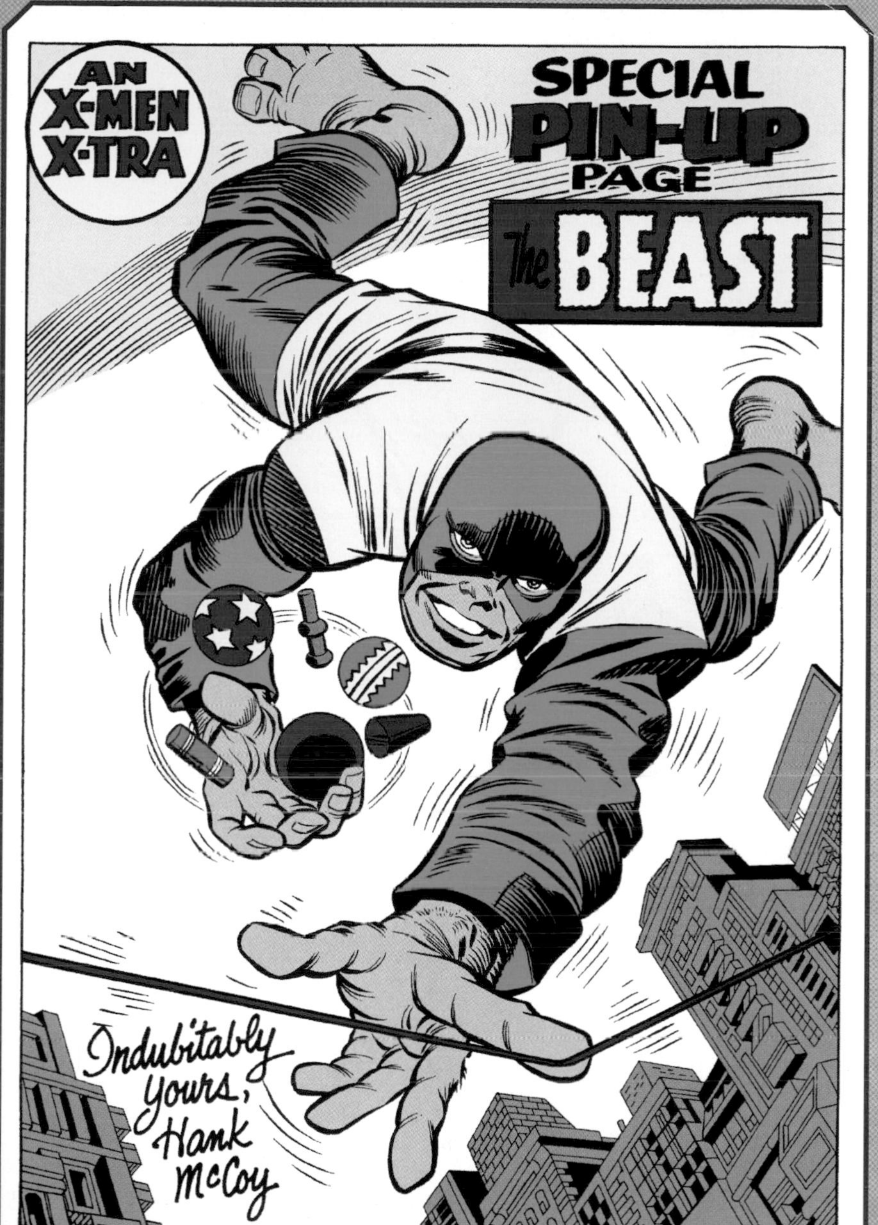

AN X-MEN X-TRA
SPECIAL PIN-UP PAGE
The BEAST
Indubitably yours, Hank McCoy

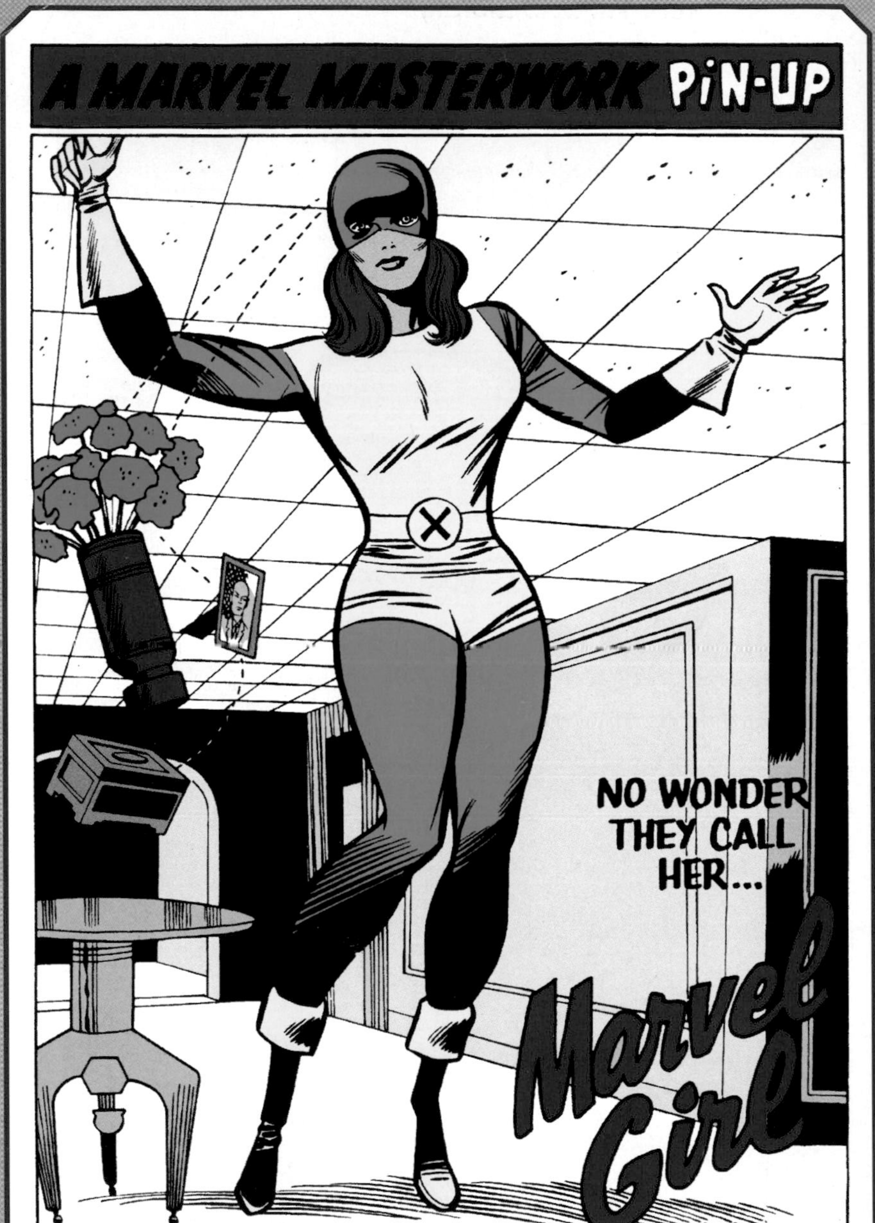
A MARVEL MASTERWORK PiN-UP
NO WONDER THEY CALL HER...
Marvel Girl